D0891491

August

GERARD WOODWARD

August

Chatto & Windus
LONDON

Published by Chatto & Windus 2001

2 4 6 8 10 9 7 5 3 1

Copyright © Gerard Woodward 2001

Ray Bradbury and R.S. Thomas are quoted with the kind permission of
HarperCollins and Bloodaxe Books:
R.S. Thomas, *Selected Poems 1946–1968*, Bloodaxe Books, 1986
Ray Bradbury, *The Martian Chronicles*, Flamingo, 1995

Gerard Woodward has asserted his right under the
Copyright, Designs and Patents Act 1988 to
be identified as the author of this work

First published in Great Britain in 2001 by
Chatto & Windus
Random House, 20 Vauxhall Bridge Road,
London SW1V 2SA

Random House Australia (Pty) Limited
20 Alfred Street, Milsons Point, Sydney,
New South Wales 2061, Australia

Random House New Zealand Limited
18 Poland Road, Glenfield,
Auckland 10, New Zealand

Random House (Pty) Limited
Endulini, 5A Jubilee Road, Parktown 2193, South Africa

The Random House Group Limited Reg. No. 954009
www.randomhouse.co.uk

A CIP catalogue record for this book
is available from the British Library

ISBN 0 7011 7111 1

Papers used by Random House are natural,
recyclable products made from wood grown in sustainable forests.
The manufacturing processes conform to the environmental
regulations of the country of origin

Typeset in Bembo by SX Composing DTP, Rayleigh, Essex
Printed and bound in Great Britain by
Mackays of Chatham PLC, Chatham, Kent

Contents

To the memory of my mother

'Tush.' The old woman winked glitteringly. 'Who are you to question what happens? Here we are. What's life, anyway? Who does what for why and where? All we know is here we are, alive again, and no questions asked. A second chance.' She toddled over and held out her thin wrist. 'Feel.' The captain felt. 'Solid, ain't it?' she asked. He nodded. 'Well, then,' she said triumphantly, 'why go round questioning?'

'Well,' said the captain, 'it's simply that we never thought we'd find a thing like this on Mars.'

Ray Bradbury, 'The Third Expedition'

There is no present in Wales,
And no future;
There is only the past,
Brittle with relics . . .

R.S. Thomas

1955

1

The coastal plain to the north of Aberbreuddwyd seems, at first sight, to do little more than fill an awkward gap between the sea on one side and the mountains on the other. It is a thorny strip, a mile and a half wide, of marshy fields, small tenant farms, clumps of Douglas firs, abandoned aerodromes, toppled cromlechs and disused sheds of black tin. By the sea the land rises to a lengthy range of dunes tufted with marram grass, providing shelter for the broad acreages of caravans, tents and mobile homes that tessellate the seaward fringes of the plain. Further inland a single-track railway cuts a dead straight path across the land, accompanied by a small bundle of telephone wires mounted on crooked poles. Still further inland, where the densely wooded foothills of the Rhinogs begin, the coast road carries an exhausted straggle of cars and lorries past the unfrequented roadhouses and small stone villages between Aberbreuddwyd and Brythwch.

Llanygwynfa is one of these villages. It consists of three buildings – a chapel dedicated to St Hywyn, a farmhouse (built, according to some, in a single night) and, half hidden behind beech trees on the opposite side of the Aberbreuddwyd road, the gatehouse of Llwydiarth Hall.

The chapel and the farmhouse, both marked by the pretty

plague of yellow lichen that freckles all the stonework in the district, stand side by side next to the main road, and bear a twin-like resemblance to one another. The chimney of the farmhouse is the stumpier sibling of the chapel's bell cote, and both buildings are squat, sturdy and square, like loaves from the same tin.

The tenant of the farm is Hugh Evans who, with his wife Dorothy, tends seven fields between the road and the railway. They have twenty-three sheep, a flock of hens, assorted cats and dogs, and eleven cows. Hugh is with the eleventh cow and her mother in the first field, where he is trying to encourage young Cochen to take her mother's milk. He is strong, surprisingly strong, for a man so tall and lean, but he is having difficulty moving Cochen, who seems more interested in the hem of Hugh's mackintosh than her mother Frochwen's bloated teats where drops of milk are hanging like grapes. Often she tries suckling at the wrong end of Frochwen, poking her pale tongue hopelessly at her mother's breastbone, which would have been correct had she been a human child. Hugh has to turn Cochen around, picking her clean off the ground, and steer her like a wheelbarrow towards her mother's milk. Each time he does this he straightens up afterwards and wonders at how a creature so young can possess such weight.

People who know Hugh Evans only by sight are uncertain about his age. His toothlessness gives his face the sunken, hollow look of the very old, and his voice has the whistling timbre of the grandfathers of the parish, who speak as if to the accompaniment of invisible flutes. Yet he can lift a young cow off her feet, or spend a day dry-stone-walling, or bale hay so that any of his younger farmhands has trouble keeping up. Then there are his children, the twins Gwen and Barry, who can't be more than ten. But then there is Hugh's white hair flowing from under his cap and his fondness for banana sandwiches, and his memories, which seem to reach back to the previous century.

Having regathered some of his strength Hugh prepares for

one more lift of his clueless youngster. Before he bends he notices a black-coifed human head sailing along the top of the wall at the higher end of the field, which borders the Aberbreuddwyd road. The head is travelling with the smooth nonchalance and speed that only a cyclist's head can possess. Hugh encircles Cochen's girth with his powerful arms for the final lift, pulling her clean off the ground, but the child struggles and kicks. Hugh drops her and falls over backwards. Frochwen walks away haughtily.

Then, from the distance, comes a noise – a grinding of gears, a spurt of exhaust, a howling scrape of tyres on tarmac, the dull crunch of metal against stone and a shout that sounds like the word 'Ouch!' yelled at full force, an 'Ouch!' that seems to fill the countryside, bouncing off Rhinog Fawr and Rhinog Fach, skimming the choppy tarns of Y Lledrith, resounding from the walls of Brythwch Castle, the cliffs of Cadair and out to sea.

Hugh leaves his sulky mother and child and runs towards the source of the noise. Nimbly climbing the wall in the upper corner he leans over and looks down upon a scene that makes him tip his cap back off his head, then hold it over his mouth.

William Vaughan's pride and joy, his freshly waxed Armstrong Siddeley Star Sapphire Saloon, is askew to the road but parallel with a cyclist and his bike, its off-side headlight crushed against the chapel wall. The cyclist is lying on his back, his eyes closed. Hugh recognizes the black-coifed head he noticed only a few seconds before. He seems to be smiling, this man (he'd thought him a boy before), as though in the midst of a pleasant dream. The front wheel of his bike is twisted into a figure eight. Bags and leather-strapped panniers are scattered about him. It reminds Hugh Evans briefly of the burial he saw uncovered when the archaeologists came from the university to dig up one of the mounds on his land. There was a man lying in much the same position, just his bones, with pots and swords all around him.

The cyclist laughs suddenly and grows from his nostrils a moustache of blood. In his right hand he is holding something very tightly. Hugh thinks it might be a pocket watch. *What the hell's time so important for?* he thinks to himself.

William Vaughan, a handsome young man with hair scraped back and heavily Brylcreemed, steps out of his car and runs his fingers lightly over his damaged headlight. He moves a piece of chrome bumper gingerly with his foot then goes over to the cyclist, his feet almost cradling the wounded man's head, like a footballer impatient for the kick off.

'Can you believe it?' he says to Hugh, whose much higher head he has just noticed. 'I was on my way to see a buyer for my little darling. A man in Shrewsbury. He's promised me *x* amount of pounds, and I've told him it's in mint condition. Spent the whole bloody morning waxing the bitch. Now this happens.'

Hugh Evans has known William since he was a baby. He is now the sole occupant of Llwydiarth Hall, the last scion of an ancient family that once owned nearly all the land in Y Lledrith and some beyond. Hugh is a tenant on his estate, as was his father and his father before him. But times are hard now for the Vaughans. In the nineteenth century half the estate was bought up by the Wynns of Wynnstay and a wing of the Hall was turned into a farm. The elegant courtyard became a muck-splattered farmyard. Small portions of the estate have been sold off regularly ever since. There isn't a great deal left now and Hugh is hopeful that he can buy the freehold of his tenancy before long. William has been wooing him recently to this end.

'I was going to ask you, Hugh,' he says, stepping over the body of the cyclist, 'if you and Dorothy would care to come up to the Hall one evening next week for supper. I realize you must be busy with the hay . . .'

Hugh, who has never been keen on William, not since he once caught him bending back the fingers of his boy Barry when Barry was only four, nods towards the cyclist, shocked at William's lack of concern.

'You're going to let that man bleed to death are you?'

William turns.

4

'Sorry,' he says to the still recumbent cyclist, 'but you did come out of nowhere, sort of thing. I always have trouble with that turning. I keep telling them they need one of those mirrors there, but they expect me to pay for it. You should tell the bloody council. Actually, better not. Just cuts and bruises isn't it?'

He reaches inside his jacket for his wallet.

'And your front wheel. Shall we call it twenty pounds?'

The cyclist coughs, sending up a spume of red bubbles.

'Call it thirty shall we?' William goes on, extracting a third note.

The Brythwch bus, perfectly on time, steers carefully past the jutting rear end of William's car. On board three men are standing with their six hands flat and white against the glass. They watch carefully as they pass.

William bends down and stuffs the money into the cyclist's breast pocket.

'We'll say no more about it,' William smiles, reaching out for the cyclist's hand, lifting him up.

'You nearly got your wings there eh? The way you went flying. Did you see the way he went flying Hugh? Like a bloody bird.' He describes the cyclist's flight path with his right hand, a graceful arc through the air. Then he offers him his hanky. The cyclist holds the crumpled white thing to his nose. William brushes some dust off the man's jacket, thinking he looks like he's dressed for church, then makes the flying gesture again, accompanying it this time with a quiet, whistling noise. Then he says 'What's that you're holding?' noticing how he has something tightly gripped in his right fist.

'A coincidence,' the cyclist replies.

'What? What's that? What's a coincidence?'

'What I'm holding.'

The cyclist seems mad. William shrugs, smiles nervously at him, then at Hugh, who is still watching over the wall.

An awkward silence falls upon the three. The cyclist, recovering himself a little, dabs at his face with William Vaughan's hanky, then looks at his jacket elbows to see if they are torn. Hugh Evans, who hasn't changed position through-out the conversation, continues to observe, motionless, from his vantage point. William pokes and prods his headlights and fenders, strokes his chromium beading, rests a while his hand on the sphinx that reposes on his bonnet, tuts, shakes his head, mutters the words 'mint condition' quietly to himself several times, sighs and then, with a final repetition of his invitation to Hugh and his wife, skips into his car saying he doesn't want to be late for his 'coincidence' in Shrewsbury, and scoots off.

The silence that follows is broken by a cackle of laughter from the cyclist, who then copies William's flight gesture, and says, 'Whoosh!'

Hugh wonders if he has suffered some damage to his head. He looks like a fairly normal middle-aged man, a little over-dressed for cycling, perhaps, in his grey suit, grey pullover, white shirt and blue corduroy tie, but sane, one would have thought.

He is still gripping the thing in his fist which he now brings to his mouth, as if to eat it. *An oyster?* thinks Hugh as the cyclist sucks it in.

The cyclist, as if noticing Hugh for the first time, smiles broadly at the farmer and clicks his teeth together quietly. Perfect teeth.

They weren't there before.

'I suppose God could jump over the fence,' said Janus as he served underarm a baby apple he'd just picked from the Ellison Orange. The tennis racquet gave a taut twang and the fruit arced gracefully over the fence into Mrs Peck's garden.

His mother, her back to him, momentarily wrapped up in the sopping length of the black dress she was pinning out on the line, didn't notice this small crime and said thoughtfully 'God could jump over the house, Janus, if he wanted to, though why he should want to I don't know . . .'

Colette's dress was white, pleated, low-cut, gathered in at the waist by a thin beige sash. The opposite of the dress she'd just rigged out. Colette was a collector of clothes, especially dresses, most of them second-hand, many of them passed on by her mother or sisters.

Janus looked at the house. Colette could see that he was trying to imagine a robed, flowing-bearded figure springing up from the lawn and passing in a single leap over the pointed rooftop.

She laughed secretly. She could barely control her laughter, so that when Janus then said, 'Do you think God could jump over the oak tree?' which was perhaps another twenty feet higher than the house at the end of the garden, she had to bury her face in a damp skirt. The skirt, a blue and yellow patch-work, soaked up her laughter and she was able to say, with due thoughtfulness, glancing at the oak tree, mentally triangulating its height, 'I think so, Janus, even the oak tree.'

Janus swished his racquet through the air, twirled it, tried to catch it by the handle, dropped it.

'What about the tower blocks at Edmonton Green?' he said, a narrow-eyed challenge in his question.

The blocks, still unfinished, had arrived unannounced and, it seemed, virtually overnight on the charming remains of the village green at Edmonton, thoroughly obliterating it. The triangle of small friendly shops and market stalls with the park wedged between them, the old level crossing with its creaking white gates and sonorous bells, all these had been subsumed by three burly, bristling, windowed monoliths and a tangle of freeways, roundabouts and elevated walkways. The shops had now become cells set in concrete malls beneath the tower blocks. The market inhabited a damp, dimly lit, roofed plaza that smelt of urine.

Colette and her family had moved away from Edmonton Green just as this eruption of ugliness was breaking. From the leafy upper end of Fernlight Avenue the tower blocks were visible as white stumps on the lowland areas towards the Lee Valley, a constant reminder of their successful escape.

'Even the tower blocks,' said Colette, slotting pegs into her mouth so that what she said next was only partly intelligible, 'though I'm not sure it would be right to describe it as "jumping". It would be more like flying. I don't think God jumps . . .'

'I saw God,' said Janus, as if to himself, 'jumping over the tower blocks at Edmonton Green.' Then, directly to his mother, 'Do you mean God can't jump at all?'

'I don't mean that, Janus. I mean he doesn't need to jump, if he can fly. But then he doesn't beat his wings like a bird. When God flies he's thinking. You can call it jumping or flying, but he thinks his way around. And he can think himself anywhere. You could say he jumps over the universe every day.'

8

A baby apple gently knocked the back of Colette's head. She turned in surprise. It seemed to have come from Mrs Peck's garden.

'Don't do that to the sunflowers, Janus,' she said to her son, who'd just atomized one with a perfect backhand, sending a rich shower of yellow petals falling like welding sparks.

Her other son, James, too young at three years old to be very interested in God, walked through and through the washing, as if taking a series of curtain calls, while Colette hung up the last of the dripping clothes. She tickled the crown of his head as he passed beneath her. Then she noticed that Janus, behind her, was laughing. She turned and saw that he was looking at her, one eye clenched against the sunlight, chuckling to himself.

'What are you laughing at?' she asked.

'Nothing,' replied Janus, moving away towards the sunflowers, shaking his head pityingly.

Colette picked up James. He settled into her body comfortably, embracing her neck with his arms, her waist with his legs.

Janus launched a sequence of baby apples into graceful trajectories that took them to the end of the garden. Only a whisper of impact could be heard from there, an answer to the tense drumbeat of the racquet.

Colette had always had the feeling, ever since Janus was a baby, that he was laughing at her. The derisive laughter that came from his cot, those knowing smiles he gave her from his pram. At the same time she was bewilderingly in love with this tiny person, and tried to put the condescending laughter down to her own imaginings. Janus's first smile came on the fourth day of his life, and its arrival shocked her. It seemed too grown up, too big to fit on that little face. It was as though it had been pinned there, she thought. A baby's smile was an involuntary facial spasm that produced, almost as if by accident, an expression of pure, uncomplicated delight. Janus's smiles were brimming with meaning, self-awareness, they were too practised, too well observed. They always brought Colette

9

sharply up against herself, and she shied from entertaining her baby with silliness, as other mothers do, because it made her feel foolish. She felt that her son was mocking her.

When he was three or four a frequent question was 'Am I very clever, Mummy?'

'Yes, very clever, Janus.'

'How clever am I?'

'Cleverer than me.'

'Am I cleverer than Daddy?'

'Probably.'

Too clever, she always felt like saying. She was delighted to have such a clever child, but sometimes his cleverness worried her. He was going too fast. He had more knowledge than he knew what to do with, more skills than he knew how to use. She could barely remember a time when he couldn't talk. Perfect but meaningless sentences came from that soft little face.

At two he was doodling doorways with poster paint, at three whole houses, then streets and cities. His numerical reach doubled every few months. At three and a half he could count to infinity. At four he was painting orreries, galaxies.

His school reports stated that his mental age was one, two, three years in advance of his physical age. The thought that he had some brainy double, a clever doppelgänger always a few paces ahead of him troubled Colette. She wondered why schools had to measure development in that way. Surely it wasn't a good thing to have the mind and body out of synch with each other, even if the mind was ahead. Janus's numerate, literate ghost seemed to be racing into the future. At such a rate he would be dead before Janus's body finished school.

The Jones's garden slotted neatly into the ninety other gardens of Fernlight Avenue and Woodberry Road, its parallel neighbour. It was awkwardly shaped, given a narrow panhandle at its far end where the gardens of Hoopers Lane intruded, and its geography was marked by the sites of ambitious schemes that had failed. The spectacular herbaceous border that had an array of sunflowers but nothing else. The trellis for a rose that hadn't taken, now used, and mostly broken, by James as a climbing frame. The rockery on the opposite side which managed some alpine flourishes but was slowly succumbing to the spreading wave of ivy that was taking over the whole of that side of the garden. The lawn was threadbare, drought-cracked earth showing through. The narrow part of the garden, beyond the winter jasmine, was thick with black-berries and raspberries whose fruit was never made into jam or pies.

As gardeners the Joneses conceded that they lacked vision. Before moving to this house they'd never had land to organize. They thought perhaps they should leave it to chance. Colette only knew she wanted trees and lots of them. Their hopes mainly rested on a number of young saplings – a Warwickshire Drooper, a Pershore, Ellison Orange, cherry tree, Judas tree, sumac and two lilacs, one purple, one white (the purple one having germinated from the bones of the buried family cat). If all the trees they'd planted grew to maturity they would have a dense, dark forest for a garden.

The house itself stood alone from the other houses of Fernlight Avenue, the only detached house in a road of semis. A gloomy, sheer canyon of brickwork and drainpipes separated it from number 87. Including its narrow, violet toilet it had eight rooms beneath a pointed slate roof and three tall chimney stacks. The Joneses had moved in three years ago but the walls still bore the fading yellow paper that was the previous owner's choice. Mr Sealy had died in one of the bedrooms (they didn't know which) and everything of his had been removed apart from the decorations, a heap of junk in the loft (including a tailor's dummy) and a heap of rubble at the bottom of the garden. The wiring was pre-war round pins and black twists of flex. The floors were cold expanses of lino and everywhere there was pipework, some of it dripping, in long, intestinal runs across ceilings, down room corners, along wainscoting. Janus had said, on first seeing the inside of the house, 'Mummy, it's like a factory.' But they would cover the pipes, carpet the floors, repaper the walls. That was for the autumn. For the summer their main concern was a holiday. They hadn't been on holiday for three years, and to this end a voice was now calling Colette from the house.

'Whoo-oo, Mrs Jones,' came the voice, in at the front door, out the back, as though the house was an enormous megaphone. Colette recognized the voice as that of Mrs Baker, their neighbour opposite, owner of a telephone. 'There's a call from Mr Jones,' Mrs Baker went on, 'from Wales . . .'

Mrs Baker always called Colette Mrs Jones. Colette always called Mrs Baker Mrs Baker. She didn't even know her first name. She was told it once but had forgotten and didn't think it polite, after so long, to ask. It was the same with most of her neighbours. Next door were Mr and Mrs Peck. Mr Peck had lumbago, was a fanatical 'comper' and had once won a sports car by inventing the phrase '*makes the better spread*' to describe a margarine. He rode to work on a bicycle that looked like two monocycles welded together, following a round-the-houses route that visited all the public conveniences on the way. There was something wrong with Mr Peck's waterworks.

Mr Peck was just that, not even an initial. But Mrs Peck was Viv. Colette knew this because Mr Peck's chirpy calling of that name from the far end of their garden, usually requesting tea while he bent with trouble over his rhubarb, was a constant and strangely reassuring sound on weekend afternoons.

Beyond the proximity of next door Colette didn't even know her neighbours' surnames. She invented names for them herself. Next door but one were Mr and Mrs Goofyteeth, whose prim suburban manners and petty snobberies Colette found repulsive. He would strut past the house in the morning with a briefcase, bowler hat and umbrella and cast a withering look at the wilderness of the Jones's front garden. Mrs Goofyteeth was short haired, large busted and long nosed. She kept her house in an order that could only be achieved through childlessness. The painful tidiness of their domain seemed to Colette like a fortress built against childhood, full of

12

thorny traps waiting to snap children up.

Opposite was a lone elderly gentleman called The Gorilla, whom Colette had some fondness for. He was a linguist who, in the greengrocer's, would ask for bananas in Esperanto. Tall, broad and hunched, he had a heavily featured face as cracked as the poet Auden's, with a voice slow and droll.

Next door to him on the right were Mr and Mrs Cortina, named after the sleek, grey company car, renewed each year, which reposed outside the house of this travelling vacuum cleaner salesman. They, too, were an ageing couple, either childless or with a departed brood. Colette, as a young mother of young children, felt somewhat outcast in this little avenue of barren couples. But at least there was Mrs Baker who had two young children of her own – Andrew and Susan – and who was now leading her across the road to her own house.

The Bakers were dull but friendly. He was a mechanic with his own garage somewhere in Barnet. She was a sensible-looking housewife. Their son Andrew sometimes played with Janus and James, sharing Dinky Toys, building traffic jams and designing, under Andrew's studiously older instruction, various forms of road junction.

As she entered Mrs Baker's hall, where the phone was, Colette felt a slight sense of relief at its gentle disarray, the traces of children evident in its smudges and subtle mis-alignments. The floor was black and white tiles, like a monstrous chessboard.

The voice on the line spoke across an ocean of static.

'Darling, it's me. I've found somewhere.'

'Where are you?'

'I'm in Mr and Mrs Evans's farmhouse. It's in a place called Llanygwynfa. I don't think I said that right. I had a tumble on the bike. They patched me up and gave me some tea. She opened a can of pineapple chunks for me. She said they only do that on special occasions. They're very nice. He's out in the fields now – he was actually carrying one of those crosier things, like a bishop. She's in the farmyard collecting eggs. They said we can stay here . . .'

'What do you mean tumble?'

'Nothing. Just a forward summersault over the handlebars, then over the bonnet of a posh car that came from nowhere. Just like Lesley in Ireland.'

'Oh yes. He was knocked down in the Knockmealdown Mountains . . .'

'That's right, by a Bentley. The driver gave him ten pounds. This driver gave me thirty, just fished it out of his wallet.'

'And you haven't broken anything?'

'Only my front wheel. But I've got a lot to thank that driver for – not only the money, but if he hadn't allowed me to crash into him I would probably have passed this place without giving it a second glance. But I've landed head first in paradise . . .'

'Don't you think you're too old for this sort of thing?'

'Don't talk to me about age. Mr Evans looks a hundred but he sprang down from the wall like a boy. This telephone's incredibly heavy. Can you hear the sheep? There's one outside the door. Mr Evans showed me a field we could have – a whole field to ourselves with a stream in it . . .'

Her husband went on to a rapturous description of the farm and its surroundings. There was a childish triumphalism in his voice which Colette enjoyed. She had objected when he first proposed cycling alone to Wales in order to scout out a suitable camp site, she and the children following by train. He was forty years old and hadn't cycled long distance for sixteen years. His body had thickened and so had the traffic. If a heart attack didn't get him then a juggernaut would. When he phoned her at the end of his first day he had sounded quiet and shaky. When he phoned her from Dot's bungalow in Llanidloes he'd sounded louder but gloomier. He hadn't phoned yesterday and she had worried. But now he was chattering like an exhausted, overexcited kid.

She returned to the house in a flush of excitement to find Janus and James hiding from the voice that was booming from an unseen source at the end of the garden. Their opposite

14

neighbour, a stranger, was complaining about the shower of baby apples that had landed on him and his wife while they were sunbathing.

3

Aldous Rex Llewellyn Jones stood alone on the platform of Llanygwynfa Halt, finding it hard to imagine that the rails below, dead straight in both directions, provided an unbroken line of bolted steel between Llanygwynfa and London Paddington.

Behind him rose the hill called Moelfre, massive and bald, roughly the shape an egg yolk will take if cracked, raw, on to a plate, the huge cousin of the feeble dunes that swelled the horizon in front of Aldous. The sea could be heard even from here, like radio static. A drought had fallen upon the land of Y Lledrith and the grass all around was dying slowly. The air above the rails was curdled with heat. Crickets rasped sambas everywhere.

Aldous, sometimes called Aldo, as in the film star, more rarely Rex but never Llewellyn, was enjoying the feel of his dentures as they sat in his mouth and thinking how lucky he was to have saved them. A mid-air catch, at full stretch, as he arced across the bonnet of an Armstrong Siddeley, reflected in it, of the teeth he'd somehow shouted out of his head. It was the second time in his life he'd saved his teeth.

In 1939, at Blackwater Bridge, near Sneem, County Kerry, he and his friend Lesley Waugh, having cycled from London, pitched a tent of white canvas and wooden poles in a field provided by a kindly farmer who'd also supplied them with a hot meal – two willow pattern plates brimming with a greasy stew and bruised, purple potatoes, which he and his wife carefully conveyed across two fields without spilling a drop. The meal turned out to be so foul they'd had to bury it, presenting the farmer with two gratefully clean plates. They'd eaten instead their last tin of corned beef, taking turns to rake forkfuls of meat out of the tin.

The early evening after a day's cycling was nearly always silent for Aldous and Lesley. Neither would feel much like talking. They were together but alone for a while, as though each was pitching an invisible tent of personal space, hammering in unseen pegs of identity. This was because cycling blended them into a single person. A whole day of cycling – of trying to match each other's pace, freewheeling side by side, becoming mirrors of each other's movements, made them almost into a single cycling entity which, in the evening, had to be unglued back into two individual people.

So Lesley sat, his braces hanging down and his shirtsleeves rolled up, his bicycle inverted before him, its rear wheel between his raised knees. He was going through the spokes with a spoke key, tightening some, loosening others, trying to rid the wheel of a kink he was sure had developed. He looked like a harpist tuning his instrument.

Aldous was standing near the entrance to the tent. He had changed out of the grey flannels and shirt of the cyclist into his evening clothes – tweed jacket and plus fours with tartan socks and brown, patent leather shoes. He'd just lit his pipe and was contemplating the view which was unremarkable – some clumps of yellowish trees, low, dark hills in the distance, to the left a lot of farm clutter, and was wondering if he had the energy to get his watercolours out and do a quick sketch. He hadn't.

Lesley, after twenty minutes of spoke-tuning, pushed his back wheel and let it run – tick tick tick – on its spindle and seeing that it was running true turned to Aldous and was about to say something profoundly sensible and dull, something like *that's that little job sorted out* but instead all he could say in a voice almost exaggeratedly calm, as if making the most commonplace of observations, was *Good Lord. The tent's on fire.*

The memory of that fire came vividly back to Aldous as he waited in the heart of that heat-shimmering landscape. There had been a drought that summer as well. The fire was like a flaring up of the land's own thirst. The landscape of Y Lledrith reminded him of Kerry, where human presence had only a tenuous hold. Walls, some fallen. Lean-tos of black tin. Odd clumps of rock that might be sites of forgotten ritual or, more likely, displaced results of glacial drift. Gorse.

Everything was destroyed in the fire. Everything apart from the clothes they were wearing, their bicycles and Aldous's false teeth. Almost without thinking, Aldous had dropped on all fours and crawled into the fiery house to save them. Lesley had pulled him out by his feet, calling 'don't be a damned fool', thinking he'd gone in to save his sketch book which only had a couple of drawings in it, but when he'd fully extracted his friend and he lay sprawled tummy down on the grass, what he held in his right hand was not a block of watercolour paper but a set of nearly new dentures.

It was Aldous's habit, at the end of a day's cycling and after the successful pitching of the tent, to take his teeth out for a while. He would rest them in a cleaned-out pipe-tobacco tin which he would place near the door. Their newness still blistered his gums occasionally, and the relief of toothlessness after a day in the saddle was a great pleasure of the evening, but he still looked on his false teeth as the most precious thing in his life. A thing without which he could not face the future.

At twenty-four Aldous didn't have a tooth in his head, had kissed them all goodbye, one by one, in a three-day orgy of blood-letting his dentist had recommended, somewhat reluctantly, after a decade or more of trying to save them. Aldous's teeth had been bad almost since the day of their arrival in his pre-adolescent mouth. To him they had been nothing more than a fount of natural agony alternating with clinical torture. When his dentist said 'there's nothing for it but to have the whole bloody lot out', tapping them hopelessly with something like a silver tyre lever, he could have yodelled with joy. The cycle of pain ended in that massive excision after which his dentures were presented to him like a champion's trophy. To hold that charming grin in his hand, representing, as they did, a life free of pain, was an experience only slightly bettered when he held Janus's tiny body for the first time.

The journey back from Ireland, having only a half-burnt five pound note to pay their way, no ferry tickets or spare clothes, Aldous recalled as one of the great adventures of his life. They slept in dry ditches by roadsides, on wet nights in barns full of damp straw. They washed at public fountains and village pumps, begged for unsold salted meats and stale soda bread from village shops, drank unfinished glasses of stout left outside pubs. But then, half way back to Dublin, feeling very low, they had a miraculous stroke of luck. Lesley was knocked down by a rich-looking person in a chauffeur-driven Bentley S2. Aldous couldn't recall, now, if this had really happened in the Knockmealdowns, but it had happened somewhere in the middle of nowhere, not the sort of place you would expect to meet any sort of car, and certainly not a sleek, recently waxed Bentley. And barely before Lesley had time to pick himself out of the bracken into which he'd been tipped, crisp notes had been stuffed into his pocket by an impatient, jack-booted chauffeur under instruction from the rich-looking man, who peered over his black sill with disdain as his car purred away.

The money was enough for a swish journey back to London; platefuls of oysters in Dublin, smoked salmon on the steamer out of Dun Laoghaire, a first class couchette on the overnighter to Paddington.

The following summer Aldous was a soldier.

Aldous now realized that the past ended with the outbreak of war. Everything since then was the present. Those cycling holidays seemed to belong to a different age altogether.

Lesley Waugh had been Aldous's English teacher. A young man in his first teaching post, he had discovered, he believed, a boy with great artistic talents when he passed the art room one day and noticed eleven-year-old Rex Jones's paintings of cowboys heroic on their horses, candlestick cacti, monumental mountains and red prairies behind them. Aldous (who called himself Rex at school) had first begun painting cowboys while convalescing from an 'appendicitis with complications' which kept him away from school for nearly a year and robbed him of the chance of going to the grammar. Twice the surgeons had chloroformed the child and made an attempt to excise the burst, infected shred of an organ and twice they'd failed, leaving deep, knotted scars on his body. While the poison slowly drained out of his system Aldous read cowboy comics and copied with coloured crayons pictures of cowboys, horses, cacti, feathered red indians, wigwams.

Fearing that the boy's talents were likely to wither in the sterile and philistine atmosphere of Tottenham Technical School, Lesley took Rex under his wing and set about developing the aesthetic sensibilities of his young protégé. He showed him the big art books he had at home where he still lived with his mother and father as part of a large Catholic family. Titians, Raphaels, El Grecos and Tintorettos illustrated with large monochrome plates that peeled away, except for one edge, from the page. He took him to the National Gallery and showed him the Monets, Cézannes, Turners, to the Tate to see the newest art – Sickert, Picasso. They lingered over the Rembrandts in the Wallace Collection and at Kenwood House. He took him to plays at The Old Vic and concerts at the Queen's Hall. Eventually he paid for him out of his own pocket to study art at Hornsey. For four years he funded Aldous as he tackled painting, drawing, sculpture, ceramics, printing (lino, litho, woodcutting, etching, silk-screen), graphics, calligraphy, textile and furniture design.

They shared lodgings and a life of suburban high culture in

Crouch End, Hornsey, Muswell Hill, with long, meandering cycling expeditions in the summer.

Until the war came.

When, in the summer of 1940, Aldous found himself posted to Colwyn Bay for an interminable army induction course, Lesley, too old for call-up, cycled to North Wales and camped in the hills above the town in a sad attempt at continuing their tradition of cycling summers. It hadn't work out. Aldous was the object of mockery from fellow squaddies for taking leave from the barracks to walk with his male friend on the beach or in the hills. Lesley packed up early and cycled home.

Never in the decade they'd shared lodgings together had anyone suggested that their relationship was improper and it was only in that summer of 1939, a few days after their return, charred, bleary, constipated and weak, from Ireland, that they'd kissed.

It was their first and last kiss. It happened without warning, so quickly Aldous hardly knew where it came from.

It had been an ordinary evening on the evening of the world. The armies were amassing across Europe, and Aldous and Lesley were lying on the floor of their upstairs room in Muswell Hill, in a nest of Shakespeare, Schubert, lapsang souchong and Schiller – *O friends, No more these sounds! Let us sing more cheerful songs, more full of joy!*

'Shall I wind up the Trout?' said Lesley affectionately, as if to a baby.

Aldous worked his knuckles into his eyes and yawned. Both men lay on their backs, straight, their heads almost touching, like the pivoting hands of a clock. Their heads almost simultaneously tipped sideways so that they were face to face. They noticed each other with a sudden intensity. They looked at each other as if into mirrors.

Aldous's usually carefully oiled hair hung loosely in sharp black strands like Japanese brush strokes. Clark Gable at his most dishevelled. His grey eyes looked into Lesley's and Lesley's green eyes looked back. Lesley's face was ruddier, more used and scuffed, with that heavy Waugh brow, those straight Irish eyebrows, like a single line broken in the middle, and the eyes themselves, rarely out of shadow, rarely seen.

From nowhere that kiss came. Aldous couldn't recall the actual moment of contact, the lip-to-lip touch. All he could recollect was the moment immediately following when Lesley withdrew his face sharply, shock now in his eyes, sat up, coughed and then blew his nose loudly. Aldous felt a strong urge to wipe his lips but resisted, thinking it would be rude. Only later did he think that Lesley's nose blowing was in fact disguised lip wiping.

Lesley fiddled with his hanky, poked it back in his pocket.

'Just to thank you, you know, old chap . . .'

'Yes,' said Aldous.

Lesley crawled on his hands and knees to the gramophone and turned its brass handle quickly. He placed the heavy silver stylus arm on the furiously spinning black disc, releasing the cacophony of dust that preceded the opening bars of the Trout Quintet.

Aldous felt not repulsion, only emptiness. Kissing Lesley had been like kissing a photograph. There was no life-spark in the moment of touching. It was only then, when he walked to the window where a miniature forest of cacti grew, that he realized what he wanted more than anything in life was a family.

So at the height of the blitzkrieg Aldous married Lesley's younger sister Colette in the Catholic Church of Our Lady, Tottenham, a building of concrete and glass three decades ahead of its time. Colette thought it looked like a cinema.

Lesley, aware that Aldous was friends with his sister, seemed genuinely bewildered when Aldous announced that he and Colette were in love. 'Colette? I don't understand, Rex. She's just a girl.' He had that look about him, of someone hit on the back with a pillow, for quite a few days.

Thrown into a panic, Lesley blundered about for the first marriageable female he could find; this was Madeleine Singer, a prim bank manager's daughter from Ealing who'd manoeuvred herself into such a position in Lesley's social landscape that marriage was almost inevitable. They moved to High Wycombe in the heart of the Chilterns where, with a swiftness that surprised everyone, not least Lesley, they produced a family.

The Chilterns had a special meaning for Rex and Lesley. It was among those cretaceous hills with their red villages and hanging beech woods that they'd cycled nearly every week-end for half a dozen summers, exploring every dry valley, climbing every sheep-shorn hill, following every twisting lane, taking greasy black brass rubbings from all the stumpy little churches, picnicking on hillsides, Lesley reading aloud from Palgrave, Rex oil-sketching a farmstead or village, their bicycles lying beside them, a shambles of spokes and handlebars.

Lesley once eulogized the bicycle as they rode side by side along a Chiltern lane,

'What is it about the bicycle,' he said, 'that makes people so good? No one can do bad things if they are riding a bicycle. Is it because they are all about balance and that if you try to fight someone while riding a bike you'll only fall off? You cannot go to war on a bicycle. And one's thoughts, when one is cycling, are never mean thoughts. You have no delusions, ambitions or jealousies when you are on a bike. I think it must be the case, Rex, that we ride bicycles with our hearts.'

Unless, thought Rex to himself, it's uphill and the wind's against you. Such times can bring on a longing for bicycle armoury – handlebar-mounted machine guns, bazookas on the cross bar.

But High Wycombe, although surrounded by those meaningful hills, was a long, thin, ugly town. The manufacture of furniture had given it a bourgeois prosperity, producing acres of dull suburbs and a noisy commercial centre. Lesley never learned to drive so rarely saw the hill country he was in the heart of. Madeleine boxed up his books ('they collect dust, dear') and stacked them in the garage ('all labelled, dear, just let me know what you want and I'll pop in and get it for you').

Aldous always felt slightly guilty for taking Lesley's sister and turning himself into his brother-in-law. They remained on good terms, the families visiting each other once or twice a year, but occasionally Aldous would catch a glimpse of that look in Lesley's eyes, the shock and desolation and sometimes the accusing glance, the 'you've abandoned me, you've betrayed me, after all I did for you . . .' look across the tea table. And when Aldous visited his friend's now bookless house (when before they'd lived in a home that seemed made almost entirely of books) and saw the born bachelor making such a valiant effort at being a good family man, his sense of guilt increased.

Lesley never cycled again. Nor did he ever attend art exhibitions, concerts or plays. He settled into a quiet life of schoolmastering and fatherhood. His bike reposed, unused for many years in the cavernous space of the garage with his books.

At one time, Aldous thought, it seemed they would go on cycling for ever. That they would cycle to the end of the world.

They'd covered most of the British Isles in those Thirties summers, from Cornwall to Scotland on dusty roads where motorized vehicles were still rare, celebrated events. Their tour of Ireland was their most ambitious. They'd planned to take in not just the Ring of Kerry but north to Galway, Donegal, perhaps even into Ulster. It was a stepping stone, they both thought, to future expeditions into the European mainland. That it all ended so abruptly and disastrously had caused Aldous ever since to feel that he was in the middle of something he needed to finish. The feeling hadn't gone away in sixteen years. It had become stronger, in fact. Going to Ireland and picking up where he'd left off, at Blackwater Bridge, near Sneem, County Kerry, wasn't a realistic option, but when, after a string of dull holidays in Devon, the idea occurred to him of cycling alone to Wales to reconnoitre the terrain and look for somewhere idyllic and isolated to camp

24

with Colette and the children, there did seem a real chance that he'd complete, at last, that unfinished journey. His wife had thought him slightly daft and had doubted his fitness. But he'd cycled to work and back every day for eight years. He believed he could do it.

He'd set off, as always on these occasions, at first light so as to escape London before the morning traffic. Colette was still asleep upstairs. He'd left a pencilled note on the table – *Will phone Mrs Baker tonight, love Aldo.* Then he cycled a hundred miles, sapping his body almost to nothing, collapsing in bracken on Bromyard Common. The next day he crossed the border into Wales and stayed with his Aunt Dot and her son Geraint at their bungalow in Llanidloes. Exhaustion caused him to stay there two nights and have a day's rest. After that his strength mustered and there followed a day of long, slow ascents and brief, eventful plummets, eventually to Bontagendor on the shores of the Breuddwyd Estuary where he camped beneath a bluff of dying rhododendrons. The tide brought the river to the door of his tent the following morning.

That day, fatigued and hungry, he cycled carefully along the Aberbreuddwyd road, a blessedly flat road in a mountainous landscape, the swirl of estuary waters and sands to his left with the teetering cliffs of Cadair above, slopes of fir trees to his right, half concealing vertiginous cottages; ahead of him the sea with the town of Aberbreuddwyd hanging on a spit of land.

He was quite overcome by the beauty of the landscape, having never explored this portion of Wales before. There was something about its complexity, its range of colours and shapes, that reminded him of the landscapes he used to make out of books, sheets and assortments of household paraphernalia for his toy trains to pass through. It looked, this landscape, as though it had been designed by an over-imaginative child.

When, finally, a few miles north of the town, he was knocked down, picked up and offered a field to camp in, he felt compelled to stay. The double coincidence of saving his teeth and colliding with a luxury car did indeed make it seem as if he was picking up the thread of his life that had been abandoned in the fire in Southern Ireland, while Mr and Mrs Evans and their farm seemed gatekeepers to a new, enchanted era in his life, just reward for daring to cycle again.

He was heartened enormously by their hospitality, the thoughtful and gentle first aid they applied, the simple but beautiful food they fed him, the humour and warmth they showed him. The fact that he'd been knocked down by William Vaughan, in effect their landlord, seemed to endear him to them. Aldous felt somehow that he'd been knocked on to their side of some ancient territorial quarrel.

Aldous, although born in London, liked to think of himself as a Welshman at heart. His father was born, illegitimately, in the Montgomeryshire mill town of Llanidloes (where Aldous and Colette honeymooned). Tom Jones came to London in 1910 and married Edith Alice Hobbs, a girl from the Kentish North Downs who was in domestic service. He worked as a painter and decorator after an attempt to set up a garage business failed. Far-sighted enough to see that the motor car, at that time still a gadget for eccentric toffs, would eventually take over the world, he failed to see that the talented mechanic he'd gone into partnership with was also a crook. Tom was double-crossed, betrayed, stitched up. His partner skedaddled with all the profits, leaving Tom with appalling debts. He was declared bankrupt and became a very bitter man. By the age of twenty-five he looked twice that age. The stuffing had been knocked out of him. He drank heavily, sang operatically and developed a lifelong love of Shakespeare. He'd turned to Shakespeare originally out of a desire to improve himself. He set about stoically the task of reading all the plays and poems, memorizing all the famous speeches. What began as a tedious trudge turned quickly into a labour of love.

Tom Jones by daytime wallpapering terraced houses in Tottenham, daubing varnish on window frames and tottering on ladders with brimming buckets of whitewash, by evening sipping a glass of brandy and reading *A Midsummer Night's Dream*.

Every summer Tom took his children, Aldous and Mfanwy, back to Llanidloes to stay with their grandmother, Mary Jones, at her nook-ridden, alcove-rich house in Short Bridge Street. Idyllic summer weeks full of gooey food and exhausting walks up Penralt, the Gorn, the Fan and the Sugarloaf, and then evenings with cakes and sandwiches among a menagerie of china cows and porcelain birds, sonorous clocks.

In later years, embittered by his business failure and bothered by the twin stigmas of his bastardy and his Welshness, which had cost him much work (on first arriving in London he'd considered changing his name to Smith, killing both with a single stone), buoyed up by a deep but incommunicable love of Shakespeare (it wouldn't do, he thought, to go on about Edgar and Edmund to his Tottenham clients while pasting up rolls of rose-covered wallpaper) he slowly grew less and less attached to Wales. When his mother died he never visited Llanidloes again. When he talked about Wales he talked about it as though it was an island, literally.

'We should go to Llani again soon, Dad,' Aldous would say.

'I couldn't manage the crossing, son,' his dad would gasp in reply, 'not at my age.'

This brought to mind Aldous's earliest memory of his father – being lifted out of his cot and wrapped carefully with newspaper and scotch tape, his father muttering drunkenly 'have you had a good crossing?'

In old age Tom walked hunched and grey, always with a cigarette in his mouth, always scented with whisky. He talked a lot about that remote, mountainous island off the west coast of England and the cruciform mill town at its heart, at the confluence of two rivers, the first town on the great snake-like loop of the Severn in its progress from the moonscapes of Plynlymon to the Bristol Channel.

How many houses, thought Aldous, how many rooms still bore the trace of his father's hand? Twenty-three years had passed since he last brushed paint on to a stranger's wall. In that time it would have cracked, discoloured, flaked. Then it would have been scorched or wire-brushed off, painted or papered over. There couldn't be much of his paint or wallpaper left in Tottenham now, thought Aldous. But he couldn't believe there was none. There must still be a few houses, perhaps just one, perhaps just a single room, somewhere, that still carried his mark, for a few years yet.

4

The train arrived, the 4-6-2 green-boilered, copper funnelled *Caernarfon Castle*, a volcano in an iron shell, a blast of industrial noise in a silent landscape. It juddered and slammed to a halt at the Halt, only two of its six carriages alongside the weedy platform.

Aldous felt a curious affinity for this train as it wheezed and gasped at the station after its great journey. He had similarly traced a path from London to Wales avoiding steep hills where possible, following faults and fissures in the terrain, seeking out flatness. The locomotive seemed resplendent with exhaustion.

No one got off the train. The guard, emerging from one of the front carriages, was about to tell the grimy driver to press on to Brythwch when they noticed a door open on one of the carriages further down, beyond the end of the platform. A suitcase was hurled out, landing in the deep grass by the side of the track. The guard, a portly man, ran as best he could, down the platform and on to the track, hollering urgently.

Aldous knew that it was his wife who'd found herself stranded at the end of the train. He recognized the suitcase. Of course, she explained later, she'd been told which carriage was the one for Llanygwynfa Halt. She'd been told several times by several people. They'd said different carriages, she was sure.

At Shrewsbury the train had flipped around, the locomotive changing ends. The first carriage became the last carriage. It was very confusing.

Eventually the guard managed to dissuade Colette from jumping down on to the clinker with her luggage and children and told the driver to take the train the necessary few hundred yards further up the track. The guard waddled quickly past Aldous, shaking his jowly red face despairingly, giving Aldous a brief, accusatory stare, carrying the suitcase he'd retrieved from the trackside.

The *Caernarfon Castle* stirred, expelled steam in a deafening rush, whistled, exploded and then moved the small distance needed to bring Colette into alignment with Llanygwynfa. Aldous could see, before the train had quite stopped, that she was laughing.

Out of a terrace of fifty doors hers was the only one to open. Janus jumped out first, followed by James who bravely leapt the gap. Then two leather suitcases, a large wickerwork hamper, a canvas rucksack, a crocodile skin shopping bag, a grey valise, a red cardboard case and two school kitbags, one of which shed a small library of books on to the platform. Finally Colette gracefully lowered herself from the train. The guard wheeled two bikes, one boy's racer, one child's tricycle, with difficulty towards the family.

Colette was wearing a red short-sleeved dress stitched with a motif of golden horses around the cuffs and hem, made narrow at the waist by a gold belt. Her long hair was tied back in a ponytail, spirals of rolled gold swung from her ear lobes and she wore pink and cream stilettos.

Janus was in his school uniform (tie, slightly loose, blazer badged with two red dragons dancing either side of a black cauldron, scuffed shoes). James was wearing a hand-knitted pullover and white shorts that were almost down to his feet which were shod with brown leather sandals.

Aldous and Colette hugged. Janus and James jumped up and down. Colette was startled by her husband's face. The day before he'd set off his face was the colour of stale milk. This afternoon it was the colour of onion skins. The journey had seasoned him. His eyes and his saved teeth were shining.

At first she felt like a guest of her husband at his private, other residence. Even as they managed the lane, he with two suitcases, Janus dragging the hamper, she felt, bizarrely, that she needed to be on her best behaviour. Aldous described everything they passed unnecessarily: 'This is a wall', or 'this is one of the trees, this is the gate to the farmyard . . .'

The ironwork of those gates, all looped and curled metal, reminded Janus of the signature of Elizabeth I.

As they progressed through the farmyard Aldous named each building they passed – cow shed (called cow house by the Evanses; Aldous and Colette laughed when they heard it), chicken coop, barn, grain store and so on. When Colette asked him about a small, windowless stone building he hadn't named, she heard irritation in his voice when he had to admit he didn't know that building's use. 'Probably just a . . . I don't know. A storage thing. I don't know.' Colette paused by its low door. Perhaps four feet high, a wooden door of flaking red paint set in a deep recess of licheny stone. A thick rusty padlock the size of a heart hung from it. She was sure she could hear a whimpering noise within. Something scraping and sniffing at the door. 'Funny to build a building without windows though,' she said. But Aldous was hurrying on, taking pigeon steps under the great weight of his suitcases.

When they arrived at their field, the third field down from the road, reached by a double bend at the end of the farmyard, through a red gate and over a narrow bright stream by means of a plank bridge, she felt she was being shown around an enormous drawing room.

And this is the grass in small hillocks except for the flat area where the tent is pitched, and these are our walls, tastefully hung with mosses and lichens, and this is the orange harrow that last made hay a century ago, and these are the scattered monoliths that might be the remains of a Bronze Age burial site, and this is the bare patch under the hawthorn clump littered with flecks of wool and round conglomerates of sheep dung like magnified blackberries that mark the favoured resting site of the sheep that sometimes live in the field. And here is the view we enjoy, the haulm of chimneys and spires that is Llanygwynfa, and above it, the domed mass of Moelfre.

Colette's heart lifted when she saw their tent occupying this place. It was on the far side of the field, its flysheet pegged to the grass on long guy ropes. It looked like the single sail of a ship come adrift from its vessel to be fastened to the world. It looked like a fallen kite, or an early and unsuccessful attempt at a flying machine. When she unlaced its entrance and recognized some of the furnishings of Fernlight Avenue (a blanket, some books, a framed photograph of herself taken twenty years ago), all lit with green, she felt she was discovering the lost treasure of her own life.

Colette had a genius for packing. Aldous thought this when she unpacked the hamper. She reminded him of a stage magician he'd seen somewhere who, from the splintery interior of a similar hamper, had extracted a stepladder, a tall lamp standard, a set of golf clubs, and a beautiful woman. Colette produced clothes, bedding, a small tent for the boys which was swiftly poled and pegged into shape, pillows which were plumped up, lilos which were breathed into, a lavatory tent like a Punch and Judy stall, folding chairs, crockery, Snakes and Ladders, Monopoly, Totopoly, lamps, cameras, binoculars, books, sketch books, canvases . . .

Once Colette had transformed the mostly empty interior of the tent into a small home and had set up a kitchen area within the tent's door guard, and once James and Janus were busy with ball games, Aldous wrapped his arms around his wife's waist from behind and rocked against her.

'I've found it haven't I?' he half whispered into her ear. 'This is the place.'

Colette turned within the circle of her husband's arms and faced him.

'Yes,' she said, and kissed him.

'Am I very clever?' Aldous went on.

'Very,' said Colette.

'You told me to go and find somewhere and I've found it.'

'Yes,' said Colette, who hadn't. 'No more sharing wash-rooms with loose-bowelled Brummies or trying to get to sleep in a field full of teddy boys.'

Aldous pressed his face into Colette's neck and laughed. Colette's neck absorbed his laughter. And then she laughed.

She laughed a lot. There was something in the air. She found Llanygwynfa very funny. She giggled helplessly when she was introduced to Mr and Mrs Evans. Their asymmetrical, tall and short stances, his long mac worn even on the hottest days, Mrs Evans's little round spectacles, her ankle socks, her grinning mouth of tiny teeth, Colette found all these caused her to laugh. When Colette laughed it was as though she'd pegged herself out on her mirth, she hung there helpless with it, swinging. She found the farm and its playful, attentive dogs funny, the haughty, nervous sheep funny. She even found the beach funny. The sand, piled up in soft mountain ranges, was funny. So was the sea, retreating, at low tide, to a strip of glitter on the horizon beyond a perfect desert of beige sand.

'She's good at laughing, that Mrs Jones,' said Mrs Evans to her husband, hearing the jocular approach of Colette through the farmyard one morning.

The two children on the farm were roughly the same age as Janus. Barry was energetic and serious. He had a small, tight face; his eyes and mouth were like holes made by a pencil on a ball of soft clay. On Gwen these holes were larger, softer. They were plush sockets containing eyes and a plump, pink tongue. She had liquorice-coloured hair down to her shoulders, a dark frame for the rosiness of her face, the white-ness of her teeth and eyes. Janus found her physicality disconcerting. When they first met she took his hand and shook it until his fingers tingled. She used her hands to direct him where she wanted him to go. She pushed him around as if he was in a wheelchair. The pressure of female hands on his body was a new sensation for Janus.

Their first meeting was for the twins to show the Jones children the lamb. The Evanses always kept one of the year's lambs on the grass by the back yard as a form of family pet. 'Beauty' was a grounded cloud walking on legs of black velvet, a little half smile on the end of her long face, a barrister's wig of wool between her ears.

The twins were puzzled by the hesitant clumsiness of the city children. It was as though they were being introduced to a prim and stern relative, a great aunt. They were shy and embarrassed. They seemed confused by the lamb's friendliness, the fact that it didn't run from them. They looked suspicious, as though they sensed trickery.

'It's our lamb,' explained Barry, earnestly, 'he's called Beauty. Come on, give him some petting you daft children. You, you're the biggest, you show your little brother how to give Beauty some love. Go on now . . .'

Janus put out his hand as if towards something that might bite. Beauty sniffed his fingers and whispered to them, nibbled at nothing. When Janus reached the wool he was shocked and had a brief sensation of falling. It was as though the lamb had no body beneath its wool.

'Is it a real sheep?' asked James.

Gwen approached the lamb quite differently. She treated it like a plump, upright baby, embracing it with both arms, hugging it, pressing her face into its wool, kissing it. Beauty threw her head back and nibbled at Gwen's dark hair.

'That's disgusting,' said James.

'No it's not,' said Janus, who was mesmerized by the embrace of Beauty and Gwen. He had never seen into the face of a lamb before. Those eyes – horizontal slits for pupils, like the eyes a robot might have.

Gwen showed Janus the whole farm. She guided him round the dark, muddy spaces of the cow house, the golden, prickly spaces of the barn. She sat him on the rusty seat of a disused tractor from whose stalled guts grew traveller's joy. The gear lever, a ball on a stick, could still be pushed around, and together they spent afternoons ploughing imaginary fields. Gwen wore boys' clothes (grey shorts, a white shirt, black shoes tied with broken laces) but had a girl's face and a girl's

34

hair. This unsettled Janus at first. He didn't know how to play with her. He'd encountered very few girls. St Edmund's was a boys' school, as was St Francis Xavier, where he was due to start in September. He found the best thing was to behave with her as if she was a boy, and Gwen seemed to accept this. He preferred to think of her as a boy disguised as a girl, or a girl disguised as a boy, he wasn't sure which. Sometimes the disguise slipped and her girlhood was revealed, like the time they found themselves trapped inside the prickly canopy of a hawthorn ten feet from the ground, scratched all over, their bodies as entangled as the branches. Janus noticed her waxy odour and the developing softness of her body. If they wrestled in the grass or in the hay of the barn he hugged and pinched her as if she was a boy, until once he squeezed her body until tears came out of it and she suddenly became delicate and breakable and angry and he couldn't understand why.

A favourite game of theirs was called corpses, where one had to pretend to be dead while the other tried to make them laugh. Janus was good at being dead because he didn't find Gwen at all funny, even when she was babooning her body, gurning, blowing raspberries. Gwen was very good at being dead as well because Janus couldn't think of any ways of making her laugh other than telling her droll, punning jokes.

'Did you hear about the scarecrow who won the Nobel Prize? He was outstanding in his field.'

'We don't have scarecrows on our farm. It's a dairy farm. We don't grow any crops.'

'You're supposed to be dead.'

'Try and make me laugh then you dumbo.'

Colette and her family passed three weeks of almost pure contentment in the hills or on the beach. The processes of the farm went on about them, an impenetrable mystery. Animals were moved from field to field for no obvious reason. Pieces of machinery were hauled by tractors. Mr Evans spent long periods of time engaged in what seemed to be pointless tasks – looking at a wall, walking up and down a section of field staring intently at the ground, opening and shutting gates without passing through them.

Colette felt at home with the cows. Once, at school, she had written an essay about cows. It began '*I can never understand why the word "cow" should be used as an insult, when these beasts are the most shy, sensitive intelligent creatures in the animal kingdom.*' Her English teacher marked this essay with a red A followed by a string of pluses. She read it out to the class. Sister Margaret often did that with her essays. Colette was good at English. She sometimes thought, if things had turned out differently, that she might have been a writer.

By the end of the second week Colette felt she understood the farm, even if she comprehended few of its procedures. She knew the names of the cows – Cochen, Penwen, Frochwen. She knew which were the best milkers and even tried to help with milking sometimes. She noticed that the cows were spoken to in Welsh while the horses were addressed in English and had English, aristocratic names – Prince, Duke, Captain.

Colette was glad that Janus had made some friends. She was starting to worry that he didn't seem to have any. He never invited anyone home from school. But here at the farm he seemed a more social creature. At times, when the farm children and her own were all playing together, along with the dairymaids, farm boys, sheepdogs, hens and lambs, she felt that same sense of being part of a complicated, sprawling family she'd felt as the youngest child of a large household. It was a sensation, she now realized, that she'd missed deeply since her family had dispersed. As a child she'd grown up amongst giants, she always felt. Lesley was a full-grown man in her earliest memories of him. Her other brothers and sisters were always tall for their age. Now, as a mother, she still felt uncomfortable towering above her children.

Aldous once confided to her that he was terrified on his first visit to her home, as a guest of Lesley's. The house was a rambling terrace in a Tottenham cul-de-sac that spilt its contents, human, animal and inanimate, out on to the street. Dogs (a fierce Airedale on a chain, a dizzy piebald mongrel always on heat), cats, rabbits, sisters, brothers, toys and furniture seemed heaped or scattered in all the rooms and on the pavement. On hot days they would put an armchair out in front of the house. There was always noise and motion, very little of which came from Lesley's father, a stern-faced man who said little, in contrast to his wife, a lively, hospitable and funny woman full of jokes and stories who always made Aldous feel welcome.

The house was so different from Aldous's family home, which seemed dim and shadowy, silent and empty by comparison. It took several visits before Aldous began to discern, in what seemed at first to be as chaotic as a rubbish dump, a quite elaborate and carefully structured order. That pile of paper, for instance, was not old newspapers waiting to be dumped, but homework awaiting Lesley's attention.

Aldous and Colette's first meeting was in the dusty concrete back garden. Colette couldn't remember, but Aldous described it many years later. She had been wearing only a pair of knickers, a cut down, collarless man's shirt and a cowboy hat. In her hand she'd held a silver pistol which she'd pointed at Aldous's head and fired five times, five sharp cracks and some blue smoke from the amorces smelling of fireworks.

'Get out of town stranger,' she'd said in a thick Wyoming drawl, 'I don' wanna see you roun' here no more.'

Aldous, the youngest in his own family, was nervous of any human beings smaller than himself and so, lofty and aloof, had feigned ignorance of her existence, though painfully aware of the still smoking gun following his head as it passed into the house. Colette had twirled and deftly holstered the weapon.

Colette remembered their second meeting, however. She was two years older and her passions now were for African exploration rather than western adventure. In the back yard at Howard Road she'd knelt in the dust with her chum Vivienne and an assortment of Bakelite big cats. As Aldous passed through the yard Colette aimed a tiger at him and roared tigerishly, then giggled head to head with Viv who twirled a leopard by the tail. They ventriloquized leonine snarls.

37

This time Colette noticed the black, glossy hair swept back and the rather dapper clothing of her brother's young friend. And this time he condescended to cast a glance in her direction, which lingered upon her, and suddenly had Colette feeling foolish, on her belly in the dust with her toys.

A few years later they were cohorts in the same loose circle of friends that centred on the Waugh family, who would go together to dances, country pubs, picnics and the pictures. Aldous, Lesley, Colette, Viv, Lily, Janus – Colette's closest brother after whom she would name her son – Janus's twitchy girlfriend Mary, and his friend Albert who saw Aldous as a rival for the hand of Colette.

Aldous didn't realize he was a rival, nor that he was participating in anything that could involve rivalry, until a visit to the zoo.

Viv ate bananas all day, bananas they'd intended for the chimps and gorillas. Aldous was amused to find that Colette had brought with her two shopping bags heaving with fruit, vegetables, sausages and fresh sardines. She could hardly carry them. He helped her.

He laughed as Colette tossed a cauliflower at a camel, the vegetable bursting into florets at the disinterested animal's feet. He applauded the accuracy of Colette's sardine-lobbing, the polar bear hardly moving his head as he took the little fish out of the air. He chuckled as Colette passed tomatoes one by one through the bars of a chimp's cage where a black leathery hand received them.

Albert, however, only managed to demonstrate how animals bored him. He protested that the zoo was a place for kids, criticized Colette for wasting good food on a lot of mangy animals and wrinkled his nose with disgust at the smell in the elephant house. But Aldous entertained Colette with stories of field trips to the zoo when he was a first year art student, how the keeper provided him with a Tasmanian devil to sketch, an unconscious ball of fluff with no discernible head or tail. 'Quite a challenge to draw,' drawled mysterious, erudite, dapper, bohemian Aldous. Colette laughed melodiously and allowed suave Aldous to take her to the pictures the following Sunday.

Colette always felt lucky to have married Aldous. Among her circle he was sought after, and her sisters were jealous, she could tell. She felt, as the youngest and plainest (she believed), like Cinderella to have won the heart of a handsome artist. And Aldous always seemed so concerned to please her. She had never felt so loved. He was always making things for her: paintings, exquisite vases, batik wall-hangings. She was the subject of countless portraits, her likeness was on every wall of the house and her face filled many sketch books. Everything he did was a gift for her, a love token.

That was how he seemed to think of the farm, and the landscape itself. Continually he talked about the fields and the mountains as though they were things he'd found specifically for her, as gifts. And she accepted them as such. She enjoyed the camomile-thick farmyard with its waddling hens, the golden cliffs of hay in the barn, the ponderous cows just as much as the vases he made for her.

There were only two things about the farm that slightly soured Colette's delight in it. One was the sight of Farmer Evans hacking to pieces a family of hedgehogs with a peat spade. 'They take the milk,' he grumbled at Colette when he saw her distressed, observing face. The other was when she discovered, from Mrs Evans, the purpose of the small, locked, windowless building she noticed on first arriving at the farm.

'That building? Oh, we call it the old school house because it's where the pups learn to be good sheepdogs. They have to be kept in darkness for the first few months of their lives, away from their mother, so we lock them in there. We feed them, of course, and look after them, but we don't talk to them or pet them. When they come out they are much faster at learning than the soppy dogs who've been suckled all their lives. It sharpens their brains.'

So whenever Colette passed the old school house and no one was around, she knelt by its small door and whispered to the trapped puppies and they answered her with quiet paw scrapings and whimperings. And she wondered if she should take a chisel to that heart-shaped padlock and set the bleary, dazzled puppies free, or whether she should leave well alone, because the sheepdogs on the farm seemed happy enough, despite their lightless childhoods.

1963

1

Hugh Evans's brother, Howell, had the sort of face you might see in a child's book of optical illusions, the sort of face that is still a face when turned upside down. With eyes set low down he was bald and bearded with a deep, mouth-like furrow in his forehead. It was sometimes said, not least by Howell himself, that his upside-down face was better looking than his right-way-up face. At least it had a full head of hair.

Howell had a tenancy near Brythwch but had come to Llanygwynfa to help his brother put a drain into the third field. The far corner, near the ash trees, had become so waterlogged that the cows sometimes sank up to their bellies in the mud. Twice that year Hugh had had to use the tractor to pull one out.

Hugh and Howell were walking across the field to inspect the ground when Howell suddenly interrupted their conversation about dogs to say 'That family that always stays here. They're not here this year?'

Without breaking his stride Hugh gestured towards the western wall and said 'They're here.'

By the far wall nothing was visible apart from some dark patches in the grass. As they came nearer Howell saw these patches as two rectangles of ash and cinders. They were roughly the shape of two tents, one large, one small.

'What's been going on, Hugh?' said Howell out of his lower mouth.

'That family is what's been going on here.'

They paused at the edge of the ashes. Hugh kicked, a little disrespectfully, a charred piece of something.

'Been an accident has there?' said Howell.

'Their tents burned down last week, but they're still here.'

Howell swallowed.

'You don't mean,' he said, looking frightened, 'you don't mean . . . not here in the ashes you don't mean do you Hugh?'

Hugh's eyes smiled.

'They're in the barn,' he grumbled happily, 'they hadn't been here an hour when the tents burned down.' He noticed the half-burnt head of a toy cat among the ashes and chuckled. 'It went up like a bonfire. The whole thing took less than a minute, I should think. The big tent went first, whoosh, and sparked off the small one. Do you remember the *Hindenburg*?'

'No.'

'It was like that. But they seem to like staying in the barn.'

For eight years the family Hugh Evans allowed into one of his fields every summer had been the gossip all through Y Lledrith, from Aberbreuddwyd to Brythwch.

— *Hugh Evans has got that English family on his land again.*

— *What are they paying him? That's what I'd like to know.*

— *I went through Brythwch yesterday and they were in the butcher's, and the mother was all dressed up like she was going to a ball.*

— *Yes, Mr Evans, sorry. Your brother Hugh putting up with the English again is he?*

— *What's it got to do with you?*

— *Nothing, Mr Evans, of course not. I just thought they might be spoiling the grass.*

— *It'll need cutting again soon.*

— *I've had to cut it four times this year.*

— *What are the National Park people saying about it though?*

— *Your brother can't open a camp site on his land without their say-*

so you know. Heaven knows I've put in four applications to let out the field behind the barn and four times the devils have said no. I had one come round in his car, and what did he do? He crashed his coupé into Brenda, my best milker, carried her upside down on his bonnet for half a mile, said he couldn't think where the brakes were. That was the end of Brenda's milk. So what if I just do it anyway I say? They say they can fine me thousands of pounds or even put me in prison like they did Mr Holywell who tried to pretend his house was a museum. So I should have said why don't you put Hugh Evans in prison then? They'll say Hugh hasn't opened a camp site, it's just one family he has staying there. It's casual isn't it? He doesn't advertise. It's like having friends staying isn't it? Well I could have a hundred friends staying . . .

'I know all about that,' Hugh said to his brother, 'I've had those National Park fools down here sniffing around. I can let people put up a tent if they are what they call "bona fide wayfarers" or some such nonsense. Not tourists. I don't know.

'Barry's nagging me all the time, Howell, to do something with the land here. He says we could open up the first field by the road. Turn the cows out. Convert the old barn into a toilet block. We could put a tea shop in, he says. He wants one of those things the kids have nowadays, discotheques or whatever they're called. Dances. He's mapped out the field and put a price on each space that could take a tent or a caravan. He tots up the figures and shows me a sheet that tells me how much money that grass could yield during the holiday season. But the National Park people won't hear of it. Barry says they've got caravans in every field from here to Aberbreuddwyd, why can't we have some? But it's the fields down by the sea that get turned into camp sites. Who wants to camp next to the road? Or even in this field, although the Joneses like it well enough. Anyway, we have to sort the lease out with William before we can do anything like that. I'm not making piles of money out of the family, I can tell you that.'

Hugh allowed himself a flute-like laugh.

'I didn't think you were, Hugh. Are they rich anyway?'

'Well, they're from London. Mind you, the father's a

43

Welshman, from Llanidloes. Or his father was anyway. They have a cousin there who's training to be a preacher. He comes over and stays sometimes. A very good organist, Geraint. A very good organist and a very good preacher. He played the organ here once, and then he asked if he could have a turn preaching. Father Rees wasn't very happy about that. And Janus, the eldest son, he's a very good organist as well. He plays in the chapel some Sundays, if Mrs Morris is down with her legs. But there's something a little bit wry about him otherwise. A bit daft. The very first year they were here Gwen came running up to Dorothy and said – Ma, Janus has killed himself. Down on the railway. We said what do you mean? She was crying to heaven. She said his head had been cut off by a train.

'Well, it happened that the pair were playing down in the fourth field – you know the line's just on the other side of the hillock, and they were playing dares like we used to on the cliffs at the back of Ronnie Staples', and they were jumping off the wall, swinging by their feet from hawthorn branches, lifting heavy stones. Then they got to running across the railway lines, then sitting down on the tracks. Then Janus laid himself out across the rails. Of course a train comes along. The Cambrian Coast Express – puff puff puff, you know how fast they come round that bend. Poor Gwen closes her eyes and screams. She hears the train go past – chuffa chuffa chuffa, and when it's gone there's Janus lying on the track, no head on his shoulders. Gwen runs away screaming.

'Of course he'd rolled away before the train came, saw that Gwen wasn't looking, so pulled his jersey up over his head and laid down when the train had gone.

'It wasn't the last daft thing he'd done. No matter how much we told him off, or his Mum and Dad scolded him, you could see he didn't think he'd done anything daft. That was the strangest thing.

'You can see he thinks a lot of himself, the way he struts around the place. He used to have this silly habit of hiding around the farmyard making animal noises when I walked past. He did fool me now and then I have to admit. I'd think, hallo, a sheep's got trapped in the cow shed, hearing this baa-baa coming from the door. I'd have a look inside and find the lad hiding in one of the stalls.

'Gwen used to think the world of him, moping around all year waiting for August. I'd worry when she went off with the family, which she did now and then, down to the beach, or into Aberbreuddwyd. Blessed relief now that she's engaged to Clive. They've put the wedding off till next year, now. Did I tell you? Clive's got his eye on a place near Bala. I expect the lad Janus will be glad. I expect he thinks it would be beneath him to marry a farm girl. Him a famous concert pianist with his studies at the Royal College of something. I don't think he knows yet. The fire interrupted all their plans I think.'

'That's the thing about fire,' said Howell, a finger in his beard. 'Blessed thing no one got hurt.'

'It was a miracle they didn't,' said Hugh, his voice a loud whisper, 'when Mrs Jones jumped into this burning tent to rescue some clothes and she came out with her hair on fire . . .'

'Like an angel of death?' said Howell, adding vividly to an imagined scene.

'I didn't see, that's what the scoutmaster told me. You know they've got the scouts on one of Bernard's fields, a whole troop of them – huge marquee, buglers – reveille every morning, last post at night. They were the first on the scene. They got buckets of water from the stream, tipped them over the flames. But by that time there weren't any. People up on the road were stopping to have a look. One daft Englishman came running, all red in the face, over the fields. You know what he'd brought from his car to put the fire out? A bottle of bloody lemonade. Half full. He said every little helps.

'Anyway, after Mrs Jones had ducked into the tent and come out on fire, Mr Jones just wet his hand and patted her on the head. Like snuffing a candle. I don't think the fire could have lasted more than a couple of minutes. The scouts were running around with bandages but there was nothing to bandage. One scout made a tourniquet for another scout, just to use them up.

'In the end they made tea for them, brought a massive urn over the fields, set it over a fire. Hot tea. The kids put six sugars in each one, plop. I had one myself. They said they had to have lots of sugar. So we all sat around on camping chairs drinking sweet tea, watching the smoke rise from the ashes.'

'There's nothing like emergency tea,' said Howell, smiling with his upper mouth, which always happened when he frowned.

2

When the fire broke out, all Colette could think of was
Juliette's pullover – a Fair Isle blaze of orange, brown and gold
that she'd spent the whole spring knitting, finishing it properly
only the night before they set off for Wales, tying up the last
loose end of cuff, close-stitching the ribs around the neck.
Juliette had watched the progress of the garment on her
mother's needles, delighting in how the various balls of
coloured wool took form in Colette's hands, grew empty
sleeves all chevroned and zigzagged with vivid, autumnal
colours. She couldn't wait to wear it. So Colette had risked
her life to save it.

Then, once her hair had been extinguished, she stood there
with a colourful pullover in her hands, a tent of ash before her,
and thought – *this must be where it ends.*

She was already beginning to say goodbye to the farm, and
to recollect the eight idyllic summers they'd spent there. At
times the third field had seemed more crowded than their
house in London. One summer her brother Lesley had come
for a week, camping for the first time since his cycling holidays
with Aldous. Away from his family he'd seemed like his old
self again. Her mother was with them that year as well. Nana
had slept in a special tent Aldous had borrowed from a school

colleague, John Short, who claimed it had been used in the Antarctic on a failed polar expedition. Nana had thought this hilarious, and every time she set off to bed would say 'I may be gone some time.'

After the fire Colette found those years coming back to her, as she sat in a camping chair drinking sweet tea, being fussed over by boy scouts and their scoutmaster, a brisk, matter-of-fact man who told her 'no woollen's worth your life'.

She found herself remembering the time a hen snatched a piece of bacon out of the frying pan and ran across the field with it. Aldous had chased the fowl across the grass, incensed because money was low and that was the last scrap of food in the tent, and the hen had swerved and dodged and side-stepped like a rugby player until Aldous finally went in for a running tackle, diving headlong, sending the bird up into the air in a cloud of orange feathers. He'd retrieved the bacon. It had a clean, perfectly triangular cut out of it. Then there was the year of kittens on the farm. That had been Juliette's first summer, tottering through deep grass leading a troupe of tottering baby cats like a miniature shepherdess. How Colette had longed for a daughter, but by the time one came along she was so used to boy children she found her new girl something of a puzzle, an anatomical anomaly that she soon began dressing in Janus and James's cast-offs. Juliette's character, as she'd grown older, had become increasingly boyish, and Colette was starting to feel a sense of guilt, as though she'd betrayed her own gender by giving one of its members to the other side.

The pullover was really the first garment since babyhood that was to be Juliette's own. Now that she'd saved it from a burning tent she was prepared, that evening, to take her family back to London on the night train, and never set foot in Llanygwynfa again. Her children were sullen and silent. Only Julian looked happy, sitting on Janus's arms.

It was the little boy, still really a baby, that Colette thought would be the problem when Mrs Evans suggested they use the barn.

The barn was the last in a sequence of buildings whose

48

purpose was to protect, in different ways, the raw materials of the farm, and to extract from them their profitable yields – the cow house, the chicken coop, the grain store . . . It was semi-redundant since the building, a decade earlier, of a Dutch barn – a barrel-vaulted roof of curved, corrugated iron high on six tall iron posts. The old barn, a much smaller, squat structure of randomly sized yet perfectly fitting boulders with a small wooden door set deeply in a recess and thin, fortress-like slits for windows, now existed only to hold any rare surplus of hay, to store odd assortments of equipment and materials and to provide shelter for ewes in labour and new-born lambs.

That summer it was only a third full of hay which was piled into an arrangement of giant steps, plateaux and terraces of gold in gentle gradations from the floor to the roof beams, twelve feet above. In addition there were two tractor tyres – huge loops of serrated rubber – a roll of wire netting, some sacks and assorted pieces of wood, the stored remains of an old outhouse. Colette could not see how Julian could be safe amongst all these potential dangers. She had thoughts of her child falling off a shelf of hay, tumbling down the fluffy stairs, bouncing his way to the bottom.

But then, as Colette stood in the farmyard by the open barn door, Julian with all four limbs embracing her, alert and attendant to his surroundings like a sailor in a crow's nest, she had seen an extraordinary sight. She thought at first that a thin, stray cow had entered the farmyard through the gate at the far end, but it was Janus and Mr Evans walking in tandem, carrying between them a cot of wrought iron. They slowly cantered through the farmyard, like the skeleton of a pantomime horse, Hugh taking the lead. Orange hens waddled out of the way. The cot was a contraption of looped and twisted ironwork crafted in the same way as the gates to the farmyard, with little brass urns at the four corners. It looked like a miraculously scaled-down version of an imperial four-poster. Julian was delighted by it, a little open prison with a plump hair mattress and a menacing web of springs beneath. With his toys he played its bars like a glockenspiel.

The family had set about the domestication of the barn with a cooperativeness that was so coordinated it seemed rehearsed. Within a few days they'd established a living space that was a rough echo of their house in London, with Aldous and Colette in the large front bedroom (the largest and flattest of the upper plateaux where they'd spread a groundsheet out, unfurled two swiss rolls of foam rubber, a white bed sheet, two blankets and an eiderdown of yellow imitation silk with pheasants and gun dogs meticulously embroidered on its buxom surface), and the children in the smaller bedrooms – the various levels and recesses about the mass of stacked hay – with Julian on the floor in his stately cot.

Janus had taken the uppermost flat area of the golden escarpment, a platform ten feet above the stained floor of the barn. He slept in a velvet sleeping bag eighteen inches from a sheer cliff. His mother objected at first and continued, even after a week in which Janus had slept safely.

'You can't sleep there, Janus. You only need to turn over in your sleep and you'll be over the edge.'

'I don't move in my sleep,' replied Janus shaking husks of wheat out of his wellingtons, 'I sleep completely still.'

'Do you?'

'I fall asleep at night and in the morning I wake up in exactly the same position. The bedclothes aren't even crumpled. I only need to make my bed once a week.'

'Even so,' said Colette, who had been about to repeat to him what her mother had often told her – that it is a sign of madness not to move about in your sleep. Instead she said, 'You might have a nightmare.'

'I've never in my life had a nightmare,' said Janus, 'not once. And I've slept on mountain ledges before now. It gives me beautiful dreams of flying.'

None of what Janus had said was true, although it wouldn't have surprised anyone if it had been.

'You're lucky,' said Colette, meaning to imply that her sleep was plagued by nightmares. She was sitting in her high bed sewing buttons on to a tiny cardigan.

'I've had nightmares,' said James, who had chosen for his repose a shelf of straw on the same level as his parents but half round a corner so that he was mostly invisible, only his feet peeking out from behind the soft wall.

Colette was still thinking about Janus's claim to live free of nightmares. When he was very young – five or six – he would wake up in the middle of the night whimpering like a puppy.

Having met with no response, James tried again.

'I've had loads of nightmares.'

'So have I,' called Juliette, who was lower than her parents, eighteen inches off the ground. She was tucked into a thickly blanketed nook in the straw. She shared this space with a small company of teddy bears – principal among whom were Wendy Boston, a large yellow bear with straw leaking from her paws, and Toffee, an inherited bear who was worn out and dishevelled in everything but his amber and black eyes, which were perfect.

'On a hot day,' commenced James, 'I was freezing cold . . .'

'Mine was about a tree,' said Juliette.

'And I went into the house to get warm, and there was a pair of hands with white gloves on, sweeping up the ashes from around the boiler.'

'Just hands?' said Colette.

'Yes, just floating hands with gloves on.'

'How do you know there were hands inside the gloves?'

James didn't say anything.

Juliette went on.

'It was a gigantic apple tree and the apples were falling off the tree on to the grass . . .' Juliette, who'd previously felt she was talking to no one, became suddenly aware of an attentive audience, '. . . and when I looked at the apples . . . they turned into faces . . . and then they disappeared.'

The whole family laughed.

'You made that up,' said James.

'I didn't,' Juliette screamed.

'Okay,' said Colette.

Juliette was furious. She had made it up, but how did they know?

They knew because she'd unconsciously based it on a real nightmare James had recounted a few months earlier in which he'd been walking near a large cherry tree. There was a presence in the tree whom James could only see as a dark shape who was shaking the tree and causing ripe cherries to rain down on the ground.

What angered Juliette most was the fact that she had had a real nightmare but had thought it would have sounded faked in the retelling. Also, it involved disembodied hands, so James would have claimed she was copying his nightmares. Her nightmare was of walking into a beautiful cottage garden. In the garden there was a bush of red roses. Over the roses hovered a pair of hands, their fingers moving as if playing a piano. Piano music was coming from the cottage.

Having invented a nightmare she knew it was too late to tell the real nightmare. It seemed very unfair.

Colette had also had nightmares about hands. In these she was seated before a dressing table, naked, applying make up to her face, looking carefully at her reflected image, opening one eye wide, arching her eyebrow, combing black on to her lashes, daubing the pouting oval of her lips with crimson lipstick. Then she would realize the hands that were so carefully enhancing her face weren't hers.

She didn't mention this dream. Instead she said to her husband, who was embroiled in the ordinariness of the *Daily Telegraph* crossword, 'What about you, sweetheart? Are your forty winks ever troubled by five-legged beasties?'

'No,' replied Aldous, taking his glasses off, 'you know what my nightmares are about . . .' Janus struck a match, applied it to the tip of his cigarette, providing a backdrop for Aldous's next word, '. . . fire.'

Aldous wrinkled his nose as he said the word.

'Funnily enough,' said Janus.

Two tent fires were not the only conflagrations Aldous had experienced. He had survived a house fire when he was a small boy. He'd woken with a hot, choking sensation in his throat, his eyes weeping. His room was full of smoke. Until then he'd always found comfort in the odour of smoke – autumn bonfires, railway stations, Guy Fawkes Night, winter chimneys. Now it was a frightening smell that made real the possibility of death. He'd had to wake his parents who emerged from their beds as breathless silhouettes. Mfanwy, Aldous's older sister and cause of the fire, was downstairs obeying the voices she'd heard instructing her to set fire to their rented house in Tottenham. When they stumbled into the parlour they found her crouched in a corner, a look of terror in her face while her rocking horse, his mane ablaze, grinned as he burned busily in the opposite corner.

'That was the last time Dad left his Swans lying about. I saved all our lives that night. It's given me a lifelong awareness of how dangerous an ordinary house can be. Or tent for that matter. Which brings me to this question I've been pondering – what is the opposite of a house? Any guesses?'

There was a pause before anyone realized a question had been asked.

'The opposite of a house?' said Colette.

'Yes. Ha-ha.'

'A bungalow,' said James, with sudden decisiveness.

'A bungalow is a house,' said Aldous quickly, as though it had been the first thought to occur to him as well.

'What do you mean "the opposite of a house"?' said Juliette.

'A greenhouse?' said Colette, half smiling.

'Not really.'

'On the basis that vegetables are the opposites of humans, so a greenhouse is the opposite of a house.'

'Impeccable logic,' said Janus.

'It's not quite opposite enough, if you think about it,' said Aldous, 'a greenhouse is really an extension of a house.'

'A tent,' Juliette suddenly cried, then 'No.'

'Could be,' said Colette, 'a house is hard, a tent is soft.'

'A tent falls into the same category as a greenhouse,' said

53

Janus, letting it sound as though he knew the answer but couldn't be bothered to say it.

'A barn,' Colette suddenly laughed, making the word huge and rolling her eyes.

James, who'd been thinking carefully, said 'A hole.'

'Not quite,' said Aldous, 'something more than a hole.'

'I can see why you said that,' Colette cooed encouragingly to James.

A silence as ideas dried up.

Janus, who'd had his answer carefully prepared, thought it might be the right moment to strike.

'The sea,' he said.

'The sea?' said Colette, 'why did you say the sea?'

'Because a house is a place where people live, and the sea is a place where people cannot live.'

'You might as well say the moon,' said Colette.

'Janus is on the right lines,' said Aldous, 'you have to define a house first. Think of the house as an environment designed to protect and shelter and nurture its inhabitants. What would be the opposite of that?'

More silence.

'It comes into this crossword actually. Four letters – "part of the house opposite".'

Colette got it instantly.

'Trap? Is that it?'

'I don't understand,' said Juliette.

'Trap, yes,' said Aldous mischievously, 'and the worst thing about fire is that it turns a house into a trap, its opposite.'

His family didn't seem impressed.

'You made that up,' grumbled Janus.

Colette then recalled what Julian's cot reminded her of, and why she so gingerly lowered her youngest child into it. With its tensile networks of sprung metal, its iron rods, loops, bars and levers, it had the appearance of some kind of ruthless trap, as if Julian's weight on the mattress might trip a hair trigger and bring the whole thing snapping shut around him.

But he looked peaceful enough now, splayed in sleep-

54

fulness, his mouth a quarter of an inch open, his eye just a line of lash.

Julian had been an unexpected finale to Colette's reproductive years. She genuinely believed that at forty-two she was no longer fertile and, moreover, that a contracted cervix had, after years of making conception extremely difficult, withdrawn fully its obligations in the reproductive process.

It was this condition, a kind of corkscrew effect on the neck of the womb caused by the birth of Janus (as though that child had tried, in leaving the uterus, to close the door on any future siblings), that was responsible for the wide chronological spacing of her children. Janus had arrived promptly enough, within a year of marriage, in the closing months of World War II. Colette had been evacuated to a maternity hospital that was a Georgian limestone mansion in the heart of Cotswolds countryside, and had spent a beautiful month convalescing after Janus's difficult birth amongst rose gardens, fountains, stone hippopotamuses and the incessant calling of nightingales. Conceiving a second child proved more difficult. Two miscarriages followed, in which unnamed children quietly and slowly bled to death, and it was six anxious years before James finally arrived, and four more after that when Juliette was born. Julian's arrival, six years after Juliette (making Janus old enough to be his father), unplanned and defying the laws of nature (so it seemed to Colette), proved the most difficult. Early bleeding meant Colette spent most of the pregnancy on her back with a bucket next to the bed ('If anything comes out,' her doctor had told her, 'keep it there until I can have a look at it.'). The birth itself was traumatic. Julian weighed ten pounds and Colette needed eighteen stitches. Furthermore, she developed an embolism which meant another month of hospitalization on her back, during which she came close to death, or so she believed when, late one night on the ward she caught the wafting scent of her dead father's pipe tobacco.

Despite Mrs Evans's plea that there should be no smoking in

the barn, Colette could hear behind her the soft whisper of a packet of Weights being thumbed open, a cigarette extracted, then the tap, tap, tap of the fag on the box to settle the tobacco. Janus's smoking was full of these quiet but intense noises – sudden inrushes of breath, long drawn out exhalations with overlong pauses in between. The smacking together of lips. He seemed sometimes to spit the smoke out, as though it was a semi-solid substance, exuding between pursed lips blue clubs of mist.

Janus's smoking had become breathier since Gwen's visit three mornings before. Janus was out alone on his bike and Colette was sitting with Julian on one of the granite mounting stones that punctuated the farmyard. Gwen walked with a beautiful feminine swagger that her farm clothes couldn't disguise. When on the farm Gwen often wore her father's old clothes – his second best black wellingtons, his old collarless shirts, even his trousers which, being too big for her, gave an exaggerated but still comely shape to her hips, before they narrowed sharply to her belted waist. The volume of her body moved charmingly within the fragile shell of these clothes, which illustrated a rather shocking fact of biology – that if old Farmer Evans could be put through a sieve and all his male characteristics be sifted out, this would be the remainder.

Gwen, extremely beautiful, a creamy white face flecked with natural rouge; oval, symmetrical features; plump flounces of black hair, was beginning to acquire the toughness of her mother.

'You're looking well, Gwen,' said Colette, always unnerved by pretty women.

'Thank you Mrs Jones.'

Gwen didn't notice Julian until she was a few feet from Colette. Then she stopped and her face seemed to enlarge, her mouth and eyes gaping, and she reached out to touch Julian's hair.

Colette was glad when Julian's hair began to grow, after what seemed like an awfully long period of baldness, the dark birth hair having fallen out within a few weeks. A baby without hair looks shockingly vulnerable, a delicate little shell of skin and bone with a gaping fontanelle that all but exposed the brain. Now Julian's hair was coming in with lush flicks and curls of gold, an angelic halo that would often have the old ladies cooing.

'Will you promise to cut a lock for me to keep?' said Gwen, smiling as she tangled her finger in Julian's curls.

'I will,' said Colette, 'though if I did that for everyone who asked he wouldn't have any left.'

Then she noticed a mark on Gwen's fingernail that made her smile. A little white fleck, three quarters of the way to the rind. She didn't say anything. She didn't think Gwen knew that Janus had told her about their fingernail races.

It must have been his idea. They each took a small-bladed penknife and cut a notch above the lunule of a corresponding pair of fingernails – the right index finger. The idea was that they would race these notches to the tops of their nails to see who got there first. Janus claimed it was the slowest form of competitive racing known to man. They'd originally planned to compare progress the following summer, but by Christmas the notches had passed beyond the pink field of the nail bed and had tipped over into the white hinterland, eventually to be clipped (Gwen) or bitten (Janus) off. By the following August each could only compare unmarked nails. Janus had no idea nails grew so quickly. 'I cut mine off on Guy Fawkes Night.' 'I cut mine off on Christmas Eve.' Arguments ensued. Eventually they agreed to try again. This time, as soon as the notch reached the end of the nail they had to cut it off and post it to the other as proof. As soon as an envelope containing a marked crescent of keratin arrived the recipient knew he or she had lost the fingernail race.

Janus elaborated this story so much he made it sound very convincing, but even so Colette was never sure that these races ever really took place. She doubted much that Janus had told her about Gwen.

'We're getting married,' he said once on top of a dune, breathless after swigging lemonade from a glass bottle, 'next

57

year,' he burped, 'when we're of age. Look.' He flourished his fourth finger which was hooped with a Christmas cracker novelty ring. 'Gwen says she'll marry me even though she doesn't love me. I told her it doesn't matter as long as we're together.'

'Do you love Gwen?'

'Of course not,' Janus laughed as he brought the bottle to his mouth again, the laugh becoming huge and echoey within the glass, 'but she needs to be with me. And I could use her.'

'Where will you live?'

'In London.'

'Won't she miss the farm?'

'Why should she? She wants to get away. She's always telling me that.'

It was true that the friendship between Gwen and Janus had caused both sets of parents some concern. Mr and Mrs Evans once told Colette how some local boys from the village had thrown a dead rat in through Gwen's open window. That was an accepted sign of disapproval for a girl who'd courted someone from outside the village. 'It doesn't happen so much now, but in the old days any girl who went with a boy from a different village could expect things like that. Dorothy's sister had a hen put down her father's chimney for seeing a lad from Llanfair, and there was a boy from Llanhud who was rolled in cow dung and dipped in the Cynddeiriog for seeing a girl from Llanygwynfa. So you see, Janus being from London, that makes it even worse in the eyes of some of the boys here, and it can do a girl's reputation serious damage in the long run . . .'

But as far as Colette could see, there was nothing courtierly in Janus and Gwen's relationship. They played like brothers most of the time, climbing trees and cliffs, hefting hay, fighting, chasing. Or had she missed something? It did surprise Colette that Gwen had become a woman so suddenly. It seemed almost improper for her to arrive with that voluptuous figure without having given some sort of warning.

What had worried Colette about Gwen and Janus was that

her son didn't seem to recognize the fact that his friend was female. When she watched them playing together there was something odd. It was as though Janus was encouraging Gwen's masculine side by enticing her into ever more boyish roles – mock gun battles, sword fights, military marching. It was this that caused her to consider, not for the first time, whether her son might be homosexual.

The thought that he might be didn't bother her. In fact, she found herself rather attracted to homosexual men. For years she'd cherished fantasies about the painter Francis Bacon and the composer Benjamin Britten. She'd even written to the latter enclosing a photo of Julian sitting on a haystack near Thaxted in Essex with a note thanking him for composing the Spring Symphony as it made her two-year-old son very happy. Britten sent back a signed photo of himself leaning suavely against his Aldeburgh studio wall. This made Colette very happy. She once wrote to Bacon also but had received no reply except in the form of dreams in which she was posing nude in his studio and he was producing grotesque images of her, as he would, and whole crowds of people were laughing at these horrible parodies of the female body. At the time she hadn't realized either man was homosexual.

Whatever their concerns, however, Gwen seemed to have come to no harm and indeed was now wearing a real engagement ring on her finger. The ring chilled Colette, who sensed the instant evaporation of branching lineages that might have sprung from Janus and Gwen.

Gwen straightened herself and looked at the barn.

'How's the barn?'

'It's different from the tent.'

'Bigger, certainly.'

'The walls are thicker.'

'That shows how much we value our grass here. Grass has better houses than people do. That's an old saying . . .'

Gwen was disappointed that Janus wasn't there, she'd wanted to invite him to tea that evening.

'Ma and Da are going to have dinner with William at the

Hall (they still haven't settled on a price, it's ridiculous isn't it?). I thought Janus might like to come over to the house to meet my fiancé, Clive. We're getting married next summer. Not in August though. August weddings are bad luck, did you know that? Clive would really love to meet Janus. If he can't come tonight, do you know if he'll be playing the organ in church on Sunday? Clive could come and hear him play . . .'

Colette passed on all this information to Janus who absorbed it without comment. He didn't go to the farmhouse that evening. He stayed in the barn reading maps by oil-light. Nor did he play the organ on Sunday. Mrs Morris's legs held out. Nor had he been out in the fields helping the farm boys at all. It had become something of a tradition that Janus and James would help with the collecting of the hay. It was heavy work lugging the stooks along a chain of people to the cart. They'd taken the hay in yesterday and Janus hadn't helped. Gwen was down there, adding her considerable muscle to the effort. James didn't go because Janus didn't go. Since then he hadn't said anything about Gwen.

When Janus read maps he tended to spread his fingers, fanning them out across the paper. It had given Colette the opportunity to look at his nails for the telltale nick or cut that would mean Gwen still mattered to him. She was shocked when she saw his nails – they were bitten down almost to nothing, little stumps of gristle. The flesh of his fingertips bulged over the ends. The last time she looked she was sure his nails were long and tough. She felt compelled to comment on it. He didn't seem concerned.

'It helps with the piano,' he said without looking away from the map. 'I got fed up with my nails click-clacking on the keys.' Then he looked at his nails. 'It's odd isn't it, how the fingernails are the same shape as front teeth.'

Thinking back to Gwen's fingernail, Colette figured it must have been caught in a door, or perhaps she was lacking certain vitamins, or calcium, or whatever it was.

The barn was lit by tilley lamps, gifts of Geraint who collected them. When the Joneses visited he would light his entire collection so that Dot's bungalow shone like Bishop Rock, so intense Aldous could see his own silhouette cast across the pine forests on the slopes of Penralt. Whenever they visited they left with a lamp.

One was on the floor three paces from Julian's cot, the other was hanging from a nail on a roof beam a foot from Janus's head, thus illuminating for him the pages of W. A. Poucher's *Wanderings in Wales* from which, in a reclining position, his head on a pillow of straw, he read. An ashtray (a scallop shell) was balanced on his chest. He uttered an occasional 'Christ' or 'fffff . . .' of incredulity whenever Poucher's pedantry over, for instance, the correct configuration of hobnails in a walking boot, or the ideal loading of a balanced haversack, became excessive.

The previous winter Janus had amused himself by writing a parody of the legendary hillwalking perfumier's prose, detailing the exact process by which a haversack containing one ham and cheese sandwich too many upset the equilibrium of man and bicycle, causing the cyclist to do a slow and graceful backward summersault, '. . . now in the inverse position I was able to take hold of the rear wing nuts of the bicycle for support while steering with my feet . . .'

Janus had personalized his space in the barn. The roof beam next to him acted as a bedside table into whose ridged oak he'd pinned photographs of Chopin, and Colette's best friend, Vivienne. ('To remind me of what a real mother looks like,' he replied when Colette asked him why he had the picture.)

On top of the shelf were a series of objects – a bottle of lemonade, a toy telescope, a cup.

He snapped shut his book suddenly and said 'I think a hut in a concentration camp is better.'

'What?' said Colette.

'As an opposite of a house.'

But the rest of the family had moved on from that conversation or rather had looped it back on itself and were talking about the fire.

No one had admitted responsibility and speculation about the cause had flourished. The favoured theory was sunlight refracted through an empty lemonade bottle. Though James thought that Juliette might have been playing with matches and Colette thought that James might have been experimenting with home-made fireworks.

Janus suggested that his father (who was supposed to have given up, again) was having a secret fag.

'Well, I didn't see you anywhere, Janus, when the tent was burning down,' said Aldous.

'What do you mean by that?' Janus laughed coldly.

'He was holding Julian,' Colette said, surprised by Aldous's sudden accusatory tone.

'Was he?'

'Yes, I was actually.'

'Let's stop talking about who burnt it down, shall we?' said Colette.

'Why?' said James.

'Let's just say the tent had had enough,' said Janus, returning to his book, 'let's just say the tent killed itself.'

As a joke, this drew some cautious laughter, and then a long silence, during which the tilley lamps whistled softly.

1964

1

For Aldous the journey to Wales always ended like this; the discovery of coal deposits beneath the soil of the third field, later found to extend beneath the chapel of St Hywyn itself, the farmhouse as well, the first, second, fourth and fifth fields, up as far as the skirts of Moelfre right down to the dunes. Nearly all of Y Lledrith, in fact. The construction of a colliery in the third field, with adjacent steel works, chemical processing plant and car manufacturing complex. The stone walls dismantled, replaced with tall fences of barbed wire. Searchlights and Alsatians. Mr and Mrs Evans enjoying rustic pomp in their new home, Llwydiarth Hall, Mrs Jones tiaraed, twinkling with industrial diamonds. In his dreams the journey to Wales always ended like this.

Aldous had come to believe that Llanygwynfa and Fernlight Avenue were balanced around a common fulcrum, and that any change in one might cause a similar change in the other. It was as though they were geographical twins, separated at birth, but still linked by a common geological ancestry. He felt that any blemish, nick or scar on the face of Llanygwynfa might engender a sympathetic counterpart in Fernlight Avenue – roofs damaged slate for slate, neighbours dying symmetrically, one in Wales, one in London, the coordinated falling of trees.

Selfishly, and against all practical sense, Aldous and his family regarded change at Llanygwynfa, however slight, as something to be feared. The journey there was undertaken much in the spirit of Scott's journey to the South Pole – great excitement, but an underlying fear that the pristine acres of snow will carry the blemish of Norwegian footprints. So the first few days after their arrival always turned into a cataloguing and celebration of sameness. They reported to each other that the people in the neighbouring village were the same people as last year. The Ginger Boy was still in the newsagent's. The Genius was still in the sweetshop. Mr and Mrs Evans still looked like Mr and Mrs Evans. Younger, if anything.

The fine details of the farm, its buildings and machinery were also carefully noted. Change here was so slight as to be barely perceptible. The blocks of hay in the Dutch barn might be stacked a different way. A piece of rope might be hanging from a door handle. There might be nettles growing where there weren't any last year.

But this year there was a change at the farm it was impossible not to notice. An entirely new building had been erected in the farmyard opposite the cow shed. Mrs Evans called it a milking parlour. It was a small, squat structure built of orange bricks on a concrete plinth. Its interior, lit by a neon strip that remained on all day and night, contained stainless steel cylinders, glass silos and black pipework which somehow sucked the protein out of Mr Evans's cows and pumped it into steel churns. It looked to Colette like a public lavatory. It gave a continual, low electric hum. Nothing else in the farmyard used electricity.

Aldous felt that they had caused the building of the milking parlour by acquiring, for the first time in their lives, a car. Since the spring this vehicle, itself a small, movable building of steel and glass, had taken up a position in the road outside their house – an outpost of the house, as the milking parlour was an outpost of the farmhouse. The car was a Morris Oxford Brake, in dark grey with pale yellow woodwork framing the rear side windows and double van doors at the back. Its front was a broad chromium grin and it announced left and right turns by the raising of semaphore indicators from side slots. Already it had been decorated with window stickers, little triangular flags, one with the word Aberbreuddwyd, the other, a black one, Llanidloes.

This car had caused such a transformation in the lives of the Joneses, had opened up so many new landscapes for them, bringing within easy reach of a day's drive the previously inaccessible valleys and churches of Essex and Suffolk, and making the Chilterns a regular weekend haunt, that Aldous couldn't help but imagine that this unfolding of technology in their lives would cause a similar disruption in Llanygwynfa. And here it was. While he'd been learning to drive in the cul-de-sacs and gentle gradients of Windhover Hill, Mr Evans had, brick by brick, been building this ugly, incongruous little building.

Colette didn't see the relationship between the car and the milking parlour. Instead, appalled by the disruption to the lives of the cows, the culling of the dairymaids (Mrs Evans, her two sisters and Gwen), the subjection of the cows to the industrial processes of modern agriculture, the abandoning of the old cow shed which now stood empty and unused, a series of oak enclosures, dark spaces, pounds and lofts, she imagined that something equally disruptive would happen at Fernlight Avenue, some old process, a way of doing things, would be changed beyond recognition. And she was right.

The phone call came in the early afternoon. The Joneses had just had lunch and were packing the car for an afternoon in the hills when Mrs Evans assailed them with loud yoo-hoos from the gate, saying that the phone in the farmhouse, a heavy ebonite and silver contraption that was almost always silent, had rung and was asking for Colette.

Colette felt ridiculous as she walked with Mrs Evans through the farmyard. The farmer's wife walked with a slight roll to her hips and with a buttoned-down purposefulness. She was wearing a thick woollen skirt and wellingtons, a cardigan over a checked shirt. Her grey hair was tied back, as it always was, in a bun. Colette became conscious of her own walk as a parody of elegance – toes turned balletically out, each foot placed in line with the trailing foot, as if walking a tightrope. Her earrings swung from her lobes like pendulums. Her necklaces and bracelets clicked and clacked.

'Are you going to a dance, Mrs Jones?' asked Mrs Evans, in all innocence believing this might be the case. Colette felt her jewellery weighing her down. It seemed to drag behind her. Most of it was worthless – fake gems, rolled gold, big chunks of glass that, had they really been rubies, could have purchased cities.

'Actually we were going to climb a mountain,' she said.

It was Lesley on the phone. Colette's older brother, Aldous's best friend, sounded like a fly buzzing too close to her ear as he told her about Nana's death.

'In her sleep,' he said, 'no pain at all, dear . . .'

'I'll come home tomorrow . . .' Colette was clenching her teeth to keep her voice steady.

'No, Colette,' Lesley whined, bouncing off windowpanes, 'no, no, you've only just got there. Leave everything to me. To Agatha and me. You stay where you are.'

'No, I must come back . . .'

Mrs Evans was standing close by as if ready to catch Colette should she fall. As she spoke she could see, through the deeply incised window, Mr Evans's head bobbing along the top of a wall. For a moment it seemed odd to her that Lesley should refer to their mother's funeral as 'everything'.

'I'd advise you to stay. At least until everything's arranged. That should be some time next week.'

Lesley's voice was too calm. Too steady. Colette didn't like the steadiness of his voice.

'You advised me to put her in that home, Lesley.'

She instantly regretted saying this. Lesley was silent. She could hear him sigh in that older brother way he always had. Even in the deepest grief she was capable of saying the wrong thing. She was aware that droplets of moisture were forming in the mouthpiece of the telephone, as though it was sweating.

'I'll discuss it with Aldous.'

Colette had to sit down in Mrs Evans's kitchen. She explained to her what had happened and Mrs Evans was very sympathetic. She'd met Colette's mother five years ago when she'd come to the farm and liked her. Although Nana was twenty years older than Mrs Evans they seemed to be of the same generation. They both had small, tough bodies and sharp senses of humour. Mrs Evans made Colette a cup of tea and went to fetch Aldous.

While she was gone Colette felt the atmosphere of the farmhouse. It was a house of rooms, each leading to the other, without intervening passages or hallways. On the walls were Victorian pastoral scenes, an original pencil sketch of trees by a distant relative, pictures of Gladstone, Lloyd George, an array of non-conformist preachers, long bearded and camera shy. There was a photo of a tall, serious young man with black hair and deeply recessed eyes she presumed was Mr Evans, standing by a wall. Framed needlework. A grandfather clock. A weatherglass. A piano accordion Janus had once played. The walls of the house were so thick and solid they surrounded her like a vast overcoat. There was a meaty smell in the air. The furnishings seemed enormously, unnecessarily heavy – the table, the chair she was sitting in, the cast iron range, the oak dresser. She wondered how the farmhouse didn't sink into the ground under its own weight.

Aldous came to the farmhouse and they walked back together through the farmyard. Colette still hadn't cried. They walked silently, their feet brushing little sprigs of camomile. They passed the barn that last year had been their home and at this point she slipped from the ledge of her self-control and fell against her husband, undone, flailing, watery.

This was how the children, who'd been playing stone-age cricket, saw them enter the field. At first they seemed normal because they were balancing in turn on the single plank that bridged the stream by the gate, but as they walked across the grass they became unusual. They appeared to be limping.

They were leaning against each other like the crowning pair of a house of cards. Their mother had one arm self-protectively across her waist, the other was holding her hand across her face, first to her cheek, as if she had toothache, then to her eyes, as if they hurt. Aldous had his arm around her shoulders and she was walking half turned towards him. She stumbled frequently as she was paying no attention to the uneven ground and several times she nearly fell over. Their father's face was serious, concerned, frowning.

The older children, for whom this approach seemed to take hours, could guess what had happened.

'Nana's dead,' said Janus.

Julian laughed and bowled a stone at him.

It was decided, after much quiet discussion, that they should remain at the farm for the rest of the week, travel back to London on Tuesday for the funeral, and return on Thursday to the farm for the rest of the holiday.

As if in disagreement with this plan, the weather mustered clouds from nowhere, hid the mountains, took the top off Moelfre like a boiled egg. The Joneses had long, slow, quiet breakfasts and filled their mornings with chores – fetching milk from the farmhouse, water from the old cow shed. The children climbed walls, played slippery games of football while Aldous and Colette washed clothes, patched inner tubes, darned shirts and read stories of eccentric aristocrats. In the afternoons they filled the Morris Oxford and went, dutifully, somewhere. To Aberbreuddwyd for shopping and a saunter through grey, busy streets, a precipitous wander around the cliffs at the back of the town, or to Dolgellau to become lost in its little granite piazzas and alleyways. Cadair Idris had entirely vanished, as had the great mountains to the north.

Sometimes they went for gloomy walks up foothills until their heads were lost in the underside of a vast roof of cloud. Sometimes they would brave the beach and sit fully clothed in the blustery dunes for gritty picnics.

Aldous would sit on a wall and paint the farm. Although painting by daylight, he painted visions of the farm on a winter's night, blue-lit, broken snow on rooftops, silhouetted, insomniac cows.

At night Colette was sleepless. The interior soft architecture of their tent glowed with starlight (the clouds mockingly withdrew at night). Two hours before sunrise she would feel a strong urge to urinate. She would unzip the mouth of the tent to make the dark journey to the lavatory tent, guided by the yellow beam of a bicycle lamp.

Always she felt a shock at the greatness of the spaces outside the tent. The three-dimensional sheer fall of stars above her head with the vast backbone of the Milky Way holding it all together. Planets, galaxies, nebulae. Moelfre visible as an absence of stars. The sheep in the field, motionless yet vividly present. Once, half dreaming, she thought the field was full of elderly, grey-haired ladies sitting in armchairs counting through pursefuls of change.

The same night she saw the lavatory tent as a Punch and Judy stall in which the puppets were sleeping. Inside she squatted above an oblong ditch of mauve chemicals.

Outside the tent she paused again to contemplate the view of the nomadic complex containing her family. Two tents – one large, one small, a car with a cluster of bicycles propped against it, all drained of colour. A stack of dirty crockery at the mouth of the tent. All this beneath the starlight. The immensities heaped upon these fragile structures filled her eyes with tears. She parted the dark curtains of the tent door and crawled into the small space within, on all fours, tears dropping off the end of her nose.

Aldous, awake, asked, as if it needed asking, what the matter was. Julian lay sprawled in slumber, limbs askew like a starfish. Undisturbable.

'I have put a pillow over her face,' said Colette in a wavering voice, just above whispering.

Aldous tutted, appealed to God, sighed, tried to think of something else to say. Colette brought up more tears, strangled a cry just as it was about to leave her throat, whined quietly instead.

'No you haven't,' said Aldous, reaching out to touch his wife, noticing how her whole body was vibrating like a motorbike.

'I've killed her,' said Colette, a high pitched voice rising higher still. In grief her voice had become very musical.

'You haven't,' said Aldous, aware that he sounded irritated and impatient. It was only to emphasize how untrue he thought her statements were.

'I put her in that home. I should have stayed with her. Someone should have stopped me from putting her in that home. Why didn't you stop me?'

Aldous lifted himself on to his elbow, jabbed the next words at her, 'Blame your bloody brothers and sisters if you must blame anyone.'

Aldous had said this before. He'd said it nearly every night since the telephone call. Every night Colette was kept awake by these thoughts that overspilt into hushed, urgent conversations, then into weeping. How Aldous envied Julian's mastery of sleep. Colette's breathy sobbing couldn't wake him. Sometimes, disorientated with grief, she would stumble over his sleeping body, and still he would sleep. It frightened Colette. Only the dead are so insensitive to the world. She could no longer distinguish between sleep and death. Waking in a tent of two sleeping bodies she sometimes felt she was the mistakenly entombed inhabitant of a family vault. So she would push Aldous over the edge of his unconsciousness and talk to him.

'You nurse her day in, day out,' he said, 'as if you haven't got enough on your hands with three kids and a baby. The one time you want to go away they've all got their excuses.'

'It wasn't their fault. She was my responsibility.'

Every spring Colette wrote to her brothers and sisters letters along the following lines:

Dear Meg/Agatha/Lesley/Janus B.,

*Any chance you could take Nana for the first three weeks in
August, or for any period, no matter how brief, during those
weeks?*

*Aldous/Aldo/Rex, the children and I are hoping to go to
Llanygwynfa for our one holiday of the year. Mumma is too frail
to come with us these days.*

How are the children? [letters to her brother Janus did
not include this line]

Love

Colette.

In previous years it had worked out. One or several of
Colette's siblings had taken their mother while Aldous and
Colette were in Wales. But Nana was deteriorating. By now
she had the brain of a five-year-old girl, the grip and stubborn-
ness of a twelve-year-old boy and the frailty and pathos of an
old woman.

This year Lesley was making a pilgrimage to Lourdes for the
sake of Christine, his daughter, who had pneumonia. Janus
Brian and his small, twitchy wife were touring the golf courses
of Spain. Agatha already had an ailing father-in-law in her
house and her husband's cricket season to organize. Meg and
Sid were booked into a hotel on Guernsey for August.

Lesley and Agatha, brimming with guilt, undertook detailed
research into the rest homes, retirement homes and residential
care homes of north London and found a cheap one in a jungle
of rhododendrons with rooms full of budgerigars. They signed
up Nana for three weeks and split the cost five ways.

Colette was reluctant. She would rather have stayed at
home with her mother while the others went to Wales. The
children protested. They wanted their mother with them. She
enjoyed, secretly, the hurt they were showing and found
herself surprised by it. If only Nana had protested. If only she
had begged Colette to stay. But Nana existed in a vague world
where there was little trouble and little delight.

Taking her to Sunnyridge Rest Home was a painful task.

Nana believed she was going to Broadstairs. She'd been to Broadstairs once, with her older daughter, Meg, before the war. Why that holiday should suddenly come alive for her again was a puzzle to Colette. She found herself telling white lies.

'Are we going to Broadstairs now?' said Nana as Colette helped her down the front path to the throbbing car where Aldous sat in the driving seat sleepily. Horrible, thought Colette, that one of this car's first tasks was to take her mother away. Nana was in her carpet slippers and white woollen stockings, taking only pigeon steps as she gripped Colette with one bony hand, an unlit cigarette in the other. In Colette's other hand was Nana's suitcase – a tarnished, white, snakeskin valise full of dresses, cotton underwear and sweets.

'Yes, we're going to Broadstairs now,' said Colette, as if to a child.

'I remember Bleak House,' said Nana. 'Is Meg there now?'

'Yes, Meg's there waiting for you,' said Colette, making a mental note to remind Meg to visit Nana before leaving for Guernsey.

Colette always felt a little jealous of the affection Nana showed for Meg. She knew it was stupid. All her life she'd been told by her mother that she, Colette, was her favourite child. Her youngest, her prettiest, her little angel. She would confide to Colette the failings she saw in her other children. Lesley was tight-fisted, aloof, a little devious. He had ideas above himself. He was a schoolteacher who saw himself as an Oxford don. He was hopeless with women. Terrified of them. It was Madeleine who had proposed to Lesley, Nana confided, and Lesley was too frightened to say no. Mumma (as Colette called her mother before she herself became a mother) and Colette tittered together. As for Agatha, she had no sense of humour. Jokes told to Agatha found themselves knocking soundlessly at immovable doors. Nana and Colette enjoyed telling Agatha jokes for the bewilderment and frustration they caused her. Janus Brian (the second name now used by Colette and her family to distinguish him from Colette's son) was introverted and odd. But Meg, tall, graceful, ballroom dancing champion Meg who, had life been fair, would have married Humphrey Bogart and been a screen legend, was regarded by Mumma with awe. She always had to know what Meg was doing, where she was, when she would be coming to visit.

Nana looked an incongruously frail content of the strong, hard car.

She showed no surprise when the journey to Broadstairs took fifteen minutes when it should have taken a day.

'Where's the sea?' she kept asking as she went from window to window in the large day room. 'Where's Meg?'

'There's the sea love,' said a Scottish nurse pointing to a washing line of white sheets that billowed in the grounds. Nana seemed satisfied. The other nurses sniggered.

'Where's the Matto Grosso?' said Nana.

The Scottish nurse was stumped.

'Brazil,' said Colette.

'Shall we go there now?'

'I don't think so.'

'Where's my cigarettes?'

'In your bag.'

'Where's my son?'

'Which one?'

'My youngest of course. My baby, Julian.'

'Julian's not your baby, Mumma, he's my baby.'

They'd found it funny at first, the way Nana had insisted Julian was her baby, but the tenacity of her belief soon became exasperating. 'Bring me my baby,' she would demand, mon-archical in her armchair where she spent most of her waking hours, haloed with smoke like a carnival mock up of Queen Guinevere. 'Where's my baby?' Such a loud, full, basso profundo voice (which Meg had inherited) from so small and thin a woman. Her vocal range was extraordinary – high-pitched, owlish shrieks if something shocked her (a hamster in her handbag, Juliette in a gorilla mask), excruciatingly wheezy laughs, knowing cackles, saucy whoops. Only the placing of Julian on her knee would allay these demands. Then she would sit with the abstracted indifference of a tired and overworked mother while Julian played for a moment an equine game on her knee before climbing down.

It annoyed Colette that her mother claimed detailed knowledge of her son's habits, the way she feigned fluency in his prelinguistic babble, to know what his favourite noises, jokes and animals were.

Aldous also found her pseudo-motherhood irritating. Once, resisting her demands while Julian was being bathed in a plastic washing-up bowl on the kitchen table, he took Baxbr, their sleek, slender, black cat, placed her on Nana's lap and said 'There, that's your baby.'

Unexpectedly, for a few moments, Nana seemed satisfied with this cat, and stroked Baxbr thoughtfully, before peering long and hard through wire-framed glasses at her baby and saying in a voice loud and haughty – 'He's all black!'

Sometimes her dementia seemed to blur for her the boundaries between the animate and the inanimate. Often she seemed to think that the boiler, a muscular piece of brown cast iron the size of a fridge, was Julian. On top of the boiler was a small circular lid which could be levered off with the handle of a fork and coal fed into the furnace beneath. Sometimes Nana would drop carefully unwrapped sweets through this hatch, one by one, and listen to them crackling in the fire. She believed she was feeding sweets to Julian.

Nana spent most of her time in the kitchen armchair next to the boiler, whose luminous orange firebox warmed her feet in winter. Here she would sit, legs crossed, her silver hair tied back in a bun, her currant coloured eyes vague behind her round glasses, her toothless mouth occupied almost continually by a cigarette. At her feet, propped against a chair leg, was a leather handbag with a buttery gold snap-buckle, always open, filled with packets of Player's No. 6, mints, cough candy and chocolate limes.

Colette would have felt devastated by her mother's deterioration had it not happened so gradually, and had it not seemed to cause her so little distress. It was not happiness that her mother was experiencing exactly, but an easiness. An absence of worry. If children could be cast iron stoves, if cats could be babies, there was little the material world could do to upset her. If problems came, they dissolved into babies. If disaster struck, she would feed it sweets.

As if to compensate for her slippage away from her known world she'd developed a magpie tendency to collect trinkets, to hoard anything bright. Her bedroom, intended for children, was an Aladdin's Cave of silver apostle spoons, compact mirrors, keys, sweet wrappers.

As Nana retreated further and further into her shrunken world, Colette found it ever harder to recall the mother she'd known. It was similar to the loss she felt as her children grew up. It was hard to remember them as babies. Watching a child grow up is to watch it die a hundred times, each new self overlaying the old, concealing it. If she watched carefully she might catch a glimpse of the hidden baby in Janus's smile, but for the most part that child was gone and a tall, confident man had taken its place. In their first weeks, Colette always felt, babies are birds. More bird-like than human. Flightless, of course, as are baby birds, but chirruping, watchful, simple. They seemed trapped within an invisible caul of dumbness, incomprehension, namelessness. Sometimes Colette found babies terrifying. They were human beings stripped of personhood, utterly naked, raw and blank. And it was towards that state that her mother was now taking pigeon steps. Nana's selfhood no longer adhered but had become something loose and flimsy, and layer after layer was peeling away. Time was running backwards for Nana. She was somehow less than a child now, because she lacked the child's huge thirst for information. She was shedding knowledge, losing names. Colette at first had wondered if she was being given an insight into how her mother was as a little girl, and wished she could imagine Nana's girlhood. But she felt now that this new state was a parody of childhood rather than a reprisal.

Colette was continually under pressure from friends and relatives, even, occasionally from Aldous, to put Nana in a home. But she refused even to entertain the idea. Perhaps it was because, as a child, she'd been harboured by her mother for over a year with a non-existent appendicitis, which grumbled but never flared. Mumma had selfishly kept her at home for company, though Colette never saw it as selfishness. She missed out a year of her schooling, her life at this stage oddly paralleling Aldous's, except that Aldous was suffering genuine illness. It was strange when she thought of it later, the two children who would eventually marry, both arrested in their early education by these pointless, devolved organs, one real, the other a phantom.

Now Colette was returning the favour, protecting her mother from the cruel institutions of the homes, as she'd been protected from school. She'd neglected this protection out of a selfish desire for a holiday and during that time her mother had died. She had killed her. She and the mountains had killed her.

The journey to London took place on an overcast August day. The mountains had been thoroughly erased by cloud, only their damp, brackeny stumps remaining. In such conditions the descent of the land from Wales to England was less noticeable. There was no flattening out. The change was in the flora – from grass to corn, bracken to barley, heather to wheat.

The funeral service was the De Profundis, a swinging of smoky censers, a sprinkling of holy water, then a hoisting aloft of the dripping coffin on to the shoulders of sons and grandsons (Agatha's sons, Mark and Paul, Meg's Mathew, Janus and Janus Brian). The most distinctive genetic trait passed on by Agnes Waugh was height, here accidentally celebrated in her tall, pall-bearing offspring and the altitude of her casket as it passed slowly out of the church.

It is a marvellous thing to be tall, thought Colette. She herself was tall for a woman, at five foot ten, though not as tall as Meg at six foot one inch, who in turn was dwarfed by her son Mathew who'd reached six foot four. The precipitous, vertiginous families that old lady had engendered. Here she was, sealed up in a coffin in order, it seemed, to render her ineffective, to withdraw her capacity to influence, if only by the presence of her body.

It was an ugly church. With a tower barely higher than the nave there was an odd shapelessness about it. A modern version of a medieval parish church, it struck Colette as a building that had been brainwashed, its history wiped and then rewritten in cheap, gaudy materials. The thickly varnished, machine-turned pews, the Day-Glo plaster tableaux depicting scenes from the Passion, the brash brass lectern and the east window of stained glass the colour of lipsticks and eye shadows.

Colette sat directly behind Lesley. She'd never noticed the back of his neck before. It was red and raw looking with horizontal creases in the skin like cracks in old plaster. It looked as though he'd survived a clumsy attempt at beheading. He'd said very little to her all day, just small talk. He hadn't mentioned Nana once. A pink triangle had appeared on his forehead, point downwards, as it always did when he was embarrassed, or was lying. All through the service Colette's eyes burnt into the back of Lesley's neck. He didn't even scratch himself.

The interment itself was a dismantling of Nana's height, from the shoulder height of her grandsons inch by inch down to ground level, then a threading through the brass handle-work of tough black straps before she entered negative height, foot by foot below ground level, shrinking.

Perhaps everyone was shocked by the depth to which their loved ones are lowered. Colette hadn't been to a funeral for twenty-four years (her father's, in 1939, who'd thus fulfilled his prophecy that there wouldn't be another war in his lifetime), but surely his grave wasn't as deep as this. Nana's coffin was going down and down, shrinking into the shadows of a muddy abyss. When was the lowering going to stop? The undertakers allowed yards and yards of strapping to slip through their hands before the coffin finally settled, a tiny, adumbrated oblong of boxwood at the bottom of a chasm.

Colette looked around at the other mourners who teetered on three sides of the grave edge to see if they shared her surprise. Lesley was standing with his hands clasped and his head lowered, but Colette could still see that pink, triangular blush marking his forehead.

A funeral supper of Twiglets, ham sandwiches and sweet white wine.

The following day the Joneses returned to Llanygwynfa, taking the whole journey in one go. There, on the farm, in the third field down, they found the green prism of their tent safely tethered and pegged down. Inside, its rolled up and bundled luggage still intact. Their home from home. Somehow it seemed impossible that the tent could have remained there while the family were away.

For the first two days the clouds remained a low, sombre presence. The family, as always during these spells, became cloud experts, able to distinguish cirrocumulus from nimbostratus, to understand their weight, temperature, density, their rain-bearing potential. The second day was more frustrating because there was brilliant weather out to sea, with white, towering clouds floodlit in gold and clean sweeps of blue sky, but the cloud lingered low over the land for the whole day. Looking along the coast it could be seen how the edge of the cloud mass mirrored perfectly the coastline. Inlets, coves, and spits of land had their counterparts in the clouds. Julian could even see vaporous villages and steamy farmsteads up there, with a family camped in a fold of cumulus. Cloud had become everything.

Never had the family abandoned a holiday, even if it was three weeks of drizzle. Even week after week of wet and wind was worth enduring, they felt, for a foggy walk up Glyn Cynddeiriog or a misty soiree on the promenade at Aberbreuddwyd, a ride on a miniature train, even a visit to the only cinema in a thousand square miles. But now the family had little spirit for the endurance of bad weather. Even the children, immune to the poignancy and loss of the days leading up to the funeral, were mildly stunned by the event itself and seemed to have forgotten how to play.

On the evening of the second day Aldous said quietly to

79

Colette, realizing it was what she wanted to hear, 'If it's like this tomorrow shall we call it a day?'

She nodded, adding 'If that's what the kids want.'

Aldous put the suggestion to them as they sat in the misted-up car, rain crackling quietly on the roof. They nodded earnestly, shocking themselves.

But on the third day Aldous unzipped the door of the tent to find a world of brightly lit mountains beyond, sheep casting sharp blue shadows, everything shining. Moelfre's every grass blade seemed defined. In two days the skin of the family reddened to the colour of boiled shrimps. For the rest of the week they climbed mountains, rode bicycles, ate twilit dinners amid fireflies and moths, and spent whole days on the beach.

The beach was entered by a small valley in the dunes. Here the sand was loose and piled in small heaps. Near the seaward side of the dune line were large grey pebbles distributed in the sand like currants in a cake. Approaching the sea, when the tide was out, one's feet encountered the feel of many different sands. A little way from the dunes was a continuous bank of pebbles, round-edged oblongs like well-used erasers. The sand then became flat and smooth as freshly laid cement. A belt of broken shells that felt prickly underfoot. Then an inner channel of water over serrated sand had to be crossed before an area of boundless manila sand was reached. Here the only marks were isolated flecks of bladderwrack, kelp, mare's-tail. It was as though a rich woman, undressing, had discarded mink stoles, kid gloves, silk stockings, pearl necklaces on her way to bed. The sand curved into gentle knots around these lonely discardments. They were the only landmarks. Mountains in their own way. These, and the odd single shell, as ridiculously alone as a single footprint might be.

Only when the sand developed a ribbed texture, further out, did one cease to drift out of the world altogether. Aldous often felt like this on the beach. The continuous, enthusiastic blare of the ocean reducing all noise in the world to a single pulsed roar, people reduced to shimmering ants, the landscape two vast flatnesses, one beige, the other blue, like the world must have been in that first week of creation, when the earth was separated from the heavens.

Here Julian delved with a small red spade, digging a hole, flinging the spoil high over his shoulder, digging with a skill and intensity of purpose that seemed entirely natural. No one had taught Julian how to dig. Perhaps we are natural burrowing creatures, thought Aldous. Perhaps our true habitat is underground. He helped his son fill a bucket with sand twice and turn out two Martello towers. They walked, Julian letting the spade trail behind him so that it scored a line in the perfect parchment of the sand. The sand was so compact Aldous and Julian left no footprints. There was just the line which Julian began turning into a wave, then loops and great interlocking scrolls. Finally Aldous helped Julian write his name, and his own, which, for Julian, was Daddy. The words were taller than Aldous. The beach now looked like this

They had drifted so far in this beach writing and the creation of what Julian called their 'sea-names', Aldous felt he was floating in a sandy nowhere with just these marks for human presence, and he had to follow them backwards, picking his way Theseus-like along the thread of the line, out of the shifting, uncertain space of the beach. As he did so he picked out members of his own family scattered and clumped around the beach. It amazed him how different they looked, not like people at all, but precious, exotic birds or butterflies.

'Everything has turned out okay,' Aldous thought to himself as he watched his wife dip Juliette's feet in the sparkling rim of the ocean. 'Everything has turned out better than I could have hoped. A beautiful, funny, interesting wife. A music room. A job that I enjoy. I have a son who is studying the piano at the Royal Academy of Music.' (When Janus was first accepted there Aldous found himself repeating that particular phrase over and over to himself.) He did feel as though he'd been blessed to have a son who could play Chopin's Etudes or Beethoven's Diabelli Variations so exquisitely it was as though Cortot or Schnabel or Geiseking was in the room.

Janus had brought music they'd never dreamt of into the house. Aldous had rarely listened to any classical music more recent than Brahms, but since his son had been at the Academy he'd encountered Rachmaninov, Ravel, Prokofiev. There was an exquisite pleasure in producing a concert pianist in the making, hearing the ponderous scales and arpeggios of their practice slowly transform into etudes, polonaises, concerti.

Now the pianist was carrying Julian on his shoulders as he paddled in the shallow waves. James and Juliette were chasing each other across the sand. Colette was laughing as she returned to the little encampment of towels and cushions that marked their space on an almost empty beach. The wind had caught her dress and her hair. Ripples were passing through her. She was shimmering.

Sand, feathered, indoors. Nana's bedroom, floored with beige lino. A little desert.

Colette had been home for three weeks and hadn't opened the door to her mother's old room until now. The back bedroom had been Nana's for five years. The smallest of the three bedrooms. Colette, when she found the strength to open the door, had forgotten its littleness. The single bed. The wardrobe that had come from the old house, that Colette had known since childhood, that was Janus Brian's favourite hiding place in their childhood games of hide and seek. A chest of drawers. A dressing table. And between all these, a beach of cold lino.

The museum stillness of the room made Colette feel she was disrupting a carefully settled presence as she edged herself into the space. The room was all greens and browns, a concentration of earthy colours, unlike any other rooms of the house. It smelt of moss.

Had not other pressures intervened Colette might never have set foot in this room. But in their crowded house the fact couldn't be ignored that Nana's death had freed up some space. Janus, James and Juliette were sharing a single room. Julian had spent nearly four years as a guest in his parents' room. Now there was an opportunity to filter off the youngest children to their own room. Juliette and Julian could share Nana's room, James and Janus could have the bigger back bedroom, and Colette and Aldous could have their room back to themselves.

So Colette, nagged daily by children excited by the impending changes to the geography of the house, had to sort things out. She had to move furniture, change old bedclothes, decide what to do with her mother's things. There wasn't much. The wardrobe yielded a few floral ghosts, the dressing table a brush matted with silver threads, the chest of drawers seemed to hold nothing but rolls of white cotton socks. Her mother could be contained in two small grocery boxes and a suitcase. She stacked them on the landing for Aldous to take up to the loft later, and returned to the room to air the mattress. Already the room was easier to be in. Colette even began to feel comfortable there. She smiled as she bent down for the mattress, inserted her arms beneath its weight and lifted. It was as though she'd opened a door on a star.

Beneath the mattress was a treasury of silver paper – foil sweet wrappers, milk bottle tops, lids from yoghurt cartons. A trove of them, so many they spilled over the edge of the mattress and trickled on to the floor, sparkling, like a jackpot. It must have taken her mother years to accumulate such riches. Colette knelt down in the frail pile of glitter and sobbed, picking up and spilling handfuls.

1965

1

Julian and his mother are standing at the entrance to the bus depot on the North Circular Road. Before them are two rows of red Routemaster buses parked side by side, forming an avenue of buses that seems to recede into infinity, as though one bus was reflected in a double mirror. It is a vision of buses for ever. An endless corridor. Julian thinks he has never seen anything so big.

All the buses are motionless, unlit. Some have numbers and destinations on their fronts, some are blank. In the far distance Julian can see mechanics in blue overalls working on a stripped engine. There is laughter and shouting, distant and hollow, as if from a dream. An inspector with a clipboard and a mug of tea walks past and winks at Colette, clicks his tongue at Julian, leaves a little trail of steaming splashes on the greasy floor. Colette says something Julian can't understand. There is a joke about the tea. Then one of the ranked buses suddenly starts into life, filling the vast hall with an echoey, gargling noise. It unslots itself like a volume from a shelf of red diaries, turns and rolls towards Julian and his mother.

Colette is dressed from head to foot in dark grey. A double-breasted jacket, a straight skirt cut to just below the knee. She looks like one of her husband's pencil sketches of her. She is wearing a brown leather harness, the straps of which make an elegant X between her shoulder blades, coming together at the front of her body in a leather breastplate from which silver buckles hang. She has Julian in one hand, a small and roughly made leather case in the other. As though she is going away for the weekend.

Julian is wearing his school uniform. It is the last day of his first year at school. He hasn't enjoyed the year much. From the first day things seemed to go wrong. It started with a bus. In class 10 there was a red Routemaster bus, small enough for a child to sit on and push around with his feet, steering by means of a white wheel that came out of its roof. He wasn't to know that a black wax crayon was stuck under the front wheel. He wasn't to know that this crayon was recording, as a thick black line, his journey round and round the classroom. It wasn't as though he'd done it on purpose. But when Rolf Slatten, an amber-coloured boy with freckles and an old man's face, drew their teacher's attention to what Julian Jones had done, Julian felt unable to protest his innocence. It was the first day. Miss Clarke was as shocked as she was cross. 'I thought you were such a good boy.' The singleness of purpose, the sheer effort, the concentration needed to draw that continuous line in its snaking course around and in between tables, looping, spiralling, figure eighting. It looked as if it might be a mile long if straightened out. Such a dedicated piece of vandalism.

Miss Clarke kept Julian in during break, provided him with a basin of cold water and a stack of green paper towels, telling him, in a voice ugly with coldness, to clean that line off the floor. It was a futile task. The oily substance of the line shrugged the water off. Julian cried, wondering how many days it would take him, wondering why it was so important that he remove traces of himself.

That was the first day. The last day was a little better. Miss Clarke had, rather mysteriously during the course of the year, become Mrs Laponte, and had nearly doubled in size. It wasn't just her body that had grown, waiting to add to the tally of the world's children, but her face as well. It had started the year narrow and pale but was now broad, round and dark, like a piece of carved wood. It smiled almost permanently. The class had come to love her and she loved them back, even Julian. She wore diaphanous, floral nylon dresses that floated and crackled around the classroom. On the last day she took each child on her knee in turn, kissed it and gave it a stick of barley sugar.

Julian waved his like a magic wand as he rushed out of the school gates to meet his mother, who stood somehow alone in a small crowd of mothers. The flood of little children that came from the gates was absorbed by this crowd. Some of the children held aloft orange batons of sugar. Some had already broken open the Cellophane and begun eating them. Julian presented his barley sugar to his mother as though it was an important trophy he'd won. His mother hardly noticed it. He could see that she'd been crying. He couldn't understand why the barley sugar didn't fascinate her. A twisted rope of amber glass that tasted sweet. A gift and a kiss from Mrs Laponte had dazzled Julian.

Colette didn't say much. On the way home they visited the cemetery. Julian liked the cemetery because it reminded him of the countryside. Grass, hedgerows, trees, small fields, half-hidden cottages, winding paths. At the centre of the cemetery, like the prize at the heart of a maze, was a set of wooden benches under a rustic roof of thatch. House martins built daub and wattle dwellings in the eaves.

Colette and Julian walked silently along one of the paths, then picked their way between headstones until they were four rows back from the path. By the time they had come to the headstone Colette wanted, Julian had lost interest. He was still holding his stick of barley sugar. He'd unwrapped it and had tasted it but had decided, rather reluctantly, that he didn't like it. He tried rewrapping the end that he'd sucked, but it became a sticky tangle of sugar and Cellophane. He didn't know what to do with it.

Colette began crying again. She fell down on her knees in

87

front of the headstone. Julian wasn't sure what to do. He felt embarrassed and looked around to see if there was anyone looking. Then his mother whispered with a clenched urgency to Julian, as though she was angry, for him to do the same.

'On your knees,' she whispered through her tears, giving equal emphasis to each word.

There was a gardener nearby, an old man in a flat cap and waistcoat clipping grass with a long pair of shears. His jacket was hanging from one of the gravestones as though it was the back of a chair. Julian hesitated, then knelt. The grass was damp and cold against his knees.

On the headstone Agnes Waugh's name was above another name. A woman's. This woman was a complete stranger to Colette. She was a stranger to Nana. Below her name there was still some blank stone that was waiting to be filled with a third name. When this name came, of the woman who was to be buried on top of Agnes and her unknown companion, it would also be the name of a stranger. Three women who in life knew nothing of each other now formed an intimate subterranean trinity, set to allow a posthumous merging of their flesh and bones. Sisters of the earth.

Colette and Julian stood up. Four circles of mud on their knees.

From the cemetery Colette took Julian home, and from there, after a wash and change, to the bus depot for her afternoon shift on the 102. Julian's final day finished too early for anyone else to collect him from school. The only solution was for Colette to bring him home herself and take him on the bus with her. She'd had him on the bus before and he enjoyed it. He would sit quietly on one of the benches on the lower deck. Only once had he caused her a problem, when he tied a strand of a young girl's long hair to the chrome handle of a seat back. When the girl rose to get off she was yanked back into her seat by her own hair. No one could untie her and the bus was delayed for several minutes. Colette had to resort to a pair of scissors from her first aid kit in the end. The girl was in tears. So was Julian.

And so they wait by the entrance to the huge depot while Jack, Colette's driver, swings the bus over to them. As he approaches, Colette lifts her leg, hitching the skirt up to the thigh, balancing an elbow on the lifted knee and then flicking her wrist, thumb outstretched, three or four times. This complex gesture of the whole body bewilders Julian who ignores it. It delights Jack, however, and he pips his horn and laughs wide-mouthed through the cab window. Colette's impersonation of a siren-like hitchhiker always makes him laugh.

'Cheer up mate!' he shouts to Julian, who pretends not to hear.

It is Colette's last day on the buses as well. This evening she will hang up her ticket machine for good. Tomorrow she and her family are leaving for three weeks in Wales.

To celebrate this fact she allows all her passengers to travel half price (she would have allowed them to travel free but handing in a blank cash sheet at the end of her shift would have caused problems). She also casts to the wind all standing restrictions. People can fill the lower deck until they hurt. They can stand on the platform, the stairs, the upper deck, she doesn't care. Her bus can fill to the brim with people. This is her last day.

Julian can see that his mother has a special skill as a bus conductress. Her siren-hitchhiker routine is just one example of how the job employs her whole body. A bus conductress like Colette is a type of dancer, scaling the spiralled heights of her blood-red staircase, leaning forward against an invisible wall of acceleration, or supporting herself against the centrifugal thrust of a sharp bend, skipping, almost, along the top deck from front to back, gripping quickly in turn each vertical silver bar, like a monkey swinging through a precious playground, clutching her Sanderson ticket machine with her other hand, pausing at the stair-head to push the bell that signals the driver to go. Her movements around the bus are accompanied by this rhythmic ringing of bells. There are bells all around the bus: at the top of the stairs, on the platform, in the luggage space under the stairs, at the end of a bell-rope threaded through a series of silver loops along the ceiling of the lower deck. Music and balance. She comes down the stairs with such speed she almost slides down the silver banister. And she can banter with passengers, carrying on several conversations at once like a chess grandmaster in exhibition, while keeping track of where the bus is on its route, how many stops to the Cambridge Roundabout, The Angel, Muswell Hill, Silver Street.

Colette herself is surprised at how easily she slipped into this new role. If it was possible for someone to have a natural gift for conducting a bus, then Colette had it. From the first day of her training she seemed ahead of her fellow recruits, who were nervous, sluggish, slightly dopey men and women. When their lecturer, a man whom Colette saw as a giant ladybird, held aloft a small blue book of rules and regulations and asked his audience what they thought might be this book's name, Colette's was the only voice to break the baffled silence.

'The Busman's Bible?' she laughed, her seizure laugh that lifted her shoulders up to her ears.

'You are exactly right, my love,' the lecturer replied, genuinely delighted, directing his well-worn index finger at Colette. 'In twenty-two years of giving these talks you are the first one to give me the right answer.'

Her first journey in sole command of a bus, however, was, like Julian's graphic journey around his classroom, a small catastrophe. The sun not yet risen, she left the depot unable to find the light switch and the bus worked its route unlit. She couldn't load her ticket machine, which was buckled into a papoose across her middle and looked like a small silver samovar. Somehow you tipped the handles of this object and paper, not tea, poured out of it. That morning it wouldn't respond to her touches. Her passengers, mostly early shift workers at the Standard Telephones and Cables Factory (manufacturers of the first transatlantic cable) had free but dark rides. They laughed at Colette. 'Never mind, love, you coming this way every morning?' A bus of dark laughter, a dark bus sailing along the empty carriageways of the North Circular. The biggest stone circle in the world.

These were nothing more than teething troubles, however. First morning nerves. She quickly and easily slipped into the routines of her job, its odd rituals, tricks and traditions.

She learnt to warm her feet on the flywheel casing, taking her shoes off, if the bus was empty, and resting them there. She learnt Jack's tricks for avoiding the drunks on Friday nights, slowing the bus down as he came to The Angel where the stop was always teeming with hoodlums, then pulling away at the last moment, to jeers and howls. Colette never had any real trouble on the late shifts. Just cheekiness. Although there was one time when she was conducting the last bus on a Saturday night, after the pubs had emptied and most of the drunks were asleep, a man scuttled on to her almost empty bus and hurried upstairs, hiding his face behind upturned lapels. When she went upstairs for his fare she found him sitting at the front, leaning heavily against the window. As she came round to the front she saw that his face was caked with blood and that his torn shirt was leopard-spots of red. She asked him if he would like her to call the police or an ambulance. He shook his head slightly but emphatically, and held out the correct change for a ride to Edmonton Green. When they passed the North Middlesex Hospital she advised her blood-soaked passenger to alight there but he just shook his head again, covering his face delicately with spread fingers saying 'Just get me to The Green, sweetheart.' At Edmonton he got off, still hiding his face, as though he was famous.

Too many adventures to remember. Too many jokes, odd characters, happenings.

The bus is now full of laughter because Colette has broken all the rules of the Busman's Bible and is allowing people to crowd the bus up to its physical limit. It was the worst thing about bus conducting, denying access to needy travellers at bus stops. The disappointed faces. The gloom she caused. Limiting entry to a number equal to those who had alighted. 'Two on top only.' 'Three inside,' ding ding. 'There's another one behind.'

91

Colette often thinks how like a ship her bus is. The decks, the stairs, the bells, the bell-rope, the rocking motion, the way the bus steers along paths of busy currents (cars/water), pauses at edges (kerbs/quays). Like a ship the bus is a whole world, a self-contained community overlaid with intricately drafted rules, regulations and commands which are posted in elegant sans serif signage all around the bus – *push bell once, used tickets here, no standing on upper deck, push chairs must be folded.* If the bus is a ship then Colette is the captain (her driver is merely the helmsman). If the ship is a world then Colette is Empress.

There was, deep in Colette's blood, a maritime pulse that she couldn't ignore. It came from her mother's people who lived at the mouth of the Tyne. Her mother's father, Granda Kent, was a ship's captain. When Agnes was a baby, and before she was born, her father would be away for months at a time, commanding trading steamers in the Far East, the Philippines, Hong Kong, Java, across the Baltic to Helsinki, or across the Norwegian Sea and the Barents Sea to Archangel. What cargoes he carried Agnes never knew, but he brought back gifts for his wife, Colette's grandmother, from all these places, and she filled the house with them. Russian icons dominated one wall of her parlour. Ivory ornaments and raku vases populated a mantelshelf. There was a cabinet of netsuke. From Helsinki there was a ceramic bust of Our Lady looking like Queen Guinevere with a white coronet about her head. There were pieces of inlaid work from Cochin-China, Persian carpets, woodcarvings of primitive gods from Sarawak, packets of tea, bottles of scent, oil, pots of spices that had never been opened and never would be. Their modest house in South Shields seemed to contain the whole world. But by the time Agnes was old enough to wait at the pier end (at a mile, the world's longest, she was always told) for her father's ship, the *Vauxhall*, nicknamed the *Coffin* because it had sunk several times, her father's voyages were coastal trudges back and forth along the spine of England with a hold full of freshly mined coal. 'Shall I hail her for you hinny?' the coastguard who manned the lighthouse at the pier head would say when the *Vauxhall*, low in the water even when unladen, entered the shelter of the mouth of the Tyne. A coded series of blasts from the foghorn would be answered by the ship's mournful, steamy call.

Colette has only the vaguest memories of Granda Kent. By then he had retired from the sea altogether and lived rather like an exalted guest in his wife's house with Teddy-I-Did-Tell, his simple brother, and cousin Ernest. Granda Kent had a brass hook where his left hand had been, severed in a maritime accident, which in turn severed his musical abilities on the piano and squeezebox. He'd carried into his domestic life many of the habits acquired in a lifetime at sea. He never washed, for instance, maintaining the sailor's need to conserve fresh water. He never looked dirty, nor did he smell, and if asked why he never washed, would reply 'The dirt keeps you warm.' Granda, Teddy and Ernest would play whist in the evenings while Grandma made suet puddings and biscuits. They would tease Teddy mercilessly by blatantly cheating, tucking cards up their sleeves while he was looking ('Ma, Ernie's cheating, I did tell him . . .') and Grandma would scold them for teasing the simpleton.

Colette was never sure exactly why her mother left Tyneside to come to London, but it was there that she met and married Jack Waugh, a schoolmaster. Jack was from County Sligo, a Catholic like Agnes. Colette and all the children grew up in fear of him. He treated his boys, Lesley and Janus Brian, with brutal discipline, thrashing them for the least misdemeanour.

When she thinks about her father Colette stops thinking about the past.

The bus, having brimmed during the steep approach to Muswell Hill, has now emptied slightly, enabling Julian to spend some time on the platform, which he enjoys. He hangs on to the white pole that is sheathed in spiralled white plastic and pretends, with one leg over the side, to scooter the bus along. When the bus slows he straightens his leg at an angle

93

against the motion of the bus as though he is slowing the bus by digging his heel into the road.

Julian wants the passengers to know he is the son of the conductress. She has never seemed, to him, so important as when she is conducting a bus. She has never seemed so in control. People do what she says. He thinks it must be the perfect job for a mother to do, and for a while he assumed that everyone's mother was a bus conductress, and that all buses were conducted by mothers. For a while, buses, bus drivers and bus conductresses (the drivers were always men, the conductors always women – in locomotive parentis), seemed to him the most important, powerful and interesting things in the world. When, a few years later, the first one-man pay-as-you enter buses appeared, Julian couldn't help feeling orphaned.

Colette has been a bus conductress for little less than a year. She took the job shortly after returning from Wales. She'd spent the week after the funeral in a daze, not fully understanding what it was that was troubling her. And then, watching Julian delving on the beach, digging a hole deep enough to vanish into, she realized. That hole they lowered her mother into was too deep. Too deep.

Once she was back in London she began making enquiries. She talked to the cemetery officials in their Alpine log cabin at the cemetery gates and learnt, to her horror, that her mother, Nana with her silver hair and little eyes, the fountainhead of five separate families, had been buried in a common grave.

She phoned Lesley from the phone box at the top of the road.

'You rat. You swine.'

'Dear?'

'How could you do that to our mother?'

There was silence before Lesley's voice came through slowly and carefully, as though trying not to wake anyone.

'I advise you to think very carefully about what you say next.'

'You're the one who should have thought carefully before

94

tipping Mumma down that hole. Do you know they've already buried someone on top of her? A complete stranger.'

Lesley's voice came across as exaggeratedly tired, as though he was having to explain something for the thousandth time, a voice he'd developed for the classroom, Colette thought.

'My dear, there simply wasn't the money available for a private grave . . .'

'So it all comes down to money does it?'

'Do you have any idea of the costs of these things?'

'You really are a vulgar little man aren't you?'

Even Colette realized the word 'little' was absurd when applied to Lesley.

'I didn't want to raise the subject of money, dear, but you gave me no alternative. Everything costs money. Nearly everything. Private graves are very expensive. Mumma had no insurance. She'd made no arrangements. How could she? Why should I . . . I'm the eldest so . . .'

Sentences usually came out of Lesley's mouth as though they'd been penned in advance. They were complete. You could almost see the punctuation. So it was slightly shocking for Colette to hear his sentences break up like that. It pleased her. He was floundering, and she let him flounder until the pips went. She had another sixpence but she didn't push it in, instead she called through the double stammer of Lesley and the exchange

'She always said you were mean. You are. You're a tight-fisted pig.'

The fact that someone was already buried on top of Nana caused an immediate problem for Colette's plans to have her mother reburied. She had to contact the widower of the dead woman to gain his permission to carry out the exhumation, since it would mean also exhuming his wife's body.

Fortunately he was a man in a similar position to herself, having left the funeral arrangements to miserly daughters. He too wanted to move his wife to a private grave.

They met in the art gallery at Broomfield Park. An

exhibition of clumsily executed watercolours was on. The artist was sitting next to the visitors' book. She was a plump woman in her sixties with a frilly dress and a mauve tidal wave hairdo.

The meeting between the two recently bereaved was brief and awkward. Two strangers thrown into contact by tragedy and the random allocation of spaces in soil. You never know, in death, who you might end up lying next to. It was rather like travelling by bus.

The widower was a pale old man, grey faced with a bald, wispy head. There were freshly picked scabs on his scalp. He was wearing two wristwatches – on his right wrist his own, a stout, roman-numeralled gadget in gold and leather. On his left a fidgety little silver watch, its face hardly bigger than the stones on an engagement ring. It was his wife's. Continually throughout their conversation he checked the time on both his wrists, pointing out, on each occasion, that he was wearing his wife's watch. Colette tried not to look at it. He seemed to think that for as long as he wore her watch a little piece of her, a little pulse, still lived. Time had become twice as important.

The meeting depressed Colette, despite the widower's cooperativeness. More than his cooperation was needed, however. Permission had to be sought from the Home Secretary himself. Letters arrived at Fernlight Avenue with the state portcullis on the envelope.

And then there was still the cost. If a private grave was expensive, exhumation and reburial was twice as expensive. A year on the buses was the only way Colette could think of paying for it.

There was something odd, Colette thought, about the way her mother's death and bungled burial had landed her in this job, conveying souls back and forth across a stretch of the North Circular Road, a Stygian current whose flow never ceased. Every day she was ferryman to hundreds of strangers, taking their change, touching them (she could now identify dozens of different palm types, from linen-soft to ape-rough). Sometimes they were shadows, hardly human coin-bearing dummies, sometimes they were warm and bright, sometimes they were shy, incomprehensible. Always they were her cargo, which in turn would fill another boat, the one that would take her mother the few yards out of the earth, across a river of grass, to her place of rest. Her last stop.

On the return from Muswell Hill Colette's bus joins the thickening flows of the rush hour. Her bus fills quickly. It is starting to get out of hand. Passengers can't get down the stairs for their stop because the stairs are choked with people. Colette herself can't, with all her practised nimbleness and dexterity, squeeze herself along the narrow gangways to take fares. She gives up and stands on the edge of the platform, travelling almost outside the bus. From being a farewell gift to her passengers the journey has become a sort of ordeal. Julian is relieved when, at Bowes Road, his father is waiting at the stop for him. As agreed Aldous collects Julian while Colette carries on with her last shift. She blows a kiss at her husband between the bodies of passengers, then rings the bell twice.

2

A ladder of worn and splintered wood stood on the landing, its top leaning into the open loft hatch. At the foot of the ladder Julian gazed up into the dark square of the roof space where he could hear his father shifting soft, weighty objects. A groan, a wheeze, a puff, then the abrasive sound of coarse fabric being dragged across wood. Shortly a fat green shape was rolled to the lip of the hatch, like a vast, thick liquid about to spill from a cup.

'Stand back Julian,' Aldous called invisibly from within the loft. Then his face appeared above the bundle to make sure Julian was clear. A last careful push, the bundle rolled over the brink, and then a rush, a hissing of air, and the rolled-up tent collapsed vertically down the column of the ladder, landing like a parachute that had failed to open on the green carpet. A crump of fabric against fabric, an uprising of dust and silence.

The tent, which had reposed unvisited in the loft for a year, had re-entered the world with a soft crash.

Thinking it must be very light Julian tried pulling it away from the ladder, taking hold of one of the orange nylon guy ropes that were splayed, squid-like, about the amorphous mass of canvas. But the tent wouldn't budge. It was heavier than it looked.

It smelt of Wales. The canvas, itself a pungent fabric, was saturated with smells – of the grasses, sedges and mosses of Llanygwynfa, its flinty air. And when later the tent was unrolled, pressed grass, a year old, turned to straw, fell out.

Aldous was still in the loft. Julian could hear his movements. He clambered over the small hill of the tent and stood on the bottom rung of the ladder.

'Daddy,' he called. The hole swallowed his voice.

His father's reply was a groaning, yawning sound, as though he was wrestling with unconscious opponents.

Julian began climbing the ladder. He heard the chiming of tent poles, more weight being shifted. He looked down nervously. The landing carpet was a small putting green opening at the stairwell to a perilous drop through the house. His head was close to the ceiling. He saw for the first time the thick crust of dust on the upper surface of the landing lampshade. Then, as if breaking the surface of a pool from beneath, his head passed through the ceiling and into the clammy, warm air of the loft.

The space he found up there was dark and chaotic. The roof sloped, forming the inside of a perfect pyramid propped up with thick timber posts at odd angles. He could see the underside of the slate plating that dressed the rooftop, how each was fastened to a thin wooden baton, overlapping like the cards he remembered in Nana's long games of patience. Horizontal timbers formed barriers and gangplanks. The floor was an array of parallel joists with plaster bulging between them, like a store of ancient eclairs. Near the hatch was the water tank, a sarcophagus of liquid, a rising curl of pipe dripping, rippling it. A little way away, under the silver glow of the skylight, was the headless body of a tailor's dummy, a gift from dead Mr Sealy. Much of the loft clutter was his. The dummy housed an abandoned wasps' nest in its chest space. Silent archways, balconies and crescents of paper. A city of origami.

The internal structure of the roof, its sloping walls and the upright posts supporting it, reminded Julian of a tent. It was as though an enormous tent of slate and wood had been pitched on top of the house.

His father, bent double over a green canvas sack the size of a man, half in shadow, looked through his armpit at Julian, straightened, banged his head on a strut and said 'Julian!'

'Daddy, I've come up the ladder.'

'I told you to stay at the bottom.'

'I wanted to come up.'

Aldous walked like a cat, stepping only on the thin edges of the joists as he approached the hatch.

'Be very careful where you step, Julian.' Aldous verbally underlined the word 'very'. 'Step on the joists. Don't step in between them or your foot will go through the ceiling. You might fall into the bedroom.'

After this Julian would always think of the loft floor as a type of quicksand.

There was the crash of the front door downstairs (downstairs twice), then the softer, hollower slam of the music room door. The doors of Fernlight Avenue were always loud. They couldn't be closed quietly. A normal closing of the front door shook the windows upstairs. The internal doors too were heavy and swung to with a thud and click of latches. The movements of people around the house were punctuated by the abrupt barking of unintentionally slammed doors. Julian, when he visited the houses of his young friends, was always slightly shocked at the flimsiness of their doors and fittings. The way their banisters wobbled.

Music from the piano came up the stairs, telling them that Janus had come into the house.

Aldous lifted the canvas sack upright. Metal jangled. It contained, Julian could see, a sheaf of tent poles. It was like a model of a cathedral organ, a cluster of differently sized circles, some neatly fitted with little pale cylinders of Welsh mud.

Aldous didn't recognize the music. At first he supposed it some cacophonic, atonal piece by one of the many modern composers Janus had introduced him to. But the music Janus was playing downstairs had somehow broken up. As they listened at the loft hatch they heard the music disintegrate until it was nothing more than random crashes of strings. Not even Bartok managed such ugly abstraction, thought Aldous, who'd yet to be entirely won over by the Hungarian. It sounded as though Janus was bashing the keyboard with his fists. There was a loud crack of wood. The sound of the keyboard lid being slammed shut. Then again. Other noises. Something being thrown. Julian looked at his father.

'What's he doing, Daddy?'

Aldous called down into the house that had been empty 'Janus!'

The noises stopped. It seemed that Janus had thought himself alone.

A few seconds later he appeared on the landing, looking pink and ruffled.

'I'm in the loft,' Julian shouted to his brother, delighted by the bird's-eye view he had of him. He felt as though he was in an aeroplane, or at the top of a tall tree.

'Two Gods,' said Janus.

'What were you doing?' asked Aldous, a strange gurgle of embarrassment in his voice. He noticed that Janus looked up into the loft as though he couldn't see them.

'About what?'

'With the piano.'

Janus paused as though he hadn't heard the question, and then said 'Experimenting.'

'We're getting the tent,' said Julian.

Janus moved to the foot of the ladder. His brow was deeply furrowed with the effort of looking upwards. Aldous shifted the pole sack on to the top of the ladder, gripping its neck with both fists, then slowly lowered it. The poles clinked quietly. Janus reached up with both his hands, as though to receive a child rescued from an earthquake, and took the weight of the sack into his body. Aldous saw that his knuckles were freshly cut.

In the garden Janus inverted the sack of poles and let them spill out, unsheathing themselves like an armoury of blunt swords. They jangled on the grass, lay in crisscross hap-hazardness.

The afternoon and evening before departure were always concerned with extracting carefully an inner house of canvas from the outer house of brick and slate. In the evening it would be pitched in the garden and the children would play in it as though rehearsing for the real holiday. Its walls would be inspected for holes. Rips and tears were patched. Bent tent pegs were straightened. Fractured guy ropes were reknotted.

The tent filled almost entirely the lawn in the back garden. The guy ropes reached into the depths of flower beds and rockeries, right up to the fence.

In Wales, however, these boundaries receded into the distance. The tent could almost become lost in a huge oblong of pasture.

James would always claim to know the exact patch of grass they'd occupied the year before. He would say he could still see a trace of flatness in the sward, that he could remember the precise angles of the landscape, the alignments of trees, buildings and mountains. No one else was convinced but they would pitch the tent there anyway. Later in the holiday someone would always make the observation that confirmed the tent was misaligned with the previous year. The farmhouse was behind that tree last year. This year it's to the right.

This year, however, as the tent was lifted out of its bundle, unrolled, unfolded, spread out, there was no doubt that they'd found the exact spot, because James reached his finger into the ground and, as though uncorking a particularly old vintage, extracted a peg from the earth, orphaned since last summer.

Poles were matched against each other, like an enormous drawing of lots, were slotted together, held like javelins. Aldous lifted the supine door of the tent while Janus nosed his spear into the unzipped gap, parted the loose sides and eased himself into the limp space, moved through an almost two-dimensional corridor of canvas, found the hole at the back gable into which he fitted the point of his tent pole, lifted it. Suddenly that which had fallen about him now stood and an embryonic space was defined. Aldous and James hammered pegs on the other side of the canvas. When Janus let go of the vertical pole it stayed miraculously upright, like the Indian rope trick. A second pole was brought into the tent, inserted into the front gable. The walls of the tent separated further. Janus found himself in a room. More pegs were hammered in, giving a slicing sound as they sank. To hammer in the pegs they used stones from the walls which gave orange sparks as they struck the curled heads of the pegs. The pegs themselves were an assortment of different types accumulated over the years. Among them were some kebab skewers from Colette's kitchen.

The inner tent structure was now complete. It struck Aldous as being not greatly different from the stone cromlechs that stood on the hillsides above Llanygwynfa. Uprights and horizontals.

Now the ridge pole was fitted on to the protruding metal spires at either end of the tent, and this thin brace was extended on two more vertical poles beyond the front of the inner tent. The framework was flimsy and James was charged with supporting it while Aldous and Janus dressed it with the flysheet. The huge expanse of canvas, twice the length of the inner tent, slithered over the ridge poles and was pegged tightly to the ground.

That was the tent finished. When the flysheet was first unpacked it was as crumpled as a heap of dead leaves. Now it was pegged so drum-tight there wasn't a crease or wrinkle anywhere.

Janus and Aldous had handled the flysheet with the deft cooperativeness of sailors unfurling a topsail. They could erect the tent without the need of exchanging a single word. Colette watched them. She hadn't noticed before how closely Janus copied his father's mannerisms, his facial and hand gestures, his expressions. The wrinkling of the nose. The peeling of imaginary cobwebs off his face. The drawing in of breath through clenched teeth. The finger-raking back of hair from the forehead. It unsettled her a little. Those mannerisms looked wrong on Janus. He didn't wear them properly. They didn't fit. It was almost as if he was parodying his father. Then she felt ashamed for thinking this.

Colette filled the bare interior of the tent with bedding. She unrolled blankets, sleeping bags, eiderdowns, plumped up pillows. Arranged cushions.

Aldous thought how easily they'd altered the landscape, creating that tiny mountain, the tent, to mirror microscopically the peaks beyond the farm. How this empty field was now filled.

Aldous and Julian went for the milk and water. Julian carried the chipped pot of red enamel that was for the milk, his father sauntered along with the white plastic water carrier in his hand. They crossed the stream, undid somehow the knot of metal that held the gate shut, let it grind open. They walked the warm, pebbly ground of the farmyard, where the cow pats had dried into huge scabs, past the old barn that had been their home once, past the cattle shed, milking parlour, Dutch barn, chicken coop, old school house. Through another gate (black), past a forgotten pen crammed with mulberries and flies, over the lane, round the curved wall of the burial ground, through the courtyard beside an older barn, to the wall of the farmhouse, thickly rendered and pebbledashed like a gateau, round the side, past the tiny but deep kitchen window, along the cobbled path and a border of wallflowers, the house on one side, the coastal plain on the other, round the corner to the back yard where chickens strutted and a couple of dogs clinked in their chains and wagged their tails, where there was a barn door into the house, the top half open, yellow light within.

'Hallo,' sang Aldous into the house and almost instantly there was an interior reply, not a word, but a musical call, bird-like, that was Mrs Evans, whose face, smiling, appeared at the door, her teeth, hardly bigger than a baby's, twinkling.

'Hallo Mr Jones. All pegged down are you? And now you want some milk?'

Mrs Evans always seemed to speak as though she was narrating a story in which Aldous was the main character. She was also one of those people gifted with the ability to smile and talk at the same time. Aldous could never quite understand how some of the rounder vowels could come from that broadly smiling mouth. She turned to Julian and said 'Is that for me, angel?'

And Julian, realizing that by holding the milk jug he'd unwittingly involved himself in this exchange, flinched as Mrs Evans reached over the door and took hold of the spout in her fingers and eased the handle out of his hands, as though painlessly extracting a milk tooth.

'He's a lamb,' she said to Aldous, 'isn't he a lamb? But growing so fast. They grow so fast now don't they Mr Jones. What have you been feeding him, compost?' She reached out again, teased Julian's curled hair in the same way she'd taken the jug. Julian felt she might lift him into the house. 'Soon be able to help with the hay, like his brothers. Soon be able to follow the tradition, like Janus and James. James makes us laugh, Mr Jones, when he comes for the milk. Clump, clump, clump over the stones come his footsteps, then a bang when he bangs down the jug on the step. We look out of the door and there is James sitting on the step with his back to us, arms folded, head resting on his arms, with the jug next to him. He doesn't say a word. I fill the jug, put it down on the step. James hasn't moved a muscle. Waits till I've gone. Then clump, clump, clump, off he goes, only a little slower. Bye-bye, I call. Nothing. It makes us laugh, Mr Jones.'

She withdrew into the house. No sound, but for the soft clink of dog chains, the cautious murmur of hens. Distant birdsong. Aldous has never known silence like the silence of waiting for milk. Mrs Jones returned with the jug, the same jug as before, the same in every respect, except for this – its weight. Without hesitation she offered the milk to Julian, straining slightly to hold it across the threshold. Some spilt. Julian took the jug, handle in one hand, spout in the other, and felt the weight of the milk sink into him. A little lick of milk spurted from the spout and hit his eye. Aldous and Mrs Jones exchanged more words. In the ten years that he has been taking milk from her, Aldous has never seen precisely where this milk came from. He imagined a churn in her kitchen, her tipping it, the milk pouring into the jug. But he had never seen it.

'Mr Jones, I want to ask you something.'

'Yes?'

'Do you mind?'

'No.'

'What I want to ask you is something we've wanted to ask you for a long time. You only ever come here in August Mr Jones, and it is the worst month of the year. It is too hot. The air is thick, you can't see through it. The flowers start dying. And then it rains. Rain in August, Mr Jones, we always have rain in August. The clouds can be down for the whole month. You know that yourself. You've been lucky recently. And then the town is so crowded and the buses are full and the lanes are full of caravans, and you can't move on the beaches. Sometimes it's caravans from the chapel down to the sands. Have you never seen our part of the world at Easter, Mr Jones, when the air is like glass and there is still snow on the hills and ice in the rivers and the bulbs are out. Why don't you come in June, Mr Jones, when the rhododendrons are out? Before you die, Mr Jones, you should see Bwlch-y-goedleoedd or Farchynys at rhododendron time . . .'

Janus and Colette were at the tent. Janus was sitting sideways in the front passenger seat of the car. Colette was in the doorway of the tent unpacking crockery and food.

Janus had a map spread out on his knees, a small blue book in his hand, and binoculars strapped around his neck.

He had an idea that the farm and other buildings of Llanygwynfa were arranged to align with the stars of the constellation Ursa Major. He'd noticed it on the last night of the previous holiday when he'd been out in the field after dark with the Plough bright above the softly glowing hump of

Moelfre. Suddenly, in the landscape beneath, there appeared its reflection, its earthly double. The stone buildings, silvery in starlight, themselves became stars in perfect symmetry with the stars above. Now he was trying to check this with the star charts from the *Observer's Book of Astronomy*, which was his little brother's. As he saw it the star called Dubhe was the farmhouse, Merak was the chapel, and then the farmyard was composed of the stars that were the tail of the Bear, or the handle of the Plough – Alioth, Mizar, Alkaid. Strangely, Mizar, a double star, was the cow shed, and there were now two cow sheds on the farm.

Colette came out of the doorway of the tent, looked at the tent for a little while, and then said 'I miss the house.'

Janus didn't reply but lifted the binoculars to his eyes and suddenly found himself face to face with a bull two fields away.

'I just don't like thinking of it empty,' Colette went on, 'and the garden growing out of control, and the letters piling up. No one to read them. Flies buzzing around the rooms, dying of thirst. I wish we could bring the house with us when we come on holiday.'

Janus was elsewhere, far afield, his vision augmented by the prisms and lenses of the binoculars, transported. He was on the summit of Moelfre. He was climbing the narrow gully above Ty Meddal. He was among the prickly dunes by the beach. He was on the roof of the chapel. He spoke.

'The man who invented binoculars is a fool. To think anyone would want to see more of the world than they already can. With their own eyes.'

'Don't you ever feel that?' said Colette. Janus swung his binoculars towards her. They brought his mother, huge and blurred, right into his head.

'Feel what?'

'Don't you ever feel sorry for the house?'

'Houses are for idiots. If mankind still lived in tents we wouldn't have tanks and bombs lined up along all the borders. Think about it mother. How could you invade a city of tents?

If the tanks roll in the city packs itself into a rucksack and goes somewhere else.'

Colette laughed.

'I spend the whole holiday worrying about the tent blowing away and the house burning down.'

'That should be the other way round,' said Janus, enabling his mother to recall that odd coincidence the year the tent burned down. When they came back, dusty and dishevelled from nearly a month in the barn, they found that a small suburban tornado had passed through the gardens of Fernlight Avenue, flattening the fences and toppling the fruit trees of nearly a hundred gardens. The tall poplar, which grew in a garden that abutted theirs at right angles, had let one of its many trunks fall across the garden, smashing in half the Pershore and crushing the fence. It took them weeks of sawing and chopping to get rid of it.

Remembering the symmetry of damage Colette also remembered the piano. Broken wood.

'Janus, what did happen to the piano?'

She hadn't noticed until the morning of their departure. Breezing through the music room in search of Julian's shoes she'd seen how the keyboard cover of the piano had been taken out and was lying on the floor. The music rest, a delicate web of black fretwork, had been broken. Pieces of it were scattered on the carpet. For the first time, she'd seen the actual wood the piano was made from, beneath its black, lacquered skin. The wood was dark red where the music rest had splintered.

'It can be glued back together.'

'But what happened? Daddy said he heard you downstairs, he said it sounded like you were smashing it up.'

Janus didn't reply for a few moments. He still had the binoculars to his eyes, sending his mother in and out of focus. To his mother he seemed to have acquired the compound eyes of a housefly.

'We had a disagreement,' Janus said.

'You and Daddy?'

'No,' he laughed, 'me and the piano. An altercation. A rumpus. A lovers' tiff. We'll make up. Kisses and glue will make up.'

'Janus, you don't realize what we went through to get you that piano. For God's sake, we even moved house because of it.'

Janus was not sure if this was true. He vaguely remembered that the old house could hardly contain the Bechstein. It had to double as a dining table. He remembered Sunday lunch around the piano, no tablecloth big enough so an old curtain with a pattern of monkeys escaping their cages was draped across to protect the woodwork, Dad carving the joint somewhere around middle C. He even remembered playing table tennis on it one Christmas. Then there were the complaints from next door. The party wall was so thin you could hear Mrs Ellis brushing her hair. Janus practising scales hour upon hour must have passed through that wall barely dampened, to jangle in their living room like a cacophonous ghost. The Ellises complained on a daily basis. In the end they didn't so much complain as beg, plead, implore, beseech. They never actually got down on their knees but it wouldn't have surprised Colette if they had. She could see that it was making them ill. 'It's not that we don't appreciate the music,' they would always point out.

The wall of the music room at Fernlight Avenue, however, was a wall that faced on to a stranger's garden, whose house was a hundred feet away at the other end of a lawn. Number 89 was the highest numbered house in Fernlight Avenue, the last house in the road. After 89 the houses stopped as far as Hoopers Lane. Not only did it have a room big enough to devote to a piano, it had space around it that could absorb any amount of noise. They were beyond the reach of eaves-droppers.

Aware that his mother wasn't satisfied, Janus continued.

'A musician and his instrument are bound to fall out now and again. It's such a claustrophobic relationship. At the Academy people are always having punch-ups with their instruments. I had a friend called Eric who kicked his cor anglais through a window. And a girl called Fiona sawed her cello in half. I'm not joking. She went out and bought the saw specially.'

As if to conclude this conversation Janus swung his binoculars away from his mother and directed them at the farm. He could see, as flat and silent as paintings, his brother and sister climbing on a rock. James was almost upside down, his feet working a narrow crevice. Juliette was vertical on a lower ledge. The farmyard itself looked like a chasm between rock faces, a crack in the landscape. At the far end, only just visible, the receding figures of his father and Julian. The slow semibreve paces of his father matched by the semiquaver dash of Julian's little legs.

'I think you've been irresponsible in having that child, mother.'

'Julian? Why?'

'Can't you see what sort of world this is? Do you know what they did the year he was born, 1961?'

'What who did?'

'They made suicide legal.'

'I didn't know it was illegal.'

'Rats off a ship. Who'd want to be born into a world that thinks its okay for you to hang yourself? The first society in history to allow self-extermination. They're responding to public demand. The world will end in 1970 anyway. It's the overdose or the H-bomb.'

'H-bombs,' Colette said wearily, as though they were a mildly irritating fad, and then quoted a rhyme she'd heard somewhere:

> I'm an old man now and my hearing's gone,
> But when I wear my hearing aid
> I can hear the hydrogen bomb.

And she laughed. Janus shook his head sternly at her laughter.

Colette had no interest in politics. She would happily

pretend to know nothing about it in order to avoid political discussions and by this route she had discovered an amusing way of teasing her serious children. She would infuriate them by talking about politicians solely in terms of personality and appearance. ('Why do Kennedy and Nixon both have such jowly faces?' and of Harold Wilson, 'I couldn't cast my vote on such an ugly little man.') This annoyed James and Juliette especially, who were on the cusp of left-wing politics, soon to cut their teeth on Marxism. It annoyed them further when she professed a deep fondness for Edward Heath, purely because he could play the organ and conduct orchestras. If Wilson was the Beatles, Heath was Purcell, Tallis, Bliss. In sourer moods she would expound a totally irrational xenophobia and declare her intention, if ever the power was to come her way (which she had to concede was unlikely), of dropping H-bombs on France, America, Germany, Hong Kong, Australia, Belgium, and any other country that had for some reason aroused her displeasure. But never Africa. And never Italy.

Apart from a week when she was a child among the fuchsias and chines of the Isle of Wight, Colette had never been abroad, and, apart from childhood holidays on the mouth of the Tyne, Wales was the furthest she'd ever been from home. They spoke another language there. The land was a different shape. It was foreign enough for her.

Every year, around Easter or late spring, the Joneses would informally discuss their plans for a summer holiday. For ten years they'd spent their summers in Llanygwynfa. Perhaps it was time for a change.

'What about the Lake District?' Aldous would say.

'It's too packed with tourists,' Colette would reply.

'What about Scotland?' said Janus, who'd heard that Scotland was more beautiful than Wales, though he did wonder how that could be. Perhaps the sheep there were blow-dried.

'All those midges,' said Colette, 'and all the land is owned by big estates. You can't walk anywhere in August without being shot at by a minor member of the Royal Family.'

'What about Ireland?' said James.

There were murmurs of interest but no great enthusiasm. Aldous felt ambivalence towards Ireland. The fire at Blackwater Bridge. The saving of his false teeth. The start of the war. The end of that idyllic part of his life. He had a strange feeling that Ireland was the crystallized landscape of his own memory and that if he went there he would damage it. It would be like walking through a landscape made of glass.

Lesley Waugh had been back there. Last year a card came from Kenmare that read

Rex,
    Just for you. Do you remember this? This place is sheer heaven. Beats Wales to a frizzle
    Love
    L.

The front of the card was split into four tiny views – hills with cars in the foreground and families picnicking. The card managed to make Ireland look very dull. It looked like an enormous municipal park. Where were the crofts, the crannied coastlines, the looming purple mountains of Aldous's memory? Even the card caused damage.

Lesley often sent postcards from places that he claimed to be more beautiful than Wales. It annoyed Aldous. Why was Lesley being so competitive? He seemed hell-bent on boasting a richer aesthetic life than himself. Cornwall. Devon. Corfe Castle. The Norfolk bloody Broads. He was exacting a slow and rather feeble revenge on Aldous for marrying his sister.

Finally, when it seemed all the alternatives to Wales had been discussed, Colette would put forward her own.

'How about Yugoslavia?'

'Yugoslavia?' came the baffled response, 'Why Yugoslavia?'

'I've heard it's very like Wales.'

'Do you think the dinosaurs had H-bombs?' said Janus.

'I doubt it.'

'But it could be why they died out so suddenly. They might

have had a technological society like our own. We would never know. A hundred and fifty million years is more than enough time to turn cities to dust. There would be no trace left of dinosaur skyscrapers, or dinosaur motorways. So why not?'

'Do you think they had a dinosaur Beethoven?'

'Probably. And a dinosaur Beatles.'

Colette thought, as though giving it serious consideration, and shook her head.

'I don't think so. I just can't imagine there being a diplodocus version of Paul McCartney. Ringo maybe . . .'

She noticed that Janus, even though he had his back to her, his binoculars still to his eyes, was laughing. They often had these nonsense conversations, in which they would develop a half-ridiculous premise into fully-fledged absurdity. Colette felt, though, that somehow she always came out of these conversations rather badly. It was as though Janus was permitted to say ridiculous things because they were steeped in irony, but it was Janus's trick to take Colette's absurdities literally, which made her feel foolish. He was very clever.

'At least the H-bomb is an answer to the population problem,' she said.

'An answer to the population problem would be for you and people like you to practise contraception, or preferably abstinence. You pollute the world with children.'

'I don't think that's a nice way for you to talk about your little brother.'

'I'm talking about overpopulation. It won't be long before we'll have to start eating each other. Actually I'm all for it. I'd have no qualms about having one of your breasts for lunch. I'd have even eaten one of Nana's. What a waste putting her in the ground.'

'You resent people don't you? That's how your mind works.'

Again Janus laughed. It was a laugh he'd developed recently, a sort of lecherous cackle, sometimes very loud, that Colette hated. All his arrogance and cheekiness seemed packed into it.

'We'll end up eating our own shit,' he said.

'You want the world for yourself. That's it isn't it? You want it all for yourself. No people, no love, no nothing.' Colette accompanied each negative with dismissive hand gestures.

'I don't care,' said Janus.

'You resent Julian, and you resent James and Juliette, and you even resent your father.'

Colette was standing with her hands on her hips and staring with her whole body at Janus. She hadn't taken enough breath for this last sentence so that its final word was said only with her throat.

Janus replied with that laugh again. A one-syllable laugh, loud and crackly. Unruly.

'But you didn't want Julian, did you?' he said, turning his binoculars towards her again. She stared back at his huge eyes.

'Of course I wanted him.'

Seeing her face huge within the long tunnels of his sight, Janus could see that her face was an exaggeration of shocked indignation. She was a very poor actress.

'I can remember you reducing Juliette to tears by telling her that she could never have a little brother or sister.'

'That's because I didn't think I could have any more children. Not because I didn't want any.'

'So Julian was a mistake?'

'Not a mistake, just unplanned.'

'I'd like to know why you did it.'

'Did what?'

'I'd like to know,' Janus lowered his binoculars, the eyepieces having left a pair of red pince-nez on his nose, 'why you were intimate with my father.'

Janus's eyes looked stupidly small. Colette bent forward with incredulous laughter and repeated the word 'intimate' to rehear its quaintness.

'Am I embarrassing you?' said Janus.

'You are embarrassing yourself.'

'Am I causing you pain?'

'Only of laughter.'

'Sometimes I feel it is my vocation to cause you pain to counterbalance the pleasure you had in conceiving me.'

Colette tried to kill the conversation by busying herself with something. She rummaged through a bag that had to be unpacked. Her hands came upon a bag full of apples. She pulled it out and tipped the russets on to a plate. Janus carried on.

'You did have a lot of pleasure conceiving me didn't you? I think I have a right, since it was the event that set my existence in motion, to know about it. I want to know every detail. Every last kiss and lick and stroke of it.'

Colette remarked, without looking away from the apples, 'Why are you so mixed up about sex?'

'I'm just talking about the moment of my creation. What is wrong with wanting to know about that?'

'Janus. I think you need a girlfriend. A girl could tell you everything you wanted to know. She could show you, you wouldn't have to be frightened.'

'Don't be so putrid, mother.'

'If the only lovers' tiff you've had is with a piano . . . You are nearly twenty-one.'

'I know about love. Don't worry about that.'

'Who've you loved?'

Janus fell silent. Looked back at the farm. Having looked at it for the last few minutes through binoculars, now with his naked eyes it seemed to be hundreds of miles away.

'Not Gwen?' Colette said, her voice delicate and worried.

Janus was silent. He was silent with his whole body. It froze. Colette probed nervously,

'She's a married woman now, Janus. You can't imagine it ever would have worked. She's an uncomplicated farm girl and you, as we all know, are a complicated genius.' Still Janus was frozen. Colette had meant that last phrase as a warmly patronizing jibe, but it came out strangely. It sounded as though she could have meant it. 'She was your childhood friend. Childhood friendships never last. She's probably got a baby by now anyway.'

'More pollution,' said Janus. 'That's another thing about 1961. It was also the year that the birth pill was put on the NHS.'

'The birth pill?'

'Don't you know what it is?'

'Yes, do you?'

Janus sighed exasperatedly.

'How many thousands of murders does that amount to over the last five years, to add to the suicides?'

'You can't murder something that's not alive, Janus.'

'You can murder the idea of life,' Janus responded quickly. Colette suddenly thought about the house and its garden, empty and alone. The far end of the garden would now be teeming with ripe blackberries, shiny and plump.

'Life.' Janus said. 'You happily talk about the pill but you won't let me know about how you fucked me up.' He said this sentence softly and quietly, and concluded it with a smile. He'd been born with a quiverful of those smiles and had fired them at her regularly throughout his life.

'Describe it for me, mother,' he said, 'describe how you conceived me.'

Colette didn't know what to say. She wondered whether she should call his bluff, outembarrass him by offering a vividly detailed description of her sex life. She couldn't.

'They're coming back,' she said, and walked, stooping, into the tent.

Aldous had given Julian charge of the milk. Carefully he held the brimming jug with both hands, one on the handle, one on the spout. The milk was an inch below the lip. He'd left a trail of little white splashes through the farmyard. On their way back to the tent they stopped to get some water.

The tap for the water was in the old cow shed, whose bright stone walls concealed an interior of dark, filthy shadows, oak stalls long abandoned by the cows, crooked, crazy floors, and an iron chest full of cattle nuts, their winter feed supplement, stinking of yeast. In the corner was the brass tap that held back a tower of water that reached a thousand feet into the mountains and the little choppy lake called Llyn Cain. One turn of its stiff handle and the water came out with a vicious force, as though a mountain had sneezed. It could knock a pot out of someone's hand.

Julian insisted on holding the water carrier underneath the tap while Aldous turned the handle. The carrier which, even to Julian, seemed virtually weightless when empty, was instantly caught in the grip of this water, and then a tug of war ensued, as water pounded into the vessel, the level rising alarmingly, gravitational force accumulating, bubbles bursting, so that Julian felt his arms could be torn from their sockets if he didn't let go, which he did. Or rather, it was snatched out of his hand and thumped on the floor, water bubbling at the brim, overflowing like champagne. Aldous lifted it by the wire handle. Julian watched his knuckles whiten, and followed him with the milk, his shoulders aching. He'd arm-wrestled the mountain and lost.

The smaller children slept in the car, Juliette on the back seat, Julian on the front. Julian loved sleeping in the car, especially on its front seat. The front seat was where the important people sat. His father driving, Janus or Colette, or sometimes James, beside him. Julian was never allowed in the front seat by daytime. By night, however, the front seat was his. He slept with his head an inch from the grey rim of the steering wheel, with its chrome inner circle that powered the horn. The dashboard with its array of dials and yellow-handled knobs, the same substance that could be found on the handles of their cutlery at home, was his night-time bedside company. The gear lever was on the steering column, and the handbrake on the door side of the driver's seat, so the front seat was an uninterrupted length of brown, stuffed leather, like a chaise longue. For Julian, the car was another member of the family. In shape and colour it was like a small elephant. The exterior was a warm grey with chrome bumpers and grill, headlights like skulls of cut crystal, light clusters that bled scarlet when the brakes were applied, semaphore indicators that flipped like the cocked ears of an interested dog. The left one stuck. Somebody had to reach out of the window and tap it each time. The bodywork of the car was outlined in timbers that had lost their varnish. The wooden window frames were beginning to rot, moss had grown in the runners, and in spring small white flowers appeared that Colette identified as wood sorrel. The car could sleep almost the entire family. If the back seat was pushed down, the rear van space opened up to an area that could sleep three adults easily. Triangular stickers now filled all one side window, souvenirs from places visited, nearly all in Wales – Aberystwyth, Criccieth, Caernarvon, Pwhelli. When, each evening, the car trundled slowly through the farmyard, James and Juliette would stand on the back bumpers like postilions in clouds of sweet-smelling carbon monoxide, jumping down to open the three gates they had to pass through.

Julian loved to sleep in the car, but one night towards the end of the holiday it felt like an unsafe place. He'd woken from a dream in which the car had been in full motion and he'd been desperately searching for the brake with his hands. In reality there was a powerful storm unfolding about the farm, and the car was rocking like a boat. Convinced the car would be blown away, he opened the heavy door, admitting a portion of the storm that was building, stepped out into the strong currents of air and made his way to his parents' tent. The tent was usually such a welcoming space in the daytime, its entrance open, furniture and food spilling out of its porch. At night it looked quite different, pegged down and zipped up. It had the smooth, windowless impenetrability of the flying saucer in *The Day the Earth Stood Still*. Julian found the metal catch of the zip at grass level and he lifted it so that, with a delicate tearing noise, a door appeared. He opened it only enough to crawl through to a gloomy vestibule floored with grass. Folded camping chairs, inverted pots, stacked dishes, boxes. His parents were beyond the inner door of the tent which, unlike the outer door, was vertical and perfectly bisected by the fastened zip, which Julian now lifted. It made a small ringing sound, like a distant alarm clock. Within, a small space like a chapel. Two figures in repose. They could have had their hands joined in prayer like figures on a medieval tomb. They seemed to be dead.

Julian found a foot next to him. He picked it up and shook it. The other end of the body lifted.

'What's that?'

'Daddy, I'm awake.'

'I thought you were a cow.'

'I'm in here.'

'Can't you sleep?'

'No.'

Aldous shifted sideways creating a little valley between himself and Colette into which Julian crawled. Aldous laid a blanket across him. Julian didn't say anything so Aldous drifted towards sleep. Then Julian asked his father to tell him a story. So Aldous woke just enough to tell him one. Normally he had such a full store of tales, able on demand to supply stories about the pigeons who live in the oak tree, the dragon who lives in the railway tunnel, the hedgehogs who live in the ivy, the only story he could think of now was 'The Burrow' by Franz Kafka.

'. . . and all he could hear,' concluded Aldous as best he could remember, 'was this whistling noise, coming through the earth, nearer . . . and nearer . . . and nearer . . .'

Julian was asleep.

3

It is November. The tent is wrapped and back in the loft. The family are asleep. It is three o'clock in the morning. In the front bedroom the acacia tree scrapes and squeaks at the window. Aldous and Colette lie parallel in their double bed.

In the large back bedroom Janus sleeps in his single bed by the window. James sleeps on the other side of the room by the fireplace, at right angles to his brother. In the small bedroom Julian and Juliette have their beds aligned with opposite walls, the door between them, like the benches on the lower deck of a Routemaster bus. Baxbr the cat is a black, glossy circle at the foot of Julian's bed.

At the back of the house the garden is a hundred feet of dead leaves. A hundred other gardens are silent beside it.

There is a knock at the front door. The heavy knock of metal against metal splitting the silence like an axe through a log of dark wood. Eyes in all the bedrooms open. Baxbr unloops himself and slithers on to the floor. The knock seems to echo silently for ages. Aldous is wondering if he heard the knock in his dream.

As if in order to reaffirm its reality the knock comes again, louder. Three loud bangs, rat-a-tat, crashing through the house. Aldous lifts himself out of bed and walks carefully to the window. He parts the curtains and looks down. He knows he can't see the front door from the bedroom window but he looks anyway. The road is empty and silent, lit by the sodium glow of street lamps. Colette is sitting up now.

'What's that?'

'There's someone at the door,' said Aldous, putting on his jacket. He has never owned a dressing gown, nor pyjamas.

'It sounded like the police,' murmured Colette.

That had been Aldous's first thought, but there would have been a police car outside, surely.

On the landing Aldous meets James and Janus.

'Did you hear that?' says James uselessly.

For some reason they are hesitant about going downstairs and answering the door.

Juliette appears. The boys laugh at her nightie. Julian sleeps on soundly.

Aldous descends the stairs slowly, suddenly thinking about the door at the back of Llanygwynfa's farmhouse, how it always glows within, not the glow of electric light, but of daylight. Those tiny, deep windows, and yet the house was full of sunlight. It was like an inside out house. Now, on the inside of his own house, the window of the front door, its lattice of leaded glass, is a big black square. For a second he thinks he can see the shadow of a face close to the glass, looking through.

He finishes his descent. The house is very cold, and it is colder downstairs. It is as though he has climbed down a ladder into a pond of cold air. He can see his own breath. As he approaches the front door he can see there is no one there. He opens it.

The front door step, three empty milk bottles, one with a note tucked into its neck, like an SOS. The path and the street beyond, twinkling with frost. Air as rough as sandpaper brushes his cheeks. He shivers.

Colette and Janus have also come down the stairs.

'Have a look down the road,' says Colette from the comfort of the deep red, quilted dressing gown that was her mother's.

'I'm not dressed.'

'Have a look,'

Aldous passes through the door, feeling ridiculous in his jacket with no trousers. The quarry tiles of the path are freezing beneath his feet. He walks right to the end of the path, on to the pavement. It is a starry night. The street is entirely empty. Cars parked either side of the road are blind with frost. A hundred houses are dark and silent.

'No one,' he whispers loudly to his wife and son at the other end of the path. He shakes his head. 'No one,' he repeats, and walks quickly as a cat back into the house.

In the morning there is the usual activity. The kitchen is crowded. The radiogram is talking in lively voices. Kettles and pans are boiling on the stove. James is packing his briefcase with last night's homework. Juliette is combing her long hair forward over her face then shaking it back. Aldous is drinking coffee and putting spoonfuls on to a sheet of newspaper and twisting it into a little parcel to take to work. Julian is playing with Baxbr. Janus is brushing his teeth at the sink. No one uses the bathroom. It is too cold.

They leave severally, James first, in his black school uniform, Juliette with her satchel over her shoulder. When Aldous leaves he wheels his bicycle along the leafy path. Colette runs after him urgently, as though he's forgotten something. She grabs his sleeve. He is alarmed by the contact.

'Last night,' she says, 'that knock. Do you know who it was?'

'No. Do you?'

'Last night. You know what was happening last night?'

'What do you mean?' He has never seen her quite like this.

'Last night they were exhuming Mumma. I've found the letter, look. Sixteenth of November was the date they set for digging her up and putting her in the grave we bought.'

'Don't,' says Aldous, 'that's silly.'

'They always do these things late at night Aldous, after the cemetery's closed, in the small hours so no one will see . . .'

'It was just kids playing, darling. Practical jokers . . .' Aldous is in the saddle of his bike now. It seems only Colette's grip is keeping him there.

'She was saying thank you to us.'

They look at each other, speechless for a few seconds.

'She was saying thanks,' Colette repeats. It is a plea.

'Maybe,' Aldous reluctantly concedes.

They kiss. Colette releases her grip and her husband freewheels down Fernlight Avenue.

1967

In the tent (a spread eagle in the lozenge over the porch with the legend *Bukta, Braves the Elements, Defies the Storms*), visible through the splayed doorway, Colette outstretched on a plump, flesh-coloured eiderdown. Her ankles are crossed, Christ-on-the-cross-like, her feet are in cream-coloured, open-toed sandals. She has an above-the-knee white skirt that is embroidered with gold thread. The skirt is rucked up, unintentionally sexy, revealing stockinged thighs, thinner than they should be. She has a pale mauve blouse open to the third silver button, a thick, white cardigan. A string of mock pearls is around her neck. Her head rests on a rainbow pillow amid a radial mass of hair dyed deep auburn. In her right hand is a carefully folded wad of pink lavatory paper.

Her view is of the parted curtains of the tent's inner door, the taut, green membranes of the door-guard, and then Moelfre. Normally a blend of moss greens and lime greens, this afternoon the bald hill was changing colour from the top down, slowly, a brilliant fluorescent orange, as though a spoonful of syrup had been tipped over it.

But she recognizes this liquid encroachment for what it is – a tormented eruption of molten rock gushing from an unseen vent in Moelfre's summit. Lava is oozing gently down her grassy slopes. Moelfre is a volcano.

It was a world of volcanoes they lived in. Extinct and plugged, these smashed peaks had all once gargled with magma. Fountains of white-hot rock. Blossoming fruits of ash. The landscape could only be understood as a series of violent events, of upheavals and inversions, or terraformations, meta-morphosings, the smashing together of landmasses.

Colette understands this. Once, she'd watched her husband trying to transfer the visual spectacle of Cwm Bychan on to a piece of hardboard using a few tubes of oil paint. She came over to him and stood on her head, letting her skirt fall up to her face. The kids giggled.

'You should paint it like this,' she said, 'that's how it should look.'

And Aldous laughed so suddenly his cigarette, usually such a steadfast fixture in his mouth, fell into his turpentine-filled Marmite jar, causing a small but intense violet explosion.

But now all the stress and pressure that had congealed in that landscape had found an outlet and the turmoil of geo-logical eras had regained a fluidity and Moelfre, that green and motionless hill, was moving, rippling like a liquid mountain, yellow and orange lavas, white canopies of smoke rising.

O the slow process of lava! Here it was, arriving like the leading edge of paradise, a tropical garden full of winding paths, pushing before it a front of incalculable warmth, gently toppling oaks, encasing the farmhouse, the barn, the chicken coop, the milking parlour, the chapel, casting them in a bronze glow, consuming the walls and the grass and the streams, tumbling and rolling, molten rock coming head-over-heels across the pastures.

Colette welcomes its luminous approach. She thinks of Mr and Mrs Evans preserved for two thousand years, hollow spaces beneath a volcanic plain on whose thin, cindery soil stumpy apple trees might grow. Their cows would become bovine spaces, as if from lost wax. The sheep and hens like-wise. One day someone might fill those spaces with molten bronze, chip away the rock, and have a monumental Mr and Mrs Evans and their animals fit to grace whatever museums there might be. And then herself and her tent preserved in rock for all time. A triangular space in pumice and her spread-eagled figure within. 'I am returning,' she thought, 'to my stony origins. I am becoming, once again, a geological feature.'

But at the door of the tent the approaching lava stops, cools, becomes glass and thoroughly vanishes. Colette sees the familiar green space of her field again. The whaleback hump of Moelfre.

A spasm of ordinariness passes through Colette's mind and she brings her right hand, the hand that is holding the carefully folded wad of pink lavatory paper, to her nose. The oily perfume held in this paper emits a powerful, spirity odour, a venomous scent that stamps through the corridors of her nose and enters, by some secret hatch door, the fragile canopies of her brain.

No lava this time, but a tilting sensation, and the knowledge of the close proximity of wings. A rustle of feathers, a great beating of pinioned limbs, and a gnat dithers past her head and out of the tent.

That morning Aldous had caused his midnight-blue Claude Butler racer to do a handstand, her saddle and handlebars seated and gripped by the world, her wheels poised upon the hazy sky.

It was an awkward puncture to mend. A first inspection of the tyre (hunched up by the tyre rim, pawing at the wheel, his nose to the tread, he couldn't help reminding Colette of a hamster in its treadmill), yielded no sharp instruments, splinters of glass, wire, pointed grains of grit. This meant the inner tube had to be taken out and for this the wheel had to be removed.

Colette felt nothing but admiration for her husband's skill. His ability to apprentice his eyes and hands to his brain. What was it about him that enabled him to render exquisitely lit landscapes in oils and watercolours, to catch a person's likeness in a few minutes' scratching with a pencil, to craft pots, form patterns out of wax and dye, to calligraph and etch and glaze, to fix doors, make cupboards, roof houses, secure guttering, cure bicycles? Was it just a way of thinking about the world, or were these skills things he'd had to learn, one by one? Was it an attitude, a way of seeing, or was it something to do with the sort of body he had? He gripped the wheel with his knees and twisted the wing nuts off with a spanner, levered the stiff skirt of the tyre out of the silver lip of the wheel, excised the frail black loop of the inner tube, immersed it, as though carefully drowning a runt, in a tin enamel bowl of stream water, found the source of the rising trail of bubbles, dried it off, marked it with a chalk X and then took out his tin.

His puncture repair kit. Colette had known these little metal caskets all her life. Her older brothers, Lesley and Janus Brian, had used them. They were fascinating and incomprehensible to her. Rolls of bandage, cubes of chalk, tubes of glue. There was something almost holy about them. Puncture repair kits were never new, it seemed, but were formed organically from the remains of previous puncture repair kits. It was a continuous, hereditary chain of healing. It was impossible to date accurately the contents of a puncture repair kit.

She knew them chiefly as a source of perfume. Whenever anyone was mending a puncture, a beautiful smell arose, a tempting, delicious smell that was equal parts sweet and bitter. She'd enjoyed this smell all through her childhood, whenever one of her cycling brothers was laying a tacky oblong of glue on to a roughened patch of vulcanized rubber. Now, forty years later, the smell had become a type of memory. The patching of inner tubes was an irregular occurrence. It might happen three times in a month, and then not for another three years, so that each time she encountered the smell she encountered it afresh, as a surprise bouquet, haunting and eloquent, suddenly flourishing in her environs.

Now, in the third field, in this entirely alien country, the smell had laid itself down over the grass and camomile as a doorway back to her childhood, to the back yard of uneven, cracked concrete, the sycamore tree, the clothes line hoisted on a block and tackle from two tall wooden masts that wasps gnawed at in the summer. And Lesley, black-fingered and clever, mending the flat tyre of his heavy, gearless bike.

It caused her to follow the smell, to linger within it, to lie down on pillows of it.

Aldous had the wheel back in its forks and was tightening the nuts as Colette came over, admiring the last moments of his work. He was worried because Colette wasn't busy. Colette was always doing something; if not some manual activity like dressing, washing and playing with her children, then she was reading, making lists, knitting, pressing grasses and sedges in unreadable books. But this morning she seemed to be doing nothing. She'd just been sitting in one of the camping chairs, smoking, looking at the hills. But a little girl had woken up in her when the scent of the glue reached her. She had followed its winding path to its source, to the tube of glue that nestled in the repair tin. She picked it up.

The tube of glue was called Romac. It was the size of the little fish Colette used to catch in the Lee Navigation, holding them by the tail as they yelled silently with their tiny, silver mouths, before throwing them back. This tube was half squeezed out, pressed to a creasy flatness at the tail end, swelling towards the neck. The bulk of the remaining glue was sealed in by a black, octagonal screw-top.

To be half empty indicated a long history for this glue. A single repair used a tiny amount, a blob that wouldn't cover a little fingernail.

Carefully, as Aldous pressed the restored inner tube back into its tyre, Colette unscrewed the top of the Romac. Like some Duchess at the perfume counter of Harrods she lifted the neck of the tube to her nose and breathed in the scent. Her thoughts became trees. Towering canopies of memories branching and leafing, falling. The leaves falling.

'Can I borrow this?' she said to Aldous, now screwing the pump on to the valve. He'd said yes without knowing what she'd taken.

In the tent Colette sat cross-legged and unwound a length of pink lavatory paper from a nearly full roll. She took the length and gently folded it back on itself four times until she had a quadruple thickness about twelve inches long. She then took the tube of Romac and daubed quick, sickly streaks of glue back and forth, as though garnishing a dessert with caramel sauce. Folding the paper over on itself, she bundled the glue up like a sticky baby, and held the drenched paper to her nose.

Glue, paper, origami, pictures.

The first sniff of the glue had come like a physical blow, as though someone had, with a single stroke, hammered a tent peg into her head. This was immediately followed by a sensation of leakage, as though she was spilling out of the small hole left in her unpegged head. She trickled quickly down herself and on to the tent floor. Somehow she mopped herself up and regained her body. She sniffed cautiously the second time, and already her brain had adapted itself to the power of the odour. Her brain accepted it. Colette imagined her brain as a greenhouse, gabled panes of glass nurturing trays of seedlings – the glue – which flourished into flowers.

There came a sense of the close presence of children, thousands of them, filling the field outside the tent to its stone-walled brim. She could hear but couldn't hear their hearts.

Then an odd sensation that the tent was airborne, sailing like a kite above the clouds. Genies out of bottles. Flying carpets. The groundsheet billowed as the air currents coursed beneath it, churning like the sea, and Colette felt a sudden vertiginous fear and gripped the tent pole next to her, terrified by the thought that she might roll out of the tent door and plummet thousands of feet to the ground. But then the tent descended. There was an upward rush of air as it approached the ground and Colette braced herself for the impact, which was as soft as an egg breaking into flour. Colette laughed, rolled on to her back and laughed, lifted her legs into the air, rode an imaginary bicycle and laughed. She laughed until she was washed out with laughing. She lay on her back, took another draw on the glue, and witnessed the eruption of Moelfre.

Once that threatening encroachment had faded she saw Janus standing alone in the field.

Colette quickly rolls on to her hands and knees and crawls out of the tent. Her hair hangs down either side of her head like flames. Her string of pearls clacks like an abacus.

Janus, who, for the second year running, had not come with them to Wales, was standing alone in the centre of the field, wearing a dark suit, a plum-coloured shirt, no tie, the neck open. He had grown a moustache, the silky, wispy moustache of the young adult. He was smoking a cigarette, lifting it to his mouth between finger and thumb, frowning as he drew in the smoke, tightening his eyes, concentrating everything into that dense breath. He seemed devoted to his cigarette.

Earlier that summer Colette and Janus had had an argument about a cigarette. It was more than an argument. Colette had shocked herself by losing control completely, giving herself to a ferocious tantrum because Janus wouldn't lend her a cigarette.

'I'm out of fags,' Colette said, shaking a silent packet of Player's No. 6.

They were in the kitchen. Colette was sitting in the armchair, the new armchair, replacing the old one Nana used to sit in, between the boiler and the sink. It wasn't an armchair literally, in that it lacked arms. It stood like a purple amputee, a back and a seat with four legs.

Nana had gone and her chair had gone. It would have been appropriate, Janus thought, if she'd been buried in her chair. A vertical coffin. Nana and her handbag embalmed and seated.

Colette had become a sixty-a-day woman. She never smoked during pregnancy. In fact it was by an aversion to tobacco that she would know she was pregnant. She would go to the doctor and tell him she was pregnant and the doctor would smile patronizingly and say something like 'I'll be the judge of that my dear', but Colette would always be right.

The tobacco aversion would last for two or three years after the birth. Then she would gradually be drawn back to their breathable comfort. With Julian a six-year-old Colette was into her third year of postnatal smoking. Each revival of her habit came with greater intensification. The birth of each child led to even greater heights of smoking. Now she was a chain smoker, lighting each cigarette with the dying moments of its predecessor. If she used a match she extinguished it by a broad waving of the stalk, too slowly to douse the flame, which usually burnt her fingers.

The smoke would find its own level in the kitchen, sometimes forming an unbroken sheet of blue from wall to wall, until someone walked through it and casually tore it to shreds.

'They're bad for your health, woman,' said Janus.

Janus had taken to calling his mother 'woman' over the last few weeks. She didn't like it.

'Give us one of yours.'

'I've only got three left.'

'I only need one.'

'Go and buy some.'

'Just one,' said Colette, raising her voice slightly, 'till Aldous gets home.' Then, more calmly, 'I'll pay you for it.'

Janus was sitting at the kitchen table, sideways in his chair, one arm on the chair back, one arm on the table, the posture causing one of his shoulders to sit higher than the other. His head was tipped back, resting against the wall. He laughed as Colette reached for her purse, clicked it open and stirred the loose change around.

There then followed a teasing process of bartering during which Janus took a cigarette out of its packet – a filterless Woodbine – tapped it on the sleeve of the packet, inverted it, tapped it again, mouthed it. By which time he'd raised Colette's original offer of 2d. to £1. Tight though money was she actually found herself unfolding a pound note from her purse and holding it out towards Janus, who then said 'You don't smoke Woodbines.'

'I'll smoke one now.'

'If you get on your knees.'

Colette gripped her money with a sudden tightness, as though afraid it might drift out of her hand.

'You rat. I'm giving you a pound.'

'I'm just interested to see what you'll do for a fag, woman,' Janus said suavely.

Colette stood up, then knelt with a suddenness that hurt her knees.

'Now you can kiss my feet,' said Janus, extending one out from under the table, twirling it.

Colette stood with difficulty. Her knees made a cracking sound. Then she made a sudden clumsy lunge across the table for Janus's packet of Woodbines. Janus snatched them before she could reach, as though they were playing snap, and put them in his breast pocket. Colette knocked over a packet of salt.

She was leaning with both her hands on the table. She was grinding her teeth together, the sound of plastic on plastic. With a sudden sweep of her right hand she knocked an assortment of table things to the floor – the tipped salt packet, an empty cup which didn't smash, some books and a newspaper. It was a powerful gesture, like a general sweeping the flags of foreign armies from the chart of his campaign. Janus laughed to cover his shock.

'You want to see what I'll do for a fag? Here's what I'll do . . .'

To Julian, silently watching this confrontation from a green wickerwork chair next to the radiogram, the conversation came across as a reasoned, though lively, discussion. He missed entirely the blurting irrationality of it, the stabbing, staccato violence of it. Not until Colette began throwing things did he sense that something had gone wrong.

An egg cup was the first. Colette had walked over to the

sink and was picking things off the draining board. The egg cup hit the wall a few feet away from Janus. He wasn't laughing now. He wasn't even smiling. He was trying very hard to look bored, raising his eyes to heaven, shaking his head pityingly. A fish slice and some forks came next. An apple corer. They jangled on the wall or bounced on the table, as ungainly in flight as newly winged ants. They weren't thrown with any force, just casually lobbed. They couldn't have hurt.

'You want to see what I'll do for a cigarette?' came Colette's call again, like a battle cry. Her voice had become high and ugly. Janus had now stood up, with great reluctance, and seemed about to take his mother in hand.

But the next object, a metal saucepan, was flung with great force and accuracy, missing Janus's face by three inches it pounded into the wall and chipped off some plaster.

By the time it struck, Colette was already throwing the next object, repeating her battle cry through tears, mantra-like, so that it lost coherence. Pots, pans, plates, saucers, cups, knives. A rain of them showered across the kitchen. Janus ran to the door for cover. This shielded him. He watched from behind it, ducking each time an object struck. The door was painted in antique gold with a small picture of a lion, profiled and Assyrian, at eyelevel. When this door, ten years later, was painted, and five years after that, repainted, the silhouette of this lion was still visible. Julian and Juliette measured and marked their increasing heights against this door.

Finally, Colette took an empty milk bottle by the neck, smashed it against the stone lip of the sink and brandished the shattered stump.

Janus, from behind the door, and Colette at the sink, looked at each other for a few seconds, he with nearly tearful disbelief, she with waning hatred, before Janus slammed the door shut and left the house. The front door's slam was a fainter echo of the kitchen's.

My brother, thought Julian, is a coward. Running away like that. It shocked him more than the violence. He yawned and asked his mother if he could have some Nesquik.

Colette laid her weapon carefully on the now empty draining board, cried, and made a glass of Nesquik.

'Mummy, why did you throw those things?'

Colette wanted to say she didn't know, but she thought that Julian needed a reason.

'Your brother was teasing me,' she said, picking broken glass out of the sink, 'just as he has always teased me. From the day he was born to this he's done nothing but laugh at me, sneer at me, criticize me, lecture me . . .'

She knelt down before Julian who sat with his knees to his chin in the chair.

'You won't be like that will you, Julian.'

Julian thought carefully before replying.

'I'm going to live on the Isles of Scilly.'

Julian had been reading the atlas and had decided he was going to begin his adult life on those islands, and then every five years move house eastwards, then northwards, until he lived, an old man, on the Orkney Islands. Then he said 'Were you going to kill Janus?'

'No,' said Colette, remembering a time when Janus was her only child. For six long years Janus was her only child. Precious. Fragile. He was an undemanding boy, quiet, serious, studious, his only cause for concern being those occasional night terrors that had him sitting upright, blindly wide-eyed in his bed, howling like a small, puny wolf. Colette would rush to his room as if the house was on fire. She would have done anything to stop that noise.

Colette looks at the young black calf that has strayed into their field. Only a few weeks old, yet confident on its long legs. It tears skilfully at the already cropped grass. So young, yet able to feed itself. Colette turns over and lies on her back, so that her head pokes out of the tent door. Her head had started to ache. She took another draw on the glue, the headache vanished.

'What are you doing?' Aldous says. He has finished mending his puncture and is standing next to her, his feet almost touching her head. From Colette's viewpoint he is a tower of tweedy clothes. She can't see his head properly.

Colette doesn't reply but sings quietly, a tune Aldous doesn't recognize. He kneels down and looks closely into her upside down face. There is a shred of tissue paper stuck to her upper lip. From her breath there comes a strong smell of glue. She laughs. To Aldous, inverted, her laugh has the appearance of a viscous, searing snarl.

'I wish Janus was here,' she says.

'Don't start that again,' Aldous groans, standing up.

'It's because of you he hasn't come,' she calls after him as he walks away, 'you know that don't you?'

Aldous doesn't reply but for a faint, dismissive grumble.

The previous summer Janus became a graduate, a licentiate and a gas man.

Aldous was cross at first, then went into a long sulk. He hadn't expected his son to become a pianist of world renown, celebrated in the concert halls of five continents, although that would have been nice. That would have been agreeable. A minor turn on the world's concert platforms, or the provincial town halls, perhaps some recordings. That, surely, had always been a possibility. It was visions of such a life that had sent him to sleep every night for nearly twenty years. Applause, bouquets, encores. He had expected his son to become someone who made a living by music. He had not expected him to become a gas man.

The years of training that had gone into those hands. The money he'd invested. Thousands of hours of expensive piano lessons. The pianos themselves. Their house. Each finger of Janus's hands represented a small fortune. He hadn't wanted to think about Janus's hands like that but now he was forced to. The years he'd spent strengthening them, loosening them, the sheer hard slog of building up strong hand and finger muscles.

'We have caught him just in time,' one of Janus's teachers had said to Aldous, picking up and waving the boy's hand as though it was a dead fish, 'another year or two and it would have been too late. The bones are like the mind, they stop developing in early youth. We have to get them while the hands are still growing, you see. While the bones are still soft.'

Those hands. Awkward, slightly medieval in their straightness. Janus's hands were like the hands a child might draw, five lines fanning from a circle, rigid yet graceful, the nails short, bitten, the ends of the fingers broadening slightly – spatulate, in the language of forensics. All so that he could grip a torch to shine in the spider-infested cubbyholes of unmusical strangers.

Aldous's hands were short and square, the fingers stumpy and plump. Mickey Mouse hands. You were surprised, when you saw him playing the piano, that he was able to separate his fingers enough to play chords, or that a single finger was narrow enough to depress a key without bringing down those either side of it.

They were not artist's hands, as he was frequently told by various people – artists, sculptors, girlfriends, piano teachers, his wife. And yet he could use them to lift a perfect pot out of a shapeless handful of clay, as well as play the piano. He could play only in a vague way, slowing down for no apparent reason, accelerating like someone who's just realized the train is leaving, slowing down again when he realizes he won't catch it anyway.

One of Janus's teachers noticed this when he chanced to hear Aldous playing one of Schubert's *Moments musicaux*.

'Your father,' he said in a confidential whisper, 'has no sense of time, if you'll forgive me for mentioning it.'

This enabled Janus to feel, not for the first time, that he had abilities and talents his father might envy.

That year there had been a summer of rows with Janus. Aldous could not accept that his son was so defiantly intent on squandering his abilities. Only a month before he'd been at the BBC recording a piece for them as one of the Academy's outstanding graduates. He'd gained a distinction in sight-reading. There had been much shouting and door-slamming.

Janus was stupidly, naively enthusiastic about being a gas man. He went into rapturous descriptions of his work, the fascination he felt for seeing inside people's houses, which exasperated Aldous all the more.

Janus further annoyed Aldous by blithely announcing only a couple of days before departure, that he would not be coming to Wales this year, as his job at the Gas Board was far too important. And then Aldous found, in Janus's bedroom the day before they were due to leave, something that disturbed him.

Janus had accumulated a small library of books on Wales, stiff-covered, glossy paged editions lavishly illustrated with monochrome photos. Poucher's *Wanderings in Wales, The Welsh Peaks, Snowdonia*. For all his pedantry the Surrey perfumier could take a good picture. H. V. Morton's *In Search of Wales* Janus found disappointing in comparison. Like Borrow he wasn't interested in landscape but had instead a journalist's interest in people, from whom he would extract stories as ruthlessly as a child prising mussels apart. Poucher was shy, the only conversations he had were hushed pleasantries with fellow diners, usually anglers or archaeologists, across the guesthouse tables. His real company was the mountains, amongst whom he was magnificently alone.

Aldous was immensely proud of the fact that he'd instilled a love of the Welsh landscape in Janus. One evening, while Janus was working late, Aldous picked his way through his son's library and found a carefully pencilled note inside the back cover of the pocket edition of the Bach B minor Mass

Janus Jones
Favourite composer – Chopin
Favourite writer – Conrad
Favourite brother – James
Favourite cat – Baxbr
Favourite occupation – hill-walking
Favourite mountain – Cnicht

It made him smile. But when he picked up *Wanderings in*

Wales, its pages fell and hung in lacerated shreds, like a child's paper chain. *The Welsh Peaks* did the same. Several music books had also been cut up. The Chopin Preludes, the Mozart Piano Sonatas (Aldous's own copy, passed on from his mother, who couldn't read music, rebound in his own hand and dedicated to his wife, monogrammed with her initials), their well-thumbed pages had been sliced with the clean, straight, determined strokes of a very sharp blade. A razor, or a Stanley knife. Some records had been damaged as well. The highlights from Carmen and some of the Beethoven Late Quartets had been etched with ugly, jagged Vs, deep broad scars across the whorled discs, like nicks on a thumb print.

It took a while for Aldous to accept that this was Janus's own work. At first he thought perhaps some maniac with a hatred of music and mountains had broken into the house. When he mentioned it to Janus his son's only reply was one of his new boorish laughs and an exit from the house. Colette said it was probably something to do with him growing up. Becoming a man. Putting away childish things.

'I didn't slash my books when I grew up,' said Aldous, 'I kept them. I thought he loved those books.'

'I don't know,' said Colette, answering a question that hadn't been asked, 'he likes to test himself. He likes to know what he can do without.'

But she knew it wasn't an answer. There was something else happening. One afternoon, alone in the house, she went through all the records, all the sheet music, to see which had been damaged. What at first seemed to be a random knife attack on the papery body of their music library turned out to be a very selective annihilation. The damaged pieces were all ones that had a special association for Colette and Aldous. Music they'd discovered and shared over the now silver years of their marriage. The versions of the Mozart Symphonies for four hands which Colette and Aldous played side by side at the keyboard, unhitching their tempos almost within the first four bars, drifting further apart until they collapsed into laughter. Janus could barely tolerate this display of wanton amateurishness, his mother with a cigarette in her mouth, a long crooked finger of ash at its tip, due at any moment to crash in a dusty heap on the keys, Aldous trilling clumsily, his wife lurching around in the bass registers. It infuriated him that people could have such pleasure playing the piano badly. And so the Jupiter Symphony had been knifed. If music was one of the bonds that kept Aldous and Colette together, Janus, Colette could see, was trying to cut through it.

Aldous was unaware of this. He still saw the incident as a self-destructive act. Janus destroying what he most valued. Like the time he'd broken the music rest on the piano. Petulance. Frustration. He felt that things were beginning to mend when, a few weeks later, he found that some of the books had been repaired with carefully applied strips of Sellotape. He failed to take it personally.

This summer there had been the trouble with Christine, Janus's cousin, daughter of Lesley Waugh. Over the spring she had become friendly with Janus, who by that time had left the Gas Board and was trying to supplement his dole money as a pavement artist.

It annoyed Aldous even more, who could see his son had no real ability in that field. 'All those years training to be a musician, now he decides he wants to be an artist.'

Janus's interest in visual art was sudden, intense and brief. Altogether it lasted for six months. In that time he'd amassed a pile of frenzied pencil drawings and pastels on curled and dog-eared assortments of paper.

It started shortly after a visit from Father Webb, the local Catholic priest who'd befriended the family after the death of Nana, and who regularly dropped by for evenings of sherry (usually leftover Communion wine) and sophisticated chat.

Father Webb was tall with dark hair, thinning slightly on top, and had a face that was a soft, velvety square. The children knew him as the Man in Black.

Aldous, Colette and Janus were talking with him one evening when somehow the conversation settled on the subject of imitation, the Christian life, and art. Father Webb then made some remarks that Janus interpreted as a direct attack upon himself.

'A pianist is merely a mimic. A pianist playing a piece of music is no more creative than a person reading a book. It is only that the reading process is a little more technical and specialized. It is specialized, but it is nothing special.' Father Webb was sitting with one leg crossed over the other, the upper leg hanging forward into the middle of the room, the foot at the end of it clad in polished black leather like a stag beetle. Father Webb had a long, heavy body that its black garb somehow made seem bigger. He filled the room. 'Imagine, if you will, that human beings can only communicate by playing the piano. Our mouths are stitched up, and we are each given our own piano when we are born, which we carry around with us until we die. Don't you think we would, every last one of us, be brilliant pianists? There would be a range of abilities, of course, but even the worst talkers would be up to concert level. Now imagine that we could only talk by means of painting and drawing. Each of us given an easel and box of paints when we are born. Some of us, many of us perhaps, would become excellent talkers in paint. But some of us, most of us, probably, would never manage anything more than some clumsy splodges and squiggles, no matter how hard we tried. Like myself. We would, in effect, be dumb.'

Janus's long years in a Jesuit college made him nervous of arguing with priests and so he didn't attempt a defence of pianists, seeing that the priest was deliberately trying to cut him down to size. He noticed instead Father Webb's sock, revealed by the hitched up trouser of his crossed-over leg. It was black. Once Janus supposed that priests wore black underwear, until he saw Father Nunn changing for rugby. White underpants and a white, string vest. Very disappointing, somehow.

'My problem,' said Aldous, who was totally uninterested in any comparisons between painters and pianists, 'is that I'm not sure if I make paintings, or things that look like paintings. If something looks enough like a painting does that make it a painting? Take me and Cézanne, for instance. I'm a great admirer of Cézanne. He was so concerned with getting precisely the right shade of a colour that if he couldn't get it he left that particular patch of the painting blank, rather than fill it with an approximation. You can see these blank patches all over his paintings. Now if you look at my paintings you'll see the same thing, colourless patches where the primed canvas (or hardboard, usually, in my case) shows through. Cézanne would have regarded these blanks as faults. Unconsciously I've mimicked Cézanne's errors in order that my paintings gain some of his authority. I sometimes think of my paintings as a type of camouflage, like those stick insects who mimic faults and blemishes on the leaves in order to look more like leaves.'

'The same could be said of people,' said Father Webb sipping his transubstantiated sherry, his voice deep and melodious, like the lower registers of a church organ. 'How do we become human beings if it is not through a form of mimicry? We are, all of us, subtle, complex, overlapping collages of the people around us. Individuality lies in the permutations and combinations of those imitations. Imitation is a vastly underrated skill. No one is quite sure how we do it, convert something we observe into an action that comes from within, but it is central to our lives as human beings. We just have to be careful that we imitate the right people,' he chuckled.

'The Imitation of Christ,' said Colette.

'Well, he's not a bad model,' said Father Webb, 'and Christ had his faults, his blemishes, I'm sure.'

It was this conversation that suddenly had Janus filling sheets of cartridge paper with deeply scored patterns in pencil. He was bothered by the twin ideas that pianism was uncreative, and that he was an imitation of his father. Somehow they worked on his mind so that he had to explore and try to excel in what had previously been his father's domain – visual art.

Aldous would have been delighted, had not he sensed a challenge to his own authority in this sudden efflorescence.

He sensed this because Janus never asked his father's advice about drawing, nor sought his opinion on his work. He just produced it and covered walls with it. His fingertips were permanently stained with the reds, ochres and greens of the box of pastels he found in one of the bedrooms, an old biscuit tin heaped with worn-out coloured shards, husks of colour, most of them aggregated to a common muddy brown on their skins but which, when touched against paper, would flare into vivid colours. It was a pleasing sensation to have colour flowing from his fingers, instead of music.

He made violently Fauvist pastel drawings of trees, all reds and yellows and blacks. But the first anyone else knew of these endeavours was the appearance on the walls of the music room of a series of collages using cigarette packets (Senior Service, Woodbines, Weights, Player's No. 6) which also made use of their internal linings of silver and gold milled paper. These collages were embellished with intricate patterns inscribed with pencil – networks of tessellated shapes that looked, unintentionally, like the patterns of crocodile skin. This pattern became a kind of motif, appearing in different forms in many of his works. There came a series of abstract designs, developments of the crocodile skin pattern, dozens of them, some on little scraps of notepaper, some on A2 sheets of card. Janus never used paint. These images were always in pencil, Biro or pastel.

Later he developed an interest in drawing from life. Not people, but clothing, furniture, umbrellas, anything with clearly defined lines, especially striped or ridged objects. His best drawing was of a corduroy jacket hanging over the ajar edge of a wardrobe door.

The intensity of these drawings produced a deep scoring of the lines. Janus pressed with as much weight as it could take on to the pencil to get a line which cut a deep, grey furrow into the paper. You could feel his drawings as though they were a form of artistic Braille. It was as though he wanted to get every last shade of blackness out of the pencil.

He always brought a great weight to bear on any graphic

exercise. His postcards were written so heavily the words came through, back to front, as embossed lettering on the pictures themselves. His punctuation was always very prominent. His commas were thick curls of ink, as big as letters.

And so for six months Janus laboured to transfer the bewildering arrays of his visual life on to paper. Lightning sketches of his mother cooking or asleep, of people on tube trains, of random scatterings of clothes, of views through windows. After six months it seemed to him he had drawn everything in the world twice.

And it was in this envisioned, heirophantic spirit that he met the miraculous daughter of Lesley Waugh. Miraculous because her life had once hung on the thread of pneumonia, and her father had made a pilgrimage to Lourdes, returning with a phial of water which had been blessed by the Pope himself, and which Lesley dabbed every night on Christine's rattling chest while he prayed over her. And against the odds she lived and grew into a teenager with a stocky, athletic but not unshapely body, which she seemed fond of displaying to the fullest the fashions of those days allowed – mini-dresses, mini-skirts, low-cut T-shirts.

Was it, Janus thought, really out of a strange sense of concern that Christine had been making so many visits to Fernlight Avenue recently? Had his parents, in some well-intentioned but sleazily underhand manner, really invited her over in order to introduce him to female company? Was she a pawn in some squalid little experiment in socialization his parents were conducting?

The children of Lesley and Madeleine Waugh had never been close to the Joneses. Strange how friendships don't seem to repeat in the next generation. The Joneses were closer to Agatha's children – Mark, Paul, Douglas, Kevin and Judy – and yet Colette and Agatha despised each other when they were young. And the close friendship between Aldous and Lesley had produced two sets of children who neither knew nor cared about each other.

Until Christine's appearance that spring in the garden at Fernlight Avenue. Where had she come from? He never felt quite sure why she was there. Did she want to see him, Colette, the whole family? She had a black dress on that day. She had dark hair in shoulder length flick-ups. She amazed Janus by walking around the garden in bare feet. Julian was collecting, as he usually did, the ripped-up corpses of mice and birds caught and then discarded by Baxbr, their cat. Julian scooped them up on a trowel and Christine helped him bury them. Janus watched, and felt touched by the way she made crosses out of two twigs bound by straps of grass. He was fascinated by the way the trees cast a dappled light on her giving her body leopard spots.

He invited her up to his room. He was absorbed by the presence in his room of her body. It confused, silenced him. It was the dress, sleeveless, black, low cut. It had a single silver zip at the back, holding it together. It was a tiny metal spine tracing the path of her own spine. She sat on the bed. He sat next to her. Her zip was a quarter, perhaps half an inch undone. The set of two metal tracks peeling away from each other like the petal edges of an about-to-bloom black rosebud. It made him think that Christine was unfinished.

'Are those your drawings?' said Christine, looking around her, a tight, over-controlled smile on her face. The tone in which she said this was too jolly, too head-girlish.

'Yes,' said Janus. They were surrounded by his drawings. They were on every wall, scattered on the floor. There were even a few pinned to the ceiling.

'I thought your father was the only artist. We've got one of his paintings at home.'

'Lifeless,' said Janus, a snap in his voice.

'Sorry?'

'Dad's paintings. They're dead. There's no life in them. Nothing. He paints too thickly. He uses all those old tricks they taught him at art school but they are just museum pieces. There's no feeling in them. There's no passion.'

Christine was still smiling, her eyes were lowered.

'I rather like the one we've got at home. A waterfall falling through trees. You get the feeling of light hitting the leaves, of the water frothing and bubbling.'

Janus felt a little annoyed that Christine was talking about art in such a superficial way. Surely it was about more than conveying a sense of light and froth. Surely it was about conveying an emotion felt by the artist at a moment of intensity. That's what his own drawings were about. She was surrounded by them. Why couldn't she see them? But Christine changed the subject.

'I hear you are going to be on the television soon.'

Janus thought carefully. What did she mean? Last year he'd recorded a piece for the BBC as part of a programme about Paganini. A well-known television arts producer and presenter had wanted him to play one of the variations on the 24th Caprice, along with a selection of other recent graduates from the Royal Academy (one variation each). It was generally thought that this would be a dazzling launch for Janus's career as a concert pianist. Performance tours and recording contracts would soon follow. He'd spent a whole day at the TV Centre in Wood Lane sweating under intense studio lights, suffering the penetrating intrusion of vast cameras focusing on his hands. He'd drunk coffee from a cup with 'BBC' on it and had seen a number of minor celebrities in the canteen doing the same.

Christine wouldn't have heard about the letter he'd received shortly afterwards in which the well-known television arts producer and presenter thanked him for coming to the studio, but that unfortunately, due to pressures of timing, his particular variation had to be left out of the final programme. He hadn't told anyone about the letter.

'Yes,' said Janus, quietly, 'it'll be on soon. BBC2.' It was what he'd said to everyone who'd asked for the past year.

'That's exciting. Are you going to be very famous?'

She said this so bashfully, reddening, looking down at her fingers, as though she was in the presence of greatness, that he

146

could only make a brief, pitying laugh of air through his nose in reply.

He had tried to dismiss the letter, the whole enterprise, as unimportant, trivial. Mr Oh So Bloody Self Important Television Producer. Who cares? But something deeper in himself was shocked and a little frightened by this letter. It was the first time in his life he'd been told he was worthless. Up until then, continuously, he'd enjoyed the immense luxury of feeling valued.

They were silent for a moment, before Christine said 'I'm hopeless at all those sorts of things. I had cello lessons but I gave them up. I can't draw.'

The bed rocked as she talked. Janus was fascinated by the way she used her whole body to talk; twisting her torso, lifting her hands to tuck strands of black hair behind her ears (black hair that was treacly brown in strong sunlight, like Baxbr's), rocking from side to side. Her silence was also a stillness.

He wondered if, by saying that she couldn't draw, she was also saying that he could. Although full of the glamour of self-confidence about drawing, he sensed, though only half acknowledged, that his drawing skills had severe limitations. He couldn't quite understand it yet. It was something to do with how all his drawings had outlines, edges. If his father didn't have a sense of time, then he, Janus, had no sense of space. He couldn't draw things with poorly defined lines, like faces. The best face he ever drew was one that used his crocodile skin motif, dividing the face into areas of scaly textures. He could draw human crocodiles, but otherwise his faces were clumsy, childish scrawls.

He wished he could draw Christine, but he wouldn't have dared. He wouldn't dare draw her. Her face was too pretty. Her face was accurate. In its form there was somehow a sense of a direct hit. Her nose wasn't big, but it lodged in the centre of her face, proudly asserting its presence. Her eyes and ears, unlike Christine herself, were finished perfectly. To draw her would be to disassemble that face, to see it wilt, dissipate and topple into roughly shaded, shaky graphite lines. She went on 'You are a very talented family aren't you?'

Again he felt he could only agree through clenched teeth. Her assumptions about his family exasperated him. How were they talented? His father painted thick, oily landscapes that were never exhibited. His brothers were still at the level of chemistry sets and toy trains. His sister was a spluttery asthmatic whose only talent was for annoying practical jokes. Janus, however, was one of the outstanding pianists of his generation. So how, exactly, was this family of his so talented?

Janus suppressed his indignation and flattered his family for Christine. He understood how praising his blood kin would set himself in their good light. He described how his side of the family could trace artistic and musical talent back for generations, how South Shields, where Colette's mother was born, was dotted with gifted Waughs. You couldn't go in a cinema there or music hall or pub without the accompaniment of a Waugh on a piano. The brass bands also were conducted and peopled by Waughs. Music came from his mother. True, he thought to himself, Christine shared that same grandmother, Nana, and the Tyneside ancestry, and yet Lesley, himself an amateur pianist, had hatched a little brood of tone-deaf children. An unlucky meld of genes.

Janus was glad to have Christine to practise on. Practise, practise, practise. At the Academy there had been frightening girls with long, waterfall hairdos and bodies as taut and poised as crossbows. They had an awesome confidence about themselves, as musicians, as human beings. Their voices were loud, they laughed easily. They played instruments that were golden, sparkling mysteries to him: French horns, trombones, coiled metal from which he was unable, with all his breath, to get a sound. He was amongst women who were all gifted, experts, adepts. Women who could pull him, he felt, into the hearts of their instruments and keep him there, tiny and preserved.

With Christine it was different. She was uncomplicated, unfinished, inept, and he felt that he fascinated her. Despite thinking that he'd frightened her on their first meeting, she returned to Fernlight Avenue several times, and on the last occasion he took her to the Tate Gallery.

Janus had returned home alone from that visit. On his way up Fernlight Avenue from the bus stop he had picked flowers from all the front gardens as he passed by and fastened them to the inside of his jacket. The gardens were lush enough for him to assemble an impressive collection. He became a walking flower bed.

When his mother opened the front door for him he opened his jacket to a blaze of colour. He grinned. But Colette wasn't happy.

'What have you done with your cousin?'

Janus laughed, made some clicking noises with his tongue and swished past Colette, leaking petals. He was heading for the music room. Colette overtook him and blocked the doorway.

'No you don't. You can't hide for ever behind that piano.'

'I've got to practise, woman.' Janus's voice was unnaturally loud. He'd been drinking. She could smell it.

'She came back here, you know.'

'Who?'

'Christine. In tears she was, poor darling. Poor girl. Her feet were bleeding in those sandals. You'd left her in the middle of London without any money. She had to walk nearly all the way, got lost in King's Cross. She had to ask a policeman, and they brought her back here she was in such a state. And now your father's taken her back to High Wycombe. What's the matter with you? What did you do to her? You were supposed to be looking after her.'

Janus's face reddened.

'She's a grown woman, mother, not a little girl . . .'

'She told us you took her to the Tate Gallery, and that you started pinning your pictures to the walls.'

Janus laughed again. Colette went on, 'You can't do things like that to people, Janus. The poor child was so embarrassed. She said she was taking them down as fast as you were pinning them up.'

★

149

It had happened in one of the quiet rooms. Nineteenth-Century English Painting. Turner. Constable. The attendant was out of sight. There was no one around. Christine was slightly bored, contemplating *Rain, Steam and Speed*, thinking what an awful mess it was, how the train wasn't even in perspective, when she noticed her cousin begin unrolling the tube of paper he'd mysteriously been carrying around all day. Then he lifted to his mouth, as though they were peanuts, a handful of drawing pins, which he held between his lips as he positioned a large pastel drawing of an oak tree in the empty space between Constable's *Salisbury Cathedral* and one of his cloud studies. Then, to Christine's horror, he pressed a drawing pin into each corner of his vividly colourful sketch, one of which buckled and fell on the floor with an unexpectedly loud clatter. It sounded to Christine like a gong falling on the floor. The attendant wasn't alerted, however, and Janus dashed to the next portion of empty space, leaving his oak tree slightly crooked, drooping down in one corner. He then began pinning up a smaller pencil drawing of an umbrella. Christine tried to take down the oak tree, but the drawing pins were deeply embedded. She couldn't get a fingernail beneath them. She took hold of the paper itself but couldn't bring herself to tear it from its fastenings.

She was appalled by Janus's behaviour. She could perhaps have found some admiration for its audacity and daring, but there was something about the furtive way Janus carried out the operation, working swiftly and clumsily with a schoolboyish panic, constantly watching over his shoulder and fumbling with his drawing pins, like a kid stealing apples, that she found pathetic. He actually ran out of the room of Nineteenth-Century English Painting, which caused the attendant to take notice. Christine hesitated, wondering if she should stay behind to excuse her cousin's behaviour, wisely thought better of it, and ran after him, but became lost in the maze of galleries.

'I waited for her outside the gallery,' said Janus, 'I waited for an hour. I had to have three choc ices.'

By the time Aldous returned from High Wycombe Janus

was still at the piano. The floor of the music room was strewn with wrecked flowers: dahlias, roses, lupins, hydrangeas. There were dandelions inside the piano, still bright and pungent. Tulips wilting in the shade of its opened lid. Sunflower petals haphazard, like confetti, littering the beautiful stringwork. A rose on a long stalk was placed across the music rest. Delphiniums, trodden on, ragged, torn, lay on the rug.

Aldous entered the room just as Janus was beginning Albeniz's Navarra. He had recently become obsessed with this piece, decorating the manuscript with pastel squiggles and baroque tin-foil cutouts pasted in the margins. Those opening chords, two octaves apart, bounding leaps from one end of the keyboard to the other, four bars that set the whole room ringing like a bell, did any piece of music ever open so boldly, so defiantly, ecstatically? Were there any four bars of such terror and might anywhere in the cannon of western music? To play it was like mountaineering with a blindfold. Music of such breadth employed one's whole body in its performance. The essence of playing this piece, Janus felt, was in how one carried one's shoulders. He'd practised it for hours before realizing eventually that one had to lean into the piano slightly, as though about to leapfrog over it, a lot of tension going into the upper thighs. As he prepared himself, picturing a silent shoal of faces filling an unidentifiable but famous concert hall, and launched himself into those chords, his hands rooted, then flying, then rooted, flying, rooted, his father walked in. Janus's hands missed the eighth chord by a semitone, sending him over the edge.

'Your hands,' Janus recalled his tutor saying, 'are walking a narrow ledge before a precipice. You must know every nook and crevice of that ledge, the memory must be in your bones. One finger out of place, one slip, and you are over the edge, falling.'

Janus had inherited his mother's hands. Colette's fingers were long, slender, smoothly hinged, they could spread themselves like starfish, the thumbs, double-jointed, curling back to touch the wrists. Her hands were magnificent toys to her children. She could lock them together to make small, knuckly chapels, quickly build spires by the isoscelesian joining of her index fingers, unfold them to create a congregation's legs marching out of church. Her favourite was the 'flying thumb', a digital *trompe l'œil* in which she joined her thumbs together in such a way that she had one thumb made of two, an index finger covering the join. Then she would lift the top half, making it appear as though her thumb had severed itself bloodlessly. This trick frightened Julian when he was a baby.

In 1943, however, Colette foolishly operated a machine in Sperry's gyroscope factory with its guard up, and a small automated hammer mistook her middle finger for a rivet, breaking the first joint and giving it a permanent kink. Janus found his mother's crooked middle finger very irritating, he wasn't sure why. It made everything she did with her fingers seem exaggerated, affected, mannered, especially when she was vamping at the keyboard. That middle finger seemed to lead a dance all of its own through the already chaotic extemporizations of Colette's boogie-woogie. It amazed Janus how someone could hit so many wrong notes and not seem to care. For his second year examination he'd played the Liszt B minor Sonata and afterwards was handed a sheet on which his examiner had listed every wrong note. There were four.

His whole body contracted with irritation.

'Sorry,' said Aldous, 'carry on.'

Janus slumped, the posture of performance completely erased from his body. He waited to see why Aldous had come in. Normally it would have been to find something, a book or a record or a piece of music. But Aldous wasn't picking through the cabinets and shelves. He was standing beside Janus, looking at him. This never happened. His father was never an audience, unless invited.

'Carry on,' Aldous repeated, gesturing towards the keyboard, then looking around the room, as if he'd only just noticed how it was full of dying flowers. Janus thought, shrugged, straightened his back, brought his hands to the keyboard. Just as he was flexing for the first chord, his father said 'Would you like me to take you to see a prostitute?'

The sentence froze Janus for a few seconds, his hands motionless in their spread, an inch above the keys. Then he withdrew them from the instrument, rested them shapelessly in his lap. Aldous went on.

'I could take you down to Soho. Greek Street. Or King's Cross. Anywhere you like. I'll pay for it all.'

Janus looked sad. His father could see the sadness suddenly condense on his face. It was punctuated by an inward laugh that seemed to comment upon Aldous's last sentence. He was looking at the music before him, on the rest that had been glued back together. Aldous looked as well. He wasn't surprised by the curious decorative graphics that Janus had applied. Most of Janus's favourite pieces were so adorned. He'd chalked 'Navarra' in huge pink letters across the top of the page, the lettering vaguely Celtic, outlined in black. Silver and gold cutouts of the milled paper from cigarette packets adhered to the margins, like something excavated at Sutton Hoo. What did surprise Aldous, however, were the words Janus had written in green ink block capitals just below the printed title, like a direction. They were Welsh – *DYCHRYNLLYD, GALLUOG.* Aldous didn't know these words, and wasn't sure if they were place names or something else.

Janus had only had the manuscript for a few months, but already it was looking worn. Pages turned with the snapping urgency of a pianist in full flow. All the music in the house was like this. It was easy to tear a page clean in half horizontally in a panic to get to the next bar without breaking one's stride. The older books were in shreds, nearly. The Beethoven and Mozart Sonatas, the Bach Preludes and Fugues. Janus had sellotaped the torn pages back together, and had taken the trouble to reinforce the page edges of some books with Sellotape. Already these repairs were old enough for the Sellotape to have dried to crisp splinters of cellophane that fell off the pages, brown as autumn leaves. Then there was the constant problem of the books not staying open at a page, the infuriating ability some books had of very slowly turning their own pages, or closing themselves as their spines gradually gave way to the pressure of leaves. So these books were continually folded back on themselves, flattened against the rest, splayed like the skin of a dissected and labelled rat. This meant the spines were soon broken, and the pages began falling out, which meant more Sellotape. The music book case was a heap of frayed paper and Sellotape. No one really minded about this. It was taken as inevitable damage. Music books, like cookery books, were inevitably damaged through use. One didn't read them like other books. They were guides to a particular very physical activity. Colette's cookery books were likewise albums of stains, – gravy, oil, blood, and torn margins.

Seeing Janus's lack of enthusiasm, Aldous tried dampening the bluntness of his offer.

'Perhaps we could go to a strip club or something, to begin with. You know, they're not all sleazy dives, so I've heard . . .'

'Have you ever been to one?' Janus suddenly interrupted, without taking his eyes off the music.

'A strip club? No . . .'

'I meant a prostitute.'

'No, but I mean, in the army. You know, in France we went to some cabarets, you wouldn't believe. There was one that had a man and a woman actually doing it on stage, and one of the squaddies climbed up on stage with them and started joining in. Only he was so drunk he just fell about and was actually sick over them. The woman, poor girl, had vomit all over her private parts.' Aldous laughed, but his laugh quickly died. Janus was looking unhappier. 'Though afterwards they found these flowers from nowhere, some of the stage hands, and they threw them all around the theatre, to try and cover the smell. Then it turned into a sort of riot, the soldier who'd been sick was beaten up quite badly, as I remember, and the audience, angry because the show had been stopped, ran amok, and there were fists flying and flowers being thrown, I was lucky to get out. Amiens, that was. That's the French for you. I think it was after that that I became interested in Fatima.' Aldous's painting of the miracle at Fatima hung on the back wall of the music room. It depicted a brilliant sun whirling like a Catherine wheel, and flowers falling out of the sky, onlookers in the foreground backlit, silhouettes, the colours all reds and yellows.

'I think you'd better leave,' said Janus, not looking at the painting to which Aldous had turned, thoughtfully.

'What? What's the matter with you?'

'Get out now.'

Aldous sighed.

'I was only trying to . . .' But he shrugged and walked away from the piano at which Janus continued to slump, and left the room.

Aldous was occasionally capable of these blundering indiscretions, these crass interventions. The odd and sometimes objectionable behaviour Janus was showing he thought must be down to a lack of contact with women. A lack of sexual experience. As far as he knew his eldest son was still a virgin. A couple of incidents recently, which they'd put down to drunkenness, had upset Colette. There was the time he lurched into their bedroom one night, completely naked, and stumbled about on the bed. And he'd written an overtly sexual love letter to Vivienne, Colette's childhood friend, now a breeder of borzois in Northamptonshire, married with twin daughters. Colette and Vivienne had been particularly close when Janus was a child, and she was like an aunt to him. Colette noticed that Janus had pinned an old black and white picture of his eight-year-old self and Vivienne to the wall of his bedroom. Vivienne wrote to Colette about the letter, expressing deep concern about Janus's state of mind. '*He seems to have an unhealthy interest in unavailable women*', she wrote, '*which he might be using as a way of deferring his ability to form meaningful sexual relationships.*' Always something of the amateur shrink, Vivienne

Christine never returned to Fernlight Avenue.

Yet that visit to the Tate Janus had rehearsed in his mind

hundreds of times. It was to be his moment of declaration. The pinning of his drawings to the walls was a fanning of his peacock's tail. In the midst of the operation, however, a panic had overcome him, not of being apprehended for criminal damage, but for displaying his own weakness before his cousin. His pastels seemed so puny and gauche pinned crookedly between the great English landscapes. And as he ran from the gallery he knew she would interpret his exit as a cowardly retreat from authority. What he'd meant as a brave assertion of his presence turned into a shameful farce. He didn't wait outside the gallery. He hadn't eaten three choc ices.

Over the days following the incident Janus sent Christine long, passionate, rambling letters. The language was formed under such pressure the lettering was rendered in deep grooves that almost cut through the paper. He wrote letters in black ink, each letter formed with architectural certainty. If his words had been buildings they would have stayed up. Indeed they were castles, forts, jails.

Her letters came back, brief but polite, in handwriting like balloons and feathers, eventually requesting that he stop writing to her.

Janus went on writing, in red ink, and then in coloured pencils, rainbow letters. He bombarded her home in High Wycombe with the brightly coloured spectra of language. Their hues matched the vividness of the content, their green and yellow declarations of love spooling into lush purple and blue descriptions of the landscapes he'd like to take her to, to undress her in, to see the pink (he always thought women's bodies must be pink, the flesh tones that a child will mix for his first renditions of people) nakedness of her body. He can't go further than this, since it is an undiscovered place for him, but its implicit awakening is there in the lines of brown and orange in which he describes her face.

No letters came in reply from High Wycombe. Gradually Christine as a living presence faded, her voice quietened to silence. He was writing letters to an invisible, voiceless woman, and this enabled his imagination to wander, to soar. He wrote of a bold, childish place where he and Christine could be in love without responsibility, where they could have children who would grow into astronauts and violinists. He declared a bicycle love for her, dreamt of riding in tandem with her, of pushing her over the Malverns, the Mendips, the Welsh Marches, of freewheeling with her down Dinas Mawddwy, of pedalling in first gear over the Berwyns, around the liquid hem of Lake Vyrnwy, of toiling up the one-in-sixes of the Nant Francon Pass. Of being free of his family. They could all go to hell. To be with her was his only desire. Greater than music, mountains.

Just before they were about to leave for Wales a parcel arrived at Fernlight Avenue addressed to Colette. Postmarked High Wycombe she assumed it was something for the children (unusual though gifts were from Lesley), so she opened it and found instead a bundle of letters, all the multicoloured letters Janus had sent to Christine, opened, fastened with paper clips to the ripped envelopes. The letter accompanying them was from Lesley, not Christine.

> Dear C.,
>   Thought you should know about these. Chris is distraught. He's sending her up the wall. Could you have a word? She's very scared.
>   Do visit soon, we're all flourishing
>   Love to all
>   L.

Colette did have a word with Janus. She showed him the letters, which she had read. She was disturbed. They seemed to portray a child wandering in a world of useless, vapid adults for whom he had no regard. They shocked her with their lack of social insight, their ignorance of people.

Janus was silent when she showed him the letters, although she saw a hardness settle in his eyes, a tremor of disgust move at his lips.

He didn't say anything for the rest of the day. That evening, while everyone was busy packing the car, he took the family photograph album, a marvellous historical document charting in sepia, black and white and then colour photos the progress of four generations of his family. He took each picture of Lesley Waugh, from doted upon baby to doting father and, very carefully, meticulously, with an old school compass, picked the eyes out of each one.

Colette can see her children. Julian in a loose purple pullover that is unravelling at the sleeves, Juliette behind him, with her hands on his shoulder, James beside Juliette. Julian is holding a metal bucket and spade. The bucket is crimson, decorated with a motif of sailing boats. All three have the sunburnt and windswept look that they always bring back from the beach. Colette speaks to them but is not aware of what she says, and they give no response. She wonders if they are real children, or merely pictures, like Janus. She had seen Janus so clearly, and yet he hadn't been there. He was to have come to Wales this summer, but on the morning of departure he didn't even get out of bed. Colette had pleaded with him, had told him how much he would regret not seeing the farm this year, when he had already missed last summer, but he refused to budge, deeply sulky. In the end they had no choice but to leave without him.

Colette speaks to her children again. They are looking at her with what seems to be contempt. She becomes aware, suddenly, that the glue pad is over her nose, and she takes it away and speaks again, but it comes out as song. No words, just a song that she has invented, and which goes up and down in long vocal glissandos and which she finds unspeakably beautiful. If only she'd known earlier what an exquisite voice she had, and what genius she had for inventing songs, she could have built a career on stage. As it is, her children are her only audience, and so she sings to them. But they walk away, one by one, and leave her on her own. She sings anyway.

1968

1

Colette discovers that she has no breasts.

She is looking at her nude self in the wardrobe mirror. Normally she would have been animated before this mirror, twisting and pouting, shifting her weight from this hip to that hip, bringing forward her shoulders to deepen her cleavage, experimenting with different poses, stances, presentations, as she'd done since she'd first discovered, as a child, that her body was a private place, a little park all to itself, in which she could be nearly anything – film star, cowboy, astronaut. But today she is standing still before the mirror, still as a photo, face to face with her double, her arms hanging loosely at her sides, her legs a little apart.

The thinness of her body reminds her of a hunting cheetah prowling the savannahs, lean, fatless, one last colossal chase left in its muscles. Her body looks proud in its hardness. She likes the hardness of it. It is hard like a mirror. She likes its angularity. Her collarbones are as prominent as handlebars. Her ribs are two sheets of curved, whitewashed corrugated iron. Her nipples are the rusted heads of nails that have been hammered into them.

Although her body pleases her, she is concerned about the loss of her breasts. What she sees in the mirror, from the waist up, is the body of a young man. If she feels for them, turning her hands, fingers spread, in on herself, like small waves curling at their tips, she encounters little pouches of softness. But they can't be seen. Her nipples, it is true, are darker and fuller than men's ever are – those sorry little flush studs that punctuate a man's chest – but for the most part, it is a man's chest she views in the mirror. While she has lost, almost entirely, any concern she ever had for the workings of the universe and could hardly care less if it was discovered there was life on the moon, that the world was about to be crushed by a comet, or that all other human beings were miraculous puppets operated by an unseen, alien master, being a woman is still important to her. Only by continuing to be a woman can she claim with any certainty to have brought four living, breathing people into the world.

When she dresses (tea-coloured tights, blue Fair Isle pullover, knee-length narrow grey skirt that is in fact a retained item of her bus conductress's uniform) she tucks little bundles of pink lavatory paper into her bra. Then in the mirror, she sees her hard, straight, flat body given a soft skin of clothing, with two pointed bumps on her chest. These mock breasts are too pointed, too separate. She unspools more lavatory paper from the roll in the toilet, scrunches it up, pokes it down the neck of her pullover, looks again in the mirror, moulds her paper breasts, shifts them with two cupped hands into a more credible arrangement. She is satisfied. They look rounder, fuller. But they feel hard. She is surprised that bunched up lavatory paper should feel so hard.

There is some lavatory paper left over. She rolls it up into separate wads, tucks them into the cuffs of her pullover.

She is still bewildered by the emptiness of the house. Aldous, James, Juliette and Julian are all at their various schools. Janus has a new job as an international telephone operator. He works at a place in the middle of London she has never seen called International House, connecting telephone calls from all over the world. He works shifts. Sometimes he leaves the house before it's light, before anyone else is awake, and comes home in the afternoon. Sometimes he will leave the house at night and come home in the early morning, just as everyone else is leaving. He will sit around in the kitchen for a while, talking, or will wander into the music room for an hour or so at the piano, and will go to bed at noon. Then she will have to creep quietly around the house all afternoon, trying not to disturb him. Keeping the radio low, not hoovering. The lavatory is right outside his bedroom door, so she always feels awkward when using it. She hates to think of him unconscious while the world is going on brightly around him. She hates the upside down life he's living.

Julian is in his fourth year at school, but still his absence seems like a shock. Taking him there each day provides her with her one solid daily routine. Two buses there, two buses back. Sometimes the conductor will be a friend from her days on the buses, and those brief chats, smiles of recognition, exchanges of memories, are things she treasures. The delivering of her son to St Nicola's Roman Catholic Primary School was a painful daily process, especially since Julian seemed unhappier there with each passing year. He'd settled into his first class, with Miss Clarke, who married to become Mrs Laponte, happily enough, but he was now in a class with a rather frightening woman, Mrs Buckley, who seemed to be of Iberian descent, her hair piled neatly on top of her head, her eyes garishly made up. Whenever Colette saw her she imagined a clacking of castanets and stamping of heels. Julian was scared of her, for some reason. Every morning he would plead with his mother not to have to go into school, would drag her into the cloakroom with him, sometimes right up to the classroom door. And it pained Colette to have to send him into that unpleasant little world, with all its miniature challenges and tests, that horrible, educational Lilliput.

She misses Julian so much that once, when Aldous came home for lunch, she threatened to kill herself if he didn't go and fetch Julian home from school. She had taken one of her husband's old safety razors, unscrewed its neck so that the steel petals opened delicately (a mechanism that had always fascinated her), and lifted the blade out from within. She held its edge against her wrist.

Aldous was just finishing his strawberry flavoured Ski yoghurt, which was all she'd provided for his lunch. He looked at Colette's wrist in a tired sort of way, the last spoonful of yoghurt still a soft lump beneath his lower lip, saw that the blade had already grazed the skin of her wrist, leaving little white scratches, and decided he'd better get Julian.

He drove up to the school a mile away and went into the classroom where Julian was sitting with twenty-four other children, listening to a story. Aldous was always surprised, when he saw his own child in a crowd of children, how different he looked from the others, but at the same time ordinary. He wondered if all parents felt like this. He was also surprised at how relaxed and happy Julian looked in the presence of Mrs Buckley, the teacher he claimed to hate. Aldous spun Mrs Buckley a lie about an overlooked dental appointment, saw undiluted, teacher to teacher trust in those heavily mascarad eyes, and took his child out of the class.

So easy. One thing about being a teacher, it made it so easy to lie. People believed you, almost without question. There wasn't the least flicker of surprise or puzzlement in Mrs Buckley's eyes. Just unquestioning acceptance of the situation. Julian, however, was horrified, since he hated the dentist, and left school with the reluctance he usually reserved for his arrival in the morning.

'You're not going to the dentist,' Aldous said to Julian's repeated, bewildered questions as he drove him home. He spoke quietly but sharply, in a way that didn't invite further questioning. It angered him that he had been led into a situation in which he had been observed by his son lying to his own teacher. He delivered Julian to his mother, who by now was sleepy with drugs, rushed back to work, and was late for his first class of the afternoon.

Aldous comes home for lunch every day now. He's been coming home for lunch since the afternoon late last year when he returned from work to find Colette unconscious on the kitchen floor with the gas stove on top of her. At first it seemed like a ludicrous scene of adultery – his wife beneath the burly weight of that yellow-enamelled body. There was a dried trickle of blood on her face. The dark glasses which she'd taken to wearing almost continually, claiming that her eyes had become extra-sensitive to light, were knocked upwards on to her forehead. Julian was playing alone in the garden with a rusted pair of shears, apparently happy.

Colette was not seriously hurt, and when she came to could give no explanation for what had happened. She had no memory of it. She thought maybe she'd been trying to get at something that had fallen behind the stove and that it had fallen on her as she was trying to pull it away from the wall. Aldous thought this possible, but he also thought it might have been a glue-induced suicide attempt. He thought it possible that she'd tried to gas herself and that in leaning on the lowered oven door had tipped the whole thing over.

Whatever it was, he feels he has to come home every lunchtime now to check on her. It was her suggestion. It gives the long emptiness of her day a focus. She usually makes something for him – a cheese omelette, steamed fish and potatoes, soup. But Aldous dreads that lunch, fearing what he might find in the house as it draws nearer. Usually there is nothing amiss. Colette will be busy with lunch in the kitchen, the radiogram will be lively and cheerful with Jimmy Young, pans will be boiling, steam rising.

Sometimes, though, Colette will be in what he and she have decided to call a trance. She will be deep in the fumes of Romac, hallucinating. She will be sitting in her chair or lying on the bed, asleep but open eyed. She may suddenly emit wheezy bursts of laughter, or fling her arms aside in a sudden, expansive gesture, her wrists twisting as though turning invisible handles. Or she will be nearer to consciousness, but still distant, staring with pointed wonder at something he can't see, the tissue paper held fast to her nose, like the chloroform pads the surgeons of Aldous's childhood would apply to his face. But he only has to take the glue pad gently out of her hand and within minutes she is normal. Intensely normal. The exaggerated normality that always follows her trances.

In some ways the sleeping pills are worse. The doctor has been prescribing these for nearly a year. The more she takes the more she needs. The doctor happily scribbles out steadily increasing prescriptions. Often she will take them in the daytime. She will take them in the morning to soften that blinding, cold wakefulness she experiences first thing. She will take some in the afternoon to help her get through those groggy hours. They retard her actions as though she is an image in a film that has been slowed down to a few frames per second. Her actions are reduced to a sequence of still moments. She becomes a series of illustrated pages that are turned slower and slower, until she stops. When she stops she could be in the middle of doing anything. Half way through a meal, a forkful of food on its way to her mouth, stirring a nearly cold cup of tea, or, more dangerously, lighting a cigarette.

Sometimes this is how Aldous will find her at lunchtime. He will eat alone at the table, his wife a silent, open-mouthed statue in the chair at the other end of the room.

Colette is sitting in the armchair now, sniffing her glue. Somehow it makes the house seem crowded. The house seems to buzz. It seems lively even though it is empty. So she sits there in her chair in the kitchen sniffing. Soon she notices there is something different about the room. She scans the space with her eyes wondering what it is. The boiler, the sink, the cooker, the cupboards, the radiogram, the table, the clock . . . these are all in place. But there is something else, something additional. Then she notices. In the centre of the red lino floor, right in the middle of the room, there is a trap door. It is covered in the same red lino as the rest of the floor. It has a little recessed brass handle.

Colette walks over, carefully fills the loop of the brass handle with her fingers, and lifts. The door is heavy. Warm air oozes out from beneath. She lifts the door right up and lets it fall with a crash back on itself. A huge space beneath the kitchen is revealed with wooden, cobwebby steps leading down into it.

How astonishing, thinks Colette, that they'd lived in this house for all these years ignorant of its cellarage. There is light down there, and voices. There is a pleasant, wholesome smell, like biscuits baking. Carefully she descends the staircase and finds herself in a low ceilinged, dimly lit space roofed with joists and floorboards. It is like the opposite of the loft.

The voices, deep and friendly, chatter and chuckle. In the far corner she can see a group of people sitting around a table. A group of middle-aged black men dressed in blue overalls are sitting around a table playing cards. Each has a steaming mug of tea beside them. As she nears them they fill out with detail, the shiny, porous skins, the dense, thick hair flecked with grey, the frayed shirt collars, the pale gums, the crimson stitchwork that marks their eyeballs. They notice her and smile, revealing teeth, some gold, some tarnished with tobacco smoke. They shift their chairs to make space for her at the table. She sits with them. They remind her of the mechanics at the bus depot, those loud, swaggering men who carried their immense skill and knowledge so lightly, who could strip an engine and put it back together in a different bus in four hours. They call her 'sister'. She likes being called sister. She spends a couple of hours down there with them, laughing, drinking tea and playing poker.

The glue can do that. Sometimes it is just a nice feeling, a musical accompaniment, everything being soft. Sometimes it is a situation, event or vision. Often these involve trans-formations of her immediate surroundings, which are usually the house. Once, for instance, she found that the kitchen was full of coats, racks and racks of them, thick tweed overcoats, woollen trench coats, polyester car coats, double-breasted mackintoshes, sheepskin coats with white, fluffy lapels. She could hardly move for them but had to squeeze sideways down narrow gangways between the coats. Near the front door she found a young girl serving at an old-fashioned counter. The house had become a coat shop. Colette tried on some coats – lovely, thick, heavy coats, luxurious minks, astrakhans, leopardskins, suede flying jackets, leather morning coats. She twirled and pouted before a cheval glass, astonished by the grace and verve the coats gave to her body.

The experience was so vivid she wondered if she'd been given a glimpse of the house's past. She made a mental note to look at the deeds to see if it had ever been a shop. She never got round to it.

Then there was the time a farm appeared in the house. She was sitting on the couch in the living room, the rest of her family watching the newly acquired television, she in gluey bliss, a wad over her nose, when she noticed animals, tiny little ones, moving slowly across the carpet. A flock of sheep, hardly bigger than white mice, and some kitten-sized cows were scattered about the floor, doing exactly what real sheep and cows do – very little. Some sheep were nibbling at the fibres of the carpet, one of the cows was licking its hind parts with its bird-like tongue, another was, with a raised tail, letting slip from its body a little fall of manure. These perfect animals so delighted Colette that she dropped down on to her knees and tried to pick them up. The animals, when she moved, looked at her with the intent wonder of real livestock, before trotting briskly away. She reached out and tried to pick up some of the sheep, but was afraid of getting a proper grip in case she hurt them. They all retreated to the narrow spaces beneath the furniture.

To the others in the room it seemed that their mother was desperately trying to pick dust out of the carpet.

Colette has been sniffing glue for a year. No one in the family knows quite what to make of it. As far as they know she is performing a unique activity. No one else in the world uses bicycle glue like this, they think. They don't know if it is harming her or not.

Sometimes Colette will recount her hallucinations, her stories of coat shops and miniature sheep, and the family will laugh together about them, but for the most part they are unhappy with Colette's sniffing. They do not like the fact that for much of the time their mother, though physically present, seems to be in a different place. The problem is that no one knows how to stop her. They can't stop her from obtaining the glue. She buys it with the daily shopping from the bicycle shop, Carnival Cycles, on The Parade. Every other day Colette visits The Parade, calls in at the usual shops – a loaf from the baker's, some chops from the butchers, some glue from the bike shop. All the family's bicycles have come from this shop. Colette knows the proprietor, a small, friendly man with poor eyesight, quite well.

Sometimes her family try and persuade her of the harm she may be doing herself. They describe what the glue might be doing to her body. James, more scientific than the rest, speaks with authority of the holes that will be opening up in her cerebral cortex, like a Swiss cheese. 'Probably big enough to put two fingers through by now,' he says, disinterestedly. Others suggest that the glue is hardening her brain. Since hardening is one of the properties of glue, it seems a possibility. Her brain will stiffen and shrink to something like a cricket ball. The glue may be having that effect on her whole body. She did seem to have shrunk, after all, and her thinness had given her body a board-like hardness. This is Aldous's nightmare, who notices, more than the others, the hardness of her body. In bed at night he sometimes reaches out and encounters a prominence of bone. It is as though her skeleton is externalizing, like an insect's. Sometimes he thinks he will wake up next to a woman-shaped mass of glue and toilet paper, from which he will have to carefully peel the adhered sheets.

Often Colette will listen to all her family's prognostications, remorseful and contrite as a child, grateful for admonishment, and agree with them that she must stop doing terrible things to her body. And she will stop, for a day or two. Perhaps a week or more. But it never lasts. She claims to have severe withdrawal symptoms – an iciness in the head, the sensation of being precariously balanced on a ledge above a precipice, a hunger in the bones, that lead her inevitably back to Carnival Cycles and its endless supply of puncture repair outfits. Aldous need never worry again about having to find a patch to cover his wounded inner tubes. The cycle, ha ha, the cycle goes on and on.

Yesterday, however, Colette made a promise to James, Juliette and Julian. They had all gathered together to plead with her not to sniff during the holiday. And she had promised. Today is the eve of the holiday. As she emerges from the cellar, settles back into the chair, settles her nose into the soft armchair of her glue pad, she relishes her last day of sniffing. Tomorrow they are going to Wales, and she has promised.

A small, silver leopard pads softly into the kitchen, looks at Colette with green eyes, sits awkwardly on the red lino, licks its lips and yawns.

Scipio is Janus's cat. A present from Colette. A gift of life.

'The child who can care for animals will never be a bad citizen,' Nana had said, quoting someone. Colette bought Scipio for Janus because she thought he needed something to care for. Some responsibility and companionship. Janus dotes on the cat. In the mornings when he comes home from the night shift he will pay more attention to Scipio than he does his mother.

He came from a breeder in Surrey whom Colette had read about in the newspaper. This woman was engaged in the task of producing the world's first spotted domestic cat. The leopard for your living room. No such cat as yet existed anywhere in the world. There were tabbies in abundance – the distant cousins of the tiger – but the domestic leopard had so far evaded the most ingenious breeders.

This woman, however, was claiming to be within sight of her goal – maybe as little as two or three generations away – and was selling off cheaply what were to be the ancestors of this new breed. Scipio was such a kitten, a runt of the litter with weaknesses that made him unsuitable for breeding, but with a pelt that was three quarters of the way towards spots. Essentially he was a silver-haired tabby, but officially he belonged to a new breed called Silver Spotted European. The breeder had christened him Culverden Nimbus, and he could trace his ancestry back for more generations than any of the humans in the house, and had his pedigree written out in an elegant, cursive hand on a pedigree certificate – Jezreel Jake (great grandfather), Hillcross Silver Flute (great great grandfather), Silver Seal Black Lion (great great great grandfather), Marguerite of Silverleigh (great great great grandmother).

His marking resembled a zebra's, more than any other creature. His forehead and muzzle were a Bridget Riley of black lines on a grey background, his back was marked by a black spine that followed the path of his real spine, branching out into delicate black ribs that did indeed disintegrate towards his tummy and down his flanks into broken lines that could be called spots. His legs were dotty and his paws were gloved with silver suede. His tail was ringed like a lemur's, with a black tip, as though dipped in ink.

There was something very feminine about the cat. He was slighter and more delicate than usual toms, with none of their heaviness or aggression. He walked delicately and daintily about the house like a nervous debutante in a silver frock, or an elegant but clumsy little duchess. At the same time, a reduced gene pool had produced a strangely uncatlike cat. He lacked feline grace and had a poor sense of balance. He was always falling out of trees and off chairs. He couldn't even attempt the tightrope-walking feat that Baxbr performed with daily casualness, of treading along the top of the garden fence. Scipio could even trip over when walking over flat ground. It was an odd thing to see a cat fall over. Most uncatlike, ungainly, clumsy, lacking in poise.

On top of this he had a talent for getting into scrapes and for vanishing. He was once folded away in the bed settee for a whole day, emerging damp and flat as a cutout when the bed was unfolded at night. Sometimes he would go missing for days and then turn up mysteriously bloody. Colette once found Scipio trapped near the old garages in Hoopers Lane by a posse of schoolboys throwing stones at him. He was too beautiful to go unnoticed. Too beautiful not to arouse strange jealousies.

Once, after a spate of long disappearances, a wealthy looking Greek called at the house, his wife hovering behind him. He lived, he said, in Woodberry Road, his garden backed on to theirs. It was on to this man's sunbathing body that Janus had once lobbed baby apples. But he now confessed to harbouring Scipio for days at a time. He and his wife (a woman laced with gold) had fallen in love with Scipio. 'We were up until two in the morning once,' he said miserably, 'your cat stretched out on the bed, me and the missus counting his stripes and spots. The wife would lift up one of his legs and tell me "Dimitri, there's more here, look", and we tot up his spots on a chart. We still haven't counted them all. Listen, perhaps this sounds crazy, but we want to buy your cat. We can pay you good money. I'll give you fifty pounds. A train set for your little boy' (Julian had just appeared behind his mother). 'We're not rich people. You want more?' (as though by her bewildered silence Colette had upped the stakes). 'We can pay by instalments. Have my watch now as surety.' He began unbuckling the bulky gold timepiece. Colette was sorely tempted by the money but the bond between Scipio and Janus was now so strong he would never have forgiven her. (The cat slithered past, his coat glossy with accrued interest.) The visitors gave little gasps and squeals before Scipio vanished into the undergrowth.

'I'm sorry,' said Colette. 'He's not for sale. We're very fond of him . . .'

'A hundred pounds,' said the man.

'Dimitri,' said his wife, who all the while had sheltered behind her husband's broad torso.

Colette was astounded to see, in the lower rims of this tough-looking man's eyes, tears budding.

'It's not fair,' Dimitri's wife went on, speaking into the back of her husband's head, 'to make that sort of offer. There are children here . . .'

'A bike for your boy . . .'

'Let's go love,' said the wife, now pulling gently at Dimitri's collar.

Colette supposed they were a business couple. Owners of a local shop or two, probably, or a restaurant. It was in the raw newness of their clothing, the brassy shine of the woman's hair, the glow of overnourishment that came from them both. It fascinated her to see how little silver Scipio could reduce to trembling mice these tough, confident entrepreneurs. So she sent Dimitri and his wife away gently. Their dejected stances exaggerated their grief to an almost comical level, she thought, as she watched their stooping bodies, heads hanging, eyes rolling, dragging their feet down the path.

The episode enhanced the general feeling in the house that it now contained something of unexpected preciousness, lustre, history, beauty and financial value. After the piano, the car and the radiogram, Scipio was the richest thing they'd ever owned. His richness made him a worrisome presence. It added anxiety to his disappearance. It was as though a piece of antique crystalware had acquired legs and was wont to get lost in tree tops. Julian had dreams that he'd accidentally damaged the cat, in the same way that one might knock an expensive vase off its plinth. He dreamt one night that he'd cut Scipio in half with a bread knife, and Scipio's two halves continued, worm-like, to live. There was no blood. Scipio's insides were like Spam – smooth, fatty, cooked meat. In his dream Julian chased the two halves of Scipio around the garden, until he finally managed to gather them up, and then he tried tying them back together with a length of clothes line, terrified that someone would come out of the house and see what he'd done. Poorly bound, tied together Scipio walked crookedly round the garden, his back half out of joint with his front, like an ill-disciplined pantomime horse.

The real Scipio was not unlike dream Scipio. A tiny panto horse, uncoordinated, clumsy, spectral. An hallucination. This product of feline eugenics, the first child of a new race. He looked, thought Julian, like a television screen. A flickering of silver lines. Something that wasn't really there.

Scipio wouldn't settle for the journey to Wales but instead jumped and danced all around the crowded car, poking around beneath the pedals, rubbing his cheek against the gear lever, balancing wildly on the seat backs, crawling through people's hair. All through Potters Bar, St Albans, Hemel Hempstead with its roundabout of roundabouts, Scipio had behaved like unhitched ballast, a grey disturbance. In Fishpool Street he'd put his head under the brake pedal, meaning that an emergency stop would have decapitated him. On Dunstable Downs he mewed mournful and deep orisons in Aldous's ear. By Leighton Buzzard Colette was reaching for her sleeping pills, her purple panaceas, chopping one in half with a pair of nail scissors, popping it down the neck of the held-open cat, stirring his throat fur to help it down. It was fascinating then for the family to see their mother's behaviour replicated in the body of a small, domestic cat. Doped Scipio followed Colette's pattern of sedation, in that his liveliness increased. As Colette would stagger, drugged, around the house picking books from all the bookcases to read in bed, ending up comatose beneath a heap of books, so Scipio staggered around the car, climbing shakily the screes of seated bodies, dragging himself with glazed determination over the summits of shoulders, falling in splayed disarray from seat backs. His movements had the same jerkiness, the few-frames-per-second hesitancy that Colette had in the final stages, until he stopped, statuesque, in the middle of doing something. Unfortunately the thing Scipio stopped in the middle of was a long, thoughtful pee, his ears back, his eyes half closed, his tail cocked, a thin but relentless stream of urine ejected backwards on to Juliette's best friend Mary who was coming with them this year. The car being so tightly packed, Mary had no escape. Though Juliette laughed, she later drank from a bottle of Tizer that was, in fact, Julian's still-warm urine. When Julian that evening at Dot and Geraint's bungalow failed to sleep, he received the other half of the sleeping pill with a glass of Nesquik, which caused him to stagger like the cat, like his mother, about the bungalow, kissing everyone. When he finished kissing the people he began kissing the furniture, then he kissed the porcelain cows, the toby jugs, the television.

Even though Scipio became something of a celebrity in the region of Y Lledrith that summer, there was always the feeling that he wasn't really there. In the early days of the holiday no one was sure what to do with him during the day. It was decided to take him out with them. He chased sheep on the farm and waves on the beach. Scipio at Criccieth kept clumsy wicket during a game of beach cricket. On his red velvet leash they would take him for walks through the town of Aberbreuddwyd, or on the promenade at dusk. For a cat he walked well, though often he would squirm like an otter to escape his collar, or loop his leash round a lamp post or people's legs. Scipio became possibly the first domestic cat to sit on the summit of Cadair Idris. On the farm he curled up on the dry stone walls, which gave him unexpected camouflage. Grey and mottled, he became, when still, a boulder. He disappeared into the walls. He once vanished for two days and two nights after breaking loose from the hamper he was stored in at night. Having searched the farm (including a close inspection and sometimes prod of nearly every boulder in every wall in case it should spring to life), the family had nearly given up on their cat and consigned him to the landscape of Y Lledrith for ever when, on the third midnight of his absence, he poked his grey, symmetrical face in through the bottom of the tent door.

When Colette was tugged gently from sleep by the kneading paws of the cat working like an organist at her midriff, she felt an uprush of joy, the sort of joy she experienced in dreams when her dead loved ones came back to life. Nana in her garden with a glass of lemonade. Vivienne in a crowd of happy dogs.

Vivienne, her childhood friend, had died in the spring, two months after Meg, Colette's older sister. Her favourite sister. The black layer of grief that had settled on her life after her mother's death was now tripled in thickness.

Contact with Vivienne had been sparse since she'd left London to breed borzois in Northamptonshire. Colette sometimes took her family to visit Vivienne at her opulent but isolated house in the middle of bleak Midland plains. Vivienne had been down to London with her twin daughters, Lucy and Laverne, a few times.

Vivienne had done well: a happy family, a large house, acres of land, dogs, stables. Then one day she went riding on her favourite horse, Coco, without a helmet, and Kwango, her prize borzoi, leapt out in front of her, causing Coco to perform an estrapade which sent Vivienne flying and falling, landing head first on the concrete drive, killing her instantly.

And Meg. Tall, beautiful, graceful Meg. A champion ballroom dancer and teacher of English. It was Meg more than anyone who encouraged Colette's interest in language, in words, stories, books. *The Water Babies*, *The Wind in the Willows*, Richmal Crompton, Ernest Thompson Seton, George Eliot, Dickens. All these had come to Colette through Meg, who took such care in the encouragement of Colette's reading that she would edit her books for her, bracketing off any dull passages of description, irrelevant padding or stuffy moralizing.

Meg died of a heart attack almost exactly a year after her husband had died of the same cause, so orphaning her tall son Mathew. He was taken in by Agatha and became part of her family. Lucy and Laverne, Vivienne's twins, were transported to Canadian boarding schools in the province of their father's people. Colette never saw nor heard from them again.

These collateral losses disturbed Colette almost as much as the deaths themselves. Wall by wall, it seemed, the acreage of her life was being reduced. Meg's death had closed down a whole field of friendships, shared memories, reciprocated favours. Nana was now some boxes stacked in a corner of the loft she never saw. Her room had been taken over by toys and teddy bears. Viv's death had removed a set of children and animals from her life. Field after field was being closed down, turned over to developers, planted with bungalows.

Whenever Colette encountered an animal unexpectedly she fancied it carried the ghost of her mother. Once, while she and her family were motoring around the Chilterns, a white cat had come to her beneath a church's richly coloured doom window. Later the same day, by an alabaster tomb that included a perfect, chubby-fingered baby, a black cat, pert-tailed and friendly, stirred itself against Colette's ankles. Like the full moon and its eclipse. Like her contradictory moods. Her mother would, of all creatures, manifest as a cat.

Or an owl. There was a church they visited in Norfolk, once, that had a double hammer-beamed roof, a vault of oaken angels with woodworm in their feathers. They'd discovered an owl trapped in that church, a barn owl whose face was a heart of white feathers flying the length of the nave from east window to west window, its talons scratching for purchase on the sloping sills of the lancets, but in flight totally silent. They'd spent an hour or more trying to encourage it to fly out of the south door, to the bird a negligible chink in a cliff, without success.

But more usually a cat. The night of Scipio's return caused Colette to imagine that her mother was tucking her into bed, when she looked up to see a small grey face leaning down to her. Scipio's preciousness was thus enhanced, and she began to think that the cat contained an essential family spirit, an ancestral endowment. Small, silver, delicate, just like Nana. She'd never known a cat capable of such affection. Often Scipio would embrace her like a child, extending both its front arms around her neck, hugging her, licking her like a loving dog. Cats were meant to be indifferent to people, but Scipio seemed full of love, a child's love.

3

The others had gone to the chip shop at Llanygwynfa-wm-Lledrith. Mary and Juliette were alone at the tent, sitting side by side in the new camping chairs – blue and yellow striped nylon strapped on to steel frames with broad armrests of white plastic, writing upon ancient postcards.

One of the shops in Llanygwynfa-wm-Lledrith stocked antique postcards – sepia and monochrome prints of local town- and landscapes taken at the end of the last century, and which mostly bore an exact resemblance to the views of the present day. The shop did not sell these cards as antiques. A job lot of them had been bought from a man in Wrexham in 1902 and the shop still hadn't managed to get rid of them. Much of the stock in the shop was like that. There were newspapers from before the war, boxes of forgotten soap powders, jars of fused together boiled sweets. Janus sometimes spent hours going through all the old postcards, magazines and other junk. The Genius didn't mind. The family referred to the shop as The Genius because sometimes on the door to the back there was a crookedly sellotaped notice saying 'Silence – Genius at Work'. On such occasions, with no one serving, it was usual for customers to help themselves and pay later. No one was sure who The Genius was. It may have been the genial, sharp-witted, grey-haired woman who usually served, but it was rumoured that the real genius of the shop was her brother, who never came out to the front, but stayed in the back, composing oratorios and hymns.

That afternoon Mary and Juliette had been to The Genius to buy some postcards. The clutter of the shop worsened each year, the floor and counter space shrinking under the spread of junk. Beside the door cans of consommé and corned beef were heaped like stones on a beach. A table was filled with old coats. There were kites, home-made from old shirts and socks, hanging from the ceiling. Oak and frosted glass confectionery stands now held displays of firelighters and candles. Bristly doormats were stacked on the counter, like the mattresses in the story of the princess and the pea. On top a jar of red lollipops, open and on its side, spilled lollipops out on to the doormats, to which they'd become stuck. Next to the doormats was an oval, viridian object that Mary thought might be a lemon. Juliette thought it was a pear. They asked The Genius, 'What's that?' The Genius replied 'Penicillin.'

Juliette was writing a postcard to Janus. Mary was writing a postcard to Baxbr.

> *Dear Baxbr,*
>   *Frightfully sorry you couldn't come with us. There are giant mice here covered in wool, and more milk than you could imagine. Never mind old bean.*
>   *Toodle-oo*
>   *Love*
>   *Scipio*

'I still don't understand why Scipio had to come with us,' said Mary.

Mary had come to Llanygwynfa with Juliette's family because her own father was too ill to take her anywhere on holiday.

Scipio was sitting on the grass in front of the tent, attentive to the quick movements of midges.

'I don't think Mum trusted anyone enough to look after him. I'm not sure really.'

Both girls were wearing unfaded jeans. Mary had a red and white lumberjack shirt. Juliette had a bottle green T-shirt under a brown suede waistcoat which ended in a frill of long tassels which, when she walked, swung like the legs of a centipede. She had worn her tassel waistcoat since the day school finished. She couldn't imagine ever not wearing it. She had brown leather sandals on her feet with chains of gold loops along the insteps. Mary had white plimsolls. Both girls had grown their hair long and liked to describe themselves as hippies.

Juliette hasn't started her postcard to Janus, although she has filled in the address panel. She followed Janus's name with his degrees, LRAM GRSM, and then with BA, MA, D.Litt., BSM, RAC, AA, BBC and so on, cramming half the postcard with droll abbreviations. She can't think what to write in the other half of the postcard.

'It's a pity Janus didn't come,' said Mary, nearly poking herself in the eye with the burning end of a cigarette. Manipulating both pen and cigarette has caused her several near accidents, once nearly writing with fire, once inhaling Biro ink.

'So you keep saying,' replied Juliette. 'He'll probably come up this week.'

'I think it's terrible a man with his talents working on a telephone switchboard.'

Mary had been to a recital Janus had given at his old school once and had secretly admired him ever since. Janus had played three of Liszt's Transcendental Studies, and four Chopin Etudes. A Polish woman in the audience had wept. Mary had never spoken to Janus, and wasn't sure that he was aware of her existence. Whenever she was at the house Janus was in his room, or playing the piano. Once she did find him in the kitchen, but he was just sitting at the table, his arm hanging loosely off the back of the chair, and he didn't even raise his eyes to acknowledge her presence. He said nothing.

When she re-entered the kitchen two hours later, he was in exactly the same position, and as silent.

'I think it's funny,' said Juliette.

'What do your Mum and Dad think?'

Juliette thought for a long time.

'They don't care,' she said, a little glow to her voice, as if relieved to have found an answer.

'I like that,' said Mary.

'Anyway,' Juliette said, 'he might be up this week. He said he might come up in the second week.'

'He loves this place doesn't he,' said Mary, 'that's what your Mum keeps saying. That he really loves this farm and the countryside. She said he wouldn't be able to keep away. She seemed upset he didn't come with us.'

Mary passed her cigarette across to Juliette, who took it carefully.

There was a pause while Juliette absorbed smoke, then ejected it. The subject was thus changed.

'Babies remind me of spiders,' she said, 'the way they crawl about. They make me shiver.'

'If you found one in the bath,' said Mary, 'would you be able to take it out?'

They both made their noses small with laughter.

'No,' said Juliette, 'I'd have to get a tumbler about this big,' she held her hands apart to indicate the size, 'and a big bit of cardboard . . .'

'And throw it out of the window,' Mary finished.

'Yeah,' said Juliette thoughtfully, taking another drag, 'let it live on flies.'

She passed the half-consumed fag back to Mary who dropped it in the exchange and had to reach down to pick it out of the grass. This caused both girls to giggle again but it also annoyed Juliette, who is irritated by Mary's clumsiness. The ability to accomplish such manoeuvres in an adult way she regards as vitally important. Gaucheness in poise, lack of finesse, general cack-handedness, such things caused the mask of their maturity to fall, revealing their true, thirteen-year-old selves. Juliette felt she had it, but was constantly let down by Mary, whose range of gestures included a large component of leftovers from childhood – the sudden nose-scratchings, for instance, or the whispering of songs quietly to herself while drumming her fingers against her lips, the childish chewing of her hair. As for Mary's cigarette smoking, it had all the grace and sophistication of a Henry Cooper piano recital.

'No,' said Mary, 'I wouldn't let one of those things get inside my body. No chance. I'd rather be a nun.'

'But how would you go to the toilet?'

'I'd do it in my jam jar like all the nuns do.'

'What jam jar?'

'Haven't you heard about the nuns and their jam jars? Sister Mary Agnes, Sister Bernadette, they've all got jam jars tied to their waists, hanging down, so they never have to go to the toilet. I can't believe you didn't know that, Juliette Jones.'

'I did know it,' Juliette lied.

'Didn't you hear Mary Feeney tell Sister Bernadette not to break her jam jar when she was shouting at her? Sister Bernadette went red as a tomato and put her in detention. Just think, Juliette, Sister Mary Francis could be standing in front of the class giving us a talk about the miracles or something, and she could be doing a wee-wee right at that moment and we wouldn't know anything about it. Don't you remember when we were playing rounders with Sister Anne O'Grady and she made a home run and she was running so fast she had to pick up her habit, she had it up higher than her knees and you could see the jam jar there, hanging down, swinging from side to side as she was running?'

'Was there anything in it?'

'No, it was empty.'

Mary takes a shallow draw on the cigarette and passes it back to Juliette. She gives out dense, uninhaled smoke that trickles up over her face.

It annoyed Juliette that Mary won't inhale. After all the trouble they went through to get those cigarettes. They had to wait for the trip to Aberbreuddwyd, then lose the rest of the family while they went to the tobacconist's. It was especially hard shaking off Julian, who seemed fascinated by Mary and was always doing drawings and paintings of her, paintings that with his unformed, childish skills made her look like a monstrous, purple bird. And they'd had to try three shops before they found one that would sell them ten Player's No. 6. This was the brand Colette smoked. At home there was a cupboard full of cigarette coupons, little, green, ornately calligraphed cards that were bundled together into packs with rubber bands. Colette must have smoked thousands of cigarettes to build up such a stash of coupons, Juliette thought, millions even. Juliette had begun smoking by lifting single fags from her mother's unattended packets. She built up small caches of them to take to school and distribute for illicit puffing in the far corner of the playground, or on the bus home. But she never smoked at home, or anywhere near home. Her smoking, a proud brag at school, at home was a carefully kept secret. Not even James knew about it.

Juliette let the cigarette hang in her mouth as she leant back in her chair and stretched her arms up above her head. Then, unclenching, she took an unnecessarily hurried pull on the fag, held it briefly in her chest, then exhaled through nearly closed lips, a long loud rush of blue exhaust.

'Men,' she said.

'Yeah,' said Mary.

Juliette coughed, spluttered, coughed again. Juliette's coughing was such a regular event that it usually passed unnoticed. Suddenly her face would redden, become embossed with veins, her rolled tongue, thin and taut like a piece of tenderized steak, would protrude from her lips, and there would come a dry series of chirrups, as rhythmic as a grasshopper, then a brief licking of lips and swallowing. Juliette had been asthmatic since early childhood, and had to feed regularly at the black teat of her bromide vaporizer, a gadget of black rubber and amber glass that sprayed a bitter, ventilating mist into her lungs.

'Your Mum's great,' said Mary, taking the cigarette.

'Is she?'

'Yeah,' Mary said with an emphasis of puzzlement, surprised at having to reaffirm her statement. 'Of course.'

'Why?'

'Christ, Juliette, you don't know how lucky you are. You can do anything. She lets you do anything.'

Juliette didn't know what to say. She hadn't thought about her mother in that way before.

'You can talk to her about anything. She's so funny.'

Juliette wasn't sure if Mary knew about her mother's sniffing. She thought she may have mentioned it to Mary, but that it had somehow passed over her head, or that she had forgotten it, or had thought she was joking. She couldn't remember if Mary had ever visited their house while her mother was under the glue. Perhaps she'd seen her entranced in her chair with the paper over her nose, and that it had not registered that anything was wrong, that her mother had just fallen asleep while blowing her nose, perhaps. So far, in Wales, she had kept to her promise of not sniffing. Mary had been in the company of undrugged Colette, who was transparent, clear, bright and fast.

'She has her moments,' said Juliette.

'Try living with my mother,' said Mary. Juliette, oddly, had often thought about it. Mary's house was so calm and ordered in comparison to her own. It seemed so plush. The carpets were thick and warm, the armchairs were as soft as sheep. It was a wholesome house, one that had spawned innumerable cakes and loaves. Though never hungry, Juliette often felt that her own house was on the edge of famine. Its larders and cupboards seemed always so depleted, scant, rancid.

They heard the distant scrape and whine of the field gate opening. Instinctively Juliette, once again in possession of the cigarette, flicked its last glowing half an inch over the nearby wall.

'Julie, there might be a sheep over there,' admonished Mary.

Scipio stood up and pointed his tail to the sky; a rope trick.

Mary and Juliette peered out from behind the tent, where they'd concealed themselves, and saw Janus walking across the field towards them, following the faint path that had slowly worn itself into the grass over the days, from the tent to the gate.

He was walking with a casualness that surprised them, as though he was strolling with a dog through a park. He didn't look as though he'd just travelled two hundred and fifty miles from London. He wasn't carrying any luggage with him at all. Not even a coat. Not even a shopping bag or haversack. He was just walking, his jacket unbuttoned, his collar open, swinging his hands, one of which held a cigarette.

He was, in fact, wearing a suit, slightly rumpled but still suave, a dark brown suit with a purple shirt. He had a dishevelled elegance; unshaven, his hair slightly ruffled.

Once, Juliette and Mary had debated which was the handsomest of her brothers (Julian didn't count). Mary found it hard to decide, but Juliette opted for Janus because, she said, 'he can look good even in rags'. The real reason being that she could never concede that James, her closest brother in age, was handsome. But now, as Janus approached, Mary could see what she meant. He did look good, even in rags.

Janus approached the tent cautiously, aware that it had become a feminine space. Two girls and a neutered cat. He greeted Scipio first, lifting the animal to his face. Scipio put his arms around his neck and hugged him. He let him sit on his shoulder like a parrot.

'Howdy brother,' said Juliette.

'Good evening,' said Janus.

Mary didn't say anything, but she laughed.

'Good evening young lady,' Janus said to Mary, looking at her for what seemed to her the first ever time, and then 'the tent looks very big.'

'They've all gone to the village.'

'Scipplepus,' said Janus.

'That's a funny cat,' said Mary.

'I'm bloody thirsty,' said Janus.

Mary took a cup and tipped water from the huge white water carrier into it, offered it to Janus who drank lustily, and when he had drained it, he twirled it up in the air and caught it, like a juggler practising.

Mary gave an awkward laugh, not quite sure what to make of the flamboyant gesture. Janus liked to tie up everything he did with ribbons. The twirling of the cup was a silk knot binding that whole water-drinking episode together. Mary didn't understand this, even though his sentences, his voice, was full of these knots, and everything he did was finished with some sort of flourish. She thought that perhaps he was trying to impress her.

At home Janus had developed the habit of catching things rather than picking them up. Instead of picking the salt packet off the table, for instance, he would, with a flick, let it jump into the air, and then catch it. It irritated his mother, who foresaw but never witnessed many minor accidents – spilt milk, smashed coffee jars, cracked cups.

'Why do you do that?' she once asked him, with a note of pleading in her voice.

He didn't answer. He just laughed, allowing a knife to fly handle first into his hand. That was it, she supposed. It made him feel that things were coming to him. It was a type of magic. He was conducting the movements of small objects by a sleight of hand, imagining himself a sorcerer breathing life into the minerals of a kitchen.

'Could I have another cup of your sweet liquid please, my dear,' Janus said, handing the cup back to Mary.

Mary gave another awkward laugh as she bent to refill Janus's cup, offering him a second glimpse of her shirtfront and the soft, shadowy, deepening skin that lay within it. Janus was shocked by Mary's development, not expecting to find a fully formed, if still unweathered, woman at the tent.

'Thank you my little angel,' he said when the second cup of water was provided.

'Haven't you brought anything with you?' said Juliette.

'Only this,' said Janus, lifting from his pocket, throwing

into the air and catching, a small but thick book that Mary at first thought was a Bible, but was an Edition Eulenburg miniature score of the Bach B minor Mass, 'this is all I need when I travel. I can use it as a hat to hold off the rain' (he demonstrated, making a roof shape with the opened book over his head) 'or to keep off the sun, or to fight off wild beasts' (he took swipes at invisible wolves).

Though he was speaking to Juliette the performance was for Mary, whom he observed out of the corner of his eye. Seeing that she was smiling, he looked directly at her. She brushed midges out of her face. A face suddenly perfect in every detail, Janus thought. Alabaster white, with toffee-coloured eyes, plump, lavender lips. An ideal face. The only thing that spoilt it was the way her ears, little rims of gristly flesh, sometimes poked through the dark curtain of her hair, making her look like a chimp. Aware that this girl had been a visiting presence in the house for some years, he desperately tried to remember her, to pick her face out of the many that drifted in and out of the house, the friends of his younger siblings. Could she really have been that girl in a gymslip he once saw on the lino playing ludo with Juliette? Was she that spindly thing he saw up a plum tree once? Then, peaking into the tent porch, he saw Julian's splodgy portraits of this girl, which were spread out on the shadowy grass. Seeing Mary through Julian's eyes somehow reminded him. Those clumsy noses and ears, the blurred, twisted eyes, blubbery mouths, recalled for him the little girl who had grown up within the range of his indifferent sight.

'I've decided to write a railway symphony,' he said to both girls, 'using the rhythms and sounds one hears on a railway journey.'

'Steam or diesel?' said Mary, surprising Janus, who couldn't answer at first.

'I don't think there's much music in diesels,' said Juliette.

'They go "ee-aww",' said Mary.

'It's a good point,' said Janus, slightly annoyed that the girls had latched on to his idea so quickly, 'diesels are brass —

trombones and trumpets, steam trains are woodwind – flutes and piccolos. I've scored the first movement already, it requires a hundred penny whistles.'

None of this was true. Janus found that the company of Mary caused him to say more and more outlandish things.

'Picture, if you will, the stage at the Royal Festival Hall occupied by a castle class Nigel Gresley steam engine. The driver and fireman are the musicians, who, with the aid of a conveyor belt contraption, drive the steam engine at a variety of stationary speeds.'

There was a tightness around his eyes as he said this, as though he was on the verge of closing them.

'The first movement is marked at 30 mph. A slow movement through the junctions of London Bridge follows. The third movement goes whooosh!'

Mary laughed, but Janus seemed offended. He turned his attention to Scipio, still on his shoulder.

'Did you know this cat is tuned to the key of B flat major?'

There was something about the way Janus said this that unnerved Mary. She felt, somehow, that he had taken offence, and was, with this last remark, setting a little trap for her. If she laughed, it might snap shut around her.

'How do you mean?' she said, treading carefully, sensing immediately that she'd said the right thing.

'If you step on his tail, that's the key he squeals in. I've tested him at the piano. Do you know the key of B flat major? What is its relative minor?'

'I don't know music, really,' said Mary.

'What don't you know?'

'I don't know music.'

'You don't know what key you are in, my dear, do you?'

'My key?'

'Everyone has a key. If I were to step on your tail . . .'

'They'll be back in a minute,' Juliette said, noticing the conversation was becoming pointlessly interrogative, stupidly hostile, and that Mary was becoming scared, 'let's surprise them.'

It was very nearly dark when they dragged sleeping things – sheets, blankets, sleeping bags – across the fields where they soaked up the dew, through the farmyard where they brushed dry muck, to the churchyard where the trio hid. Mary and Juliette draped themselves with bedclothes and waited. Janus watched over the tall burial ground wall. Refusing to get himself up as a ghost, he gave a signal to the girls when he saw the familiar face of the Morris Oxford, a jack-o'-lantern grin turning the dangerous corner. Juliette and Mary wafted into the lane, Janus followed them, stood in between them as the Morris Oxford halted, spread his arms wide in a 'here I am' gesture, but could only see that broad beaming face of the car staring back at him. A great big smile flooding the three with light. Mary and Juliette jumped up and down, two wailing, giggling ice creams, beside Janus, attracting moths.

4

Unglued, the world, for Colette, was lit glass. Daylight came into her eyes with the stealth of knife blades. Air came into her nostrils like the ingress of freezing water. The ordinary world flayed her. All food tasted of acid. She wrapped herself in pullovers, coats and scarves like soft suits of armour to shield her against the too insistent world. One day she left her dark glasses, which muted the white blare of drab daylight, on top of a mountain, and had to buy another pair from The Ginger Boy.

Juliette was in love with The Ginger Boy, although he didn't know this. He was the son of the proprietor of Llanygwynfa-wm-Lledrith's newsagent and post office, three shops down from The Genius. From The Ginger Boy the Joneses bought their newspapers and comics, buckets and spades, shrimping nets, bottles of pop, packets of crisps, bars of chocolate and stamps with little dragons in the corner, who stuck their tongues out behind the Queen's head.

The Ginger Boy had a rotating stand of sunglasses which aching Colette fingered through one morning, until she found a pair that she liked. Mirror sunglasses, two oval mirrors set within a silver frame. She wore these almost continually. Aldous found them very useful for shaving in, telling his wife to keep still while he softly chiselled at his soaped-up face. He took a photo of Colette on the promenade at Aberbreuddwyd, a close-up of her face. When he looked at the developed photo in September he was stunned by the accidental wholeness of the image. Colette's face, her lips heavily painted, full and broad like a negro's, the two big reflecting lenses of her shades making her seem like a huge wasp. The left mirror reflected Aldous taking the photo, his own eyes concealed – one behind the viewfinder, the other clenched shut. His hair was wild, frozen in a moment of breeziness. In the other mirror were reflected Juliette, Julian and James, the two older kids seated precariously on the white railings above the sea, waving frantically, the younger holding his hair as if afraid it might blow away.

For nearly two weeks Colette had been without glue. She felt there was a chance if she could keep herself busy. The only way she could possibly manage without glue, she thought, was if she climbed a mountain every day. The project absorbed enough of her imagination and energy to distract her from the temptations of scent. The planning and preparation of an ascent required concentration and memory. The climb itself needed energy, clearness of thought, coordination. The weather held good for the whole holiday. The descent of cloud and confinement to the fields could easily have led Colette back to her Romac. But the mountains were clear, bright slopes for three weeks, and she climbed. Everyone climbed. They scaled the headless Sphinx of Cnicht, which caused Janus to contrive stupid sentences around the peak's name with which he taunted Mary. 'Can I canoe you up Cnicht?' 'Can we connect on Cnicht?' Mary tried to walk ahead of him. So persistent were his taunts that at one point she expelled a brief flurry of silver tears, which had Colette scolding her son.

'Is that all you've come here for, to upset the poor girl?'

Janus had looked deeply bewildered and even a little frightened at Mary's weeping.

'I didn't even know she was here. I'd forgotten she was coming with you.'

'Well if you try anything like that again you can go straight back to London. You don't seem to be enjoying yourself much here anyway. I don't know why you bothered coming.'

Colette had been overjoyed when Janus had shown up at the farm. It would have been his third year of absence had he not come and she was worried that he might never come again. But her joy soon waned. Janus now seemed oddly out of place holidaying with his family. There didn't seem to be anywhere he could fit in. When they sat down for dinner in the evening Janus ate his standing up. He would go off for walks on his own without telling anyone, or wander off late at night into the darkness.

Mary was now out of earshot. Having composed herself she was scrabbling through heathery boulders with Juliette and James.

'I didn't do anything. I was just teasing her.'

'Try and remember she's only thirteen. If you must practise chatting up girls pick on someone your own age for Christ's sake, and preferably someone who's not related to you.'

The reference to Christine brought a silent sneer from Janus.

'You don't have to worry about me and Mary,' he said, having dropped behind his mother a few yards, 'I have no taste for virgins.'

Snowdon was climbed, where a superb coincidence meant that the Joneses met their cousins the Maguires, children of Agatha, Colette's sister, who'd ascended by train, not the Miners' Track. Mark, Paul, and Douglas had all grown Zapata moustaches. With Judy and Kevin they came back to the tent for an evening of sausages and wine. Julian was amazed by the amount of food the boys swallowed. When, last year, Agatha had moved house, she had bequeathed to Colette a little stash of crockery. Plates, saucers and cups. He remembered his mother setting them out on the kitchen table like a stock of trophies, looking at them closely, admiring them. They were all pure, plain white, trimmed with gold leaf that had faded and flaked a little. They amazed Julian for two reasons. The first was the fact that, though clearly from the wear on the glaze they were well used and had fed an entire family of burly boys and a hefty girl for maybe a decade, there wasn't a chip or crack anywhere. For the Joneses, sets of crockery were always mongrels, hybrids, composites of sets bought and broken over the years. Their dinners were served on mosaics of crockery – Midwinter, Apache; there was even a cup of wedding day Royal Doulton that had somehow survived through to their twenty-fifth anniversary.

The other reason was their size. No one in the family had experienced crockery of that size before, dinner plates of that diameter, cups so deep.

'You can see,' said James, twirling rather daringly a plate between his fingers, looking a little accusingly at his mother, 'the sort of meals they're used to getting from Agatha.'

'No wonder they all play rugby.'

'Including Judy.'

'They're good plates,' said Colette, surprise in her voice.

To Julian it looked like the crockery of giants.

The Joneses climbed mountains with a peculiar frenzy that summer, together and alone, on screes and outcrops, on gorsey slopes, in ruined valleys heaped with marble, in echoey chasms and bilberry-thick foothills. They climbed mountains as though afraid the mountains wouldn't be there next year, as though the mountains might move. – Rhinog Fawr, Glyder Fach, Aran Fawddwy, Moelwyn Mawr.

James made a solo assault on Moelfre. He followed the long, haunted lane that went creepily straight between an avenue of sweet chestnuts and, later, through dark woods, towards Llwydiarth Hall, past a farm of invisible, shrieking animals, and then on to a track that led through open countryside, across heathery fields. On Moelfre's western slopes he walked diagonally across tilting, mossy grass, found the wall that from the farm looked like a hairline, found it was made of massive boulders, wondered why this should have surprised him, and followed it uphill.

At the summit, alone, James noticed the hugeness of a cloud that had just come in from the sea. The size of a city, it appeared suddenly like a solid object, an enormous, floating hunk of rock, turning the landscape black with its shadow, which rose up the hillside, as if the mountain were a glass vessel filling with a dark liquid. James thought that the cloud and its shadow would both knock him down. So he ran down the hillside, alone through the shadow, running nearly all the way back along the track, frightened to look back at the lowering hill.

On reaching the farm (which he'd seen from the summit, their tents like scraps of confetti in the field) he looked back at Moelfre and wondered how the might of that hill had been squashed down, now, to so small a size, or how he had managed to grow from the black dot that he was when he was up there. What disturbed him most was the realization that he had left his binoculars up there. It gave him the feeling that he was being watched, that he was under constant surveillance.

He had given the mountain eyes with which to watch him, as had Colette, who'd left her first sunglasses on the meringue peaked Cadair foothill called Craig-y-Castell (anglicized to Craggy Castle). Other things were forgotten on the tops of mountains. Janus left a cloth-bound Bartholomew map on top of Craig-las. Aldous left his car keys on top of the Bird Rock. There must be something about the summits of mountains, thought Aldous, climbing a mountain twice in a day, that induces forgetfulness. At the summit of a mountain, it is as though the whole world has shrunk to the size of a garden, or something smaller, a mere pointed patch of grass and rock. A mountain summit is a moment of awful transition, where land that had been endlessly soaring now falls. It is the conclusion of a tumultuous event in the landscape. Its finish. This, combined with vistas of such boundlessness, can easily upset one's sense of time, can loosen one's grip on the world. Maps and keys are easily forgotten.

The ascent of Tryfan, a gloomy, triple-headed mass of

shattered rock, became an absurd comedy, the mountain a stage, its crevices, paths, screes all platforms on which the family suddenly found themselves acting out parts. Thus when Colette rested on a rock she was suddenly alarmed by the fact that the little rock formation on which she was seated looked very like a granite suite of dining-room furniture – a table and chairs. James perpetually took paths that led up blind defiles and bluffs with a sheer wall of rock at the end on which it was impossible to gain a single foot or handhold. The mountain continually offered terraces of rock which were a great temptation to climb, which James and Janus often did, in their slippery, ordinary shoes. Julian was delighted by the vast lumps of raw marble that he kept finding. One piece, as big as a house, seemed an impossibly rich find. 'Why can't we take some with us?' he kept saying. 'Dad, can't we take some marble with us, we'd be very rich.' Marble, to him, was of the same family as gold. To him it was as though they were climbing a mountain of pure gold.

They were looked down upon, often literally, by serious mountaineers, bearded men tubby with thermal clothing, who from beneath their lacquered crash helmets cast scornful looks in their direction. They were not dressed properly – Aldous in his grey jacket with sharpened pencils peeking above the lip of his breast pocket, the not quite matching grey trousers which were tucked, as though in cycling mode, into his grey socks. His black brogues. Colette in the green, fluffy aura of a cashmere pullover and blue nylon trousers with elasticated stirrup loops at the cuffs. Hooked over her forearm a white handbag with a long handle, which swung about awkwardly as she climbed in her beige suede shoes. Janus wearing his suit, his only clothing, James in his school uniform.

In this guise, half way up Tryfan, they came face to face with climbers decked with ropes and hooks, a butcher's shop of pitons and crampons hanging from their waists, clumpy boots and waterproof windcheaters.

'That's a young lad to be up a mountain like this,' the mountaineer said, nodding in the direction of Julian, happy in his chocolate-coloured anorak, straddling a boulder like a horse.

'He has mountains in his blood,' said Colette.

The man gave a patronizing laugh then, from his standing position, fell over backwards, and had to be helped up by two colleagues. In the fall he'd cut his hand, which offered Colette the opportunity to say 'Whereas you have left your blood in the mountain.'

The Joneses cast disdainful looks upon all mountaineers.

Two thirds of the way up, however, they lost the path and had to search for a route upwards, finding one, after many blind alleys ('Juliette, come back, you're heading for a precipice!'), that involved the scaling of a thin, steep ravine, a crack in the side of the mountain, which meant each offering hand-ups to the one behind, or providing footholds for the one in front. At one point, to a distant observer, it might have seemed that the family had formed a tower, each standing on the head of the one below, like a living totem pole.

Julian became thirsty. Janus reached into his pocket and produced a handful of bilberries, which he'd been gathering all the way up, and told Julian to eat some, as they were very thirst quenching. Julian didn't argue, although his tongue turned purple.

Whenever he could manage it, Janus followed Mary, especially when she was climbing. Scaling a tricky slope he could position himself so that his face was a mere two inches from her buttocks, or, on the more perilous, vertical climbs, his lips might come to within an inch of her undisclosed nipple. He enjoyed being so close to her when she was climbing. Her buttocks clenched and unclenched with a voluptuous firmness as she strained for footholds, reached for ledges, lifted herself. At one point, during a steep climb, his face was so close to Mary's bottom that he managed to plant, unseen by anyone and unfelt (he prayed) by Mary, a light kiss on her left buttock. It was ultimately a disappointing kiss, however, because there was no sense of flesh in it, just the rough texture of new denim. It was just like kissing a pair of trousers.

The summit of Tryfan was marked by two standing stones, like uprights from Stonehenge, side by side. These twin monoliths were known as Adam and Eve. As such they were probably the most abstract representations of the human figure ever cut into rock. Which one was Adam, which was Eve, Colette wondered? Two identical blocks of Ordovician rock. Yet there was something, if one looked long enough, about their shape. The slightly bulging waist of the one on the left, the taller, squarer stance of the other did perhaps suggest an ancient husband and wife. As the human family posed for photos against the granite one, James and Janus standing on top of the stones themselves, like sculptors who'd carved an entire mountain, Colette wished she had some device, some timer or something, that would allow everyone to be in the picture. She didn't have an entire picture of her family, because there was always one of them, usually herself, behind the camera. She would have asked someone, but they were alone up there.

Briefly, as Colette watched through the little hall of mirrors that was her camera's viewfinder her family posing amongst oblong rocks, she had a most disturbing sensation. She thought, for a moment, that she didn't know any of these people; the tweedy, dishevelled man with greying hair and a cigarette in his mouth, the young men in smart clothes, the two teenage girls, the little boy. She wondered why she was taking a photograph of them, or why they seemed so at ease in her company. But the moment in which these people were strangers was short, a passing cloud of non-recognition casting its shadow, and after it had passed she saw them again as her own family.

5

The return to Fernlight Avenue after three weeks' absence in midsummer was always to a garden of dizzy voluptuousness. Entering the kitchen they were taken aback by the thickening of greenery beyond the windows. The lawn would be a yard high with hay, the trees would be scraping the windows and would have unloaded their fruit on to the ground. Walking into the garden they would tread on fermenting apples and plums as though they were pebbles. The roses would have bloomed and fallen, leaving puddles of pink petals on the grass, and the lower end of the garden, where it narrowed to an avenue between soft fruits, would be impenetrable, the blackberries and the raspberries having closed the gap between themselves.

The lushness of the growths they encountered helped confuse their sense of time passing, because they seemed out of proportion with the actual time elapsed. It was as though, in Wales, they'd put a foot in eternity, never endingness, and they'd come back a year later. Julian was especially confused. When he returned from Wales he always thought he was a year older. He'd managed to think of the holiday in Wales and his birthday, which was in January, as the same thing.

Usually this was all put right by a vigorous session of

gardening, during which Aldous would arm himself with shears, secateurs and a blunt, rusted lawnmower and set about cropping everything in sight, producing a harvest of heaped grass, fronds, and dead fruit which he would pile at the end of the garden – a small, soft, fermenting mountain, which Julian and Juliette climbed on, but which somehow had always disappeared by spring.

This year, however, he failed. They'd returned from Wales at the last moment, the day before school began. The next few weeks were too busy with chores for anything to be done about the garden. It thickened a little more during September, but then it began to die, and so nothing was done about it. Not until the end of autumn did it become usable, when the screen of leaves against the windows began to clear, and the far end of the garden became visible. Juliette found the first growth of a horse chestnut sapling she and James had planted the previous year down there. They were almost hysterical with triumphant delight, but Aldous inwardly moaned. Another tree to deal with. How would he cut it down without hurting them? How long before the neighbours complained about blocked sunlight, or the garden itself became a darkly canopied forest?

In November, Juliette and Julian visited Carnival Cycles in The Parade. The Parade was two parallel strips of shops separated by a main road. It had two churches, a police station, and a derelict cinema. There was an ironmongers, an estate agent, two chemists, three newsagents, two bakers, a grocer's and a couple of restaurants. Carnival Cycles was at one end, next to Medlock's, where the Joneses sometimes bought paraffin.

Julian wasn't sure why they were going to Carnival Cycles, but followed his sister into the shop anyway. He didn't like it. It was gloomy and there was a strong smell of machinery. It reminded him of the spooky parts of Battersea Funfair. There were bicycles everywhere, forming huge spiders' webs of metal all around him. There were children's tricycles (he'd grown out of these), boys' racers, adult touring bikes, racks of tyres and accessories. The floor was wooden and greasy. There was no one else in the shop apart from the man behind the counter, who was filthy with bicycle oil, his shirt torn and blackened. He was fiddling with nuts and bolts and didn't notice the children until Juliette spoke.

'Excuse me,' she said.

The man looked up. He wore glasses that reduced his eyes to little points of colour.

'Yes, my darling, what can I do for you?'

'If a lady comes in here to buy glue, could you please not sell it to her?'

The man looked puzzled, and then half smiled, not sure if he'd understood.

'Come again.'

'If a lady . . .'

'What lady? Any lady?'

'No, she looks like . . . what does Mummy look like Julian?' (Julian didn't seem to know.) 'She's got long reddish-brown hair and she's quite tall and she wears a green coat.'

'Got it. And what was the other bit?'

'If she tries to buy any puncture glue, could you please not sell her any.'

'Yes, that's the bit I didn't understand. Why not?'

'Because she mustn't have any.'

'Mustn't have any?'

'No.'

'Shall I ask why not?'

'It makes her go funny and it's making her ill.'

'I see,' the man said, returning his attention to the gadgets in his hand.

'Okay?' said Juliette.

'Yes,' said the man, rummaging now through a box of bolts.

The two children paused for a moment, as if expecting some more solid commitment from the shopkeeper, but he seemed to have forgotten their presence, and so they left.

1969

1

Aldous's last will and testament, a document that so far existed only in his head, contained many unusual stipulations, bequests and requests – that Janus should not inherit the piano unless he become a teacher of music, that the house should become a retreat for distressed artists, that all his paintings should go to Lesley Waugh, and that his body should be cremated and its ashes scattered about the seven fields of Llanygwynfa. Or they should be mixed with malt and formed into pellets to be tipped into the bin in the cow house that held the cattle nuts. That would be most fitting, he thought, to be consumed by the cows, to turn those gentle, shy creatures into rapacious flesh eaters. To fall so deeply into grass. Or his ashes should be mashed with the sand on the beach and made into a sandcastle and he would sit, flags planted about his battlemented head and experience the tidal disintegration that is the fall of all sandcastles. It would be a way of gatecrashing the exclusivity of the ancient burial sites to which he could not gain legitimate access without first being a living resident. He felt that three weeks in August for nearly fifteen years, even if it was in a field in a flimsy house of cotton, qualified him, at least in part, for some form of burial rights. Not that he considered seriously the possibility of cremation. To dedicate one's body to the industrial voracious-ness of a furnace and atomize instantly one's physical presence in the world, even though he wasn't born a Catholic, went against the lingering belief he felt for the possibility of physical resurrection. He'd seen, on a recent visit to the Tate, that great vision of the resurrection Stanley Spencer had painted. If resurrection was going to happen, of course that was how it would be – a slow awakening, groggy, yawning, stretching, blinking, bleary-eyed, still in our grave clothes, still with dirt on us. How would resurrection be possible for people whose bodies had been reduced to little pots of cinders? It was in these little details that Aldous's faith was most severely tested. Increasingly he felt a need to know exactly how the life to come would work. What food would there be in heaven? Did the dead feel hungry? Did they have a sense of smell?

He watched his wife emerge from the tent, as groggy as a new-born butterfly. She'd been lying down and her hair was big and fluffy from her repose. She was wearing a thigh-length sleeveless dress covered in large, brilliant white daisies on a blue background. She was holding the pad to her nose and her white handbag was swinging from her other forearm. She had that deliberate walk she always had when drugged, as though it was a process she was trying hard to remember. Her feet were lifted an inch or two higher than necessary, as if treading uneven ground. She was heading across the field to nowhere, away from the farm, towards a wall. Aldous watched her, barely able to comprehend, for a moment, that this figure was his wife. Everything about her had been altered – the shape of her body, the colour of her hair, her way of walking. She had thoroughly disguised herself. Her thinness was shocking and gave her a masculine angularity. It made her feet look enormous. There was an abrasiveness to her body, a sand-papery roughness that made her unpleasant to touch.

Aldous had not made love to her that summer. He wasn't sure when they'd last had sex. Perhaps at Easter. Even then he'd noticed the hardness of her body. It was as though she was setting, like ice. And there was a chemical odour of glue always about her, on her clothes, in her breath. Kissing her was a fumy, headachy experience. Her face now displayed too much bone structure; deep creases had developed around her eyes. The eyes themselves had withdrawn, very slightly, as though shy of the light, into her head. It made Aldous think of the way a snail will retract, fold and tuck itself into a crisp shell. Her mouth, with its twin rows of synthetic teeth, had become large and carnivorous looking. Her temples were little sunken pits either side of her head.

Aldous wasn't sure if this thinness was related to her sniffing of glue. Was it that she had lost interest in food? She was a good cook of wholesome, flavoursome meals. She relished rich sauces and thick gravies, sweet pies, bread. Her Sunday roasts came from the oven like crocks of hot jewellery, glistening, shiny. She had a constant battle with Aldous's taste buds, which hadn't developed with his other senses. To Aldous all food could be divided into three types – salty, sweet and tasteless. Mostly it was tasteless and it was a chore to have to put it into one's body. Food didn't vary within these categories. All salty food was salty in the same way. Vainly Colette tried to waken Aldous's tongue, spiking her Sunday roasts with garlic, a flavour he particularly disliked. For Aldous a roast chicken seasoned with garlic was rendered uneatable. They rowed about it. Colette would protest that it was only the slightest hint of garlic, that she'd only wiped the raw skin of the bird with half a clove.

'But you know I don't like it,' Aldous would say, 'why do you do it when you know I don't like it?'

'Because I like it and I want you to like it. I want us to like it together.'

'You can eat it if you want, but leave my food alone.'

'You're killing my joy in food.'

'You're poisoning me with that stuff.'

Garlic became a sticking point in their marriage. Janus aligned himself with his mother by developing an ostentatious taste for the food. He liked to eat it raw.

'You're turning my son against me.'

'Thank God he hasn't inherited his father's tongue.'

What had gone wrong with the boy? He would carefully peel three cloves and slice them with a Stanley knife blade to a transparent thinness, and put them in a sandwich. He would munch this odorous snack and talk loudly afterwards, filling the kitchen with his sharp breath. Aldous would have to leave. He would sit in the front room beneath the starfish of his tie-dyed curtains and have to shut the door to keep the smell out. Aldous couldn't go near the piano after Janus had been playing. The house became segregated by odour.

But now it seemed that Colette had lost interest in flavour as well. The meals she'd prepared for her family recently were basic and frugal – luncheon meat with Smash and tinned peas. Tyne Brand Irish Stew. Goblin hamburgers. Fried rissoles. These tinned, frozen or dried foods had slowly replaced the casseroles and stews that Colette had produced with such panache throughout their marriage. Quite often Colette was not in a fit state to prepare (cook wasn't the right word) these meals. Aldous was then left to twist the wings of a butterfly tin opener around the rim of a can, or prise the key off a tin of corned beef and unlock the salted meat. Sometimes he wasn't available and so the children got their own food. Occasionally Aldous would cook his speciality, the only thing he could cook with any confidence – chips.

It occurred to him that these perfunctory, cold meals she cooked at home now were the meals they'd always eaten at Llanygwynfa. In fact she tried to make her dinners more appealing to her disappointed family by drawing on their sentimentality – *but you like it when we have it at the farm* . . . It was as though she was trying to reproduce the cuisine of the fields in the kitchen at Fernlight Avenue.

But if Colette's thinness wasn't to do with her lost desire for food, what might that glue be drawing out of her body? He thought of that glue pad, latched securely to her nose, as a wicked pink creature sucking his wife's selfhood out through her nostrils. She was the empty cup of the woman she'd been.

The most difficult thing for Aldous was having no one to

talk to about it. If he tried, people thought he was either joking or mad. Even doctors thought this. He'd tried with their own doctor, during a visit about a rash.

'By the way, I was mending a puncture the other night and I inhaled rather a lot of the glue – you know that glue you get with puncture outfits? Could that be dangerous?'

'It might give you a headache, nothing more.'

'Even if I inhaled it for a long period?'

'But why should you?'

'If I had a lot of punctures to mend.'

'As long as you do it in a well-ventilated room, or outdoors, there should be no problem.'

Dr Low had been their doctor since Janus was born. He had leathery, deeply creased skin and crinkly, greying hair. Skin and hair somehow combined to make Aldous think of a living, human-sized cigar, burning contentedly.

'Supposing I forgot to open the windows?'

Dr Low seemed amused.

'Do you have a lot of bicycles, Mr Jones? I thought you were an . . . Oh, you cycle a lot don't you, to Wales every year, and the children as well, how are Janus and, er . . .'

'You know that saying, "Mad as a hatter"? Didn't that come from something to do with milliners inhaling spirit . . .'

'I think it did,' said Dr Low, moving things around on his desk, tapping himself into an ashtray, 'though I shouldn't worry about your punctures. You'd have to inhale a great deal of the fumes to do yourself any harm . . .'

'What sort of harm?'

'Well, you'd end up as mad as a hatter I suppose.'

They both laughed, and Aldous could see his doctor had no idea.

'You're an artist aren't you?'

'Well, I teach art . . .'

'I've been doing some painting myself.'

'Have you?'

'A bowl of chrysanthemums, and a view of Holland.'

The doctor then scuttled to a corner of his surgery and

produced two canvases, clumsily executed paintings-by-numbers, and asked Aldous for his opinion. The doctor didn't mention that they were by numbers, and Aldous wondered if he was trying to fool Aldous into thinking they were all his own work.

Colette had made several attempts to give up sniffing. Earlier in the year she had managed to do without glue for six weeks. She had also got the sleeping pills under control, rarely taking any during the daytime. She took six at night, at about 8 pm, and spent two hours slowing down until she would crawl on all fours to bed, there to spend a night in motionless but noisy sleep to wake slowly the next day. But at other times she seemed continually entranced within the glue's influence. Sometimes she even sniffed in public places. In June she'd ridden the underground across London to visit Agatha, taking Julian and one of Aldous's paintings Agatha had bought (*A Smaller Cornfield*). Aldous had heard from Julian how Colette and his painting had fallen the length of the down escalator at Wood Green. At Rayners Lane she'd been gluing a pad on her lap when Julian had told her the train was coming, and in her hurry she muddled her folding and got glue all over her fingers.

As Aldous watched his wife staggering across the field towards nothing in particular he thought about the times she'd run away. It had happened on several occasions since she'd begun sniffing. Colette had taken her family's constant pleas for her to give up the drug as a criticism of her as a person. As a mother. These discussions usually turned into arguments, name-calling, door-slamming.

'Since you clearly regard me as deficient as a mother, wife, lover, cook and everything else, I have decided to leave,' she said one evening at the end of a dinner which had, for once, been exquisitely made.

Janus was on a late shift. Three children and Aldous were her audience. The evenings had become performances for Colette. She acted out a tragedy each night detailing in howling, tortured sentences how she had been betrayed: by her mother, by her friends, by her sister, her husband, her children, her pets. 'You, you have all conspired against me' (to her children). 'You are all interlopers. We didn't ask for your advice. Your father and I were in love long before you were even thought of. What gives you the right to tell me how I should conduct my marriage? I give birth to a pretty but harmless ball of fat, ten years later it has grown eyes and a tongue which it uses to tell me how to live my life. I suppose you wanted a mother like Mrs Peck or Madeleine. You're ashamed of me.' (Tears now came, such ordinary tears they were not seen.) As her sleeping pills took hold her speech became a slowly flowing undercurrent, a muddy stream of morose, accusatory language. She began placing her stresses in awkward places, her pronouns would be followed by long pauses. 'You . . . have no idea what it . . . is like to lose . . .' The vitriolic nastiness of her monologue increased as the evening progressed, and she would save her most stabbing comments for the moments shortly before her unconsciousness: 'Do you know' (to Julian) 'what your father said to me in bed last night,' her eyes would be closed by this time, her words barely audible, 'he said, and I quote, "I wish we'd never had Julian."'

Aldous, who was filling the sink with dirty dishes, said, 'What a terrible thing to say.'

'Absolutely, well, I don't know, what a thing for a father to say about his son.'

Mealtimes had once been the scene of lively discussions. For an hour after the meal was finished the family would continue sitting around the table discussing politics, space travel, art, Kafka . . .

It surprised Aldous how quickly the children lost sympathy for their mother, how swiftly they grew to a cynical dismissal of her complaints. They began laughing and jeering at her. Colette had decided to make a great display of her exit. She carefully packed the brown leather suitcase that had for a decade and a half conveyed her dresses to Wales, and she put on her viridian PVC overcoat with buttons the size of old pennies, wrapped a headscarf around her sprayed hair and said individual goodbyes to her family, who were still sitting around the kitchen table. 'Goodbye James, I know you'll grow up to be an intelligent man.' 'Goodbye mother, don't hurry back.' 'Goodbye Juliette, I hope you'll be good.' 'Grow up Mum.' 'Goodbye Julian,' she said, bending down, pressing his forehead against her cheek in the way that she took his temperature. Julian was crying and had been ever since Colette had announced her departure. 'I don't want you to go, Mum,' he blubbed. James laughed. Juliette snapped at her little brother, 'Stop crying for God's sake, she's not really going away, she just trying to get our attention. Don't you remember the last time she did it?'

It had become a fairly regular occurrence. Each one was like a rehearsal for the time when she would actually leave, each succeeding departure a little more realistic than the last. It was as though she was acting out these departures in order to feel what it would really be like to leave her family. To let her family know what it would really be like. The first few times they had pleaded with her to stay, placated her, appeased her. They quickly saw through the games she was playing, however, and now treated these theatrical exits with contempt. Once, as his mother was departing, James managed to stick a sign on her back which read 'Lost Property'.

It was usually down to Aldous to persuade his wife to stay. Nothing he could say stopped her, but just the gentle holding of her arm and drawing her back into the house was usually enough. This time, however, he decided to let her go.

He was slightly cross with her. That morning he'd been sitting in the kitchen reading the newspaper, when Colette had quietly walked over and, for no reason at all, hit him across the face as hard as she could. Her blow came through the newspaper, as it were, so that it felt to him as though the *Daily Telegraph* had punched him in the face.

'Why did you do that?' he said, holding the side of his face.

'Do what? What did you feel?' said Colette, bending over, leaning into his face.

'What do you mean?'

'Did you feel something?'

'What's the matter with you?'

'Tell me what you mean, did you feel something? What happened?'

It turned out that Colette, out of glue, had been sniffing furniture polish that morning. There was a tin of it in the house, a circular, shallow tin whose lid came off with the aid of a riveted-on lever, to reveal a creamy, violet coloured, waxy substance. The odour from this was spirity and attractive, so Colette filled some lavatory paper with it and sniffed. The effect was quite different. Instead of peculiar dreams and sensations of flight there came sudden short bursts of violence, screams, and then intense interrogations. Even Colette could see that this was dangerous territory and she never sniffed furniture polish again. It had coloured the whole day and led eventually to Colette's exit that evening.

She was going to stay with Agatha in Ickenham. 'I won't kiss you goodbye,' she said to Aldous as she opened the front door, 'I don't want to leave any marks on your face.' She left.

James pierced a milk bottle top repeatedly with a needle until it looked like the skeleton of a leaf. Juliette leafed through one of her mother's magazines. Julian sobbed quietly, asking periodically, 'Do you think she'll come back?' 'Yes,' the others replied, with bored certainty.

Aldous finished washing up, quickly dried his hands and said, 'I'd better go after her.'

'She'll come home by herself,' said James, 'it'll be "I missed the last bus".'

Aldous went anyway. He found her at the bus stop at the bottom of the road. There had been time for three buses to pass. She was standing alone at the stop. Her mascara had run down her face like the markings of a cheetah. When they re-entered the house her glasses steamed up. When she told them she'd missed the bus her children laughed loudly.

Now Colette had reached the end of the field, arriving at a

wall. Aldous had watched her journey, her elegant stagger, across the grass to nowhere. At the wall she stopped, as if surprised there wasn't a way through. She began feeling the wall, as though looking for a door. Aldous walked over and led her back to the tent by her arm. She walked sideways, crab-like, the paper to her face all the way.

Colette always brought lots of books on holiday, mostly thick Victorian novels – *The Mystery of Edwin Drood*, *The Mill on the Floss*, *Jude the Obscure*, and books she'd been reading and rereading since childhood – Ernest Thompson Seton's *Wild Animals I Have Known* with its anthropomorphic yarns about Raggylug, Lobo, Bingo and Wully. Usually she brought one large book for pressing flowers in. Flowers, leaves, grasses, Welsh petals, mountain sedges, mosses, all were compressed between two pages of these hefty books and transported back to London where they were put back into the shelves of a bookcase and then forgotten about, sometimes for years, so that they were only retrieved, if ever, by accident, slipping out like little waifs, falling feather-like to the floor. By then the source of the pressed vegetation would be a mystery – were these flattened feverfews from Wales, Suffolk or the Chilterns? The flowers became anonymous and weightless. The vague plans Colette had of making collages from them were never realized.

This year for the purpose she brought along a heavy hardback coffee-table book called *Champion Dogs of the World*, over a hundred pages of canine colour plates depicting prize-winning best of breeds. An ideal book for pressing flowers.

While the rest of the family were climbing a mountain somewhere, Colette sat in the tent, a pad of glue with her, leafing through those dogs, carefully posed in wild or artificial landscapes – the bouvier de Flandres like a Suffolk church tower, the puli like a rag mop, the shih tzu with a head at both ends. She treasured this book of supreme dogs because she knew personally the borzoi on page eighty-two, whose streamlined profile was posed in a stretch of bright winter parkland. It was Kwango, Vivienne's dog. It was the dog that had playfully plopped its paws in front of Vivienne's horse causing its successful estrapade, the graceful flight of her friend over the horse's lowered head, over the dog which cowered and watched with moon eyes Vivienne's passing body, which smashed head first on to the driveway of ridged concrete. Why hadn't anyone foreseen that this perfect dog would bring about such a violent downfall? Kwango had been Vivienne's crowning achievement, a perfect specimen (her lineage had been plagued by faults – undershot teeth, poor coats), but Kwango was perfect in every detail. It was as though, in producing the supreme borzoi, Vivienne's life's work was over, and so it ended. Colette still felt her best friend's death as a physical pain, a sour sensation in her throat. She also felt, in spite of herself, betrayed. Vivienne had always said she wanted to die young. Colette couldn't help feeling that Viv had got her way, and had left her behind.

Vivienne and Colette both had a terror of growing old. When they were children they made a pact. She remembered it clearly. They were sitting under the dining-room table which, with its down-to-the-floor tablecloth, was like a little house. Not unlike a tent, it suddenly struck Colette. Not unlike a tent at all, with its flimsy floral walls.

Colette and Vivienne sometimes spent hours in this domestic bivouac. Family life continued around them, indifferent to their presence, visible only as feet to the girls, audible as voices or the soft knocking of crockery on their rooftop. In this space they sealed a pact to die young and violently. They exchanged imaginary blood (having pierced their thumbs with imaginary knives). Colette wanted to be killed in a racing car at Le Mans. Vivienne wanted to fall to a sniper's bullet during the English Revolution (the Russian Revolution was still a much talked about event, though the girls understood little of its politics). Now Colette was left to grow old alone.

She considered her book, a gift from Vivienne three Christmases ago, a memorial to her friend, and now she was going to write a poem in memory of Vivienne on one of the blank endpapers. She inhaled her glue as she wrote.

Bat and Cat

A bat is a flying cat,
A cat is a creeping bat.
Two opposites and yet
They both attract.
The flying cat,
The creeping bat.

After writing her poem she had no memory of doing so. A few days later she pressed some oak and beech leaves in the book, put a stone weight on it. The poem was preserved with the leaves. When the book was taken home at the end of the holiday it was put on the floor behind one of Meg's enormous red armchairs, along with some of the other big books of the house. It remained there, unopened, for many years.

2

Here is one of James and Juliette's schemes for becoming rich. They noticed that since the modern tent had been invented (when, they wondered, and by whom?) it had been available in only two colours – white or green. True, horrible tents were coming into existence that did their best to be soft versions of suburban bungalows with curtained, leaded fenestration, window boxes, and even things that resembled chimneys, that were in vivid oranges and blues (designed to provide as much contrast as possible with grass, thus avoiding the problem that traditional tent owners always face – losing one's tent in a green field and having to feel all over the sward for it), however, no one had yet come up with a patterned or illustrated tent. How starkly would a tent embroidered with the Mona Lisa stand out. How distinguished would a tent of zebra stripes or leopard spots be. They would set up the first psychedelic tent company manufacturing spotted or swirly tents, *trompe l'œil* tents that looked like open gates, or awful holes in the ground. Tents that looked like cows, like purple cows, like green and purple cows. Tents that look like erupting volcanoes, like the Pyramids of Giza, like rockets. A tent that looked like the mushroom cloud of a nuclear explosion.

James always felt, when they arrived at the farm each year, safe from nuclear attack. It was a great relief. In London their house sat under an immovable cloud of violent intent. Any of the tiny silver planes that could sometimes be seen from the back garden cruising the breathable limits of the atmosphere might be carrying the city's doom within its hold. A bomb as bright as the sun. They were on the map.

But in Wales they were beyond the interest of international wars. Who would want to waste their bombs on these hills? James wondered if they would even know if there were a nuclear war. The nearest bomb would land on Birmingham, a hundred miles away behind the mountains. What would they see of a bomb landing there? Summer lightning in the sky? A faint murmur of thunder? A breeze?

The whole holiday might pass without them knowing. The Evanses had no TV or radio and never bought newspapers. He tried hard imagining, one afternoon at the beach, what it would be like to return home when there'd been a nuclear war in their absence. When would they first notice something had happened?

The Welsh hills would be unaffected. At Knighton they might notice the leaves on the oaks had turned brown. At Bromyard they might wonder why all the sheep and cows were asleep. At Stratford there would be many burnt trees. In Buckinghamshire the grass would be cindery. The Chilterns would be black, treeless ranges. Happy in their car and tanned, their tent strapped to the roof rack, everything covered with sand, they would drive through a barren, burnt-out wilderness. Hemel Hempstead, St Albans, Potters Bar, through these towns now no more than grey stains on the ground. They would stare round-eyed from the windows like the animals in the ark. At Cockfosters, once the gateway to the city, most northerly outpost of the Piccadilly Line whose underground station was like a little metropolitan fortress at the edge of the city, they would find instead the crater rim. Before them a cliff, and then a smoking, volcanic plain twenty feet below.

But in Wales a breeze, a glow in the air, nothing else. In

Wales they were safe from burning. The wind always came in from the sea. They would be upwind of the great storm. They would even be safe from fallout. Endless pure water to drink in the mountains. Livestock to live on for years. It could go on for ever. A nuclear war would mean for them an endless holiday.

But the prospect of an endless holiday was less attractive now than it once was for Juliette and James. They envied Janus his absence, his commitment to work, his independent money. Still at International House it seemed unlikely he would be coming to the farm that summer, although he had said he would if he could. Colette had wanted to persuade him to come, but Aldous had stopped her, saying that their eldest son had outgrown the farm. It was true that last summer he'd seemed awkwardly out of place and rather unhappy, spending much of the time in sulky silences when not making clumsy attempts to woo thirteen-year-old Mary. In the end Colette had to concede that the farm was a more relaxing and happy place without Janus. Juliette and James, however, tried to make up for him in sulkiness. Anxious to outgrow the farm they would photograph each other looking downcast and bored by rockpools. James would pose in his leather waistcoat and Chelsea boots on the screes of Rhinog Fach, looking meanly disdainful, and Juliette would look wanton and sullen by the brimming streams that spilt down the side of Moelwyn Bach. Sometimes they would spend a day at Aberbreuddwyd, leaving the boredom of mountains to Julian and Aldous, and go instead to the town's one amusement arcade to sit on the floor by the town's only juke box, inspiring awe in the local boys who'd never seen jeans of such frayed thinness on a girl before. The local boys sat on the floor as well, as though they'd always sat on the floor at the back of the amusement arcade. Juliette and James knew, however, that they'd started the fashion in Aberbreuddwyd for sitting on the floor. They played 'Honky Tonk Women' and smoked a communal Senior Service.

The evenings, however, were long and tedious. They spent half the holiday devising a plan for prising the money out of the honesty box at the beach car park, and one dusk went down there with a starting handle smuggled out of the back of the Morris Oxford, which wasn't strong enough to break the latch on the box. They would sometimes walk after dark across the farmlands, and lurk around the fields where Farmer Bernard still allowed the scouts to bivouac every summer, hoping to initiate some sort of adventure, but mostly the evenings were long, boring descents into darkness watching daddy-longlegs burn themselves up in the lantern.

This was why Juliette felt such hunger to be away with Steve Maher in the Norfolk Broads, and why, one evening, she began packing her things.

Juliette had met Steve Maher the previous Hallowe'en at Fernlight Avenue where she and James had held their first teenage party. The front room had been transformed with rolls of blackout drapery Aldous had brought home from school along with some advertising hoardings he'd come by. Juliette and James pinned these all over the walls – a huge eye here, some fingers there, a frying pan full of Walls sausages, a British Rail diesel loco hurtling, blurred, straight at you, snatches of vast text. They'd hollowed out a cauliflower and filled it with a cheesy dip, a huge bowl of Twiglets beside it. A punch of gin, vodka, orange juice and tinned fruit salad. Pride of place amongst the spread was given to a sheep's skull with one horn found on Dyffwys.

Two sets of friends, single-sex cohorts of quasi-religious institutions for whom the opposite gender was a rarely encountered mystery, met in this darkened room, and a clumsy, sweaty kind of hysteria quickly ensued.

A host of young Jesuit boys who looked to Juliette like middle-aged men made mostly unsuccessful attempts to woo her. Charles Hindley showed her a scar on his knee he'd got on the dodgems at Brighton. Mark Temple drank egg flip with cherries in it until he was sick. Paul O'Farrell whistled at her through his tear ducts. Graham Mort sat on and shattered a violin, like he'd hatched a rosewood egg. (No one was sure where the violin had come from.) 'I'd die if I lived here' one girl kept saying. Mary smoked cigarettes confidently at the grand piano while boys and girls tittered behind the tall green curtains. The punch bowl was emptied, leaving a sticky residue of cherries and pineapple chunks. Teenagers spilt into the garden, given eerie shadows by kitchen light through low branches, white spumes of breath mingled. At midnight Juliette smooched to The Doors' 'The End' with Steve Maher.

Juliette had been a rather worrying child, prone to deviousness and prankdom. She'd once posted a note through next door's letterbox promising Mr Peck a slow and painful death if he didn't pay her the sum of one pound. On the Goofyteeths' scrubbed doorstep she once spread a thick layer of butter which nearly had Mrs Goofyteeth skidding to her death. As a toddler she would often go missing, to be returned by a concerned stranger. She once tricycled to the shops with her grandmother's purse and tried to buy a purseworth of sweets, but the purse turned out to be empty. Days out with Juliette were likely to become tense, complicated events, as when, after a trip to the zoo, she sent a secretary on the tube into hysterics by grunting close to her ear with a gorilla mask on.

Colette decided that this behaviour indicated a strongly independent side to her daughter's nature. She'd already been to a rock concert on her own (the Rolling Stones in Hyde Park, she came home wide-eyed and wonderful – 'they released all these white butterflies'), so her mother shouldn't have been surprised when she declared her intention of going on holiday to the Norfolk Broads with Steve Maher in the summer.

The brief uproar that followed her casual announcement was abated somewhat when she pointed out that she would be going with Steve Maher's whole family, and that the holiday would follow their own in Llanygwynfa. She could go to both. Colette interrogated her. She'd met Steve Maher and quite liked him – a dreamily vague, intelligent Irishman with wan looks unblemished by teenage acne. She gave grudging assent.

Then, the night before they were due to depart for Wales, the tent down from the loft and packed, the car heavy with luggage, Julian's white chest, a mesh of bones thinly covered with skin, was freckled with pink spots that were later diagnosed as chicken pox. Julian stayed in the plush bed formed by fitting together the two enormous red armchairs that had come from Meg's house and spoke weakly in demands for Sparkling Spring (a powdered fizzy orange drink) and toy tractors. The holiday had to be delayed.

James and Juliette visited their sick brother's bedside the next evening. How touching, thought Colette, who didn't realize that their visit was to voice snarling disgust with Julian for delaying the holiday. They would have pinched and poked him on the forehead with rigid index fingers and flicked his teeth as though they were marbles if they could have found a way of stopping him from crying.

The delay of more than a week meant now that the Llanygwynfa holiday would overlap with the Norfolk Broads holiday. One of the conditions Colette had applied was that she should take Juliette to Mr and Mrs Maher's house herself and check it all out with them. It hadn't occurred to either that she would no longer be able to do this. The Joneses left for Llanygwynfa, once Julian's lesions had scabbed over, Colette having made a promise she would not be able to keep.

Aldous was heating up the dinner and Julian was painting the farm with purple and orange poster colours. Colette peeked inside the car, which in the evening became Juliette's room, and saw her daughter by the weak interior light filling a small suitcase with clothes.

'What are you doing?' She said.

'Packing,' said Juliette, wrapping her bromide inhaler inside a small bra.

'Packing for what?'

Juliette looked up, genuinely puzzled.

'I'm going to Norfolk tomorrow,' she said.

Colette needed a moment to know how to respond to this, so she quietly slammed the car door and walked to the porch of the tent. Juliette resumed her packing. Colette turned around and walked back to the car, opened the door and leant her head in.

'You're not going to Norfolk, my girl. Don't be ridiculous.'

She closed the door and walked back to the tent.

This time Juliette needed a moment before she climbed out of the car and strutted across the grass to her mother.

'What do you mean?' she said.

'You are not going to Norfolk,' Colette repeated with infuriating simplicity, raising a hand.

'What?' Juliette hollered, her brow chevroned, her throat big, like a bullfrog's.

'You're not going.' Colette seemed to be taking delight in these negatives.

'I'm running out of gas,' said Aldous despondently, shaking the contents of his frying pan around. No one acknowledged him. The boys, lounging on the grass nearby with comics and toys, tittered.

'What do you mean I'm not going? You gave me permission.'

'That was before Julian got chicken pox. How can you go to Norfolk now? We're in the middle of the holiday. We're not taking you back to London, and you're certainly not travelling on your own.'

Colette was unusually lucid. As she spoke she settled into the aluminium chair next to Aldous. They looked like a pair of enthroned monarchs at the portal of a soft castle.

A row ensued during which Juliette accused her mother of everything she could think of and Colette absorbed the insults with an exaggerated indifference, which only deepened Juliette's resentment.

Meanwhile the little crown of flame on the Camping Gaz (replacing the old primus stove) gave a final gasp, and died. With it the prospect of freshly cooked egg and chips. Aldous tried for a moment to fry the dinner over the lantern, but there wasn't enough heat to generate a single bubble of fat. So Aldous and Colette went to the fish and chip shop.

Llanygwynfa-wm-Lledrith's fish and chip shop was at the back of Mrs Roberts' house, almost opposite The Ginger Boy, in the middle of the village. She served hot takeaways from the window of her kitchen, which was under a cedar wood veranda festooned with vine leaves, and looked out on to a charmingly kept garden, thick with lupins, hollyhocks and modest statuary (rabbits, frogs, babies), with a small, constantly trickling fountain in the centre. The garden ended with a low stone wall, and beyond was open farmland, punctuated by the tilting monoliths that marked the boundaries of long forgotten parishes.

Whenever Aldous visited Mrs Roberts' chip shop there always seemed to be female underwear on the washing line, as there was now, two frilled, imitation silk bodices, one lilac, one midnight blue, that palpitated in the breeze, voluptuous one second, scant the next. Aldous found it hard to believe that these two garments contained, when dry, the torsos of Mrs Roberts and her daughter, two broad, fleshy women with tight, curly hair and small, lipless, though always brightly painted, mouths.

Sometimes there was quite a queue at Mrs Roberts'; hungry caravaners from the coastal sites whose gaz was exhausted, bright and loud new arrivals who hadn't the energy for cooking, and for whom fish and chips was a treat. Sometimes the queue snaked all through Mrs Roberts' garden, in and out of the hollyhocks, round the fish pond, and underneath the washing line, where one might get a wet slap in the face from a saucy black bodice or lacy slip. But this evening there was no one, and Mrs Roberts and her daughter were sitting on a little wooden bench on the veranda, beneath the vine leaves, enjoying a Gold Label each, and admiring the simple beginnings of what was to be a complicated sunset.

The Joneses were not frequent visitors to Mrs Roberts'. They didn't like the loud, Midlands jostle they sometimes found themselves amidst, and the tacky interior furnishings that could be glimpsed through the windows (a clock in the shape of the continent of Africa, plaster windmills, an enormous, decorated clog) were a vulgar parody of the venerable furnishings of the Evans's farmhouse. Because the Roberts made no distinction between the commercial and domestic aspects of their house, Aldous and Colette always felt like burglars when they went to buy fish and chips. And now, as they approached the mother and daughter beneath the veranda, they noticed a conspiratorial exchange of Welsh words before the two sauntered into the house, holding their drinks, the daughter, smaller but stouter than her mother, sighing loudly through her lips.

But when Mrs Roberts reappeared at the window to take the order from Colette, who was wearing her dark glasses and smoking a cigarette, she seemed full of friendly banter, which unsettled Colette. Suddenly she was made aware that their visits to this fish and chip shop over the last fourteen years had been noticed.

'Is Janus not with you this summer, Mrs Jones?' the woman said.

It took Colette a moment to answer.

'No,' she said, 'not this year.'

'Not for a couple of years now is it?'

'He was here last year. He's busy in London.'

'At the telephone exchange?'

'He's earning money.'

'That's what children are for.'

Aldous then noticed that Mrs Roberts' daughter, deep-frying fish, was attentive to this conversation, so attentive that Aldous wondered if they'd ever had some sort of relationship. Or that the girl had had a crush on Janus. And Aldous suddenly felt a hankering to have his son marry himself to this place, to take a woman from the local stock, settle here.

Gwen had come to the tent a few nights ago with her husband, a gold-complexioned man full of winks and smiles. She wanted to know if Janus had made any gramophone recordings, as they had a record player but no records. Colette

221

had been rude to her and sent her away almost in tears. Gwen looked terribly wrong as a married woman. She'd become all tweedy and made-up, like the older women you saw in the tea rooms at Aberbreuddwyd. All the roughness, the exquisite dishevelment, had been smoothed out of her.

Aldous wondered why Colette was so upset by Gwen's visit. Surely she could never have expected anything to have come from her friendship with Janus. But now he wondered if some beautiful opportunity had been missed, for Janus to engage with something warm and knowing, marry a woman rich in land, become rooted to a lush, generous landscape. With that moment lost Aldous now even fantasized about his son, the gifted pianist, marrying a girl from the fish and chip shop, a girl already old, thick set with the ingestion of animal fat. She would have made a wonderful daughter-in-law, serving up fizzing bundles of chips for his son, taking him on trips to Holland. At least Janus would have belonged somewhere.

When her food came, Colette took it with some suspicion. Mrs Roberts knew about her and her family. It made her feel that every September, when they'd gone back to London, Mrs Roberts and her daughter got together with Mr and Mrs Evans, The Ginger Boy, The Genius and everyone else they'd come into contact with at Llanygwynfa, for a long discussion and exchange of gossip on the subject of Colette Jones and her family.

It was nearly dark as Colette and Aldous drove back through the farmyard. The headlamps illuminated chickens as they waddled out of the way, and Colette as she opened the three gates they had to pass through. The tent was a patch of dim light on the far side of the field. As the car lurched across the black pasture towards it, Colette, the food hot in her lap, could sense its emptiness. It contained only James and Julian, who were reading and drawing in the mothy light.

'Where is she?' said Colette.

'She said she was going for a walk.'

'At this time of the night?'

'Where?' said Aldous.

'To the beach . . .'

'In the dark?'

'But then she did have a small suitcase and the *AA Book of the Road* with her,' James chuckled.

'She's run off,' Colette said with a clenched sureness in her voice.

'Oh Christ.'

'Did you get the fish and chips?' said James.

'Sod the fish and chips,' said Colette, to which James guffawed. Aldous tutted. Colette snapped.

'Don't you care what's happened to your sister, out in the middle of nowhere in the dead of the night?'

'Frankly, no,' said James, with an 'it's not my fault she's run away' tone in his voice.

Half an hour later the farm was alive with police – three carloads of them, their radios hissing. Sheep were given a blue, pulsing existence in their lights. Cows, interested, watched through a gate. Mr and Mrs Evans arrived in their night-clothes and chatted with one of the sergeants, who was a relation. Some boy scouts appeared. Colette couldn't help thinking the police seemed pleased to have something to do. It was becoming like a social event, a chance to catch up on the latest gossip. They interrogated James, as the last person to see his sister, and were exasperated by his indifference.

'Don't you care what's happened to your sister, boy?'

'Frankly, no.'

He did, however, recall her mentioning Aberystwyth, and Colette in turn recalled something Juliette had mentioned in passing months ago – that a friend of hers was staying over the summer with a relation in Aberystwyth. The police enjoyed this information and did everything they could with it – wrote it down in notebooks, sent it through the atmosphere on radio waves, repeated it to themselves, until finally they produced, with an efficiency that impressed Aldous and Colette, a name and address in Aberystwyth at which another division of the Welsh police called in the early hours of the following morning, just as Juliette was about to leave for Wolverhampton, where a man she'd accepted a lift from at Dinas Mawwdy had offered her a waitressing job. Parents and child were reunited tearfully at midday.

Aldous and Colette were shaken by the experience, Aldous particularly, especially when he heard about how Juliette had hitchhiked in the dark along lonely mountain roads, and about her plans to begin a new life in Wolverhampton, maybe never to return to her family again. How easily his daughter had slipped out of his world, into the darkness of mountains, swallowed by the landscape. What rare luck it was for a police light to fall on her, to pick her out of that huge blackness. A chance in a thousand against a silence that might have lasted for ever.

Colette admitted defeat, seeing how sulky Juliette was and how she was likely to run away again if she didn't have her way. She allowed her daughter to go to Norfolk.

As the final days of August approached Aldous felt less and less the possibility that they would return to Llanygwynfa. Janus had outgrown the farm. Juliette was gone. James, soon eighteen, would be likely to follow next year. Colette – would she be physically capable? Then there was the trouble they'd caused the Evanses, upsetting Gwen, bringing the police to the farm.

In the last week there was a heatwave. His family, now reduced to four, a little weary, spent a lot of the time at the beach. One afternoon he and Julian became interested in body prints. Aldous rolled the lumpy sand flat with a lemonade bottle and took full-length impressions of Julian's body. Later, when it was time to go back to the tent, Julian hid from his father in the maze of sand dunes and watched him through a frill of marram grass as Aldous scanned the emptying beach for him. Aldous, who knew where his son was hiding, indulged a moment of ridiculous sentimentality, imagining that the impression in the sand, already trodden on, was all that he had left of his youngest son. He remembered that when he first came here his family was small, and that the years had seen its steady increase, its growth, had heard its strengthening voice and admitted its crowdedness. Now, it seemed, the process was reversing, and his family was thinning out again, becoming a quieter, emptier thing. It was losing itself. So that when he looked down to where the sand had been rolled flat and there was a Turin Shroud impression of a young boy with his head in profile, his arms hanging loosely by his side, as if a child had just fallen out of the sky, and then fallen straight back into it, he imagined that this was all he had left. A weightless space in sand, already trodden over. A trace.

He was not sure himself that he wanted to come again next year. The landscape suddenly seemed too immense. He feared that he and his family might fall into it, and vanish. Not for the first time he felt the power of the landscape resided in its ability to unglue you from the world. How it caused you to live on the point of invisibility. It was like the forest of namelessness that Alice passed through.

Apart from that the landscape itself was changing. Bungalows had been erected with ghastly facing stone and bloated chimney stacks alongside the main road by Ty Meddal. The corner by the chapel had been lit that year; an orange glow now illuminated the buildings at night, and in the dark Moelfre was invisible behind the blurred twinkle of sodium lights. Stars were less. Night-time was no longer a retreat into the comfort of total darkness. There was talk of road widening. The Evanses were on the brink (as they always were) of successfully purchasing the freehold of their farm. Barry was engaged in a perpetual struggle with the National Park authorities to convert the upper fields of the farm into a proper camp site, with toilet facilities, shops, playgrounds. All these things helped Aldous feel that this was not the same place he'd fallen into head first in 1955. That his time in this paradise was up. It would be better to leave it now and have the memories intact before they got spoiled. That was the thing he could not understand about heaven, and the thing that frightened him most about death. If it went on for ever, paradise, then it would never change. If it never changed there would never be any need to remember it. Heaven, therefore, is an unremembered place, and the dead have no memory.

On the penultimate day the weather mustered itself into a powerful storm that didn't erupt fully until dark.

It had been a day of blustery showers, of clouds the colour of carbon paper suddenly appearing and rushing overhead, unloading their wet burdens as they passed, carried by boisterous, busy winds. From the tent Aldous watched little troupes of these clouds as they gathered over the Lleyn Peninsula, swirling and twirling out to sea, forming themselves into whirlwind cones, tornadoes, waterspouts, inky vortices, twisters.

The Evanses came over at twilight.

'You should have gone home today,' Mr Evans said. Aldous, even when talking face to face with Mr Evans, had no idea what he looked like. He seemed able to hide his face very efficiently. Mrs Evans had a very exposed face, every inch of it was displayed proudly, shiningly.

'You haven't done your painting of our farm, Mr Jones,' she said, 'you'll have to leave it till next year now.'

As they spoke Mr Evans's cap blew off. He didn't seem to notice for a few seconds when he grabbed wildly at the space around his head. The two of them then chased the cap across the field, their hair and clothes billowing.

It chilled Aldous a little, the way the Evanses assumed they'd be back next year. It was hardly surprising, since they'd been coming for fifteen years, but still Aldous felt that with each succeeding year the possibility of their not returning increased, not decreased.

The cycle of their relationship with the Evanses, having peaked in August, retreated into memory by Christmas, when an exchange of cards brought an envelope to Fernlight Avenue bearing a stamp with a Welsh dragon on it, and Mrs Evans's cursive, scrolled lettering, as scrolled as the ironwork of her farm. The cards were always seriously religious –

sleeping angels, Epiphanies, Magi. They were like Lesley's cards in that way. No Father Christmases on his cards, or robins, or snowmen, but infant Jesuses, nativities, stars.

This midwinter contact with Llanygwynfa had a curious effect on the Joneses. They would look at the card, its envelope, and think, and sometimes say, *isn't it funny to think that the farm's still there, even now.* Their domains were so distinct, so separate, it was hard to imagine them co-existing. Aldous sometimes thought that the farm did indeed cease to exist in their absence. Once they'd left at the end of August each year, invisible machinery was put into action that rolled up the fields, withdrew the buildings of Llanygwynfa into black storage lofts and its people – the Evanses, The Genius, The Ginger Boy, stepped out of the roles they'd so brilliantly played for a month or, in worse moments, succumbed to a stiffening and final stasis of their own miraculous clockwork and reverted to the ingenious mannequins that they were. Aldous had been influenced in his thinking along these lines by a Ray Bradbury short story called 'Mars Is Heaven'. Space travellers landing on Mars are fooled by theatrical Martians into thinking they've landed in heaven. They slowly realize that the beautiful scenery and the long-dead relatives they joyfully greet are all illusions created by the Martians, who turn out to be rather unpleasant. Aldous felt it was really happening in Llanygwynfa. He'd thought he'd landed head first in paradise. Now, fifteen years later, the props were starting to lean, the acting was becoming see-through. Particularly his wife. Colette was playing her role very poorly.

However, every spring he wrote to Llanygwynfa asking for permission to come to the farm in August. Almost by return of post would come a letter from the farm, written again by Mrs Evans, brief but friendly, granting that permission. This letter charged the house with a second wave of excitement. The farm was still there.

But Aldous was not sure he'd be writing another letter next spring. And as Mr and Mrs Evans said their good evenings, giving their final pieces of advice about the coming storm, their hair and coats billowing, he thought that this might be the last time he'd ever see them.

Aldous spent the evening securing the tent. He didn't have a hammer for the pegs so selected a small round boulder from the wall and used its mossy surface. There was the dull percussion of pegs sinking, occasional orange sparks. Sometimes the peg jarred on a sunken stone and sent a bolt of geological energy through Aldous's body. Eventually every peg was sunk up to its neck and the flysheet was as tight as the skin over a pregnant woman's belly.

James was sleeping in the small tent. Aldous, Colette and Julian were sleeping together. There was absolutely no way, Aldous said to his wife, that this tent could blow down. He'd stake his life on it.

Colette was nervous. They lay side by side listening to the thump thump of the flysheet tightening and slackening. It was as though they were in the ventricle of a whale's heart. When Colette fell slowly into an undrugged sleep, Aldous remained awake, listening to the beating of the flysheet. It was midnight when the rain came, carried on a cold front of ghastly turbulence which turned the beating of the sheet into a snapping, crackling sound. It was at this point, the rain pulsing all around him, that Aldous realized the tent wouldn't hold. Not tonight. They'd had windy nights before but not like this. Then the lightning came, illuminating the tent's rumpled human contents briefly in its glare. The family, gloved by this tent, were all awake as a corner peg of the flysheet came loose. There followed a ferocious flapping, as though a sea gull had been pegged down. A single wing was beating frantically against itself. Aldous knew he would have to go out and fasten the loosened peg. Once one went the others would be loosened, soon they would all go. He rolled back the cover and pulled his trousers on, then his coat, unzipped the tent and crawled into the enclosed porch. The free peg was at the back of the tent. He had to unzip the tent's outer door and walk, having stepped into his shoes, out into the field and around the tent. Rain hit his face. He felt as though he was cheek to cheek with a cheese grater. He walked hunched to the back of the tent, realizing he'd misplaced the stone he'd been using as a hammer and had to find another one from the wall. At the back corner of the tent the flysheet was dancing madly. The peg was nowhere to be seen. He searched with a bicycle lamp for the peg in the grass. It must have been catapulted out of range of his search. He had to take a less crucial peg from the inner tent to replace it. On his way back he noticed James's tent. It didn't have a flysheet. The rain would soon start coming through. When Aldous returned Colette and Julian were talking and laughing. Their laughter lifted Aldous, who'd until then thought of the storm as part of the natural destruction of their lives there. Julian and Colette's laughter (*we'll wake up on top of Snowdon*) made everything less serious.

Soon another peg went on the flysheet. Aldous had to make another sortie. As he hammered the peg back in, however, it hit a buried stone and bent. He couldn't straighten it and could only submerge the peg to half its depth. It came out again almost immediately. Then another. Then James came over and asked if he could sleep in the car as water was pouring into his tent. Aldous unlocked the car for him. The storm worsened. Aldous had given up any idea of sleep and was now engaged in the perpetual task of pegging down the flysheet. As soon as one was hammered back, another came out. Pegs were damaged or lost. Eventually half the flysheet had to be left to billow freely in the wind.

'I think we'll all have to sleep in the car,' said Aldous, 'the tent's going to be torn to shreds if we try to keep it up. You get in the car and I'll take the tent down.'

Colette and Julian thought this was an excellent idea. With the back seat folded down it was quite easy for Colette, Julian and James to sleep transversely across the car. Not that they slept at first. Instead they told each other jokes. The wind rocked the car.

Aldous didn't come over to the car. Colette could see the vague shape of him struggling with the flailing body of the tent, like someone wrestling with an angel. He'd decided to spend the night in the tent. It was possibly the last night they would ever spend at the farm; he didn't want it to end in defeat. Besides, there wasn't really room for him in the car, and there was too much in the tent that needed packing. Instead he took the flysheet off completely to save it from tearing and used the leftover pegs to extra-securely peg down the inner tent.

In the morning Colette woke early after a brief and eventful sleep and found herself in a car whose windows were frosted like bathroom windows with her and her two sons' breath. She propped herself up on an elbow and wiped a transparent arc across her window and saw, to her surprise, the tent, the inner section of it at least, still standing a few yards away, wobbling like an enormous jelly in the blustery wind that was the aftermath of last night's storm. She was even more surprised to see, behind one of the flapping doors, her husband busy preparing breakfast, which he brought out shortly, three enamel plates loaded with bacon, eggs and fried bread.

'We thought you'd end up on top of Snowdon.'

'There is an old Welsh proverb,' said Aldous, in his worst Welsh accent. 'Even though my house falleth down, still will I find time to cooketh my breakfast.'

The tent looked like a peeled fruit. The lavatory tent had blown away completely; they could see it fluttering in the branches of a hawthorn in the second field. A fire engine trundled slowly along the lane by the chapel. They later heard that the caravan sites by the coast had been ruined with all the caravans on their side or upside down. Mr Evans came early that morning bringing with him Julian's plastic chamber pot, which he'd found in their yard.

3

In the autumn Colette bought two mice for Julian. One was black and one was mottled grey. The mice lived in a large glazed ceramic casserole with a glass lid that was kept on the dresser. The domestic routines of the house now centred upon the segregation of these mice from the cats of the house – Baxbr and Scipio. If the cats were in the room the lid had to be on the casserole. If there were humans in the room the lid could be half on the casserole to allow some ventilation. If the cats were out of the room and the door was closed the lid could be removed and the mice even lifted out (they couldn't climb the slippery walls of their house) and allowed to scamper around the kitchen, skidding on the lino. Sometimes Julian would hold these creatures, whom he'd called Adam and Eve, in his hands and enjoy the tense, muscular warmth of their bodies. In December Adam gave birth to a brood of children and lay exhausted on his side, suckling these blind babies, who were hairless and pink, their eyes sealed pouches with colour showing through the skin. They were about the size of baked beans and looked like pictures Colette had seen of human embryos at two months.

The cats were very interested in this new, tiny family in the house. Even though they rarely saw the mice they would sit on the floor beside the dresser staring at the blue casserole with a depth of concentration that could be mesmeric to watch. They could sense either by odour, sound or some other trace, their presence. Whether they could hear the blood of a dozen tiny hearts pulsing nobody knew, but the cats knew everything about the mice.

Colette was overjoyed by this flourishing of new life in the house. She'd carefully furnished the casserole with everything she understood mice loved – lint, wood shavings, water, grain, wool. The mice busily arranged all this material into a plush bed for Adam to whelp his babies in. Colette and the mice seemed to understand each other very well. A gorgeous smell was produced by the hectic domestic life of the mice, a smell that Colette thought was very like fresh human sweat.

Colette's nose was very sensitive now that she'd given up sniffing. She hadn't sniffed since Llanygwynfa. She'd felt terrible about sniffing so much that holiday. Juliette's running away, the storm and the shock of her own gauntness in the mirror had all combined to encourage her to quit. Julian sometimes added his thin voice to those others that would gather to implore her to stop. She had stopped now, for good she believed. There had been the usual withdrawal pains. Headaches that clamped her head in a vice, vomiting that recalled the mornings of early pregnancy and the sensation that the air was a semisolid substance, as though it was full of sand. Those discomforts were intermittent and seemed now to have passed, although she was now and then placed in the grip of a hunger that didn't originate in her stomach but seemed to come from inside her bones, as though her skeleton was hungry.

But she'd survived even these awful bouts and now was left with the sensation that a little chimney sweep had been at her nostrils, had cleaned and widened them so that the air rushed in like two silver trains laden with cargoes of smells. Smells she'd never encountered before – why did Julian smell of candles? Why did she smell olives and coal a moment before Aldous came home from work on his bike? She could smell moods as clearly as she could smell food. Cheerfulness in the house raised an odour of sweet peppers, gloominess was French cheese, anger was oranges.

The olfactory gift was only temporary and was now starting to weaken. The air was beginning to conceal its information once again, although that December night she could smell something strange, a lingering smell of peanut butter, or chicken paste. She was hurrying that evening because there was something on television she wanted to watch. She'd cooked the dinner and was clearing away. She'd fed the cats and filled their saucers with milk while the rest of the family were sitting in the front room ready for the programme, which was a Tommy Cooper Special.

All the family, but Colette especially, found Tommy Cooper hysterically funny. Just his face was enough to make Colette laugh. He didn't have to do anything. He just had to appear. She didn't want to miss a moment of his show. At the same time she wanted to make some coffee for herself and Aldous, a cup of Nesquik for Julian, some lemonade for Juliette, and she had to get the cats out of the room and make sure the lid was on the mouse casserole, then carefully carry the drinks into the front room. All the seats were taken. Aldous was in the big red armchair by the gas fire that had somehow become his. Julian was in the twin of that chair, his young body almost lost in its red uplands. James, Juliette and Janus were filling the couch, so Colette sat on the floor, her back resting against the front of Julian's chair, her legs stretched out flat in front of her, her ankles crossed. Her feet were in open-toed sandals.

The person on the television wasn't the fezzed comedian she'd been expecting but a girl with prominent teeth and bobbed hair. She recognized her as the singer Cilla Black.

'What have you been making me rush for, he hasn't even started yet,' said Colette.

'This is just finishing,' said Aldous.

None of the family liked Cilla Black. In fact they disliked her quite strongly and could only just tolerate the closing

moments of her programme. They desired Tommy Cooper all
the more.

Colette felt very relaxed and happy. She leant back against the
chair and watched Cilla who was singing a final duet with her
guest. Cilla was wearing a long silver dress covered in sequins
that flashed and sparkled in random points of light all over her
body. Colette felt a little mesmerized by this dress. The song was
a slow, dreary ballad. It seemed to go on for hours. Colette
watched anyway. She found it difficult to take her eyes off Cilla
Black's sparkling dress. Then, with a casual lifting of her leg,
Cilla stepped out of the television and began drifting very slowly
towards the floor of the front room. It was as though she was
riding an invisible escalator. She was still singing, holding a
microphone to her mouth. Colette laughed and looked at the
other members of her family to see if they shared her astonish-
ment. She was briefly puzzled as to why they all looked so
bored. She shrugged and returned her attention to Cilla, saying
'Isn't it amazing what they can do these days,' as though it was
some new feature of the television, a special three-dimensional
projection facility they hadn't tried out yet.

Cilla was still small, about the size of a cat, still black and
white, still singing in her long dress, a look of emotional
intensity in her eyes as she walked on legs concealed entirely
by her dress, across the living room carpet slowly and rather
gracefully.

'I didn't think the telly could do this,' Colette heard herself
saying, at the same time feeling that her voice had come from
somewhere else. She began to feel a little bit worried. Looking
back at the telly she was sure it wasn't plugged in. She could
see the plug there in the corner, the socket next to it empty.
Some form of magic was operating the television. And Cilla
was close now. She could see the scanning lines of the
television screen still on her face as she came up to her feet and
then stepped on to them. Colette then felt the sheer panic she
would feel at the sudden close presence of spiders. It was a
horrible thing to have on your body that electrical, twinkling
figure. She shook her legs to try and dislodge Cilla, but Cilla

clung like a horrible silver insect. Colette tried brushing her off with her hands, kicking her legs frantically, doing anything to be rid of that creature that was now walking along her legs as though along a narrow mountain ridge towards Colette's body. Colette then lost consciousness.

To the rest of the family the event was rather different. Colette breezing in and out of the room with trays of drinks, forgetting things, going to the kitchen, returning, closing the door with her feet, complaining about the lack of seats, sitting, finally, on the floor.

'What's that funny smell?' she said. No one quite noticed her saying this.

Aldous then saw that Colette's toes were twitching. He thought she was keeping time to the music and was surprised she was doing it so badly. Then she began kicking her feet, as though she was trying to kick her sandals off. These odd movements were only half noticed by the family. Then she began to make a whooping noise, her face raised slightly towards the ceiling, all the conduits of her neck visible and taut. In the first moment of the noise it could have been mistaken for laughter, a rather sarcastic, mocking laughter. Everyone looked at Colette in a tired, slightly puzzled way. Julian's thought was *why is Mum impersonating a dog?* The kicking of the feet continued and suddenly extended to the whole body. The separate, high-pitched whoops collocated into a continuous, very weak cry that seemed swallowed up by the movements of her body.

The hot coffee she'd been holding dropped and spread a dark puddle that was quickly absorbed by the carpet. The family, after a moment's motionless bewilderment, sprang into animated, confused panic. Colette was convulsing on the floor, her head was working from side to side mechanically, her limbs flailing like a distressed baby, her eyes were open and seemed to be scanning invisible faces. Aldous quickly got on his knees beside her but then didn't know what to do. She was silent now, except for a kind of quiet rumbling in her throat.

'Get an ambulance,' he said, 'go next door and phone for someone.'

'Hold her head,' said Juliette. James had gone next door to phone. Juliette tried to take her mother's feet in her hands.

'What's she doing, Dad?' Julian tried to shout, but his voice wasn't working properly.

Colette was like a sleeper under the deep stress of a nightmare.

Somehow remembering an army first aid course he'd undertaken at a barracks in Wiltshire nearly thirty years before, Aldous turned his wife's body on to its side to stop her choking. Moving her body he was struck by its lightness. He'd braced himself for a heavy push and his body tensed with shock at the give of her body, as light as a bundle of dead grass.

As Colette moaned and twisted on the floor, a magician on the television performed a doomed Indian rope trick. Throwing the rope high it fell each time into a slack heap of coils. There was audience laughter.

No one in the room was talking. They were holding Colette, or watching, or walking from room to room wondering what to do.

Juliette tried to wake her.

'Mum,' she said. Colette's open eyes registered nothing.

'What's happened to her?' said Juliette to her father, both of them sharing the same frowning bewilderment, both with little Hs formed between their eyebrows, both with their tongues lolling ever so slightly from their mouths, as always when they were seriously puzzled or worried.

'I don't know,' said Aldous who'd considered, in those few minutes, every possibility from heart attack to stroke to epilepsy to brain tumour. Presently Colette's convulsions began to subside. Her eyes, instead of scanning in an almost robotic way, from side to side, up and down, now seemed to be straining for focus on real objects – chairs, paintings. The paintings held her attention for some time. Her eyes kept going back to the picture of Moelfre, half in shadow, that hung near the television. She looked at the other scenes from

Wales that surrounded her. A waterfall. Clouds caught in strands of marram grass. Suddenly she turned her head to look over her shoulder at Aldous. He looked into her eyes terrified that there would be no recognition. There was.

'What's up?' she said.

'Mum,' said Juliette, 'you've just . . .' and then she cried.

'What's going on?' Colette said.

Aldous was thinking how odd it was for Colette to be on the floor, apparently now normal. Her glasses off, she looked her usual early morning self — her eyes heavy and veined, overmoist, her lips rough and dry, her hair slightly ruffled.

'You've had some sort of . . . attack.'

'Don't be ridiculous,' said Colette, putting her hand to her cheek as she always did when something simultaneously shocked and amused her.

Aldous could see something was still wrong with her. Now she was too normal. Her manner was transcendent normality. Heightened ordinariness.

She tried to sit up.

'You'd better lie down.'

'Have I got a hat on?'

'No.'

'Why's Juliette crying?'

'You just gave her a bit of a shock, that's all.'

'I gave her a shock?'

Then suddenly she was talking about something trivial, about how she'd put black coffee in the dinner instead of beef stock and nobody had noticed. Then she was back to the summer arguments with Juliette, but actually there, talking about the Norfolk holiday as though it was still in the future, 'You've got another think coming . . .'

On the television an inept magician was trying to disentangle a knot of steel rings. The rings became more knotted. There was laughter.

When the ambulance arrived Colette was sitting up on the floor talking happily and laughing. No one had explained to her what had happened, or that an ambulance was due.

The two ambulancemen seemed enormous, like puffed-up birds. They were loud and friendly, calling Colette and Aldous by their first names which rolled off their tongues with surprising familiarity. Colette chatted with them, apparently not aware that she was the reason for their visit. When they brought in a chair which they unfolded before her, she didn't realize it was for her.

'You want *me* to sit in it?'

'That's right Colette, try it out for size. It's a clever little chair isn't it?'

Colette, who'd been standing, sat in the chair, an ambulanceman behind her with his hands on the handles; she smiled crookedly at Aldous as she gracefully lowered herself. It was the smile she gave whenever she accepted something ridiculous.

The ambulancemen wheeled her into the ambulance, telling Aldous it would be best if he followed them to the hospital in his car.

Home Farm Hospital was three miles away at the very edge of London. If you looked out of the front windows of the hospital you saw the city. From the back windows there were the fields and cows and trees of the green belt. In the blackness Aldous could see neither.

He was told to wait while a hefty nurse guided Colette into a curtained cubicle. After an hour a doctor took him aside to ask him questions, after Aldous had described what had happened.

The doctor ran through a checklist of symptoms, past illnesses. Aldous answered as best he could, providing a scant natural history of his wife. When it came to current medication Aldous became hesitant.

'She has sleeping pills – Mandrax. Painkillers sometimes – Cojene, aspirin.'

'Nothing else?'

'She sniffs glue.' Aldous hadn't meant to speak these words so casually.

The doctor nodded slowly as though he fully comprehended. He was a very small doctor, slightly built and young
looking. He had fair hair and a beard. He looked too young
for such lush, thick facial hair. It looked like a false beard.

'Glue?' the doctor said, not comprehending.

'Yes. Bicycle glue. For puncture repairs.'

The doctor scratched his chin, asked for more details.
Aldous told him everything, how she used it, in what
quantities, the effects it had on her.

'She's stopped now though. Not since August. She says
she's packed it in for good. Could it be . . . do you think it has
something to do with what happened?'

It hadn't occurred to Aldous before. Somehow he'd always
thought, as she'd been sniffing for so long, that any ill effects
would have shown themselves by now. Why, after nearly
three years, should she suddenly have a seizure like this?

'I couldn't say at the moment,' said the doctor, 'though it's
a possibility, especially if she's recently withdrawn from
inhaling the glue. It is rather unusual. I'll have to consult with
my pharmacological colleagues,' and he half laughed, as if he
wanted sympathy from Aldous for the diagnostic predicament
he was in.

It was decided that Colette should be kept in overnight.
Aldous tried to speak to her but when he approached her bed
she seemed so busy, chatting with nurses, arranging things
around her bed, that he didn't feel inclined to interfere. But as
he was leaving she caught sight of him and called his name.
She ran to him, her hair flying, and he froze for a moment,
because she looked entirely mad. But when she reached him
she gave him a big hug. It was not a wife to husband hug,
however, it was a mother to son hug and as such failed to
connect with Aldous. She quickly asked him to bring some
things from home, before hurrying back to her curtained bed.
'Like a theatre,' thought Aldous as a nurse briskly drew the
curtain, 'the final act.'

Aldous was horrified by his wife's energy.

Back home the house had the atmosphere of a place

recently abandoned, even though there were people in it. In the kitchen Julian, who should have been in bed, was crying. Aldous said it would be all right, rather unconvincingly. But it was not about his mother that Julian was crying. He pointed to the casserole on the dresser. The lid was on the floor. Adam, Eve and all the children – gone. There wasn't a trace of blood anywhere.

4

Aldous had to go to work the next day and in the evening still had an adult education class to teach. After a day of helping restless children silk screen elephants he drove home and asked Janus to prepare some dinner for Julian and Juliette. Then he drove to the hospital. She was no longer in casualty. The nurse told him she had been moved to Hope Ward. It took him nearly half an hour of walking along shiny corridors and across windy car parks, passing huge heating generators and courtyards of blind windows, to find this ward. But Colette wasn't there.

'Mrs Jones?' said the sister. 'She was transferred this afternoon.'

'Which ward?' said Aldous breathlessly, conscious that he hadn't much time left.

'No,' said the sister, 'to another hospital.'

'Another hospital. Christ. Where?'

The sister looked through a large register.

'Friern Barnet,' she said.

'But that's,' Aldous faltered, 'but that's a loony . . . a lunatic asylum.'

'I'm sorry Mr . . .'

'Why've you sent her there?'

'Dr Nixon's decision.'

'Can I speak to him?'

'Her. She's not on duty at the moment.'

Aldous didn't have time to go to Friern Barnet. He had to go to his evening class. Some of his students had been coming for ten years. For some it was the highlight of their week. He couldn't let them down. His students were mostly middle aged or elderly. Occasionally a younger person would come along for extra A Level tuition or preparation for art school entry, but mostly they were mature, calm, peaceable. There was Morris, a big old man who tried hard to be eccentric and who painted small, semi-abstract landscapes in which scenes were divided into geometrical areas of flat colour. Maureen, who painted viridian and cream silver birch forests. Mrs Essendon who painted sloping lakes. Jan who copied the scenes on greetings cards. They were, all of them, quietly proud of their unambitiousness. In the early days Aldous worked hard at opening these people up, getting them to paint real flowers instead of floral photos, to work on a bigger scale, use different media, but he quickly realized he was fighting a losing battle. Anything new or unusual upset them. They just wanted to paint their sloping lakes, their forest scenes. The point of the class, he soon realized, was not to produce great art, but to relax. To chat quietly during the coffee break. To discuss holiday plans and house extensions. And Aldous soon became happy to let them do that. It made them feel at ease with the world. He praised their sickly, clogged, lifeless images.

Aldous tried hard to convey to the rest of his family that he found his evening classes a thrice-weekly chore that he performed only for the extra money. In truth, however, his evening classes gave him a precious foothold on what he had come to regard as the real world.

The following day he spent again at school. He had no choice. A day off would have been too disruptive. He would have been confronted with chaos on his return – work in the wrong cupboards, paint in the wrong drawers, the kiln left on . . .

But while he was working he felt less and less that his presence in the school was a genuine, real one. He was, through loss of his wife, losing a sense of his own quiddity. It seemed like a loss. She'd been taken away by the men in white coats. That's what horrified him. When the sister had told him Colette had been carted off to Friern Barnet he nearly cried out loud – *You haven't put her in the Hatch?* Friern Barnet had been known until very recently as Colney Hatch, a notorious institution to rank alongside Bedlam or Broadmoor, a vast Victorian lunatic asylum with a tall, narrow dome, miles of polished, straight corridors that seemed to recede into infinity with howling and laughter echoing around them.

Aldous was terrified of madness, of going mad, of being near mad people, of loved ones losing their minds. It stemmed, he thought, from his sister's schizophrenia. He'd loved Mfanwy, who'd mothered him with the skill and sincerity of a sister five years his senior. Then, a little while after puberty, when her body was a woman's but her gestures (a sudden, frantic rubbing of the nose, following the text of her reading with a finger) remained a child's, she began to give half herself to a separate reality. She would take part in droll, tedious conversations of which, as in a telephone conversation, Aldous could only hear her end. Sometimes it terrified him to have her answer a question he hadn't asked, for her to laugh inexplicably, to see the animal in her eyes. Sometimes her eyes seemed to contain no more human presence than those of a mouse. Her movements seemed purely mechanical. She could have been a robot.

Her illness was treated with brutal simplicity – electric shocks, confinement and eventually, when the disjointed phases of her personality were interspersed with periods of black depression, surgery. Her lobotomy, which happened in her mid-twenties, stabilized her mind enough for her to marry and raise a small family, but her personality was stunned by the operation and she transformed from the bright, fizzy girl of her childhood to a slow, permanently tired, wistful middle-aged woman.

Mfanwy seemed to him thereafter always a mutilated piece of tissue globed in bone. She terrified him by revealing the cold, chemical randomness at the core of all human beings. And he was dreadfully ashamed of his terror, of the fact that he found himself avoiding her. Sometimes he pretended to new friends that she didn't exist. Colette, however, was very fond of Mfanwy and her husband Alec. Aldous had never understood the root of the affection but now he felt he'd been given an insight. Once, when he was young, his sister had spent time in Colney Hatch.

Aldous had visited her there with his father. He remembered the hospital as a system of shiny tunnels, huge oak doors with brass handles that swung back with such force you felt they could take a limb off. He remembered its smells (varnish and polish, not unlike a church but with a sour undertaste), its sounds (cacophonies of laughter, moanings, urgent babblings) and sights (old ladies tiptoeing nowhere, men with long, God-like hair). He recalled once seeing a woman in a straitjacket sitting in a chair, rocking. Her arms bound to her body she looked as though she was frantically trying to keep warm. When he saw his sister he was startled by her normality amid all the profound and disturbing madness. She talked and laughed like a real person. He didn't understand why she was there. She played a game of chess with him and won easily, effortlessly.

After that single visit to Colney Hatch Aldous never talked about it with anyone, not even his father. He hadn't even mentioned it to Colette.

Perhaps twice a year he and Colette would have a small row about Mfanwy. The row would centre on whether or not to pay her a visit. Colette would enthusiastically propose a visit (Colette's visits were always spontaneous, unannounced events), and Aldous would resist, saying they couldn't just turn up, they needed to arrange a date. Neither party was on the phone. Letters would be written but not sent. Colette would lose patience and again propose an instant visit, Aldous would argue against it. Colette would call him a miserable antisocial killjoy. Aldous would become sulkily silent.

But now he thought Colette must have seen somewhere some similarity, a scrap of affinity, because she now inhabited that place he'd last visited as a child.

As he approached the building through the frosty night it suddenly felt strange that in over forty years he hadn't seen it, yet it was only three miles from his home. If he ever had cause to visit the area, which he rarely had, he avoided coming within sight of the hospital. When he saw it now it didn't look like the monstrous castle he remembered. It looked more like the stately home of a mild eccentric. Its interior had changed greatly. There were still the long, reflective, infinite corridors but the woodwork had gone. Everything was painted a minty green, there was sensible-looking signage

PSYCHIATRY ← OCCUPATIONAL THERAPY →

The beeswax had been replaced by a sterile hospital odour. He felt less nervous as he walked along one of the corridors, probably in the wrong direction. A man walked past him in the other direction, in every way a normal looking person – balding with a well-trimmed beard, a serious frown, tweed jacket. Two features identified him as a patient: one was the glare he gave Aldous as he passed, and the other was the baggy blue shorts he was wearing.

When Mfanwy had been there the patients wore uniforms. Striped pyjamas. It was thought important that patients could easily be identified. It didn't matter that they looked like convicts, since asylums weren't very different from prisons. Now, however, it seemed that patients could wear their own clothes. Some patients could come and go from the hospital during the day. Doctors and nurses didn't always wear uniforms. Psychiatrists would sometimes leave their white coats in their lockers. In the whole hospital, Aldous was later to learn, the only people to wear uniforms were the cleaners and ancillary staff. They were the only people easily identifiable as sane.

By this blurring of identities the hospital made Aldous very conscious of his physical presence within the building. Even though there were no mirrors he felt he was observing himself. He could see his large frame walking (a double, vertically below him, walking in the illusory space of the polished floor), his heavy brown overcoat (40 per cent wool, 60 per cent acrylic fibre), his brown shoes (the left coming away at the toe allowing the freezing ingress of puddle water).

Suddenly, ahead of Aldous, Colette appeared from a doorway. She didn't look in his direction but continued ahead of him. Fear suppressed an instinct to call out to her. He thought she might not recognize him, that she had become totally insane, that she might scream or talk nonsense or cry. The awful thing was the unpredictability. To have no foreknowledge of how someone was going to behave was an intolerable form of ignorance for Aldous. And so he found himself following his wife down a long, straight corridor, thirty paces behind. From her walk she seemed sane. Drugged, unhappy, Colette's walk became slow and careful; small, cautious steps; a slight stagger. Now her walk was swift. Her confident strides swallowed the polished floor tiles. Her dressing gown, the padded silk one in deep red with black trimmings and rope belt that had been her mother's, was billowing open. Her hair was flouncy. There was even a hint of a feminine sway to her walk.

The brisk swagger of her walk reassured Aldous, although he still felt doubt. He remembered the curiously abundant energy she'd shown immediately after her seizure. This walk, likewise, had something preternaturally energetic about it. It was too normal. Aldous was beginning to feel that the territory of madness is entered by a doorway of crystallized normality.

A moment later Colette went into an almost empty day room. Aldous paused a while before continuing, so as not to make it seem he had been following her. In the day room she was talking to a woman with dark curly hair sitting in one of the many armchairs. Colette was giving the woman an unopened packet of cigarettes. Suddenly they both turned towards Aldous, who felt trapped for a moment by their faces.

They were like two beams of light identifying him in the darkness through which he'd been making his escape.

'Darling,' said Colette.

The one word, its saying, told him everything.

As they talked, Aldous realized his wife hadn't been this lucid, intelligent, funny for many years.

'Isn't it crazy,' she said, 'they've put me in the Hatch.' She had that half smile, lopsided, that she'd lost over the last few years. Recently her smiles had been fiercely symmetrical, perfect crescents filled with evenly spaced teeth, causing identical twin stars of wrinkled skin to pleat the sides of her face. Those smiles, he now realized, had been mustered with all the deliberation and rehearsal of a theatrical performance. Now, her body drained of toxins, cleansed, perhaps, by her seizure, that smile, its crookedness showing that now she could see depths in things again, had returned.

'I'm sorry if I gave you all a shock. The doctors here aren't sure why it happened. That's why they're keeping me in. I said to them, "You're not sending me to the Hatch"' (her voice did a self-parody of haughty indignation) 'and the doctor actually put her hands over her ears, screwed up her face and said, 'Don't call it that, we don't call it that any more. It's called Friern Barnet Hospital.' I said it will always be the Hatch to me. I sang her that old song about little Johnny Blunder; you know how it goes –

> *He was born one day*
> *When his mother was away*
> *In a place called Colney Hatch*

and then I couldn't work out if it meant *he* was born in Colney Hatch or his mother was away in Colney Hatch when he was born. So anyway here I am. Don't worry darling, they haven't put me in the padded cell. I've seen it though. Wendy showed me. This is Wendy.'

The seated woman, quite young Aldous now realized, with smooth skin mottled with freckles, blue eyes, thick dark loops of hair, lit a cigarette from the fresh packet Colette had brought her and exhaled smoke as Aldous smiled at her. She didn't smile back and this shocked him. The previous week she'd attempted suicide by hanging herself from a light flex. She'd brought down half the ceiling on top of her.

'They just want to keep me under observation for a while,' Colette went on. 'I'm here voluntarily, I can go home any time. It's in case I have another fit. I haven't. They want me to talk to some psychiatrists as well. You told them everything didn't you? About my sniffing? It seemed to fascinate them. None of them had ever heard of it before. I'm unique.' Here she spread her hands like flowering petals at shoulder level, a gesture that displayed her with the caption '*little me*'. She grinned. Again it was that askew smile.

Colette stayed at the hospital for three weeks. She was visited by Aldous every day and by the kids every few days. She seemed to thrive in the asylum. She busily involved herself in the lives of the other patients, learnt about their lives, their problems, their histories. She remarked to Aldous that she felt comfortable there because no one criticized her. (Aldous remembered that this was what she always said about cats and dogs, the pets of the house. *Cats never criticize you*, she would say, to which he was sometimes tempted to reply, *they would if they could bloody talk*. He sometimes imagined her tried in a court which consisted entirely of pets (cats, dogs, mice, hamsters, a tree frog) with an old Airedale as a judge who solemnly sounded his gavel and donned a black cap as he pronounced his sentence).

Wendy became her best friend. Aldous soon became used to the daily visits to the hospital. He even felt as though he was enjoying it. He once said to Wendy, 'It's quite nice here really isn't it?' 'Yes,' replied Wendy, staring at him out of cold blue eyes, 'until you see the bars on the windows.'

When Julian came he did jigsaws with Wendy while Aldous and Colette talked. Wendy had had a string of unhappy relationships with thin, wispy, unshaven men. She had attempted suicide three times (razor blade, gas oven, light flex) and she wrote in pencil tortured poetry brimming with symbolism and dark metaphors (dead flowers, worms, chains).

At the end of three weeks Colette returned home, just in time for Christmas. Aldous was not sure that her stay at the hospital had done anything other than provide a change of scenery for his wife. There had been no definite diagnosis, other than something vague about depression, no treatment other than the prescription of more drugs – tranquillizers called Valium, which she was to take whenever she felt depressed. The fit remained unexplained, although its link to sniffing was thought to be likely, She was told that she could risk her life if she took up sniffing again.

Dead flowers. Worms. Chains. Every year Colette picked a rose from the Charles Mallory in the front garden using secateurs she'd bought with Green Shield Stamps. This rose, budding, at its first moment of unfolding, was placed in a small vase in the hall. The vase was a half-cylinder, its flat side hanging flush with the wall, its curved side projecting into the space of the hall, a little stoop of water just enough to hold one flower. The rose stayed there all year. Within a month it was a shabby, wilting mess. During the winter it dried; its colour deepened; its petals hardened into curled sheaves of stiff, crisp paper. It wasn't Colette's intention to preserve the rose in this way. It was just an accidentally perfect product of forget-fulness. Once it was in the vase – a small space within the comparatively vast space of the hall – it was lost. No one saw it.

But Aldous noticed it when he brought Colette home. It had been in its vase for six months and was an exquisitely shrivelled bloom. The bicycles, in their chains, were propped as usual against the opposite wall. For some reason Aldous felt it necessary to guide his wife past them.

1970

1

Janus leant back in his chair, stretched out his feet as far as his desk would allow, lifted his arms and tucked them behind his head. The chair creaked and sounded like it was going to snap. He sat forward again, then settled back more carefully. Aware that his ears were beginning to ache, he pulled at the black apparatus that gently gripped his head – headphones at either end of an outsized barrette of adjustable plastic, a mouthpiece like the sawn-off tip of a rhino's horn – and rested it, no heavier than a bundle of knitting, in his lap.

Before him was the switchboard, a matrix of empty sockets, like an enormous and successfully completed game of solitaire. In one of these holes a voice might arrive from anywhere in the world, unheard, its presence announced by a small red light, requesting that Janus insert a pin and thus allow the voice's continued movement around the world. His days and nights were spent in making these connections, allowing the free movement of voices. It amused Janus to think, sometimes, how like an organ the switchboard was, with its stops, its vox humana, its unexpected, surprising music.

Plug 12 row 4 lit. A man in Salisbury, Rhodesia, wanted to talk to his wife in Felixstowe. Janus dialled the required number, inserted the pin, made the connection.

He then reached under his desk and felt about for a moment amongst his things, his haversack, his umbrella, his jacket, and found a can of Special Brew, which he lifted, not quite bringing it out from under the desk. He pulled the ring and there was a pleasing hiss, a gasp of pressurized gases. Glancing quickly in both directions, seeing that he was unobserved, he brought the can to his lips and drank. He drank swiftly and deeply, swallowing half the can in a few seconds. He put the can back in its hiding place and gasped, grimaced, shook his head as a prickly surge of bubbles rose in his throat and burst. He wiped his mouth and leant back again in his chair. He glanced sideways at the clock at the end of the room. He had about ten minutes to go. Then he noticed Wally, three desks away, giving him a quick glance. Had he seen him take the swig from the can? Who cared? Wally wouldn't tell anyone anyway.

There was just time, now, to make the call he'd been planning all night. He dialled the two numbers. Everything was in the timing. The first number, loaded, would ring the moment he inserted the pin. The second was already ringing. It was answered promptly.

'Hallo?' came a rather gruff voice into the headphone Janus had against his ear.

'Hallo,' said Janus, in his best telephone operator manner, 'could I speak to Mrs Gwen Hardy, please?'

'Who's calling?'

'This is International House. I have an important call for her.'

'International what?'

'Could you bring her to the phone please.'

'She's out with the cows.'

'Oh dear oh dear oh dear,' said Janus.

'Who is this?'

'This is the Milk Marketing Board.'

There was a pause. Clive Hardy's next remark was cautious. 'Is it now?'

'Yes, we have reason to believe you have been mistreating

your cows in an unspeakable way.'

Silence from the other end of the line.

'Furthermore your wife has lodged an official complaint with us regarding your activities at night in the cow shed.'

'What?'

'Diddle diddle dum, tra la la la la,' said Janus.

'Who *is* this?' Then a sudden dawning. 'Is that Janus Jones?'

Janus pulled out the pin. The line went dead. The other number, never called, had been the Prime Minister's own private line, known to very few. Oh what a beautiful trick it would have been to have Gwen dragged away from the pastures for her urgently mysterious call, and for Edward Heath, at the other end, successfully awoken by the phone that only rang when heads of state were calling, to have farmer's wife Gwen to talk to. Where would it have ended? Janus, a presiding spirit of the conversation, listening in on his headset, chortling.

Glancing to his right he saw that Wally was still watching him.

Wally was the only friend Janus had made amongst the telephonists at International House. He was already in his fifties and looked much older, with his coif of white hair and crackly laugh. He had a retroussé nose that presented, like a tortoise, two little nostrils to the world. He walked with a stoop and did everything slowly and spoke with an affected, piping lilt that was somewhere between Cambridge and Ponders End. By coincidence he lived close to the Joneses in Palmers Green, and Janus had been to his house many times. From the outside it was an ordinary suburban house, but inside it was like a palace. Wally's house had no doors, just archways sometimes hung with thick velvet curtains in deep purple. His rooms were festooned with budget chandeliers, wall-mounted lights moulded like classical Greek sculpture, spotlights. He had an electric organ that he liked Janus to play, and after an evening of synthesized Bach he would try to seduce the young and gifted pianist. Janus found this highly amusing. One time he was fingering and pedalling his way through a Bach toccata while Wally draped an arm across his protégé's shoulders, exaggeratedly interested in Janus's technique. His hand began to move in a caressing motion across Janus's shoulders, then down between his shoulder blades and towards his backside. Janus then stood up and danced a waltz with Wally across his schmaltzy living room before pushing his face into the mouldy earth of a pot of hyacinths.

Wally was old and weak and desperately in love with Janus, and Janus enjoyed the attention, and so continually enticed the old man into making foolish advances. No, Wally wouldn't tell the supervisor that he'd just seen Janus Jones take a swig of beer from a can under the desk. There was only ten minutes of the shift left for God's sake. Janus had been drinking all night. It didn't mar his performance. On the contrary, it was enhanced. He was better able to coordinate the pins with the plugs, and moreover he was friendlier with customers, those little voices, always slightly desperate, that whispered in his ear all night, asking for connections. He could chat with them once he'd had a few drinks. And in the quiet periods, of which there were quite a few now that international direct dialling was starting to take hold in some countries, he was better able to withstand the hours-on-end boredom.

Janus took from his breast pocket his pocket diary in which, at the back, was a hoard of phone numbers he'd gleaned over the years, adding new ones each year, transferring the whole lot from diary to diary, re-sorting them, grouping them under new headings. There were phone numbers of aunts and uncles he now rarely saw, phone numbers of school friends he hadn't seen since school, from work colleagues at the Gas Board, tutors at the Royal Academy of Music, students who were now violinists in symphony orchestras. There was the driving instructor he'd spent a few lessons with. There were phone numbers from people he'd met in pubs one night and never seen again. He even had his own milkman's phone number. Then there were the numbers he'd gathered over the years as a telephonist. The British Embassy in Cairo. Radio ChickenShack in north Arizona, along with dozens of other local radio stations all around the world. The private numbers of some celebrities, including Paul McCartney, Dean Martin and Nancy Sinatra. He was saving these for something special. He would have to think very carefully about Paul McCartney, because he wouldn't be able to use him much.

There was Christine's number. Janus perused it. Eight figures that had become so familiar to him he could almost see Christine's face in their sequence, as though she had reduced herself to a digital form. How magical was the telephone, Janus thought, that by running his fingers across these numbers he could stroke her voice into existence. He took another draught from the can, emptying it. He clenched his face against the burning of the alcohol and belched loudly. Wally and two other telephonists looked over. Janus put on his headset, adjusted the black plastic horn-shaped mouthpiece, leant forward to his panel and dialled. The phone rang twenty-three times before it was answered. Christine's voice said tiredly 'Yes?'

'Good morning, this is your five fifty-five alarm call.'

There was a sigh.

'Janus, I've called the police . . .'

'What for?'

'Because this is driving me mad. I'm going to change my number.'

'Don't do that my little cup cake. I can always find it.'

'Leave me alone Janus.'

She hung up.

Janus sat back, took off his headset and threw it on the desk where it clattered loudly. More headphoned heads turned. A light came on the board showing that a call was coming through from Paris. Janus yanked out the plug and let it hang. Then he stood up, wobbled and sat down again. He rummaged around under his desk, gathered his things and got ready to leave. He got more looks. He was leaving early. The morning shift hadn't arrived. Janus hooked his rucksack over his shoulder, hung his jacket over his elbow and began walking. He remembered that he'd left his beer and his umbrella under the desk. He turned, thought, but was interrupted by Norman, the supervisor.

'In my office, now,' he said, beckoning.

Janus swayed into the cluttered little office.

'Thanks for making this easy for me,' he said, 'you're fired.'

'Well I never.' said Janus.

'I don't think I need to explain, do I? Apart from the fact your breath smells like a brewery and there's a small off-licence under your desk, I've been tracking your calls for the last couple of weeks, following complaints from several members of the public and enquiries from the police about nuisance calls.' Here he produced a stapled sheaf of closely typed A4. 'This record speaks for itself, of course. A Mr Waugh of High Wycombe mean anything to you? You've called him five times in the last week, connecting him to Chiltern Radio's phone-in programme. Presumably he's crossed you at some time? I don't know why you're laughing, Janus. If you think it's just a joke, try talking to the people at MI5. Twice you put them through to a Mr James Bond, who turned out to be none other than your friend Mr Waugh again. Rest assured that once you start meddling with these confidential numbers you'll be in it up to your neck. Christ knows where it would end. I'm sorry Janus, but this job requires a hundred per cent trustworthiness. You'll be paid up until today, but your bonus will be withdrawn. From this I will take the money you owe me personally, which now totals over five pounds.'

'Smashing,' said Janus.

'Now I think you'd better leave before I'm tempted to contact the police.'

'Well, I never,' said Janus, who had collapsed into a creaky leather chair, and then slumped forward. The supervisor looked disgusted, wrinkling his face sourly and said 'Oh for Christ's sake man,' anticipating that Janus might be sick in his office.

He stood up and walked around the desk and tried lifting Janus out of the chair. Janus staggered a little, then seemed alert. He picked up from a shelf a thick ream of cartridge paper and put it in his bag.

'Put it back, Janus,' said the supervisor.

Janus picked up an earthenware coffee mug from the same shelf, a Christmas present for Norman which he'd never used. Janus pocketed it, along with a bunch of pens and pencils.

'A leaving gift,' said Janus, and left the office.

Back on the floor the night workers, including Wally, were handing over to the morning shift.

Wally walked over to Janus quickly.

'Bad news poppet?'

'I've been fired.'

'That is bad news. Come on, I'll take you home.'

Before leaving Janus took one more thing. Along the tops of the desks was a row of small wooden boxes, one for each international telephone exchange in the world. Each box was designated a three-letter code, the first three letters of the city name, which was marked on the front in white paint. Into these boxes were placed call-booking slips. The boxes above Janus's desk ranged from Johannesburg (JOH) to Nairobi (NAI). Janus took the box marked KHA.

Janus and Wally spent the day in the City, breakfasting on beer in a market pub in Spittalfields, then riding the double-deckers out of the East End and along the Strand, Wally taking the role of keeper to Janus's lunatic, annoying commuters on the top deck with ear-piercing whistles and whoops, and drunken belly-dances, whipping the opened *Telegraph*s out of the paws of accountants. They rode the Routemasters for much of the morning, the number 11s and 15s, into the City and out again, Janus teasing the conductors by ringing the bells and stamping on the floor above the driver's cab while Wally sat quietly inside. They were expelled from many buses, then walked across Waterloo Bridge to the Festival Hall, where Janus ran around the concrete piazzas, jumped on the walls, whistling and whooping, blowing raspberries, running up to people as if about to knock them over, then kissing them on the backs of the hands (men or women) instead.

'You have so much energy,' said Wally once they'd rested on a silver sculpture, Janus panting, undoing his shirt, 'if I drink too much I just fall asleep, but you get livelier and livelier.'

Janus, when drunk, could not listen to people and behaved rather as if they weren't there. Thus it was that Wally disappeared, while Janus resumed his drunken high jinks. Wally followed lamely, unseen, as Janus paraded along Whitehall, through Trafalgar Square, along Charing Cross Road. Wally was becoming tired, and continually suggested they drop into a café somewhere for some coffee, but Janus went on marching until they reached Oxford Street where, with a sudden decisiveness, he sat down on the kerb and cried.

Wally sat down beside him and put an arm around his shoulder, which staunched immediately Janus's tears, and caused him to withdraw, snail-like, into a shell of indifference. He lay down along the kerb, which had become as soft as a sack of feathers, and fell asleep.

When Janus woke up Tottenham Court Road had become a bed, its buses, lorries and taxis had melted into blankets and pillows which surrounded him like the soft shell of an unlaid egg. It was the sumptuous four-poster in Wally's house with its gold fluted columns and curtains of crushed velvet, its canopies of lace. And there was Wally, the old queen of the switchboards, the queer of Palmers Green, in bed beside him, snoring a grandfatherly snore.

Janus, never encumbered by hangovers, no matter how much he drank, took a look at the old man whose face was half sunken in the pillow beside his and thought what a treat it would be to take one of those plaster cherubs and do his head in with it. The old man would wake after the first blow and beg for more, probably, *yes, Janus, you can kill me if you want to, anything for you, Janus, here on the back of me head, you could do me in with one bash there . . .* Janus lifted the bedclothes and peered down, saw that, thankfully, he was still fully clothed, whereas Wally was a vista of sagging male flesh flecked with grey hairs. Full paps with nipples the size of ladybirds. He was so hairy, so grey, he looked like a sheep.

Quickly Janus threw back the covers and lifted himself out of bed.

Wally stirred, opened his eyes.

'What are you doing, pet?'

'What day is it?'

'It's Saturday. How do you feel?'

'Oh fuck,' said Janus, and flopped back on to the bed, held his head in his hands.

Wally sat up, the covers dropping, revealing his bare, snow-topped shoulders.

'You'd better not have done anything last night you old queer,' Janus suddenly snapped, turning to him.

'Of course not, Janus, just tucked you up . . .' then seeing that Janus was looking with revulsion at his body, 'I always sleep like this. What am I supposed to do, sleep on the floor? Anyway, you had no objection last night . . .'

'To what?'

'To my sleeping in the same bed.'

Janus sighed, found his shoes on the floor, slipped them on.

'Shall I make us a nice cuppa?' said Wally.

'I'm going home.'

'Back to your nutcase Mum?'

'Don't call her a nutcase.'

'But you always do. You said she'd been in Colney Hatch.'

'That was months ago. Before Christmas. She's better now. I told you that as well.'

'So why do you still call her a nutcase?'

Janus reached across the bed and took Wally's head into an armlock and lifted his arm up into a half-nelson. The sudden flurry of energy with bedsprings bouncing had Wally in giggles.

'You're the bloody nutcase,' said ruffled Wally once he'd been released.

Janus stood up, moved across the deep pile of the carpet against which the opening door made a stiff, brushing sound, and said 'Lend me five pounds Wal.'

'What for?' said Wally, reaching for his jacket at the end of the bed.

'I just got the sack didn't I for Christ's sake?'

'But you've got Mummy and Daddy to look after you.' He held out a carefully extracted note for Janus to take. Money seemed to work like medicine for Janus, in a sour mood five pounds would sweeten him instantly.

Janus smiled.

'Ta you old poof.'

Janus went downstairs, picked up his haversack which he found in the living room next to the organ, and made for the stained glass of the front door.

Wally came down in a black silk dressing gown that made Janus laugh.

'Will you come and see me, Janus?'

'I don't know.'

'But you must keep in touch. You can't live with Mummy and Daddy for ever. There's always room here . . .'

Janus opened the front door.

'I don't know,' he said again, and moved out into the street.

Wally came after him as far as the front step, then seemed distracted by the milk that was waiting for him, in little bottles, by the front door. He picked them up, nursing them carefully in his arms as he walked awkwardly backwards into the house.

A bright, intensely lit morning that exaggerated everything. Houses were palaces. Front gardens parks. Trees jungle. If you could take all the gardens of suburban London, thought Janus, and join them together, you would have a garden the size of Oxfordshire. He passed a hundred gardens that morning, along Oswald Avenue, Green Lanes, Dorset Street, Severn-dale Avenue, Hoopers Lane. It was such a nice morning Janus took a detour down Woodberry Road. Garden upon garden, an infinity of roses, a desert of modest lawns. And the trees. Every few yards, a tree, alternating with the lamp posts. Limes that bushed out with green foliage from their trunks in the summer that caught the blind unawares, that dropped sticky sap on to new cars, that blocked the gutters with dead leaves and caused floods.

Turning the corner of Green Lanes and Fernlight Avenue in what was early summer, Janus was confronted with leafage of such density it was easy to forget there were houses there. A linear forest in which there happened to be buildings. The parked cars, tacky with sap, formed a guard of honour for anything that travelled along the road.

As he sauntered up Fernlight Avenue towards his house, which was the utmost house in the road, the highest numbered house in Fernlight Avenue, he marvelled at a bird in flight. A grey bird. A silver bird. A little silver dove that flew in a graceful arc. There was a sound of brakes applied suddenly, the screech of tyres, then a volley of canine barks. A short scream. Janus ran.

'He's under the car,' said the woman, who was crying, and trying to pull her Doberman back by the collar, just outside Janus's house, as Janus arrived, breathless. 'The man's driven off. I don't know if he knew.' The woman was shaking. 'He didn't look good, the cat.'

Scipio had twirled in the air like a sycamore key, a graceful triple pirouette, having been first crushed under the wheel and then flicked into the air by the car into whose path he'd run to escape the Doberman that now was pushing its way beneath Mr Cortina's Cortina, where Scipio, alive, sheltered.

The woman pulled the Doberman, vaguely known to Janus as Jack from round the corner, away, and Janus crouched down and looked into the oily, shadowy space beneath the Cortina. There a silver animal panted, half visible. It seemed that its pelt, dappled with spots and rings, had become loose, and hung in tatters about its hind parts and tail, as though it was clothing, and that Scipio had been caught half undressed. His white chin was crimson and he was sneezing on blood. His tail was smooth and shiny, because it was raw skin. His legs were twisted.

'Poor thing,' Janus heard a voice behind him muttering. A small group had gathered. Colette had come out of the house. Janus stood up.

'It's Scipio,' said Janus to his mother. Then he got down on all fours again, peeked under the car, and made feline noises. Strange, thought Colette. It was as though he was impersonating a cat.

Janus reached into the shadow of the Cortina. His hand met a nest of knives and came back with four red stripes neatly drawn. He tried again with the other hand. Scipio, with the paltry strength he had left, savaged his hand, growled and hissed, a little explosion.

'They should have ambulances for cats,' said an old lady.

Janus rushed into the house, returned with a broom and a pair of gloves. With these he managed to sweep Scipio out of the shadows and on to a blanket.

In the bright, intense daylight his injuries became explicit. Back legs broken. Abdomen crushed. Skin flayed along the flanks and tail. God knows what inside.

'He's bringing up blood, dear,' said the old lady, 'best put him out of his misery. Look how he's breathing, dear.'

The tiniest breaths, little teaspoonfuls of air.

'Sad isn't it?' said her friend.

Janus looked at his mother to see if her face agreed with these grim sentiments. He wasn't sure.

'All those spots,' said the old lady, 'it's a shame.'

Janus ran into the house, returned with a bike and a bag. It was his old bike. Straight handlebars. Three-speed Sturmey archer gear.

'What are you doing?' said Colette.

'Taking him to the vet.'

'On a bike?'

'How else?'

The old women looked at each other with bemused smiles, as if someone had made a risqué remark. Scipio was breathing quickly and slightly, but in the open air seemed accepting of Janus's hands as he lifted him and the blanket together as one into the grey holdall. He gave one gasp, licked his clotted nose, chuckled with agony, then fell silent. Janus lifted the bag on to the saddle rack, looped the handles of the holdall around the saddle, mounted and set off, freewheeling, wobbly at first, down Fernlight Avenue.

'Well,' said the first old woman, 'he must think a lot of that cat.'

'Was it his cat?'

'I think so.'

'Someone who does all that for a cat can't be all bad.'

'No. The child who's good to animals, what do they say?'

'Something or other.'

Colette tried to cry while Janus was at the vet's, but she couldn't. The sight of Scipio, a little tangle of blood and broken bones, had upset her deeply, but she couldn't prevent herself from feeling relieved that Scipio's presence was gone from the house. She felt foolish admitting it to herself, but the cat made her feel tense. It was a constant source of anxiety, like a mild toothache, always there, always waiting to be damaged. Also, Janus was always spoiling the cat, lavishing silly gifts on it, coming home from work in the morning with slices of cold roast beef, packets of shaved smoked salmon, felt mice filled with catnip, toy birds with bells in their tummies. Nothing for Colette. He would sit in the chair opposite his mother, dangle Damoclesian scraps of luxury meats above Scipio's head, watch him rise on his hind legs and paw them down from his fingers. Janus might spend a whole morning doing this until the hypertrophied cat would drag its heavy tummy to a cushioned chair for a day's sleep. Colette (she knew it was stupid) felt jealous of Scipio. She was beginning to regret having ever bought him that cat.

Perhaps, she thought, the loss of Scipio would enable her and Janus to start afresh. Janus had been particularly difficult with her since she had come out of Friern Barnet (she had become used to that name by now). It was as though he hadn't forgiven her for something, though she never felt sure what, precisely.

Colette had felt lucky when she came out of the hospital. Lucky to be alive, lucky to have a family to welcome her home, lucky to be home just in time for Christmas. Julian and Juliette seemed genuinely delighted to have her back, and even James, usually rather cool in his relations with his mother, appeared to be pleased. Janus, however, had snubbed her. She wasn't expecting this reaction because he had taken the trouble to visit her frequently while she was in Friern, and had made a big impression on the residents and staff by playing Chopin and Bartok on an old upright that had been left and forgotten about in a corner of the day room. Some afternoons he had a sizeable audience gathered around him. He would politely refuse requests for popular favourites ('Give us "We'll Meet Again" will you darling?') and played instead his own concert repertoire. One evening he performed, entirely from memory, the whole of the Diabelli Variations.

Christmas Day itself had been desperately opulent, the tree almost invisible beneath a heap of presents. Janus had lavished gifts upon his family – a black velvet jacket for James, a three-foot high model of a *Saturn V* for Julian, expensive shoes for his father, tins of smoked salmon pâté and catnip toys for Scipio, but for his mother he'd bought a cheap box of chocolates. It was well known that Colette hated chocolates as presents. Chocolates were for despised maiden aunts or loathed mothers-in-law.

Janus's mood seemed to grow darker as Christmas progressed. On Boxing Day he hardly came out of his room, and when he did he would barely talk, but would sit for hours at the piano without playing it, or would slump in front of the television.

Then, one evening before the year had quite ended, the Christmas tree still lit but empty of gifts, its needles beginning to desiccate and fall, Janus and James were sitting together in the front room watching television. The paper chains and balloons hung dolefully above them, having become so ordinary they weren't noticed.

The rest of the family was in the kitchen. Julian was busy on the floor testing the hypothesis that cats' whiskers existed to enable cats to measure gaps before passing through them. He'd put Baxbr in an upside down cardboard box with a slightly too narrow opening cut into it with a bread knife. He placed a tempting scrap of bacon beyond the opening. Baxbr pushed through the gap and became stuck. Colette was reading *Dombey and Son*. Juliette was washing her hair at the sink.

They noticed noise coming from the front room. A boisterousness. A shouting. Sometimes laughter. Incredulous laughter.

Now and then James came into the kitchen to get something – coffee, a glass of water, and would report that Janus was getting stupid. Aldous hadn't taken much notice. He heard him say something about Janus being teasing, provocative. He only took notice later when the noise became obtrusive. Sudden loud cackles of laughter from Janus, a most uncharacteristic noise. A loud whistle. Janus could do those – four fingers (two from each hand), symmetrically into his lip-corners, a shrieking, screaming note it was hard to believe a person could produce. Then quieter, saner laughter from James, then whooping noises from Janus.

'Sounds like Janus has had a bit too much to drink,' said Colette without looking up from her book, her voice full of tranquillized calm.

Aldous had never been a drinker. He'd been drunk only once in his life, in the army. That experience had turned him off drinking for thirty years. The nausea. He could remember trying to climb into his bunk in the barracks feeling as though he was trying to stop the bunk from rotating before he climbed into it. Neither did he like being among drunken people. It brought out his fear of madness again. To see people out of control. Drinking, it seemed to him, was to submit to madness.

Janus had been drunk before. In the summer they'd spent an evening in the garden of The Red Lion and Janus had become slightly tipsy, and it was quite funny. He'd told his family that he was getting married to Scipio. Yes, they were in love. Arm in arm they'd walked along the banks of the New River. Together they'd gone to The Happy Fillet to buy some coley, to the Contented Sole for some jellied eels and by moonlight they'd shared a can of tuna. They were all laughing at Janus's monologue; the whole garden was laughing in the end.

But that night, the third or fourth day of Christmas, a day of calling birds or French hens, a crescendo was building in the front room. There was a new voice in the family.

When James came out again to get a drink at the tap in the kitchen Colette said 'What's going on in there?'

'Janus is just being stupid. He's drunk.'

'What's he doing?'

'Just saying stupid things. Really stupid things.'

James was walking through the kitchen with his mug of water when Colette said 'Don't go back in there, James,'

James wrinkled his nose as though bewildered by his mother's concern, as though now she was being stupid, and returned to the front room.

The calling continued for a little while and then it became quiet. It was quiet for about half an hour and everybody in the kitchen forgot that Janus was drunk. Juliette combed her wet hair. Colette read Dickens. Julian teased Baxbr with a scrap of newspaper tied to the end of a piece of string, and Aldous read a newspaper.

Then there came a sound from the front room like a wall falling. A great weight crashing into the floor, the floorboards of the whole house shaking. Unable to think what had happened, unable to imagine any furniture that could fall with such a noise, Aldous went quickly to the front room to investigate. When he opened the door he saw that Janus was lying on the floor holding his nose. James was sitting on the couch, his arms folded, watching the television with exaggerated nonchalance. Janus's nose was bleeding. He stood up calmly, spitting blood from his lips in the same way he spat smoke when he had a cigarette. Aldous found himself thinking irrelevantly about how different James and Janus had become in appearance. Janus was still a young man of the Fifties, a short back and sides hair cut, loose-fitting trousers with turn-ups, while James had grown his hair to shoulder length with a perfectly symmetrical centre parting and wore faded jeans, T-shirts, and the black velvet jacket that had been Janus's present.

Their father's presence was not acknowledged by either brother. Instead, with what looked to Aldous like a comically aggressive face, the sort of face you might pull if you were telling a group of children a story about a bad wolf, Janus lunged at James, growling. James was quick to respond, lifting his feet and pushing against Janus's midriff, propelling him backwards so that he crashed into the television which fell from its already precarious perch on a blue stool. Orange sparks erupted from its slotted back cover. The silence in the absence of the television was very noticeable.

'What the hell have you done to the telly?' Aldous said, at last finding a voice.

James had stood up.

'What?' he said to no one. His face was white and empty. He was concentrating very hard.

Janus staggered across the side of the room, sweeping a line of vases and photographs off the mantelpiece. The vases, some of which Aldous had made, smashed. He picked up the table lamp, throttled the light out of it, and hurled it at James. His growling was now done with an extended tongue as though he was pretending to vomit. He was looking at both James and Aldous with a face that said they made him sick. Then he said 'I'll fucking kill you', and lunged again at James, a hopelessly wild, uncoordinated swing of the extended arm, the fist at the end easily dodged, all the weight Janus put into it instead propelling his body across the room towards the door where Colette had just entered. He crashed into her, throwing her against the wall where she knocked her head and fell to the floor.

After that Colette couldn't remember what happened in sequential detail. There was just a series of scenes that could have happened in any order. At one point Janus, stretched out on the floor, took hold of Aldous's ankle and bit it. Aldous's only option was to stamp on his son's head, which he did hard enough on his ear to be painful without being dangerous.

The fighting went on for what seemed hours. It was prolonged because every now and then Janus appeared to calm down and to recover his temper. He would sit panting, holding his head, his eyes clenched shut as though he had a pounding headache, then suddenly he would spring into violence with renewed energy. His mother, whose head was marked by a dark trickle of dried blood, tried tipping a panful of cold water over his head as a means of subduing him. He ducked and knocked the pan out of her hands. Most of the water went over her. This happened in the hall. He took the pan and threw it through the front door window. The window was leaded, divided into a series of rectangles by thick lines of metal. The pan burst this delicate array of glass.

Eventually Janus's violence burnt itself out. He had staggered, bruised with a black eye Aldous had given him, to his bedroom. Ranting as he climbed the stairs. Repeating the phrase 'a nice Christmas this has turned out to be', several times before he shut himself in his bedroom, where he remained for fourteen hours.

Aldous told Colette, though she already realized it, that he had not hit anyone before in his entire life, but that evening he'd punched Janus in the face. Even at school he'd managed to survive without resort to violence. For ten years in a tough school, and him with a posh name. Somehow he'd always managed to avoid violence. His size helped. He was too big to be an obvious target for bullies. Inwardly he was rather proud of this achievement, although later in life it worried him that perhaps he'd forgone some crucial stage in the development of his character. His father used to comment on his softness. He

268

seemed disappointed that his son never came home with a black eye or a fat lip. He wasn't developing properly. Everybody fights when they're young. It gave you a hard edge, a competitiveness, the aggression essential to survival. Still, five years in the army had toughened him in a way equivalent to countless playground bundles. He had, however, got through World War II without throwing a single punch, let alone firing a shot.

The sweeping up after Janus's departure reminded them both of the war. It was what you saw housewives doing after an air raid, even if their houses had been half flattened they'd be out on the front path sweeping away the rubble.

And there was rubble in the house now. He wasn't sure where it had all come from. Some of the vases he recognized, his lotus vases. Some glasses. Lots of pieces of glass. Some plates.

It was while they were clearing away that they realized Julian wasn't in the house. He was found, after a brief search, in the house of a neighbour on the corner. They didn't know who lived in that house as it had changed ownership several times in the last few years. Aldous discovered that it was now inhabited by a young blonde woman who'd found Julian walking aimlessly up and down the pavement outside.

Julian had found himself leaving his own house as though he was disowning it, shrugging it off, shedding a skin. In the street he was surprised by how much noise the conflict was generating. It echoed the length of Fernlight Avenue. Passersby looked at him and he looked at them as if to say – *that house, it's nothing to do with me. I've never lived there.* There would be a scream. The sound of breaking glass. It wasn't that Julian thought he would be in danger if he stayed in the house. He never felt that. He just didn't want to be inside the house while all that was going on. He didn't want to be inside the noise, inside the violence. He'd never seen violence like that before, except on television, and that made it seem almost exciting to him. But what really frightened him was the thought that someone, or everyone, was going to be killed.

When violence like that happened in films, people died. So he said to himself as he walked up and down the pavement, 'they're going to kill each other', repeating the statement several times because it sounded incredibly grown up to him. He couldn't believe he was saying something so grown up, having such grown up thoughts.

He realized that he had nowhere to go. But it hadn't been his intention to go anywhere. He'd left the house like someone who'd been told there was an unexploded bomb on the premises. He would retire to a safe distance until the house was made safe again. It was a strange thing to feel that the street was a safer place than the house. Julian didn't know how to be in the street. The street was a place where he played when he was very young with children too old for him. Sometimes, if there'd been a good snowfall, he would create a slide on the pavement, stamping down the snow gradually as he paced back and forth until it was as hard and smooth as a butcher's marble counter. But otherwise the street wasn't a place in which to dwell. He had the problem of walking nowhere while looking as though he was walking somewhere, with purpose. It didn't fool the woman on the corner who asked him if he wanted to come inside. Almost without hesitation he accepted.

It was only the second time in his life that he'd allowed himself into the domain of a complete stranger. The other time it had been a woman as well, a motherly, older woman in a Ford Popular who'd noticed him crying as he was walking along the road home from school. Julian was crying because he was intensely cold. He was wearing shorts and in the mile he'd walked from school his legs had become so frozen they felt as though they were on fire. He refused to accept a lift from the woman at first even though she followed him in her car, stopping every few yards and telling him to get in. By this time he was in such agony he could barely walk and his face was awash with tears. So he got into the little green car and was driven safely and warmly home. He was perhaps seven years old. Now, at nearly nine, he walked into the house that offered haven having been asked only once. It seemed impossible that the house could be more dangerous than the one he'd left, whose angry noises still filled the street.

But he didn't really like the house he was taken into. Although the young blonde woman, who was rather pretty, was the sole occupant, Julian sensed a strong male presence. A pyramid of unopened beer cans was carefully set on a table, an extravagance that Julian had only seen in supermarkets before. The house, it seemed, had been carefully stocked and prepared for the arrival of 1970, in a few days' time.

'There's a bit of a commotion going on at your house isn't there?' the woman said, smiling.

'Yes,' replied Julian feeling that this woman knew in detail what was happening at his home, and therefore that he didn't need to explain anything.

'Who's making all the noise? Is it your Mum and Dad?'

'No, it's my brother.' Julian was surprised at the woman's ignorance. He wondered if she was going to ask why they were all fighting. He was thankful she didn't.

'People can sometimes drink a bit too much at Christmas can't they?'

But Christmas itself hadn't been like this. And their home had nothing like the stockpiles of alcohol that furnished this quiet woman's rooms. When eventually his father found him and took him home, thanking the woman with a nervous, apologetic laugh, trying hard to make light of the events, Julian felt relief that his family were still alive. He was glad to be back in his house, even though it was in ruins.

What surprised Julian the most was what happened the following day. Janus came downstairs in the afternoon claiming to have no recollection whatsoever of the night before. His first question was 'What's happened to the front door?' Aldous had boarded it up with one of his paintings, a view through trees of distant Welsh hills, the painting facing into the house, brown stippled hardboard facing the street.

Julian thought that everything would be changed after that night, that Janus couldn't live in the house in the same way as he'd done before. But now the whole family seemed to be treating the events as a joke. They were recounted to Janus who listened with laughing incredulity.

'And then you bit my ankle . . .'

'I didn't did I?'

Laughter.

'And you threw a pan through the window.'

'No.'

Laughter.

Julian was glad that nothing had changed.

Although he missed the glass of the front window. So did Aldous. When he came to replace the window a few weeks later, it was found that leaded light was far too expensive. He had to buy instead a single pane of glass with narrow vertical ribs that distorted the view of the street in an ugly way, as though the world had been combed with a steel comb. It was never the same house again after that window had been broken, as though some essential spirit had escaped through the glass. All the other houses in Fernlight Avenue had leaded front door windows. All of them. Aldous was amazed that they'd managed to preserve their original glass for so long. The road had been built in 1910. All his neighbours' houses had had their glass for sixty years. But he'd broken his. The house was broken.

When Janus returned from the vet's, wheeling the bike clumsily into the hall, the holdall on its saddle rack empty, Colette was surprised by the whiteness of his face, the redness of his eyes.

'Don't feel too sad,' she said, laying a consoling hand on his arm, 'I know how much Scipio meant to you, but we can always get another cat.'

Janus settled his bike against the wall and looked, first at the hand that was laid on his arm, then at his mother's face. He looked empty and Colette thought he was going to cry, but instead he laughed derisively.

'What are you talking about? Scipio's alive.'

272

'Alive?'

'The vet said he'll live.'

What the vet had actually said, after a brief examination, was 'Let's put him out of his misery.' But Janus had begged the vet to do whatever he could, and after a while the vet reluctantly agreed, as long as his internal injuries weren't too severe, that there might be a chance, pointing out that it would be expensive and time consuming. Scipio had a broken pelvis, broken kidneys, a broken tail. He was bleeding inside, like an egg timer. He would need several operations. He would need to be girdled in plaster for about three months. He would need round the clock care for at least six months. He would have to be fed through a syringe. His motions would need to be expressed manually. He would have to be fed a cocktail of pills daily. Even after all that he might not fully recover. He might never walk again. The vet wanted an assurance that Janus was prepared to care for a sick cat. He also wanted some money up front. Fifty quid for the initial operation to fix the bleeding. Who knows what else he might find broken when he opened him up? That would all be more money. He would have to stay at the surgery for the first two weeks.

How Janus could have done with his bonus. For once, however, he had some money put by. Not money he'd saved, exactly, just money he hadn't got round to spending yet.

'And who's going to look after him twenty-four hours a day? I'm sorry, Janus, but I'm not prepared to devote my life to the care of a cat.'

The first spotted domestic cat. A piece of history.

Janus told her that he would leave his job in order to look after that cat, and this sparked off a row. At first it seemed to centre around ownership of Scipio.

'He's my cat,' said Janus, 'I have final say.'

'Wrong,' said Colette, 'Scipio's mine. I bought him. I paid for him. I found out about him.'

'But you bought him for me.'

'I bought him for the house.'

'You bought him for me.'

273

'I bought him for the family.'

'Scipio's mine.'

'Remember what he did to Adam and Eve.'

'That was Baxbr.'

'O come back Dimitri. I should have sold him for a train set when I had the chance.'

'What are you talking about?'

'Have the animal gassed, Janus.'

'I'm keeping Scipio alive.'

'My god I'll kill that cat myself if I have to, with a brick when you're out.'

'You won't. He'll never be out of my sight. You lay a finger on that cat and I'll kill you.'

'You always thought more of that cat than you do me.'

'That's because he loves me.'

'Animal love is nothing love.'

'Your love is nothing love.'

'My love is everything.'

'You sound like a bloody birthday card.'

'You don't know anything about love.'

'No, it's you. You're the one who doesn't know anything about love. All the time you tell me I don't know anything about love. Why do you keep saying it?' Here Janus took his mother by the shoulders and shook her. Her glasses fell off. She pushed him and he fell against the front door, which, slightly ajar, thumped shut.

'I keep saying it because I want you to know about love. I want you to go away and find out about it.'

Janus leant with his back against the front door, with its new glass. Colette had him pinned there, her arms either side of him resting against the door. She felt small next to him. They looked into each other's faces. Her face felt small against his.

'Don't bring him back here, Janus,' Colette whispered, 'I'll kill him. I mean it.'

After a fortnight at the vet's Scipio came home and Janus set him up on a small nest of cushions and blankets in the corner of his bedroom, below the window. Three times a day he fed him, filling a large plastic syringe with liquid food. The cat gagged the first few times, but gradually became used to the intrusion of the plastic nozzle in his throat. Three times a day Janus emptied the cat's bladder and bowels. This was more difficult, especially as Scipio's lower half was encased in plaster. He had to push his fingers inside the cast and press. The vet had shown him how. He pushed the excrement out, as though getting the last few drops of colour out of a tube of oil paint, catching the shit in a plastic dish. The urine was discharged in the same way, just like squirting a tiny water pistol. Once he knew where to push, a thin stream of hot, almost clear liquid would come, to clatter quietly in another dish.

For most of the time, however, Scipio reposed among the blankets and cushions in a patch of sunlight, a coil of slack muscles and dead skin, without even the strength to wash himself. Janus did this, combing his fur twice daily, moistening the dappled pelt, just like a cat would.

He spent whole days in his room, just him and the cat. He did not admit anyone else. To the rest of the family Scipio had become a rumoured presence, a ghost, something sequestered, like Mrs Rochester, muttering in her attic, or Miss Havisham perhaps, steeped in dusty lace, inhabiting a single room at the same eternal moment.

Often, with everyone else out, it was only Colette, Janus and Scipio in the house. Colette would sit in the kitchen, aware of the remote presence of her son upstairs, and the cat, and she would experience a sense of absence. It felt as though she had been exiled in her own house, that it was she who was in confinement, and not the cat.

Sometimes, visiting the lavatory, she would pause outside Janus's door, which was occasionally just ajar, and she would hear voices. Was her son reading stories to Scipio? Was he lying down beside him conducting a one-sided conversation? If she paused too long, however, Janus's voice would come loudly, hollering for her to go away.

Would he care for her, his own mother, as much if she was

equivalently crippled? She thought not. She couldn't picture her son syringing glucose down her throat, combing her hair, emptying her. More and more it struck her that Janus's devotion to the cat was not an expression of love for Scipio, but an expression of disdain for his mother.

Aldous tried to persuade her that Scipio's illness had focused Janus's life. They had hoped, after all, that Scipio would give him some responsibility. And here it was. Janus was the cat's only hope of life. Without him he would have died. And Janus had stopped drinking. He'd given up his job at International House, a job that wasted his talents but which he seemed to enjoy, just so that he could nurse the cat. He had no money, it was true, and they missed the housekeeping that had come, more generously than necessary, from Janus's weekly wage packet. On National Assistance he could barely pay for Scipio's medicines and occasional veterinary visits. But surely the unemployment was worth the sobriety that had taken hold of Janus.

One thing. Janus, since Scipio's accident, had stopped shaving and hadn't cut his hair. Very quickly he grew a lush, dark beard and long hair that made him look like a Russian grandee of the Revolution. In certain lights he was Jesus, or Solzhenitsyn, or Brahms.

On a summer afternoon, Janus unusually absent, Colette alone in the house, she stole into his room.

She'd rarely been there since she and Aldous had moved their sleeping quarters downstairs, and she was struck by the changes in its atmosphere. How strongly it smelt of Janus, and how masculine Janus smelt. The carpet had gone, and there were floorboards of dark wood that gave the air a resonant quality, like that of a small chapel. Janus's single bed was a mess. Meg's old dressing table was heaped with stuff – music manuscripts, library books, newspapers. Shoes and clothes were scattered on the floor, along with Ordnance Survey maps, some partly unfolded. The unstructured clutter made Colette feel she was stepping through a minefield as she walked through Janus's room.

In the corner, beneath the window, in a trapezoid of July sunlight, part of the clutter lived. Scipio, a solipsism of silver fur curled up in a hoop, groomed himself with the strength he had regained. It was the third month of his convalescence. He could lift his head. He was beginning to regain control of his bowels. All this Janus had told Colette, and she had been permitted to visit him once or twice, but she had not been to him alone. She could see where the fur had grown back, refilling the empty spaces of bruised skin on his flanks with exactly the same pattern of black dots and stripes on a silver background as before.

Colette took a pillow from Janus's bed, that still carried the impression of his head, a soft pit at the centre of its plumpness. She carried the pillow to Scipio and, concentrating very hard, the pillow held in both hands, she lowered it upon the cat, who paused in his self absorption as the shadow came over him, and looked up indifferently as the pillow descended. Colette was on her knees and brought all the weight of her upper body on to the pillow, which became smooth and tight with the pressure. She felt an urgent need to control her mouth, such as one feels when taking in bitter medicine, and all she could think about was her hands, which she could see beneath her as they secured the pillow. How old they looked. Wrinkled. Veins as plump as blue earthworms. Age spots.

Drops of water fell from her eyes on to the pillow – pat, pat, like grey freckles.

No movement came from beneath the pillow, until, after what seemed like an hour of sustained pressure, a strange, tingling vibration came up through Colette's hands. The pillow was buzzing softly. It was as though she had smothered a beehive. The buzzing was rhythmic and strong. Scipio was purring.

Quickly Colette lifted the pillow and laughed. Scipio gave his head a shake, twitched his ears, licked his nose and blinked contentedly in the sunlight, like something hatched from an enormous, soft egg.

On a summer dawn in August, Aldous, alone, opened the front door of his house and moved along its path to the road, wheeling a midnight blue Claude Butler racer, his since 1950, heavily laden.

Eight years since Aldous last cycled to Wales. Eight years in which he'd forgotten about that part of his life, the part that is bicycle-borne. *We ride bicycles with our hearts, Rex*, Lesley had said. Only now did he realize that in saying goodbye to cycling he'd allowed his body to fall out of synch with some vital rhythm. Cycling had chained his heart to the sun and the moon, those two great wheels in the sky. Since abandoning the bicycle (apart from the daily flat grind to school, or the perfunctory freewheels to the shops), the chain had slipped from his life and his body had slowed and his heart had stiffened. By cycling to Wales he hoped, somehow, that he would restir those stagnant red waters, to ride a bicycle with his heart.

The house behind him closed and dark, he took a moment to appreciate his bicycle – its drop handlebars taped with black insulating tape, the gear and brake cables sheathed in white plastic, the saddle, a Brookes double sprung leather seat, as comfortable as an armchair, that he'd had since he was a boy, transferring it from bike to bike. How easily the bike accommodated its load, a bundle of camping gear and clothes wrapped up and piled on the saddle rack, secured with clothes line. The tent poles strapped to the crossbar, extending beyond the handlebars like bayonets, as though his bike had become some eccentric weapon of warfare. The sandwiches and waterproofs and other provisions that sat in a bag above the front wheel. The bike under the weight of his life seemed as bulky as a small pony, and as strong.

He mounted in the before-milkmen silence of early dawn and pushed up the slender gradient of Fernlight Avenue to Hoopers Lane. He passed endless curtained houses – Woodberry Road, College Road, Dorset Street, steered past The Goat and Compasses, turned right into Goat and Compasses Lane, by day thick with juggernauts, now empty. A long slow ascent, the first of many, took him past The Owl, the locked entrance to Redlands Park and then on to Southgate, still empty, passing the modernist tube station, rows of closed shops, the light white and milky. He cycled along the A111 to Cockfosters, past the northernmost tube station on the Piccadilly Line and then freewheeled down into the first taste of countryside: Hadley Woods to his left, Trent Park to his right and then his first real ascent, Stag Hill, a straight road that climbed between fields of grass.

He got off to walk. He could have cycled but he needed to pace himself, conserve energy. No point in exhausting yourself in the first five miles. He walked past the sign that said, on the other side, *London Borough of Enfield*, so marking the invisible boundary of London. The beginning of Hertfordshire. He walked under a stately row of pylons and pedalled on to Potters Bar. Lone lorries appeared and rumbled past him. A car passed. He noticed the drivers craning their necks to look at him. He felt out of the ordinary. A rare sight. A cyclist with a heavily laden bicycle. Hemel Hempstead with its two-way roundabout, a roundabout of roundabouts. Then a valley through the Chilterns following the Grand Union Canal between chalky hills. Here he stopped by the side of the road at an entrance to a field. He'd been cycling two hours. There were the beginnings of rush hour traffic. A trickle of cars flowing in from the Aylesbury Plain towards London. He settled into long grass, unpacked some sandwiches (cheese and pickle) ate them and drank from a bottle of warm lemonade.

He was feeling good. Twenty miles and he wasn't at all tired, although the palms of his hands were tingling. His own fitness surprised him.

He hadn't meant to go to Wales this year. The children, apart from Julian, weren't interested. Janus was too preoccupied with the nursing of Scipio. Colette was too weak, too shaky. The subject hadn't even been raised, and he was glad. Usually by Easter anticipation was rising, plans were being made, lists being compiled. This year it was as though the farm had become part of their unspoken history. Something they no longer talked about. When that time of year came when Aldous would write to the Evanses at Llanygwynfa, he did nothing. And he thought the cycle of their visits had been broken. For Aldous their years at the farm started to seem like a dream. It was as though Llanygwynfa was on an island on the other side of the world that they would never visit.

And then the letter came.

The Evanses were never the first to write to the Joneses, but one morning not long after Easter a white oblong envelope appeared on the doormat bearing Mrs Evans's scrolled copperplate and a stamp with a dragon in the corner.

Dear Mr Jones,
   Just a line to let you know that the Third Field will be available for you in August.
   We do look forward to seeing you
   Yours sincerely
   Dorothy Evans (Mrs)

Colette saw the letter and her heart filled.
'We must go there,' she said.
But Aldous wasn't sure. Too much had changed – not just

280

in his family, but in the world.

They had new neighbours. Mr and Mrs Peck had sold their house to move to the South Coast for the benefit of Robert's asthma. The new neighbours were younger; a policeman and his German wife. They had a young daughter.

Aldous and Colette had been rare visitors to the interior of their neighbours' house. Whenever Aldous went there he felt he'd stepped through the looking glass because the layout of the house was identical to their own except that it was reversed. The stairs were to the right of the hall, not the left. The door to the front room was on the left, not the right, and opened on to such a coherently patterned and coloured space – wallpaper with regularly spaced roses, symmetrically swirled carpet – it was as though the Pecks' house was a parody of their own.

Within weeks of their arrival Mr and Mrs Milliner began a sustained assault on the old spaces, taking down the wall that separated the kitchen from what corresponded to the Jones's music room, creating one enormous room at the back of the house. Aldous could just glimpse it from the back garden steps. They had lifted the lino and stripped the paintwork. Suddenly there was everywhere naked wood, knotted and grained. Colette too found the renovation of their mirror-house a little unsettling. She didn't like the wife who twice had upset her; first by asking her to clear up the rubbish in her back garden because it spoilt the view from the upstairs window, second by suggesting that Colette had the side of her house, the one that faced the alleyway, painted white, so that it cheered up the view from her kitchen. It was as though, in renewing and reshaping the surfaces of their own home, they had lost track of its boundaries and were spilling their plans over into Colette's life. It was as though they were trying to renovate her, flay her like they'd flayed their woodwork.

Elsewhere Aldous was aware of other changes, some sudden, some gradual. The coinage he'd grown up with – large brown pennies, brass threepenny bits, florins, half-crowns – had, in a single night, been swept out of existence to be replaced by ugly brash coins based on decimals. No longer was money, time, weight and length a unified system.

Somehow the country was growing up.

The Ordnance Survey had metricated their maps. The countryside was measured in kilometres. The maps were to a larger scale (two centimetres to a kilometre worked out at about one and a quarter inches to a mile as opposed to the inch to the mile of the imperial maps), and yet much detail had been dispensed with. It was no longer possible to tell if a wood was deciduous, coniferous or a mixture of both. The woods on the new maps were just plain green shapes. The orchards were green stipple, when before they'd been little drawings of apples. Windmills were with or without sails. The loss of the elegant poise of the old system (an inch to a mile, how succinct, how elegant) had somehow made the world less interesting. Aldous felt the landscape had been altered in his absence. Just as the Milliners had simplified their house, stripping its paintwork and merging its rooms, so the Ordnance Survey had renovated the landscape, made it easier, simpler.

The house next door had grown up. The landscape had grown up. The money.

Aldous had been absent from the countryside because the car had gone. The MOT inspector wouldn't even get in it. He took one look at the lush foliage growing along the window ledges and at the rusted hole in the floor by the hand brake big enough to push three fingers through and said he wouldn't take the car out on the road.

The car was saved at least from the indignity of the scrap yard. The science department at the school took it, lifted its engine out, cut through it with oxyacetylene torches, labelled it so that the children could learn about the workings of the internal combustion engine, the gearbox and the differential. The skeleton and gizzards of the old Morris Oxford made quite an interesting drawing project as well, and Aldous often took classes down to the science block to draw it. Now pictures of the interior working of the car lined the art room, the machinery that had brought so many landscapes into their lives.

Aldous didn't have the money to buy another car. He could never quite understand money. It just seemed to fall through his fingers. No matter how hard he tried he couldn't save any. He provided it, others consumed it. His friend at school, John Short, the geologist, was always surprised that Aldous wasn't rich, since, as an artist, he had a superb sense of detail. His contention was that success in money always depends on attention to detail. *'If you go into a fuming rage when you're short-changed a ha'penny in a shop, or you're concerned about the difference of a quarter of one per cent in the interest rates of two building societies, you'll end up rich, because the rich love these sorts of details. It isn't meanness exactly . . .'* Aldous wasn't sure that he agreed. It *was* meanness. Pecuniary detail wasn't interesting in the way that leaves were. Still, he could not afford what many were now considering necessities – a phone, a fridge, a car. In the summer their milk barely lasted a day. They stored the bottles in pans full of cold water under the stairs, supposedly the coolest place in the house. Milk often turned to cheese, exuding from the neck of a bottle like toothpaste from a tube. Butter became liquid in its dish. It would be better to stay at home for the summer, thought Aldous, and save for a fridge. The idea of a telephone, however, frightened him. The thought of suddenly being available to the whole world. The thought that anyone, no matter how deranged or vile, could put their voice into your house.

But then the letter from Mrs Evans came. For the first time they were being asked to Llanygwynfa. It stirred Aldous. As the summer gradually developed outside the windows the question of what to do about the holiday kept returning. In bed at night Colette would talk about the farm.

Aldous and Colette's migration to the bed settee downstairs had been caused by Juliette's increasing maturity. She was too grown up now to be sharing a room with her little brother.

Twice Juliette had caught him faking sleep while she undressed, watching her through eyes barely open. Julian had to be moved to the large back bedroom, leaving Juliette the small bedroom to herself. To make room for Julian, however, Janus was moved into the front bedroom. At twenty-five he was entitled to a room of his own. So James and Julian shared the back bedroom. There was nowhere for Aldous and Colette to go but downstairs.

They quite liked sleeping downstairs. The settee, which unfolded with a clunking, grinding sound and the yawning noise of springs extending, was surprisingly comfortable. The front room was cosier than the upstairs bedroom. There the tips of the acacia branches tapped at the window. Here they were screened from the world by the dense foliage of the front garden. They could have the television on while they were in bed. One of Aldous's paintings of Moelfre was on the wall. The mountain was seen from an unusual angle and there was a dark cloud above it casting a deep green shadow on to the crown of the hill.

Colette talked about the farm as though it wasn't even in question that they were going there in August. She said she needed a holiday. She needed to get away. The change of scene would do her good. The air would build her strength up. She talked as she drifted off to sleep.

But it was Colette's health that concerned Aldous the most. Her recovery had been slow. He thought she was still quite ill. She'd managed to keep off the glue, but she'd had two more fits: one a few weeks after Christmas, and one a few weeks after that. The January one was in the morning. She and Aldous were helping Julian get ready for school. It was a frosty morning and Julian needed mummifying in coats, scarves and gloves before he took to the bike for his one-mile ride. Colette was helping her son on with a glove when she fell to another seizure.

'Oh bloody hell,' said Aldous, who'd been helping Julian with his other glove (it wasn't that Julian couldn't put on his own gloves, but that he was so thickly clad he could barely move). Julian could see that Aldous was scared. Colette's howling came like a series of small cries – *oh oh oh oh oh oh*, like the White Queen pricking herself. She collapsed on the floor in convulsions. Julian left the room quickly. Aldous only just had time, after turning his wife on her side, to run out of the house and catch Julian as he cycled off.

The second time Colette was in the middle of cooking Sunday lunch. These meals, once reduced to the frugal level of luncheon meat and Smash, had been revived recently. She now spent Sunday mornings preparing a chicken; barding it with butter and bacon, boiling the heart and liver of the bird with its neck in a small saucepan for the stock, tying the chicken's broken ankles together with string. Aldous would go to church while the bird's skin browned beautifully. But one Sunday, while caressing the clammy chicken's skin with butter, she collapsed and the chicken rolled, its puny limbs flailing, alive in the moment of its falling. The roasting dish rang like a gong. Colette writhed.

By this time Colette's fits were becoming ordinary events. Commonplace. They didn't even call the ambulance for her Sunday fit. It wasn't even mentioned to the doctor. Aldous, always mistrustful of hospitals and doctors, thought even less of them now. It wasn't so much that they couldn't explain his wife's fits, but that they seemed so disinterested in her.

Colette was confident that the Sunday fit was her last. As the summer progressed the months clear of fits mounted up. Her strength, she claimed, was rebuilding itself. Her energy and her appetites were returning. But she still seemed awfully thin to Aldous. She still had that gauntness, her face still had that hollowness. He didn't share her confidence that her fits had finished and that she had completely recovered from glue sniffing. What he dreaded most was Colette having a fit on the train, or in the tent, or on a mountainside.

But there was also the possibility that another visit to Llanygwynfa might do her some good. The air, like she said, might reinvigorate her.

It didn't help Aldous's cause that they were surrounded by

images of Wales, his paintings which exaggerated, if anything, the summery beauty of the landscape. He wondered if he should begin taking these paintings down, from all the rooms of the house, to try and release themselves from the grip of that place.

Then one night he came to bed and his wife was out cold, a higher dose of pills than usual zapping her an hour or so early. On her back, her head tilted to the side resting in a silent, cold bonfire of hair, her arms were above the bed-clothes, and her right hand was holding a book, her left hand a pencil. She had been making a list.

The book was a book of horror stories. There were lots of these books in the house. Ever since discovering the collected short stories of M. R. James in a second-hand book shop they'd looked for stories that would be as good. The taste he gave Colette for creepy tales made her buy books of horror stories, which usually disappointed, but sometimes amused her.

The Pan Books of Horror Stories, edited by Herbert Van Thal, with their glossily macabre covers (a mummy lit with green light, a woman's face – half skin, half skull) contained stories with a curiously visceral theme. The typical story would involve the matter-of-fact recounting of torture ('*little flakes of white flesh clung to the saw blade . . .*'), which in turn usually involved the careful dissection of a living, conscious body ('*I plunged the scissor-blade into the eyeball of his screaming head . . .*' '*having removed the arms, legs, eyes and tongue of the patient, I set about the nose . . .*') There were some variations, 'An Experiment with H_2O' for instance described the boiling alive of a man in a glass tank, whilst his boilers (the woman he'd raped and her mother) took clinical notes ('*the subject is now simultaneously urinating and defecating . . .*'). They were in a different class altogether from James's understated hauntings, in which ghosts are glimpsed out of the corners of eyes, mistaken for dogs, bedclothes or knapsacks, though they were not without their own spectral violence.

Colette had fallen asleep making a list in the blank end-papers of one of these books. Aldous eased the book out of her sleepy grip and looked at the list. It was a list of things to take to Llanygwynfa. As she'd written it the sleeping pills had slowly taken effect, and the list, like a stick dipped in a pool of water, became increasingly distorted at its lower end.

Tent
Flysheet
Poles
Pegs
Lavatory tent etc
Sleeping bags
Pillows
Laamp
Gas cooker
Plaaas
Bowls
Cus
   Pins
Frying p
C H A I R S hairs
   Cloth
BOOK
     BOocus
   CCCCCCC
      K E T C H U P
Pins etc
  Ma keup
MirrorORORRRRRRRR
SOOOPPoap
owls
                apEs
LOVER
         Rain cats
  Costume

WH WH WH WH WWWWWWW
WWWWW HWHwhhh wwwwwhhhhhh

What a strange noise amongst all the animal calls must have been the human being's first whispers of language. Sometimes Aldous thought he could imagine the world before human beings. Before the apes. Before birds. The fluvial plains of old red sandstone. The creeping lava fields. The oceans building chalk beds from the skeletons of tiny animals. A foot of chalk, he'd read somewhere, represents thirty thousand years of sedimentation. Here, in the wave of chalk that was the Chilterns, he thought about the expanse of time when human beings had no place in the world. And then he remembered the summers before the war when he cycled through these hills with Lesley. Those journeys had now become, somehow, part of the history of these white hills. As Aldous continued through the fissure in the hills he passed signposts pointing along tempting lane offshoots to Aldbury, Nettleden, The Gaddesdens. When he'd cycled with Lesley the names had had an impossibly romantic allure, places remote from London, foreign almost.

At Tring, a little town of old red bricks, he reached the edge of the escarpment that marked the end of the Chilterns and the beginning of the Aylesbury Plain. He plummeted down the steep hill, plummeted through chalk, plummeted back thirty thousand years with each foot of his descent. Perhaps five hundred feet he fell in a few minutes. How many millennia was that? Just to build the chalk. The chalk was just one layer, relatively new.

Beyond the Chilterns the cycling was easy but dull – flat roads running straight for miles, an almost featureless land-scape, huge hedgeless fields, tall lonely elms and oaks, pylons. He passed through Aylesbury without stopping, on through the plain, passing American air bases, to Bicester, where he wrote a postcard and posted it to Colette. Then gradually the land began to swell again, lift slightly. A much older geology shaped the landscape now. Limestone. Ancestor of chalk. An older form of chalk. It hadn't occurred to Aldous before that in travelling to Wales he was travelling backwards through geological time. The country ages with each mile out of

London. In Wales there were mountains that were formed right at the beginning of Earth's geological history – the oldest surfaces in the world.

The route to Wales had become so familiar to Aldous he could describe it in mile by mile detail. Somehow it had written itself into his brain. The route was an integral part of his mind's circuitry, even though he'd only ever done it once a year (sometimes twice, if he went at Easter to Llani). At first he'd cycled on his own, later with Janus, once with James as well. He could spot the precise tree under which they'd once mended a puncture, or had lunch, the farms at which they'd asked for water, the fields in which they'd camped, the ditches in which they'd slept.

Now he was cycling alone again. A slow gentle course through the Cotswolds. The tucked-away toffee-coloured villages with their small but stately churches, through eventually to the procession of vast chestnut trees that announced the approach of Chipping Norton. It was in this avenue that Janus and James had, after a day of cycling almost without rest, both collapsed with burning cramps in their legs.

Aldous's sons were a ghostly cycling presence. Once, reaching the crown of a long push, he paused and looked back to see the black shape of a cyclist tiny at the bottom the hill. Aldous thought for a moment that it was Janus, that Janus had set out in pursuit of his father an hour or so later, had been chasing him since London, and had caught up. As he watched the cyclist passing in and out of the shadows cast across the road by the trees, he felt an urge to push on quickly. An urge not to be caught. But Janus was younger and fitter. He would catch up eventually. When he passed, having cycled the entire ascent, he turned out to be a bespectacled man of about forty with a cap and long khaki shorts. He nodded and smiled as he passed Aldous. The fraternity of cyclists.

Sometimes Aldous, pedalling along a quiet road, could distinctly hear a bicycle freewheeling close behind him and, turning, could only see an empty stretch of road.

Janus could have been there, but not the boy he

remembered. Not the bright, fair-headed, fringed, eager to please child, but the man only last Christmas he'd punched in the face.

Aldous dropped down the escarpment of the Cotswolds into the Vale of Evesham. Janus would have swept down this hill at full speed, taking the two hairpins near the bottom with a terrifyingly acute leaning. Aldous had his brakes on all the way down. It was the second wonderful view of the day.

He remembered, a couple of years ago, listening to Janus explaining to Julian how the land between London and Wales was shaped. He drew for him a diagram in cross-section of the two ranges of hills that were traversed

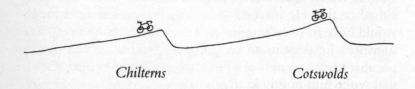

Chilterns   Cotswolds

Two slow, gradual ascents followed by a steep fall at the scarp edge. The view from the Chilterns was of the Aylesbury Plain swelling towards the Cotswolds. From the edge of the Cotswolds the view was into the abyss of geological time, the flatlands cut out by the Severn and beyond them the blue hills in which that river was born.

It was only once he'd descended the Cotswold scarp that Aldous felt he'd really left London. The landscape beyond felt like something hidden, like a secret garden.

He made a diversion to Stratford-upon-Avon, became lost and arrived only half an hour before that evening's performance of *A Midsummer Night's Dream*, for which he'd booked. He didn't have time to find somewhere to stay. He had hoped to put up at a decent B&B. Instead he had to go straight to the theatre, beg to be allowed to store his heavily laden bike in the back of the ticket office, have a quick wash in the gents and dash into the auditorium just as the curtain was rising.

It was Peter Brook's production, and the rising curtain was the last theatrical convention Aldous witnessed. On a sterile white stage characters wrestled with giant springs, swung on trapezes, walked on stilts. The moment of Titania's entrance-ment Aldous found particularly beautiful – circles of colour, pink, green, yellow disks, floated slowly down from above.

Aldous remembered going with his father to see *A Midsummer Night's Dream* at Drury Lane. He can't have been much more than ten years old. He remembered how awkward his father became when in the presence of high culture, how hard he tried to do everything correctly.

The unreal atmosphere of the play lasted with him as he went in search of accommodation afterwards. Everywhere was closed or full. He reached the edge of town and thought he would have to sleep rough when he asked at an inn and they suggested he slept in an old stable at the back. He passed a peculiar night in a nest of straw with a dozen murmuring hens that woke him noisily in the morning.

The next day the weather was dull and overcast. Aldous felt gloomy and, as he cycled, his mouth continually filled with sticky saliva which he had to spit out. Through Kington the grass rose around him, majestic rocks soared like the faces of windowless cathedrals. Nowhere else is the border with Wales so geologically marked. Now he was back at the beginning of things. The air smelt of iron. Struck flint. A long slow climb through treeless Radnor Forest, then a plummet through fir trees, lumber country, the horizon crenellated with mountain tops, rivers twisting in their hunt for the sea, villages that looked hewn from a single piece of rock.

For the first time Aldous felt uncomfortable in this landscape. He didn't know why for certain. He felt like a stranger when before he'd always felt like a returning son. The land of his fathers. He stopped for lunch in a pub in the small village of Llanfihangel-nant-Melan. The barman addressed him in Welsh. He felt like a linguistic intruder. As he ate his sandwich a friendly local chatted with him. When Aldous told him he'd cycled from London the man quipped 'So the English are invading again after an absence of six hundred years.'

'My father was a Welshman,' Aldous snapped. The man looked shocked. Aldous left quickly, feeling embarrassed.

As he cycled on he began to feel a terrible emptiness, a nauseous hunger, and his head felt as though it was filling with liquid. When he passed Rhayader he stopped and vomited by the roadside. A passing car showed the faces of two horrified children. Aldous wheeled a few yards further on to distance himself from his sick, and lay down on the springy grass.

I've overdone it, he thought to himself, *I've pushed myself too hard*. He'd planned to get to Llanygwynfa in four days. He'd done too much on the first day. A hundred miles or more, then the play in the evening, then the homelessness and a strange night in a barn. It was too much for him.

It had been Colette's idea that he should cycle. By this means she'd trumped what he thought was his winning card in the argument against going to Llanygwynfa. No car. For eight years they'd driven to Wales, sometimes taking the bikes with them in the back or on the roof, but not since the car had Aldous cycled there. James and Janus had cycled some years, but not Aldous. The car's dismembered retirement at Edmonton County School meant the end of their holidays at the farm. Until Colette suggested they go there as they'd done in the past, in their early days, Aldous cycling, Colette and Julian following by train. At first he'd laughed off the idea, but Colette wouldn't let it go, and the more he thought about it, the more the idea appealed to him. He was, as much as anything, interested to see if he could actually do it. To see if he still had it in him.

Now he was beginning to consider the possibility that he hadn't, that he'd cycled himself out. Was it possible for a man to cycle himself to death?

The postcard he'd sent from Bicester had said as much –

Darling, glorious weather, wonderful scenery. All this and the play tonight, it's too much. He hadn't sent a postcard to Colette for years. Perhaps not since they were married. It did feel strange to be writing to her like that. He didn't have a voice for postcards to Colette. He didn't have a postcard style. His words had a stiff formality to them that he realized he'd borrowed from Lesley, who peppered his brief, twice-yearly cards with words like glorious. The phrase *it's too much* was rather Lesleyish. From Lesley's cards you had the impression he lived his life in a permanent state of ecstasy. *Glorious. Heavenly. Sheer delight.*

He'd planned to make Llanidloes by the end of the second day. Then two shortish days through the mountains. But now, as he lay on the verge a few yards from a spilled portion of himself, Llanidloes only a dozen miles down a relatively flat road, he felt incapable of any further movement. He felt rather ashamed of himself. He felt like a fool, as though, as an adult, he'd played on the swings in a children's playground only to have them buckle under his weight.

When Aldous came to it was twilight. The mountains had become pointed silhouettes against a pure white, luminous sky. Standing up, brushing dust and grass seeds off his clothes, he felt he had recovered enough of his strength to make Llanidloes, but he decided to spend the night in the open. He found a spot at the edge of a forest where a river was running. He pulled out his sleeping bag and bedded himself down in long, leathery grass and suddenly felt indescribably happy. He wondered why. He thought it must be because no one in the entire world knew where he was. The nearest to total freedom that a human being can experience. It was the same feeling he felt in his cycling holidays with Lesley Waugh. No one in the world could get you. You were invisible, secret, hidden.

It was the freedom of running away. 'I could just go into these little hills and live in them for ever,' he thought. 'I could eat berries, catch small animals, cut a bivouac from larch trees or live in the shade of the spruce groves that are like houses already, deeply thatched. And who would know?'

It was a fantasy he'd entertained increasingly over the years. He and Colette upping sticks and pioneering a new life in some wilderness somewhere. A bend in the river and a hut of lumber, endless salmon suppers amid the snowy peaks. If they could just lift themselves out of the currents of history, live where the only things that grew old and died were the trees, in a cabin of things that didn't change . . . Then Colette could be a girl again, a girl until she died.

The next day Aldous called on Dot and spent a whole day recuperating at her bungalow. He found her home very relaxing. It contained much that had been in his mother's house, its porcelain cows and owls, its oak and walnut whatnots, nested tables, embroidered counterpanes. He enjoyed trying to recall the histories of its objects – which were the things he knew as a child, which weren't.

It was two more days before he reached Llanygwynfa, having crossed mountain passes and passed mountain crosses, skirted reservoirs and estuaries, before finally freewheeling past the chapel of St Hywyn and in through the cobbled courtyard of the farmhouse at sunset. Mrs Evans came out to greet him, but her face dropped when she saw his, and she took him into the farmhouse by the arm calling for her husband, because she was convinced that Mr Jones was about to die.

When Aldous tried to speak, to reassure her that there was nothing wrong, that he was just a little weary from his cycling, he discovered that he had no voice. Mr Evans appeared from round the corner of the house, still in the cap and long mac he'd been wearing for fifteen years, looking concerned. Aldous had never seen Mr Evans look concerned about anything before, not even when he first saw Aldous lying in the road, as good as dead, nor when the tent burned down, nor when the storm came, but now he looked worried, and quickly he took hold of Aldous's other arm and drew it across his shoulders. Mrs Evans doing the same, the two carried him like an injured calf into the house.

Unattended, hastily propped by the burial ground wall, Aldous's midnight-blue Claude Butler racer slowly tipped sideways and fell with an unheard clatter on the cobbles.

3

The next day, having recovered from what was only a bout of mild exhaustion and heatstroke, and having put the tent up in the dark, Aldous went to Aberbreuddwyd (the trains no longer stopped at Llanygwynfa Halt) to meet Colette and Julian off the train. It was a searingly hot day and the town was crowded with magenta-skinned English people. The train from Shrewsbury (there was no longer a direct service from Paddington) was an undignified little diesel that failed the landscape miserably, parping stupidly as it crossed the estuary bridge and trundled through the canyons and tunnels towards the harbour.

Colette looked red and shiny when she stepped down from the train. Momentarily dizzied by the height from which she had to reach down for her husband's hand, she seemed flustered, unsure of herself. She gave him an account of the journey that tried to make the best of the grim trains that had inherited these tracks, how smooth and fast they were.

He took them back to the tent on the bus. When the bus rumbled away Colette savoured again the silence of Llanygwynfa, the crooked little farmyard, the moss-thick chapel. And there, in the field, was their tent, their home from home, pegged down, tight as a drum. She unzipped it and sat down in emerald light, stretched out, and slept.

In the night Aldous woke and thought he was in the house at Fernlight Avenue. He sat up and thought about going downstairs for a cup of water. His head brushed against the inner wall of the tent, and he couldn't understand it. He felt around for the edge of the bed – there wasn't one. He reached out and discovered that he was surrounded by material. His hands knocked softly against the tent pole. It made a little ringing noise. He realized he was not in the house but he couldn't think where he was. He found he couldn't breathe properly, that he was choking, suffocating. He felt like a fly that has been swaddled by a spider. Just at the point of drowning in sticky silk he realized where he was and breathed again. But it happened every night. Sometimes he dreamt that he was back home, but that the house was all soft and floppy, the floors sagging like huge hammocks. He tried to go downstairs and the stairs folded into a smooth chute down which he slid. The house billowed and ruffled like a tent in a storm.

On the first morning the cloud descended and a fine rain fell. Aldous cooked breakfast busily in the tent mouth while Julian played alone in the field in his anorak. Colette stayed in bed, exhausted. After breakfast they realized there was nothing they could do. It was Sunday. They had no car. The buses weren't running. The only activity came from the chapel, whose one bell rung continuously all morning. Julian and Aldous walked to the village where Aldous bought a newspaper and Julian a toy tractor. In the afternoon it rained heavily.

The following day Aldous woke at three in the morning, again not knowing where he was. When the dawn came up he crawled out of the inner tent and sat on one of the chairs in the porch trying to reassure himself. In the field he saw Janus standing alone, wearing a suit, looking bizarrely out of place. Then he saw Janus as a little boy when he first brought him to the farm, turning cartwheels on the grass, chasing the sheep.

Later, walking alone through the farmyard, Aldous would hear the laughter of children coming from the cow shed, and peeking in through the half open door would see only a huddle of murmuring hens. He would feel on his shoulders the weight of the children he'd carried through the farmyard, or see little Julian spilling the milk all the way back to the tent, Janus and Gwen picking blackberries by the gate, Juliette in a torn skirt running before him across the crooked slabs chasing the hens. Soon Aldous could barely manage the walk through the farmyard without having to bite back tears, and found himself seeking reassurance in the sight of Julian, that there was still a child happy here at the farm. But Julian didn't seem that happy.

The second day was grey as well, but the rain held off. Aldous took Julian to Aberbreuddwyd on the bus. Colette stayed at the tent.

At Aberbreuddwyd they walked a little on the cliffs behind the town, scrabbled around on the rocks by the harbour. For Aldous it was the same as the farmyard. Everywhere he looked he saw his own children as they'd been, brilliantly happy, their lips red with cherryade, the huge sky shining in their eyes. He saw James clambering about on the boats that lay higgledy-piggledy on the sand when the tide had withdrawn, he saw Juliette untangling a phantom of candyfloss, Janus with a map spread on his knees naming the mountains they could see across the estuary. But now there was just Julian, alone, trying very hard to enjoy himself, awkwardly balanced on the slippery harbour rocks.

The thought occurred to Aldous that one's life was a series of little deaths, particularly the life of a child as observed by its parent. Where was the little boy he'd cradled, if not dead, to be replaced by an adult that was little more than a stranger to him? Children die within the carapace of adolescence to become, suddenly, equivalents of their parents, something that had to be understood all over again.

298

When they returned to the tent Colette was still asleep. So deeply asleep that nothing could wake her. Under the spell of her pills you could shake her, shout at her, she would still sleep. She slept as though someone had an invisible pillow over her face. She was crushed by sleep. She slept the whole evening and night, and didn't wake until next day.

Aldous was woken in the dark by noises outside the tent. Shuffling noises. Odd footsteps suddenly close. A cough. He listened to these noises for what seemed like hours, drifting in and out of sleep. He dreamt he was in the back bedroom at home, and that he had woken to find the bedroom full of birds. It was like the final scene from the Hitchcock film — there were birds everywhere, all over the floor, on the chairs, settled along the bookshelves, on the sideboard, perched in rows on top of the wardrobe. He had to lift himself slowly out of the bed and walk with tremendous care across the floor, stepping in between the birds who cooed and rustled quietly, until he made it to the door. When he was out of the room he slammed the door shut, sending into flight all the birds in the room, whose contained flutterings he listened to on the other side of the door.

When he truly woke he understood where the dream had come from, because there were birds playing around the tent. He could hear their close wing-beats as they perched on the ridge pole, invisible to him, their intense, nervous fluttering, the scrape of their little talons against the canvas. Occasionally he sensed the presence of a larger bird, a smack of wings and then the sudden gargled shout of a crow, like a drunk. If only, Aldous thought to himself, they would all settle on the tent together, grip it in their tiny feet, beat their wings as one and lift the whole caboodle up into the sky. He laughed at the thought.

The next day was again drizzly. Mr Evans visited them, bringing a playfully happy sheepdog with him. He had bought the freehold from William Vaughan after fifteen years of negotiations. He and Barry had asked for permission to create a proper camp site on the farm.

'Next year things will be a lot better for you. You will have a proper toilet block over there by the barn, and we might have a small shop next to it. There's going to be a gravel driveway circling the field and we'll probably put a new gateway in between the first field and the third field, and we'll have electricity hook-ups put in for the caravans. We'll still be taking tents, of course. You don't have to worry about that. We can reserve a space for you.'

At this point he noticed Colette who was asleep inside the tent. The sight of her, glimpsed through the doorway, seemed to render him speechless for a few moments. She was lying on her back with her head near the door, which made it seem as though she was hanging upside down. Her auburn hair, which had an inch of grey at the roots, was splayed across the lip of the tent and spreading out on to the grass. Her mouth was open, and its interior looked pale and dry.

'She doesn't sleep very well at night,' said Aldous, by way of explanation.

'Is that so?' said Mr Evans, still looking. Aldous noticed that his head was turning very slightly, as if he wanted to crane it around and look at Colette upright, to check that it was her.

'She gets very tired.'

Mr Evans didn't say anything, but finally managed to draw his attention away from Colette.

'The boys coming this year?'

'No,' said Aldous, 'Janus is . . . too busy in London . . .'

'Playing the piano?'

'Yes.'

'And James? I keep expecting to see them on their bikes coming up the road from Aberbreuddwyd.'

How could Aldous put it? That they were bored with coming on holiday with their parents, bored with the farm, bored with Wales.

'James has a job now, just a temporary thing at a wine merchant's while he wonders about applying for university. Juliette's working hard at school doing her O Levels . . .'

Mr Evans's face registered little interest in these facts. He suddenly became bashful, took hold of the peak of his cap, as if about to remove it, but just held it, as though worried, in the perfectly still air, that it might blow away,

'I was wondering, Mr Jones, if you would mind writing to the National Park people to tell them, you know, how much you've liked coming here over the years, but how it needs proper facilities, you know. It might help our application, you being a teacher and so on. Would you mind doing that?'

'Of course not,' said Aldous, 'I'd be delighted to.'

The low clouds persisted. The mountains were invisible. You would not guess that this was a mountainous place. 'We might as well be in Norfolk,' Colette said. Aldous and Julian walked the mile to the beach one afternoon and sat on a bank of pebbles watching the sky for rain. Aldous lifted and felt the pebbles. So solid and dead, but if you mishandled them – a sudden snap and biting of the fingers.

Julian was interested in dinosaurs and had brought along several colourful books on the subject, along with a couple of pocketfuls of small plastic tyrannosaurus rexes, triceratops and diplodocuses. He played with them in the back of the tent staging little fights between them, allowing them to march majestically across the groundsheet and the bedding, and to drive his toy tractors. He created a toy dinosaur farm, where dinosaurs ploughed the land, milked the cows, sheared the sheep. Aldous thought how unsurprising it would be to see a real dinosaur in this landscape. Once, walking the misty foothills of Moelfre, he saw one, a tyrannosaurus rex with its raunchy thighs and thalidomide hands and huge, prickly mouth running energetically across the rocky ground to the north. It watched them from a distance, following, but didn't come close.

The problem with tents, thought Aldous one dawn, is that they don't have windows. Once you've zipped up for the night you have no viewpoint upon the world. If only he had a window he could look out and confirm that the ambiguous pitter-patterings he'd been listening to for hours were field mice, hedgehogs or birds and not the talons of a carnivorous dinosaur savouring the stretched canvas for a moment before taking a bite. Or he could confirm whether there was a world out there at all. He could imagine unzipping the door one morning on to a white or black void, the universe having withdrawn to the primordial pinpoint of nothingness it once was.

Then dawn would come. Even on a misty day the approach of the sun was noticeable as a silvery matrix of beads seeping in through the weave of the canvas.

He was beginning to dread the night-time, the idea of zipping himself into this windowless house.

Colette spent most of her time in the tent. She took sleeping pills all through the day, and would have only brief spells of lucidity, and only once or twice ventured out of the farm. It was as though she'd come to the farm with the intention of sleeping there. As if that was her sole purpose. She'd been asleep for nearly a week, and seemed content to sleep through the rest of her life. It meant that Aldous and Julian had only each other for company. It puzzled Julian. His mother had seemed so insistent on coming to Wales this year, she'd wanted to come here at any cost, and yet she was sleeping through the whole holiday. Perhaps, he thought, that was why she'd wanted to come, so that she could sleep uninterrupted for three weeks.

By the end of the first week, however, she had finished her prescription of pills, and so she woke up. At home her GP would write prescriptions on demand. He seemed to see it as a way of paying Colette to go away. But now her doctor was two hundred and fifty miles away. Aldous hoped she might do without pills for the rest of the holiday, but she decided she would go to Aberbreuddwyd and see a doctor there and try to persuade him to write a prescription for her.

She tried to think of a plausible excuse. A freak wave crashing in from the sea and sweeping her handbag with all her pills out into the deep. Accidentally flushing her pills down the toilet. Someone stealing her handbag from the beach while she was swimming. Leaving them on top of a mountain: 'my husband went back for them but they'd gone, and there were dozens of unconscious sheep everywhere . . .' In the end she settled for leaving them on the train. The doctor, whose practice overlooked the harbour which filled his surgery with the twinkling lights Colette had called tommy noddies when she was a child, looked uncomfortable and asked her if she'd contacted the railway lost property office. She elaborated her story, described all the other things she'd lost along with her handbag – her money, valued photographs of her mother and her children, reams of Green Shield Stamps she was going to stick into albums when it rained, to eventually buy a set of saucepans with, her sunglasses, even her spare dentures. Colette burst into realistic tears. The doctor sucked his pen. He asked for the name of her GP. She told him. Colette sobbed quietly. After much silent thought the doctor eventually wrote a prescription and Colette went to the chemist's with Aldous, both laughing incredulously at her audacity.

Half way through the second week the clouds were still low, the rain kept coming back like an absent-minded guest, continually returning for some forgotten thing. Aldous's tan slowly left his skin, the ghost of summer. Colette was taking fewer sleeping pills since her fraudulent procurement of some more and was conscious for much of the daytime.

One afternoon Aldous and Colette were sitting side by side on the camping chairs in the porch while Julian was deep in an agricultural fantasy at the back of the tent. A fine gauzy drizzle was falling on the field, so light it was like a rain of cobwebs. It occurred to Aldous suddenly that they had been watching this drizzle for more than an hour. He felt he knew more about drizzle, its silvery colour, the way it fell in barely perceptible waves, than any other man alive.

Colette turned to Aldous, who seemed unable to take his eyes off the rain, and said 'Do you think it's raining in London?'

Aldous, who felt it must be raining everywhere, thought it probably was.

'It must be,' he said.

'What we need is a Sun Dome,' Colette said, and laughed. Aldous knew what she meant. Sun Domes featured in a Ray Bradbury short story they'd both enjoyed called 'The Long Rain', about Venus. There it rained everywhere without pause. All the plant life was white. The only respite from the rain was offered by the Sun Domes, ingenious buildings that recreated perfectly the atmosphere of a warm sunny day.

'Yes,' said Aldous.

They spent a little while reminiscing about past holidays, the time the tent burnt down, the time the tent blew down, the time Juliette ran away, the time Scipio came to the farm. It took Aldous a while to get used to the fact that he was having a conversation with Colette.

'Odd, isn't it,' she said, 'the cat turned out to do some good for Janus after all. Just a pity it had to get run over first.'

It was true that Janus seemed to be a different person since Scipio's accident. Devoted to the care of the cat he was calmer, less angry.

'What about when the cat gets better,' said Aldous, gloomily, 'what then?'

'Perhaps he'll have learnt something along the way. Perhaps he'll start taking music seriously again. We'll have to wait and see.'

Aldous gave a brief snort of laughter, meaning *I'll believe it when I see it*.

'I was wondering,' Colette went on, 'before the accident, whether Janus should see a psychiatrist . . .'

'A psychiatrist,' Aldous said, wincing. 'What on earth for?'

Colette sounded almost apologetic.

'To see if they could fathom him out. In Friern I found it very useful . . .'

Aldous didn't want to think about Friern, or psychiatrists.

'There's nothing wrong with Janus . . .' Aldous hesitated. Looking at his wife he could see she was disappointed with this remark, and he found himself forced to elaborate, 'I suppose he just gets a bit frustrated . . .'

'What by?'

Again Aldous hesitated.

'Perhaps he's finding it hard to accept he's not as special as he thought he was . . .'

'You mean *we* thought he was.'

Again Aldous winced slightly.

'I never expected him to be anything more than a good pianist and a good teacher of the piano,' he said.

'Just like you never expected yourself to be anything more than a good teacher of art?'

Colette had never quite understood her husband's indifference to his own talents. The way he didn't preserve or record in any way his own work, but would use old paintings to board up windows, or patch ceilings, or make cupboard doors.

'I'm a good enough artist to know that I'll never be a great artist,' Aldous said, smiling.

'And Janus isn't a good enough pianist to know he'll never be a great pianist?'

'Janus could be a great pianist. There's just something lacking here.' Aldous tapped the side of his skull. 'He hasn't got the temperament, the mental toughness. He can't handle criticism and he can't handle rejection. Don't you remember what that teacher wrote on his school report? "*Resents criticism*".' Colette nodded enthusiastically. 'That's why that BBC rejection hit him so badly. That's why he gets angry. He'll get angrier and angrier until he accepts his own limitations . . .'

They were silent for a while, looking again at the drizzle. It fell more slowly than normal rain, as though reluctant to reach the ground.

'I think there's more to it than that,' said Colette.

'Do you?'

'He seems so terribly disappointed, not just about his music, I mean, but about the world generally. It's as though he feels the world has failed him somehow . . .'

305

'He needs to fall in love,' Aldous grumbled. It was something one of his tutors at art school used to say to any student whose work was lacking in passion. 'Go and fall in love and then come back tomorrow.'

'Is that why you thought he should see a prostitute?'

Aldous looked at Colette and was relieved to see that she was smiling.

'He told me all about your generous offer,' she went on. 'Aldous, how could you?'

'It was just an idea. No worse than sending him to a psychiatrist.'

'Life's all appetites with you, isn't it?'

'I think we can overcomplicate things to cover up the basic simplicity of our desires. We want sex, we want food, we want sleep . . .'

There was a long pause before Colette asked, a slight cheekiness in her voice, 'Have you ever been to one?'

'What?'

'A prostitute.'

'Of course not,' said Aldous, slightly disgusted.

She was better. A year ago such a conversation would have erupted into a full-scale row, with bitter accusations and claims of betrayal flying around, and Colette falling into a week-long sulk. Now she seemed almost amused by the discussion. Aldous didn't like to admit to himself that his wife's spell in an asylum had done her any good. To do so would have been to concede that she was insane in the first place, and she was never that, he felt. He preferred to think of the hospital as an incidental stage in her long journey through grief, a journey she would have eventually managed anyway and which, he hoped, she was completing now.

They both looked at the rain.

After a while Aldous said 'Shall we go home?'

Colette looked at him and smiled gratefully.

'I need to see the house,' she said, 'to make sure it's still there.'

They thought that Julian might be disappointed, so they

waited until the evening to put the idea to him. He thought for a moment and then said, 'Can I stay inside the tent while you take it down?'

This had never happened before. On a misty morning Aldous and Colette were packing when there was still a week and a half of the holiday left.

They had cleared the tent, all that was left inside was Julian. He stood within its triangular, green light and waited. He could sense his father as the vaguest of shadows moving around the walls, and then he heard his voice, 'Are you ready?'

No voice sounds so close as that which speaks through the wall of a tent. It seems to bypass the ear completely and happen exclusively within the brain. Aldous thought this as well, on the outside, when he heard his son's voice come at him through the tent, 'Yes, I'm ready.'

This must be, he thought, what it is like for the spiritualist who converses with the dead. The medium at her seance hearing the close voice that comes from somewhere entirely remote. The inside and the outside of a tent are such entirely different places.

'I'll start taking the pegs out, then,' said Aldous.

'Okay,' came Julian's voice.

Julian, within, watched his father's shadow move around him, then heard the slicing sound of a peg withdrawing from the soil's tight fit. Then again, from another part of the tent, then another. Julian thought of a magician extracting the many swords from the box that contains a woman.

A slackness happened in the walls of the tent. The beginnings of the soft, green implosion that slowly gathered pace as more and more pegs were pulled out of the ground. Julian could hear his father straining at some, those that had curled around a submerged stone and wouldn't come out, like those deeply rooted saplings the plum tree was always sending up. Now everything in the tent was loose. That which had been fast and smooth now suddenly looked old, wrinkled, sagging. The tent was slowly losing its balance. The poles started to wobble, tilt, sway. Then a sudden long rush, like silk against silk, a long hiss of fabric as the flysheet was lifted off the tent, doubling the light inside. It was bright and narrow, the inside of the tent now, as Aldous pulled the last pegs out.

'Keep hold of the poles,' he said.

'Okay,' said Julian.

Finally, at the end of its tether, the tent lost itself entirely and collapsed like a parachute that has touched down, enclosing Julian within a suddenly comical tangle of fabric. This was the part that he wanted, to be suddenly trapped inside what was no more than an enormous bag.

From the outside Aldous watched the tent collapse down to nothing, then take the proto-shape of a child struggling, like something rising from a swamp of silk. Julian laughed, pretended to fall over, eventually rolled and tumbled his way to the collapsed door and emerged, dishevelled and bright.